SEAL WOLF SURRENDER

TERRY SPEAR

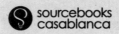
sourcebooks
casablanca

Published by Sourcebooks Casablanca, an imprint of Sourcebooks
P.O. Box 4410, Naperville, Illinois 60567-4410
(630) 961-3900
sourcebooks.com

Printed and bound in the United States of America.
OPM 10 9 8 7 6 5 4 3 2 1

To Thomas Richardson, who tells me that he goes broke buying my books but to keep them coming. Love your sense of humor, and remember, YOU are the alpha of your pack of dogs.

Chapter 1

HER PARENTS' GARDEN NURSERY HAD BEEN OPEN FOR A brief time that morning when Natalie Silverton, who was loading flowers into the back of a customer's pickup, realized it was time to leave for the airport. "Thanks, Mrs. Nesbitt," she said, barely waiting for the woman's response.

She ran back to the shop where her mom was cashiering. "I've got to leave." Having helped all she could before she departed, Natalie grabbed her purse from a locked drawer under the counter. Her dad had left to deliver trees to a customer's home, and Natalie had been handling everything else except the register. She hated to leave her mother alone in the nursery.

"Go, give our Angie a hug for us," her mom said, giving Natalie a quick squeeze. "Have a good time, and don't hurry back. Your schedule is clear for five days. See some sights while you're there. Have some fun."

Her mom knew Natalie wouldn't see any "sights" on her own. She suspected her mom was hoping she'd go out with some of the wolves of the Greystoke pack while she was away.

"Love you, Mom." As their master gardener, Natalie gave classes and tours of their nursery all the time. But she had to catch a flight from Amarillo, Texas, to Denver, Colorado, to celebrate the marriage of her best friend, who was like a sister to her. Half a decade earlier, Natalie's parents had learned Angie lived in the Amarillo area and didn't have a family of her own. They had promptly taken her in as part of their family.

Natalie rushed back through the garden to reach the gate that led to her carriage house behind the Silverton Garden Center. She should have parked her car in front of the garden shop, but she had intended to leave a little bit ago.

Her bags were already in the car, so she changed out of her jeans and Silverton Garden T-shirt, yanked on a dress and heels, and tore out of the house. She jumped into her car and drove off, tamping down the urge to speed. She would make it, but without a lot of time to spare. She would much rather arrive at the airport early and relax before she took the flight. Better yet, if she hadn't given a gardening workshop last evening, she would have just driven to Denver. It was only about a six-and-a-half-hour drive.

A half hour later, she parked and rushed into the airport, pulling her bags behind her. Inside, she paused, looking for the right airline counter to check her bag, then saw it and hurried toward it. Without warning, a little girl ran in front of Natalie to catch up with a woman who appeared to be her mother, forcing Natalie to stop suddenly. The abrupt stop caused a man to stumble over her bag and fall, sprawling out on the floor. She was so used to apologizing to customers that she let go of her bags and hurried to help him up. He looked to be in his early thirties, so it wasn't as if he needed the help, but she immediately made the gesture. Getting closer to him, she smelled he was a wolf, and that took her aback. She didn't know of any living in the area other than her parents and Angie.

"I'm so sorry." She offered her hand to him.

Blond-haired and mustached, he narrowed his blue eyes at her and cursed. "Hell, woman. Don't you ever look where you're going?" He took a deep breath of her scent, his eyes widening a little when he realized she was a wolf too. He ignored her offer of help, rose to his feet—towering over her at six-foot-plus—and brushed off his jeans.

He had the situation a little backward, since *he* was the one who wasn't watching where he was going and had run into her bag. Was he just passing through, visiting the area, or did he live in Amarillo?

The wolf jerked his bag past her and headed for the same check-in counter she had to use. Great. She smelled liquor on him. Whiskey. She sure didn't want to have to put up with a drunken wolf. Though he could be on a different flight with the same airline.

For a moment, she thought about whether to get in line behind the surly wolf or wait until someone else came up to give her some distance. She decided not to wait and moved in behind him, keeping some space between them.

He was already arguing with the agent at the counter, wanting to carry his bag on the plane, but the woman said he couldn't. "It exceeds the maximum size for a carry-on. You'll have to put it in the cargo hold."

It was the same size and style as Natalie's bag, and she knew she'd have to check hers. She would have shipped Angie and Aaron's wedding gift to them if she'd had the time. Then she wouldn't have had to check a bag.

"They let me carry it on the last flight I took it on. I had no problem at all."

"That may be, if you flew on one of the bigger planes. This one just doesn't have room." The agent wasn't backing down from the growly wolf. Good for her.

"Hell, lady." He slammed his bag on the scale. "Someone should have said so beforehand."

"I'm sorry, sir. It's just that the bag won't fit under the seats or in the overhead bin." She gave him the claim tag for his bag.

He jerked the claim tag from the agent's hand and stalked off. Natalie felt embarrassed for being a wolf, considering this man was one too. His rude behavior would have given the wolf kind a bad name, if humans had known wolf shifters existed.

Natalie checked her bag and hurried to security, where she ended up behind the wolf again. How lucky could she be?

"I always have precheck stamped on my ticket. That ticket agent didn't like that I was annoyed about not being able to carry my bag on the plane. I want to report her."

"Sorry, sir," the man said, "but it's really random."

"I still have to go through all this crap?" the growly wolf said.

"That's the rule, sir. Please remove your shoes and step through the screener."

The wolf grabbed a bin, jerked his sneakers off, then slammed them into the bin and shoved it onto the conveyer belt. Natalie wondered if he was always this disagreeable or if the liquor was the reason. She felt sorry for anyone who had to cross paths with him today.

She removed her heels and put them and her purse in a bin. After she put her carry-on on the conveyer belt, the security officer motioned her through. She grabbed her stuff and hurried to put on her shoes. Then she began looking for her gate. Of course, it had to be on the other side of the terminal.

At least she had a straight flight and no transfers. She saw the wolf ahead of her. There were a lot of gates in this direction, so he could be headed to any of them. She was counting on that, but then he took a detour to a bar. She shook her head. He'd already had too much to drink. He didn't need to make any more of an ass of himself than he already had.

When she reached her gate, the attendants were already calling for boarding. She was in group two, and with relief, she boarded the plane. If by chance the wolf was on her flight, maybe he'd miss it. She smiled. That would serve him right.

Natalie took her seat, and it wasn't long before she saw the wolf coming down the aisle. As soon as he reached his row, across the aisle from hers where she had an individual seat, he began to complain about being seated next to a mom and her toddler. Passengers were backed up behind him as he balked about sitting in his assigned seat.

The hostess hurried to see what the difficulty was, and the wolf said, "The kid's diaper needs to be changed. It probably hasn't been changed since yesterday. I can't sit and smell that piss the whole flight."

"She was changed right before the flight!" the irate mom said, her voice elevated.

Refusing to sit down, the wolf stood in the aisle, glowering at the hostess. "I demand a new seat. Anywhere. The kid smells like pee."

"The flight is full. Please have a seat," the hostess

said, her cheeks coloring though she was trying to pacify him in a cool, collected manner.

Natalie was about to offer her seat to him, just so they could get on their way. He was already delaying them, and if they didn't leave now, they would miss their place in line on the runway. Not that she wanted to sit by the mom and her toddler if the girl had a soiled diaper, because like him, Natalie had an enhanced sense of smell. But as annoying as he was, she didn't want to accommodate him. That would only encourage such bad behavior.

"I won't sit next to the damn woman and her filthy kid."

Natalie saw one of the crew members coming, and from the set of his jaw, she didn't think he'd allow any guff from the wolf. At least she hoped he wouldn't. "You're going to have to leave the plane," the man told the wolf.

The next thing she knew, Mr. Drunk Wolf was being escorted off the plane. He was cursing up a storm, but at least he wasn't fighting. Their kind could be trouble if they ended up in jail, especially if they couldn't control the urge to shift during the full moon.

Conversations filled the air while the flight was delayed about fifteen minutes. Natalie hoped no one would miss a connection because of him.

She texted her friend: Crew had to escort a drunken wolf off the plane. Arriving about fifteen to twenty minutes late.

You're kidding. A wolf? In Amarillo? No problem. We'll save you a seat. Love ya, Angie

Now *Natalie* was ready for a drink!

～

Brock Greystoke was having a beer with his twin brother, Vaughn, at the rehearsal lunch for their cousin Aaron when Angie announced, "My best friend, Natalie, is delayed, so I want everyone to give her a special warm welcome when she finally arrives." Angie was a vivacious gray wolf and had fallen in love with Aaron and the Greystoke pack right away. Brock was glad for both his cousin and the pack.

Brock knew Angie was really hoping that one of the bachelor males of Devlyn and Bella Greystoke's pack would mate Natalie, and she would move there so Angie could continue to be close to her best friend.

"You *especially* intend to give her a warm welcome, right, Brock?" Vaughn asked.

"Don't even mention it. After the mess I went through with Lettie, I'm staying clear of she-wolves for the time being."

"Hell, it's been two years."

"Yeah, which isn't long enough. And I'm certainly not going to lay claim to a she-wolf who will only be here for a couple of days. Besides, she's not with a pack, and her parents have a nursery where she serves as their master gardener. She won't want to move here and join a pack." Not that Brock hadn't liked Natalie's appearance. Dark-haired and blue-eyed, Natalie was striking. Angie had made sure all the bachelor males had seen a picture of her friend, saying she wanted everyone to recognize her when she arrived. So why had she sent *only* the bachelors Natalie's picture?

"Been thinking about this a lot, I see." Vaughn smiled, as though he knew Brock better.

Brock couldn't get over Lettie because of the crazy situation she'd gotten him into. As a PI, Brock had tried to locate and eliminate a *lupus garou* bank robber who had killed a woman and her child at a local bank. Learning Lettie was the robber's sister—who had only gotten to know Brock because he was after her brother— had really irked Brock. Hurt too. He couldn't believe she'd only had plans to convince him to let her brother disappear. Well, her brother did disappear, but he needed Brock's assistance in disappearing permanently. They couldn't allow a wolf to get away with murder and chance him getting caught and going to prison.

Brock sat back in his chair, not the least bit interested in Angie's friend. From what Angie had said about her, she sounded like fun, but she wasn't local. "Natalie's not look- ing to relocate or find a mate among our bachelors. She's staying at a hotel far away from all of us. She doesn't want anyone to pick her up at the airport. Her actions prove she doesn't want to get involved with the pack. She's only here to attend her best friend's wedding," he said.

"Right, and that's what Angie wants to change. She wants her friend to meet someone and ultimately join us. Hey, if I hadn't met and mated Jillian, I might have been interested." Vaughn waved at his mate, who was headed back from the restroom.

"You weren't looking to settle down either. I still can't believe Jillian shot you for going after her brother, and you mated her."

"Our two situations were eerily similar, with you going after Lettie's brother, though quite a bit different."

Vaughn slapped Brock on the back. "Life is really good, Brock. You just have to find the right woman. You know Jillian wasn't with a pack either. She was off working on her own."

"The two of you work all over. It's not like she's dealing with wolf politics all the time," Brock pointed out. "Besides, you work together, and her parents moved here so you'd all be close. I wouldn't expect Natalie's parents to pull up roots to join our pack. And I'm not talking about me, but about any of the bachelors who are eager to meet her. If Devlyn hadn't read them the riot act and told them they had to let her do this her way, half of them would have been there vying for the chance to pick her up at the airport."

"Maybe she would have been amused. What do we know?" Vaughn chuckled.

Jillian joined them and gave Brock a hug. "You really should join the United Shifter Force. After that wild trip to Belize with the jaguars, we wondered if you wouldn't like to partner up with us. We could use your help. And I'm sure you'd love it."

"No, it's not for me. I love being a PI. But see? The two of you are perfect for each other," Brock said.

"Has your brother been trying to convince you to make a play for Natalie?" Jillian took a seat and sipped from her glass of wine.

"He has, and I won't be trying to win her over."

"That's what I told him too. She's only going to be here today, for the wedding tomorrow, and then she's leaving the day after. There's no time to get to know her." Jillian smiled at Brock. "Besides, she's probably not your type."

Brock raised a brow. He knew Jillian was not-so-subtly challenging him to get to know Natalie better.

"Why would you think I have a specific type of woman in mind?"

Jillian just smiled. Brock wondered what his brother had been telling her about him and his dating ventures. And why she thought Ms. Natalie Silverton wouldn't suit.

Natalie finally made it to Denver International Airport. She rushed to get her bag and pick up a rental car, hoping she'd only be about a half hour late, no later.

She still couldn't believe Angie had met her mate at the Denver airport when she was flying there to go skiing. She had ended up skiing with him at Breckenridge for the whole two weeks when he hadn't planned to be there at all. Three months later, Angie was tying the knot and moving to his gray wolf pack's territory near Granby, Colorado. Aaron Greystoke was the pack leader's cousin, but he also owned a horse ranch. Angie Pullman loved horses, and Natalie wondered if *that* wasn't the deciding factor in her friend falling in love with the wolf.

Natalie immediately texted her friend: I'm in Denver, just got a car.

Angie texted her back: There are a ton of guys in the pack who were willing to pick you up.

Yeah, but you know me. I like to have my own car.

Natalie didn't like to have to rely on anyone but herself. Besides, she wasn't here to date any wolves, and she knew that was what Angie was up to. She enjoyed being an independent wolf, just like Angie. Though it appeared her friend had changed her mind about that. Natalie would miss all the fun she'd had with her back home.

Thanks for coming. I can't wait to see you.

Me too, Angie. See you soon.

Wolves mated for life, and they lived so long—aging so much slower than humans once they reached puberty—that it was important to find the wolf they couldn't live without. Natalie just hoped Angie wasn't making a mistake with her whirlwind romance.

Using her GPS, Natalie drove from the airport toward Granby, but somewhere along the way, she took a wrong turn, then another. After fifteen minutes of rerouting directions on her GPS, she called Angie. "Hey, my GPS is going crazy. Can you guide me there?"

"I'm sending a SEAL to the rescue. I'm in the middle of toasts. Here, talk to Brock."

"No, that's okay, I'll just—"

"Tell me where you are," a sexy, deep-baritone male voice said. "I'll meet you there, and you can follow me here."

Ugh, if it didn't mean so much to both of them for Natalie to be there, she would have just skipped it. She wondered if the SEAL was as sexy-looking as he sounded though.

She blew out her breath in an annoyed way. "I'm at—" She looked around. "I don't know where. I parked at a garden nursery called the Denver Garden Center."

"There are four of them."

Of course there were.

His voice calm, as if he was used to helping women in distress, Brock asked, "What are the intersecting roads?"

Oh, just great. "Wait just a minute." She couldn't see any intersecting roads! She looked at her GPS. "Um, I think I'm off North Boulevard."

"Okay, that's the nearest one to the restaurant. I'll be there in fifteen minutes."

"You can just give me directions." Otherwise, she would be thirty minutes late instead of fifteen.

"It's your call, Natalie. I'm one of Aaron's cousins, Brock Greystoke, by the way."

"Nice to meet you, Brock. Yeah, it will save us both time, so just give me the directions." And *hopefully*, she could make it there without having to be escorted the rest of the way. She could hear all the noisy lunch guests having fun without her. She preferred working with plants more than partying with people. And she had a total love-hate relationship with the GPS. She loved it when it worked. She hated it when it got her lost.

"All right, I'll stay on the line and get you here that way," Brock said.

She could listen to his calm, soothing, masculine voice all day. She imagined hers sounded frazzled and annoyed. "Okay."

"Turn right onto North Boulevard. Stay in the right-hand lane. You'll turn on the first exit to the right."

"Okay, leaving the nursery. I'm on North Boulevard, coming up to the first exit on the right."

"Good," Brock said, and she was glad he didn't sound as if he thought she was an idiot.

"Okay, exited North Boulevard."

"Go down to the third signal and turn left on Elm Street."

"Oak Street. Ash Street. Elm Street."

Brock chuckled. Okay, she knew she sounded silly, but she really, really hated getting lost in a strange city, *especially* when she was already late! She was really nervous about meeting all these strange wolves. Despite working in her parents' garden shop and being used to meeting customers—human customers—or presenting educational programs to humans, she wasn't used to meeting a lot of wolves.

"Keep going. You're nearly there. Stay in the right lane, and at the third signal, you'll turn right. Dallas's Steak House is three buildings down on your right."

"Thank you. I so appreciate it. I'm nearly there." She should have just thanked him and signed off, but he wasn't ending the call either, and she felt more at ease knowing if she missed the steak house somehow, Brock would redirect her and make sure she got there all right. "Okay, I see the steak house, and I'm pulling into the parking lot."

"You're driving a blue Toyota?"

"Uh, yeah." She turned to look at the deck leading to the front door of the restaurant, where a large fountain was flowing into a basin.

Wearing blue jeans, a dress shirt, cowboy boots, and a Stetson, Brock was standing next to the fountain, appearing bigger than life, but he looked as though he was into roping steers rather than scuba diving as a SEAL wolf. Dark hair, dark eyes, and a sensuous mouth, curved up in a slight smile, greeted her. His gaze was intense, all-consuming. She parked her car and joined him.

"You must be Natalie, Angie's best friend. Brock Greystoke, Aaron's cousin." Brock offered his hand to her and she shook it, but then worried hers was a little clammy from sweating out the drive there. She should have wiped her hand off on her skirt before she shook his hand.

"All Angie's talked about was one of us running to the airport and picking you up so you wouldn't get lost. You know, instead of staying at the hotel, you could stay with any of the families in the town of Greystoke out in Wolf Valley. That way, you won't have to make the long drive there in the morning for the wedding. I know how it is when you want to have your own getaway vehicle though. Oh, and welcome to Colorado. Angie said you've never been here before."

"Thanks, and no, I haven't." How could she tell the darkly handsome wolf she preferred staying at her own hotel because she didn't want to put anyone out? They'd insist she wasn't, but she just needed…her own space. She wondered how much Angie had told her new pack members about her.

She sighed, and Brock opened the door to the restaurant for her. The noisy conversation inside was nearly deafening, partly because of their enhanced wolf hearing. That was why she preferred her garden nursery to this.

The aroma of hickory-cooked steaks did appeal though.

"Are you ready for a good-sized steak after all the flying and rushing to get here?" Brock asked.

"Yes. I hate being so late."

"Don't worry about it. We just started at noon, and it's only a quarter of one. Everyone is enjoying cocktails and appetizers first."

Natalie figured no one would realize she hadn't been there earlier since no one even knew her and Angie would have been too busy enjoying herself. But Natalie hated arriving late to anything, as if she were the star of the occasion and needed a big entrance. Yet she was vitally aware of the man walking beside her, his arm brushing hers as they moved closer together so that customers could get by them. When a waiter nearly ran into her, Brock adroitly slipped in behind her, pulling her out of the waiter's way.

Heat spread through her whole body, and Natalie tried to think of anything other than the way his body was pressed against hers in the sudden crush of customers as a large party was leaving the restaurant. "Angie told me you and your brother, Vaughn, are Navy SEALs. Are you just here on a visit?" she asked Brock.

"No, we're both out of the navy now, retired. You know how it is. We didn't look like we were aging, so as soon as we could, we retired. Both of us had been private investigators. Vaughn hooked up with a jaguar policing force that's called the United Shifter Force, and he has a mate now. They live out here, but their headquarters is in the Houston area. They travel there whenever they need to for a mission. I'm doing the PI business on my own now."

"You look like you wrangle steers too."

He smiled at her.

She felt her face flush with heat. Maybe that was the wrong thing to say to him. She saw men wearing western wear in Amarillo too, so she was used to seeing it.

"I help out on Aaron's ranch when I can. I just like getting out and riding a bit. Do you ride?"

"Uh, no, actually. A bicycle, yes. A horse, no. Angie's the big horse nut. I guess that's some of why she and Aaron hit it off."

"Yeah, it is. And the skiing. Do you ski?"

"No. We don't have any mountains around Amarillo. I guess the closest is New Mexico. To think Angie switched her plans to go to Colorado instead of New Mexico and met Aaron because of it! I guess it was meant to be." Natalie was much more of a warm-weather person, though they did get snow in Amarillo. She really couldn't imagine falling down a mountain on two skinny skis for fun. She figured once Brock learned she didn't ride horses and she didn't ski, he wouldn't find her very interesting. Which was fine with her. She wasn't looking to hook up with a wolf, even as sexy as he appeared to be.

"Well, sometime when you come back to visit, you can ski with Angie and Aaron."

She noted Brock didn't offer. He probably didn't want to have to deal with a total newbie skier.

They wound their way through the large building until they arrived at a banquet room where the private rehearsal lunch was being held. There were about thirty people in the room, and everyone looked in their direction as they entered.

Angie quickly left her chair and gave Natalie a hug. All of a sudden, the pack members surrounded Natalie, giving her handshakes to welcome her. As stiff as she was around them, they must have realized she needed her space—so no one but Angie and Aaron gave her a hug in greeting.

"I'm so glad you made it. I told you that you should

have let someone pick you up at the airport. And you can't stay at the hotel in Denver. You're too far away from the fun." Angie glanced down at Natalie's hands and *tsk*ed. "You have green fingers. Not just a green thumb."

"I was working in the garden when we first opened, helping a customer with an order, when I realized it was time to catch the flight. Spring and early summer are such busy times for plant sales at the nursery."

"No problem at all. We're going straight to the ranch after the lunch. The ranch house has eight bedrooms, and since most everyone lives here in the area, most of the rooms are empty. You know we'll be having margaritas, and you don't want to be driving all the way back into Denver. What if you got lost?"

Natalie could never win an argument with her friend. Besides, if she was going to drink, she agreed about not driving back into Denver. "I'll have to cancel my hotel reservation for tonight, but after the wedding, I can stay the night in Denver to catch my flight the next day."

"Why don't you just stay at the ranch house, and then you can have breakfast with some of the pack members before you leave? For now, you can just follow Aaron and me to the ranch after the meal." Angie sat Natalie next to her chair, while Aaron was sitting on the other side of Angie.

"All right. But only because I *know* you. We'll be partying all afternoon. I still can't believe you're getting married."

"You can come and visit us any time you want." Angie smiled. "Now, let me tell you about all the bachelors in the pack."

Natalie chuckled. "You know I'm not interested.

Period. I love Amarillo and the garden center. What would my parents do without me? I can't plan on them wanting to relocate again either. So no. I'm just here to help you have fun."

"Well, I'll tell you one person who really, really isn't interested in finding a mate. That's Brock. Which is why I asked him to help you out with the directions."

"Oh?"

"Yeah. He broke up with a girlfriend a while back, and he hasn't been interested in one since. She's not with the pack. He met her under some rather unusual circumstances. Suffice it to say, he's not looking for a special someone right now. I figured if I sent any of the other bachelor males to help you, their tongues would have been hanging to the floor and their tails wagging behind them, way too eager to win you over."

Natalie laughed. "Thanks." Now she was curious about the experience that had made a man like Brock swear off women.

Chapter 2

AFTER LUNCH, A CARAVAN OF CARS HEADED FOR AARON'S ranch house to continue the party, but not before Angie arranged it so Brock would drive Natalie's rental car for her so she wouldn't get lost.

Brock had been up to the task; it wasn't any imposition. He'd ridden to Denver with some of his other cousins, and even if they lost the caravan, he knew the way and wouldn't have to give Natalie directions.

Natalie settled back against the seat. "It wasn't really necessary," she said as they followed Vaughn and Jillian's car to the town of Greystoke while the wedding couple was in the pickup ahead of them. "I couldn't have gotten lost, not with all the cars to follow."

Brock chuckled. "No problem. I rode with my brother and his mate, so I didn't have my Humvee here. I would have worried about you if we'd somehow lost you."

They lost sight of the first two cars in the caravan at a signal.

"I don't think my GPS works in Denver," Natalie said.

He laughed. "Mine's gone haywire a time or two. So what does a master gardener do?" He envisioned her with bright-orange garden gloves, dirt smudges on her cheeks, her dark hair pulled back in a ponytail, and a trowel in hand as she dug around in the garden.

"I teach about gardening, plants, and wildlife to a lot of groups. What does a SEAL wolf do?"

"Rescues, retrievals, and removals."

"They all sound the same."

He smiled. "They're not. Rescues of people and equipment from hostile situations. Retrieving data and other important items. Removing bad guys from the scene."

"Sounds dangerous."

"It could be. Sometimes it was just tedious. It depends on how hostile the situation is."

"Are you guys going to be at Aaron's ranch too?"

"Yeah, we're using the guesthouse to party. You ladies will be in the main ranch house."

"He's got a lot of room for visitors."

"Yeah, he's one of the most welcoming wolves of our pack. He wanted a place for visiting wolves to stay who weren't with our pack."

"Does he have them stay often?"

"They come through and check out our pack, and most move on. But sometimes we have visitors who end up staying."

"It's a beautiful area. I love the mountains as a backdrop."

"It is beautiful. I don't think I could live anywhere that's flat." He'd traveled all over, but he still loved the view of mountains.

"It would be fun to run through them as a wolf."

"If we had time, we could go there together."

She smiled at him. "'Time' is the keyword."

"Yeah." He knew she wasn't interested in staying any longer than she had to. "If you need anything, don't hesitate to ask anyone while you're here."

"Thanks, and thanks for offering to drive."

"No problem."

They finally reached the ranch, where Natalie joined the other ladies and entered the ranch house while the guys gathered in the guesthouse out back.

"You are so slick," Vaughn said to Brock as they walked inside the guesthouse. "I never thought of doing that."

"What's that?" Brock grabbed a beer out of an ice chest and joined the guys as they were telling war stories.

"Suggesting you aren't interested in a woman, but you're always there for her."

Brock smiled and tapped his frosty beer bottle against his brother's.

Their cousin Shawn joined them. "Yeah, he's slick all right. He moved in to protect the lady in SEAL-wolf mode right away."

"Hell, you're an Army Ranger. I would have thought you'd figure out how to snag her attention," Vaughn said to Shawn.

"I would have, but Angie wasn't buying it. She bought Brock's story—no more she-wolves for him."

"Natalie is so not interested in being here long-term," Brock said. "She will probably visit Aaron and Angie in the future, but you know how that goes. Everyone's busy with their own lives, so that could be rarely." Brock got a call on his cell and saw it was Angie on the caller ID. "Hey, Angie, what's up?"

"Hey, Brock, I swear I won't ask another thing of you this afternoon while you party with the boys, but we need a man to light our fire."

He laughed.

"We're all dressed up and don't want to get sooty or anything," Angie further explained.

"I'm on my way."

"Thanks, Brock. I knew you were the man for the job."

Vaughn and Shawn were waiting to hear what Angie wanted now.

"I need to light the ladies' fire."

The guys laughed.

"Do you need help?" Shawn asked.

"No. A SEAL can handle this." Brock headed out of the guesthouse and walked to the ranch house where the women were playing loud music and sounded like they were having fun. He smiled.

—⁓—

Bella and her sister, Serena, the two redheads of the gathering of ladies, were kicking off their sparkly sandals, then setting up a huge assortment of nail polishes to choose from for the nail-painting party. The pretty brunette, Brock's sister-in-law, Jillian, was preparing footbaths for the ladies. And Natalie helped Angie prepare finger baths. Natalie had never done this with anyone other than her mom and Angie, so this was fun. She removed her sandals and saw Bella and Serena making margaritas in a blender, just like they'd fixed when her mom and Angie needed a ladies' night!

"This is in memory of all the times we did this with your mom," Angie said.

"This is great, Angie. I love it." Natalie glanced at the stairs leading to the bedrooms. "You could have a ton of kids in this place."

Angie had always wanted to have more than one. Being an only child—unusual for *lupus garous*—and then losing her parents early on, she had always wanted to have more of a family.

"That's what Aaron keeps promising me." Angie laughed and so did everyone else.

Bella and Serena served everyone margaritas while the other ladies soaked their feet in the footbaths. After drinking their margaritas, the women soaked their fingers in little containers of soapy water. Natalie was glad when Angie scrubbed Natalie's fingers to remove the green stain from handling plants that morning.

After that, Angie made a call in the kitchen while the ladies began painting toenails. By the time they were in the middle of painting fingernails, Brock arrived at the house, surprising Natalie.

"I was told you ladies needed me to light your fire?" Brock asked, and all the ladies whooped and hollered, all except Natalie.

She only smiled at the sexy wolf. She imagined he could make for a sizzling encounter. Though she immediately wondered why he would have been asked when the ladies could have done it themselves.

Natalie knew Angie was up to something. She just hadn't thought her friend would try to match her with a wolf who wasn't interested in any she-wolf.

"Thanks, Brock, yes," Angie said. He started the fire for them, and Angie said to the ladies, "So, I met Natalie when I was vacationing in Cozumel. I had a boyfriend who got food poisoning at the salad bar. Such a drag. It was one of those trips that went downhill fast. Until I saw Natalie with her parents at the same resort. You know how it is when you meet others like us. We got to talking, and Natalie and I decided to go scuba diving.

The boyfriend went home early, and I eventually ended up in Amarillo to visit with her and her parents again. They realized I didn't have any family, and I just stayed. We've been best friends ever since."

Natalie noticed Brock was slow to make the fire. Natalie was certain Angie had told their story in front of Brock so he'd know Natalie was a scuba diver too.

"Hey, did you get your bags out of the car yet?" Angie asked Natalie.

"No, I was going to get them after we had our girls' party."

"Brock, can you get them? You can carry them to the first guest room up the stairs on the right," Angie told him.

"No, that's all right. I can do it." Natalie didn't want him thinking he was their errand boy.

"I'll get them." He held his hand out for Natalie's key, and she fished it out of her purse, then handed it to him.

"Thanks, Brock."

"No problem. Be right back." He left the house, and if it had been just her and Angie, Natalie would have said something to her friend about her matchmaking attempts. But she didn't want to do that in front of the other ladies, and it *was* Angie's wedding party.

Brock came into the house with the bags, and Angie said, "If you don't mind, you can haul them up to Natalie's room."

"No trouble at all. I'll join the guys as soon as I drop these in her room."

Unless Angie had other odd jobs for him to do, Natalie was thinking. Brock winked at Angie as if he knew her game.

"Oh, wait. I'll get my wedding gift for you out of the big bag. Let me grab that first. And thanks, Brock, for doing this for me."

"My pleasure."

Natalie unzipped the bag. She stared at the rolls of wrapping paper filling the bag instead of her clothes and the wedding gift. Underneath were a few men's clothes and a shaving kit—smelling like the drunken wolf who had collided with her bag at the airport.

Natalie's heartbeat quickened, and she felt her stomach turn.

Appearing shocked, the ladies all looked at the rolls of wedding and birthday paper.

"Ohmigod, I got someone else's bag at the airport in my rush. I always check the name tag on the bags at the baggage claim. *Always*. Except for this time," Natalie said, feeling like such an idiot, not only in front of all the women here, but in front of the hot SEAL wolf. First, she got lost, and now this? He must really think she was a flake.

Brock looked at the luggage tag. "Marek Jones from Amarillo, Texas. No phone number, email address, or street address."

"I need to get my bag back." Natalie was almost in tears. Her bridesmaid's dress was in her bag too.

"It's okay," Bella said, patting her on the back. "You and I are about the same size. You can wear my gown and I'll just watch if we can't get your bag tonight. No biggie for me, and Devlyn will be glad I'm helping him keep the kids under control."

"Thanks." Natalie knew Angie would want her in the ceremony more than the pack leader, since she hadn't known Bella very long, but Natalie didn't want to upset everyone's plans. She felt so stupid for having made the mistake. "I'll call the airport. Surely, they'll have my bag locked up, and I can leave this one off right away."

"It smells like a wolf owned it," Brock said, frowning.

"Yeah. It's the same guy who tripped over my bag when I was trying to reach the check-in counter at the airport in Amarillo. He was a wolf and sure was pissed off at me."

"So you met the guy." Brock pulled out one of the rolls of wrapping paper and looked it over.

"He's the reason our flight was delayed. He'd been drinking and was looking the other way—which was the reason he ran into my bag. I had to stop for people in my path. You know how busy airports are. Anyway, I smelled whiskey on his breath. Then he made a big issue with the agent about taking his bag on the plane. It was too big to be a carry-on."

"Hmm." Brock picked at the cellophane covering the wrapping paper.

"After that, he became belligerent when he had to sit by a mother with a toddler. He wanted to be moved, but we had a full flight. They ended up kicking him off the plane. They must not have gotten his bag off in time. The same thing happened to me once. Not that I was drunk or anything…"

He smiled at her.

"My passport had expired, and I had to take a train to Philadelphia to get a new passport and leave on the flight the next day. My bag ended up in Scotland waiting for me. This guy wasn't there to get his bag at the baggage claim. He must have been on the next flight out.

My bag wasn't there, just his, and it looked just like my bag, except for a few more scratches. But I assumed that was because of the gorillas who handle the luggage." Natalie was so upset over this whole fiasco.

What if the guy, Marek, took her bag? He was such a creep that he might just ditch it and go back to the airport with his claim ticket. Of course, that was saying he hadn't bothered looking at the name on the luggage tag either.

Brock nodded, but he appeared to be concentrating on the wrapping paper as if he could determine who the man was from the smell. "Three male wolves handled these."

As if that had to do with anything! Marek was a wolf. It wouldn't be unlikely that he had wolf family or friends. But Natalie delayed her call to the airport to see what else Brock had to say, as darkly serious as he was.

"Why would anyone fill a suitcase with rolls of wrapping paper?" he asked.

"Brock's a PI, if he didn't mention it to you already," Angie said. "He sees mystery and mayhem in everything."

Rolls of wrapping paper was an odd thing for the wolf to pack, Natalie had to admit. It was none of her business though. All she cared about was turning the bag over to the airport and grabbing her own.

Brock started to pull the plastic wrap carefully off one of the rolls.

"What are you doing? They're just wrapping paper, and I don't want the man to think I ruined his stuff when I turn it over to the baggage claim agent."

Brock ignored her and unrolled a section of the wrapping paper, everyone watching with interest, except for Natalie. She was irritated with Brock for ignoring her.

She could just imagine the guy who owned these needing them for something important, and she would be held responsible for the condition they were in when she dropped them off. Marek would be able to smell her scent on the suitcase because he was a wolf too. He might remember her from cursing her out when he tripped over her suitcase at the airport in Amarillo.

Brock cautiously peeled back the wrapping paper as though expecting a bomb.

"What…what do you believe is in there?" she finally asked, thinking maybe something really was wrong.

"Looks like a whole lot of money. One-hundred-dollar bills rolled up in the paper," he said.

"Oh…my…God." Natalie couldn't believe she had someone else's money. It had to be illegally gained, or he wouldn't have hidden it like that. He certainly wouldn't have risked carrying it on the plane if it was legit. The guy would come after her for sure. Not just to get his money, but to eliminate her for knowing what he had in the suitcase.

Brock was holding one of the bills up to the light, eyeing it closely. "Damn good likeness to the real thing too."

Natalie examined one of the bills. "It feels like an older bill. A real one. Are you sure they're not?"

"Yeah. I smelled fresh ink, but these are 1997 bills. A human wouldn't be able to detect the smell. I bet you anything that this is one of those cases where they're removing the ink from one- or five-dollar bills and printing one-hundred-dollar bills on the treasury's old paper. If there's a way to do it, criminals will figure out how to work the system. An eighteen-year-old girl was caught trying to pass them off at a Denver shopping center last year, but one of the clerks saw some smudges on the ink in a couple of places, and the ink was too dark in other places. There are pens that catch paper that isn't genuine, but they miss these because the paper is the real deal." Brock began unwrapping another roll, and Natalie and the other ladies grabbed one each to unwrap.

"If he finds out I have it, I'll be in real trouble. We can't turn it over to the guy or the police. Not when he's a wolf. I've got to call the airline about my bag." Natalie set aside the roll she'd unwrapped and all the money that had fallen out of it onto the dining room table. She called the airport right away and told the woman she had accidentally left her bag at the airport and needed to get it.

"We have it in the baggage office. No problem," the agent said.

"Thanks!" Relieved her bag was there, Natalie ended the call. "Okay, enjoy your party," she said to Angie. "I'll run to the airport and be back as soon as I can."

"I'll drive you there," Brock said, setting aside another roll of paper as if he had a more important mission now.

Natalie raised an eyebrow.

He smiled. "Just as a precaution. To make sure you get there all right, and if the guy shows up and thinks your bag is his, and he's still drunk… Well, I just want to be there."

She appreciated Brock for making the offer. "You can't arrest him though."

"No, but I'd sure like to get a look at him and learn where he's headed, if possible. I'm sure he's part of a group. Being embroiled in this business—losing the money—could cost him his life, unless this is his share of the money. And then he'll just want it back."

"What do we do with the money?" Natalie asked.

"Does anyone want to roast marshmallows?" Brock smiled.

"That will be the most expensive marshmallow roast we've ever had," Bella said. "I'll let Devlyn know we need to have one out at the firepit when the two of you return. Are you sure you don't want anyone else to go with you, just for extra protection?"

"I think it would raise more speculation if the guy is hunting down his bag and a whole bunch of wolves arrive there with Natalie." Brock pocketed some of the counterfeit money.

Natalie eyed Brock. "Need some extra spending money?"

"Evidence if I need it later. I wouldn't hand this stuff out for anything."

"All right, let's go." Natalie hated to ask anything more of Brock, but he seemed eager to help, and she felt safer having him go with her in case she had another run-in with the wolf. She glanced back at the table piled with money. "How much do you think there is in that pile?"

"Maybe three million." Bella was counting the stacks. "Ten thousand in each stack. One hundred one-hundreds. Only about an inch thick for that much money in a bundle."

"Amazing." Natalie just couldn't believe she'd picked up the wolf's counterfeit money. She was glad no officials at the airport had stopped her to look in the bag. Then again, she would have realized sooner that she'd gotten the wrong bag.

Chapter 3

AMAZED AT HOW CALM AND COLLECTED BROCK HAD BEEN when discovering the fake money in the rolls, Natalie walked outside the ranch house with him to his black Humvee. "You didn't seem as shocked as I was. Did you think money was hidden inside the rolls?"

"I had no idea. I hoped they were a salesman's samples, but I suspected it was more than that. It seemed odd that the whole suitcase was filled with them. And since I smelled wolves, I wanted to make sure they weren't participating in something criminal."

As Brock drove her to the airport, she finally relaxed a little. "I can't believe a wolf would be traveling with that much fake money from Amarillo to here. Someone's going to have to take him down, aren't they? We don't have a pack, so I'm not sure how that goes. But if he's coming into your territory, and he's a danger to our kind if he gets caught, wouldn't it be in your jurisdiction to do something?"

"Yeah. Anyone that could should put him down, whether he's in their territory or not. He endangers our kind by engaging in criminal activity. It would be great if we could convince the wolf not to do this any longer, but there's too much money involved. I imagine it would be too tempting to keep doing what he's doing. Unfortunately, that's the problem with *lupus garous* getting into the kind of trouble that could land them in jail. If he doesn't have wolf roots going way back, he could end up shifting during the full moon while he's incarcerated. Even if he is a royal with very few human roots, he could strip and shift and tear into an inmate, unable to hold his temper if anyone hassled him. We have an agreement now with the jaguar policing force to incarcerate certain kinds of shifter criminals. But not for murderers or anyone who tries to eliminate us. We have to terminate them; no jail terms for those shifters. It's really a shame people can be so talented, yet waste their talent on crime."

"That's what I was thinking. Plus, they probably figure they'll never get caught, and it's way more exciting than working a lot of eight-to-five jobs. Thanks so much for all the help you've been for the short time I've been here. I sure didn't think I'd have all this trouble while going to my friend's wedding."

"You're welcome, and no problem at all."

"I'm sorry I was aggravated with you for checking out the roll of paper. I guess you have a nose for crime, doing the kind of work you do."

"It might have been nothing, but it seemed suspect to me. And with the smell of the male wolf on the luggage, I had to check it out."

"I hope he's not at the airport when we arrive."

Brock didn't say anything.

She glanced at him and smiled. "You hope he is so you can see who the criminal is in person."

"Yeah, but I don't want you to be in the middle of this."

"Hopefully, he won't suspect I took his bag. Instead, that I was in such a rush to get to where I was going, I just forgot to go to the baggage carousel and grab my bag. Unless he's able to take a look at the airport video in the baggage-claim area."

"Legally, he wouldn't be able to."

"That's a relief." But now she worried that the guy would raise hell that his bag was missing, considering what was in it, and want everything investigated.

"Maybe you should stay in the car while I carry your ID and claim tag with me and retrieve your bag."

Natalie sighed. "No, that's okay. They might not turn it over to you, and I want to make sure I get it. Exactly how much combat training have you had?"

He chuckled. "Enough. I doubt the guy would make an issue with us at the airport. He'd be arrested, and none of us can afford that."

When they reached the airport, Natalie was again glad she had a SEAL wolf with her.

As soon as they were at the baggage office, she knew there'd be trouble. Marek, the owner of the bag, had sobered up, and he was berating the woman in the office for losing his suitcase.

Natalie poked her head into the office and said, "Excuse me. I'm here to get my bag. Thanks for locking it up for me." She showed her claim ticket and her ID.

Marek stared at her, and she felt a shiver steal up her spine. As if Brock knew she was afraid of the wolf, he ran his hand down her back in a reassuring manner. She appreciated it. The wolf looked down at the bag and eyed it with hard speculation. He no doubt could hear her wildly beating heart, just as Brock surely could. And he had to know their bags looked so similar that it would have been easy to grab the wrong one.

Brock seized her bag's handle and rolled it out for her, and they headed for the doors that led to the parking lot.

Marek came after them. "Hold up for a minute."

Natalie wanted to ignore him and keep going, hating confrontation, especially with a male wolf who had already been so belligerent. She had to deal with complaints at their nursery because her parents hated dealing with dissatisfied customers even more than she did, but their customers weren't criminals.

To her surprise, Brock wheeled around and said, "Yeah?"

She expected Brock to be all growly and angry because Marek was in the business of dealing in illegal money. But Brock managed a pleasant smile, which threw her and the guy off.

To Natalie, Marek said, "Your bag looks just like mine. Same color, same twenty-six-inch size. You were on the same flight as me earlier. How come you're just now getting your bag? Did you grab mine by mistake? And where's mine now?" *He* was growly.

"Not that I owe you an explanation for anything, but since I'm a nice person, I'll tell you why. I was running late because my flight was delayed. Some drunken wolf had to be removed from the plane. Which meant I totally forgot my bag when I reached Denver. I didn't even remember it until after we ate lunch, and I was going to give my friend her wedding gift. No bag, no gift."

Marek didn't look like he believed her.

She took hold of Brock's free hand and pulled at

him. "Come on, honey. We need to get back to the celebration."

Brock looked down at her and smiled and squeezed her hand.

She felt her face flush with heat. She hadn't dated in more than two years, and she had to admit Brock was total hotness.

The last guy she'd gotten close to had turned out to be using her. He'd wanted to get insight on her parents' successful garden nursery in Wichita Falls so that he could start his franchise garden shop and get rid of his competition. After she figured that out, she'd had trouble trusting men's motives, though she hadn't met any eligible wolves in Amarillo after their move there. She hated feeling that way, but it only took one lousy rat to prove not everyone could be trusted. She'd felt so bad because her parents had suffered too, not just her.

She heard footsteps behind her and was worried that the wolf was following them.

"Don't worry about it," Brock whispered in her ear, then pulled her to a stop and kissed her, turning their bodies so he could see who was following them. Still, he got into the kiss, as if he really was her honey.

Well, she was totally into going along with the game, since she'd started this anyway. She wrapped her arms around his neck and leaned into the kiss, tonguing him as his body pressed against hers. Hard muscle and the stirring of an arousal. She almost laughed at turning him on so quickly, but that would have ruined the ruse.

Their pheromones were zinging all over the place, calling for more, and she was surprised at the intensity of the intrigue between the two of them.

He smiled at her, almost looking a little sheepish, his eyes a bit glazed. Then he pulled her away to walk to the Humvee. She was dying to know if he saw Marek behind them, but if the other wolf was following them, he hadn't walked past them when they'd stopped to kiss.

Brock slipped his arm around her as they walked to an elevator and got on and pushed the button for the second floor. She didn't say a word, thinking Brock was going to the wrong floor so the guy wouldn't learn what he was driving. And what his license plate number was. When the elevator opened on two, Brock punched the button for the third floor. When they reached that floor, he pushed one.

He smiled roguishly down at her. Natalie chuckled. She really didn't believe it would work, but if the guy was trying to follow them, he'd be running up and down the stairs. When they reached their floor, they headed for their row and soon were in the Humvee and on their way. She was trying to see if the guy had figured out which vehicle Brock was driving. She noticed Brock glancing in his rearview mirror too.

"Do you think he'll suspect something more since we were trying to evade him?" she asked, worried that it might have been a little obvious.

"He already suspected you took his bag. I was trying to prevent him from learning who I am and where I live. Which would mean he might follow you there too. That's a lot of money to lose. He wouldn't know I'm with a pack here or anything about me. So he doesn't know the kind of danger he could face if he followed us out there. More than anything, I worry about you and when you need to go home. He won't know your address or name unless he tries to follow you home, and that could be a problem."

She hadn't had anyone but her parents to worry about her in a long time, so she really thought the world of Brock for caring. "But I won't have Marek's money. Not after we burn it tonight."

"He won't know that. And he'd probably figure it would be easier to get the truth out of a lone woman than it would be when you have me at your side. If he didn't make it to our parking garage level and see my vehicle and the license plate, he might hang around the airport, thinking you'll be going to Amarillo soon."

"Great."

"Well, if he does come after you here, he'll be one sorry wolf."

"Maybe we shouldn't have tried to lose him."

"Oh, I'll go after him. He's made the mistake of coming here. I've got his name, his scent, and I'll run a check on him. As long as that's his real name, I can run him down. I'll definitely be escorting you to the airport when you leave and be watching out for the guy."

"Right. You're a PI. I keep forgetting. Do you ever do bodyguard work?" She never thought she'd be asking a perfect stranger if she could hire him as her bodyguard until this was resolved. But she didn't want to bring this business home with her and get her parents into the middle of it without having some additional protection.

Brock smiled at her. "In the line of duty as a SEAL, yeah. As a civilian, not yet. But I'm up for hire for anything you might need."

Anything? Lighting her fire further? She felt she needed to fan herself.

"God, I can't believe I just came to a wedding and found I have to hire a bodyguard. I will never, ever again grab a bag at the airport baggage claim without checking the name tag on it first. My concern is when I leave here, he might have people watching for me on my return to Amarillo. They won't know my name, but he could send a description. Then my parents could be at risk, if the criminal followed me home. I'm not into all this cloak-and-dagger stuff. So I don't know what to expect."

"Can you hang out here in Greystoke a while longer? You'd have tons of protection from the pack. And there are all kinds of things to do. Too late for skiing, but you can ride your first horse. Or I could drive you home, and you could avoid the airport altogether. It's only about a six-and-a-half-hour drive from Denver to Amarillo."

"Driving would be fine. I had so much work to do before I got here that I didn't have time to drive, or I would have driven here instead of flying. Are you sure you don't mind? You don't have another job to do?"

"No, I'm free. I just finished up a case a few days ago. And anything criminal that affects the pack means I'll be working on it right away. Why did this guy come to Denver? We have to know if he's got wolf cohorts here and what else is going on. Are they working in Amarillo too?"

"I guess I should ask how much this is going to cost me to hire you as a bodyguard."

"Oh, I'll do it for free. This is personal."

"Thanks." Natalie really didn't know what else to say. She thought the world of him for wanting to help her like this. She'd never known any man who would do so much for her when he wasn't expecting anything back. But she wasn't going to let him do all this for free. "How much do you make as a PI per hour?"

He glanced at her. "Seriously, I don't need you to pay me anything."

She let out her breath. She would pay him for his time. It was only fair. She'd just ask Vaughn or Jillian, who had both been PIs, what they charged. They would know what Brock charged for his services too. Well, for that matter, she could just do a Google search. She pulled out her phone and looked it up. Between forty to a hundred per hour, plus expenses. That was highway robbery! Okay, okay, so she was still paying him. That was seven hours of travel to her home and back for him. So fourteen hours of his time. And the average was around fifty dollars, so if she couldn't find out his real charges, she'd just pay him the average. Unless he was under fire. Then she'd pay him more.

She frowned. Maybe she should be paying him for bodyguard services instead of PI services. She Googled that. Twenty-five to a hundred dollars per hour. She sighed.

He glanced at her phone and chuckled. "You're not paying me. You can buy me a nice meal on the road, if you feel you owe me something. Fix me dinner, let me stay the night, and I'll go back early the next morning. Unless there's trouble and I'll stay longer."

"All right." But she wanted to do more than that.

To her surprise, when they arrived back at the ranch house, he told Angie that Natalie had hired him as her personal bodyguard, and he had to stay with her the rest of the night.

Angie gave her a big hug. "He'll protect you with his life."

Natalie smiled. "I doubt it will come to that." She opened her bag and pulled out her gift to Angie and Aaron.

"I won't be staying in your room, of course. I'll just sleep on the couch. Unless you want me to stay with you," Brock said to Natalie.

She chuckled. "No, I'm sure you sleeping on the couch will be more than enough protection."

"This really isn't that serious, is it?" Bella asked. As pack leader with her mate, she or he had to let the whole pack know if they were going to have trouble.

"We do need to let everyone know about it," Brock said.

"Maybe Vaughn and I should go with you when you go home," Jillian said, sounding worried.

"Oh no, this guy probably won't learn where my home is, if they're even watching for me at the airport in Amarillo. He might think I live here and was just on a trip out there. If he didn't wonder why I'd buy a wedding present for my friend in Amarillo. But hey, why not? I could have been out there and found the perfect wedding gift for her. I should have told him I was going home. In any event, I can only afford to have one bodyguard." Natalie was still going to pay him to drive her home, but she didn't see any reason to pay him if he took it upon himself to sleep on the couch here. She was sure he wouldn't accept payment for that. But the trip to Amarillo would be the real inconvenience for him.

Jillian glanced at Brock, looking horrified.

He quickly held up his hands in defense. "I'm not charging her. I already told her so. She's going to fix me dinner, and I'll sleep over—"

The ladies all smiled.

"—before I return on the trip home," he quickly added, frowning at Jillian and then at Natalie as if to say she'd better not even think of offering to pay him again.

"Okay, well, if you change your minds, we're off for a couple more days before we have another mission," Jillian said.

"We've even talked of her staying here a couple of extra days, just so she loses this guy," Brock said.

"And you'll be her bodyguard the whole time?" Bella asked. "Otherwise I'm sure there are others in the pack who would be eager to make sure she's protected."

"Yeah. After I drop her off at home, if everything appears all right, I'll come home."

"Do you want me to open my present now?" Angie asked, looking as though it killed her not to see what was inside the wrapped package.

"Yeah, sure, go ahead," Natalie said.

Angie unwrapped it and smiled at a round wooden box with four cheese-cutting utensils inside, the top of the box engraved with their names and two howling wolves standing together. "Ohmigod, this is just beautiful! I'll have to have it on display."

"I'm sure glad you like it. I wanted to get you something really unique."

"I do. It's beautiful."

Someone knocked on the door, and Brock went to investigate.

"The guys must have heard you arrive," Bella said.

"I told them about the money. Everyone was waiting to hear how it went with the suitcase at the airport."

Vaughn was at the door. "Hey, we heard you come in. We're ready for the bonfire if you are."

"Yeah, we'll join you," Angie said, the women all having changed into jeans and T-shirts while Natalie and Brock were gone.

"I'll run up and change," Natalie said.

Brock immediately carried her bags up to her room. He set them on the floor and hesitated to leave, as if he was waiting for her to do or say something.

"Thanks again." She wrapped her arms around him and kissed him again. She didn't know what had come over her, except that she was so grateful to him for everything. And it seemed so natural between them. Maybe it was to see if their pheromones would react in the same wildly passionate manner as before. Maybe it was because just saying thank you again didn't seem to be enough.

He kissed her right back, his arms wrapped around her, proving he wasn't the least bit adverse to showing her more affection. "You know this is so not a good idea."

She smiled up at him. "Yeah, I know. Felt good though, didn't it?"

"Hell yeah. See you downstairs." He rubbed her arm, then turned and headed out of the room.

Wow. That was all she could think. *Just. Wow.*

She quickly slipped out of her heels and dress and pulled out a pair of jeans, sneakers, and a shirt. Once she was dressed, she headed downstairs to find Brock waiting for her. Her bodyguard.

"You take your job to heart."

"Always."

They joined the others, who were all waiting for them at the firepit since it was Natalie's "money."

The wood had already started burning, while the suitcase full of fake money was sitting on a chair.

Devlyn opened the suitcase and tested one of the bills with a pen, just for the heck of it. "We have these pens at our leather goods store, one of the outlets for our leather goods factory. Sure enough, the money looks like the real thing, paper-wise. We have a UV-light counterfeit detector too. A five-dollar bill will have a security strip that glows blue. If it's a hundred-dollar bill, the line will glow red; a twenty, green. If they used a five-dollar bill, removed the ink, and then printed a hundred on it—"

"It would glow blue," Natalie said. "That's cool. Sounds like something we should get for the garden center."

Everyone was gathered around the firepit, which was great for having s'mores and roasting marshmallows.

"Well, I didn't expect to be doing this right before the wedding—roasting s'mores over fake money—but I'll always remember it. I never expected you to bring the perfect game to the party, Natalie. Forget movies." Angie tucked her roasted marshmallow on top of the chocolate bar sitting on the graham cracker, then topped it with another graham cracker and bit into her s'more.

Aaron sat beside her and kissed her cheek. "You never told me how much excitement your friend could bring to a party."

Taking a deep breath, Natalie hoped this mess wouldn't cause real problems for any of them.

Chapter 4

IT WAS ABOUT FIVE WHEN SHAWN AND VAUGHN BROUGHT out the ingredients for taco dogs: Mexican chorizo, pico de gallo, and shredded lettuce with melted Mexican cheese, as well as hot dogs, cheese, buns, and condiments for the party, wanting something more substantial to roast over the fake-money bonfire than marshmallows.

In the meantime, Brock and Natalie were telling the pack about running into the man at the airport's baggage claim. Brock hadn't planned to tell about the elevator ruse, but he was glad to see Natalie feeling more comfortable with the pack and everyone laughing about what he had pulled off. They were drinking beer while his brother started roasting hot dogs, although others just stuck to the sweeter stuff.

"I've never been with a tactically trained guy who's good at evasion. I'm not sure what I would have done if I'd been alone. Probably walked back inside the building and tried to lose him there. So I was glad Brock was with me," Natalie said.

Vaughn was smiling at Natalie, and then he raised his brows at Brock. Brock hadn't changed his mind about her. He was a sucker for offering assistance to a woman who needed extra protection. He definitely wasn't looking at this as a possible courting. He was damn glad Natalie didn't tell about their kissing each other to throw the wolf off. Though he figured staying in the house longer with her might have led to some gossip.

When it came to males interested in a single she-wolf, gossip was a natural consequence.

"Well"—Natalie paused to sip some of a rum toddy—"we suggested we were close friends, so he might believe I had come back home here and that I wasn't from Amarillo. I really should have said something to that effect. You know, like 'I'm so glad to be home!' But I didn't think of it until it was too late."

Angie was eyeing Natalie with speculation, but she only smiled and didn't say anything, thankfully. Brock figured she knew her friend well enough to realize something more had happened between him and Natalie. He thought about the remarkable kiss they'd shared and how he really hadn't wanted to end it. Even now, his gaze drifted to her soft mouth, parted in conversation, her easy smile, and again he thought of kissing her.

Brock was drawn inexplicably to the she-wolf, her blue eyes hypnotic, making him lose all thought of anything but her. Gauging her expression, he felt she was enjoying herself.

"That would have been a good idea." Devlyn squirted a neat line of ketchup on his hot dog wrapped in a bun. "What I don't get is why the wolf was drunk going onto the flight. And an ugly drunk. That would be a sure way to get into trouble, like he did." He took a bite of his hot dog.

"Some people who drink too much are happy drunks. Some get ugly," Natalie offered. "Maybe he was having a really bad day."

"But why before a flight when he had all that money to protect?" Devlyn shook his head. "If it were me, I certainly would have waited to have a drink after I arrived at my destination and once I had secured the money."

"That's you, dear." Bella leaned over to kiss him. "That's why you're a pack leader."

Several agreed.

"I've been pondering it too," Brock said, grilling a hot dog for himself. He had offered to make one for Natalie, but she was happily eating s'mores. He thought she was cute. "Was he angry about something? Afraid of flying, and he hoped drinking would calm him? Or maybe he was celebrating."

"I think it was more likely he was angry about something. He was angry the whole time I saw him. Of course, he could be like that all the time. Some people don't seem to have a kind word to say to anyone." Natalie made another s'more.

Brock motioned to her s'more with his hot dog. "Do you want to go running after we finish burning all the money?"

She tilted her chin down and smiled at him. "Are you trying to say I'll need to work this off?"

Everyone chuckled.

"Sounds like a great idea to me," Angie said. "A nice run as wolves to finish off the night properly, then time to go to bed for the big day tomorrow."

Brock was glad he'd suggested it. He hadn't had time on the last assignment to stretch his legs as a wolf, and he was eager to do so now. With Natalie.

Everyone agreed.

"What do we do with the suitcase? I hate to throw out a good bag, the clothes, and the shaving kit, but he'd know it was his if he ever caught up to it," Natalie said.

"We can donate them to a charitable organization," Brock said.

"Good idea. I hated the idea of destroying a perfectly good suitcase." Natalie removed the guy's name card from the tag holder and tossed it into the fire. "To think, if he hadn't been drinking, we would never have known about this, and we would have just been enjoying the pre-wedding party."

"Yeah, but this made for a nice finale." Bella finished the last of her hot dog.

"Ready to go for a run?" Devlyn asked.

"I sure am," Bella said.

"Me too," Angie said. "If I eat anything more tonight, I won't be able to fit into my wedding gown tomorrow."

The women headed inside the ranch house to strip, while the men did so outside. Normally, they wouldn't have been shy about stripping and shifting in front of the others, but Natalie wasn't familiar with the pack, and Angie was still new. Before long, the she-wolves were bounding out of the house as wolves, all gray except for Bella and her twin sister, who were red wolves. Brock couldn't help but look for Natalie, the only wolf of the bunch he didn't know when in her wolf form.

She was a pretty gray wolf with black tips on her fur and a blonder chin and underbelly, running next to Angie, a pure-black wolf.

For a second, Brock thought about keeping his distance to prove he didn't have the hots for Natalie like some of his cousins did, though he noticed they were staying away from her, as if they thought he had already laid claim to her. But he *was* her bodyguard, so he was sticking close to her. He suspected a lot of the others would be watching out for her, too, because she didn't know this area and they didn't want her to get lost, should she get separated from them.

They took off running, Bella and Devlyn following behind, watching for stragglers. Natalie was sticking close to her friend, but Angie was playing with her betrothed, nipping and biting, and Brock thought Natalie looked a little lost. He had been keeping a watch over her, but now he joined her and brushed up against her to let her know she could rely on him to be her friend. That she was not alone.

She smiled at him, showing off her pretty canines. In that instant, he thought something special passed between them. He hoped she didn't feel quite so much as if her friend had left her behind. He realized being here was probably hard for Natalie because she didn't seem to be all that outgoing and it might be difficult for her to make new friends. Without knowing anyone, she had to feel like an outsider. Wearing a wolf coat didn't automatically change someone's underlying personality.

They ran with the others, but Brock stuck by Natalie's side, and she didn't bother trying to stay close to Angie and Aaron any longer. Brock was glad he'd made her feel more comfortable on the run. Then she started to really explore the area, not worrying so much about who she was with. The pack had dispersed, so they weren't all on top of one another. Though the land was their pack's property, they still had to watch out for trespassers—hunter types—and they made less of a target if they weren't all bunched up. Plus, they could let the rest of the pack know if they saw someone who shouldn't be on the land.

Natalie headed straight for the river. Others did too, but spread out from her and Brock. They were still within eyesight when the trees and shrubs didn't block their view, so it wasn't as though she and Brock were alone together. He knew his brother would give him a hard time about saying he wasn't interested in the she-wolf. But if the roles had been reversed, his brother would have done the same for Natalie, and it had nothing to do with his interest in her as a wolf.

Brock found himself hoping she liked the area, but he scolded himself for even thinking about it. She wasn't from here and she wasn't coming back, except maybe to visit her friend. He should just be hoping she was having a good time while she was here.

When she reached the bank, she stepped into the water and drank. He joined her and drank his fill.

He was thinking again about how he was going to locate the rogue wolf once he made sure that Natalie was home safe—if someone else from the pack didn't do it first. Natalie suddenly headed into the river. Their double coat of fur would keep them warm. Brock just hadn't expected her to go swimming. He joined her, as a good bodyguard would. She glanced over at him and smiled.

They swam for a bit together, then heard Angie and Aaron howl. It had been an hour, and they were heading back in. Natalie bit playfully at Brock, surprising him before she headed for the shore. He swam after her, and when they reached the shore, she shook off the water on her fur. Then he shook his off and got her wet again. She barked at him.

He laughed. The sun began to set, casting yellow and

orange across the trees, and he couldn't have enjoyed
the end of the day any more than he did now.

Then they raced each other back to the ranch. Brock
stayed outside with the other males to shift and dress
while the ladies went inside to change.

When he entered the ranch house, Angie was wearing
pj's already, looking tired and ready for bed. Natalie was
wearing jeans and a shirt but was barefoot.

"You might want to stay in Natalie's room to really
protect her," Angie said. She smiled, gave Natalie a hug,
and headed off to Aaron's master bedroom suite.

"That won't be necessary," Natalie said. "Night,
Brock. Thanks for sticking around. And for the wolf run.
That was so much fun."

"It was my pleasure." He hadn't had that much fun
with an eligible female wolf in forever.

Natalie smiled and retired to her room. Brock sighed
and made up the sofa sleeper. This sure wasn't how he
had thought his cousin's wedding was going to play
out. Hopefully, they wouldn't have any issues during
the big day.

Early the next morning, Natalie was excited for Angie,
though the whole business of the counterfeit money was
a black cloud hanging over her head. She didn't have
to worry about anyone coming for her and the money
though. Not with all the pack members here, setting up
for the walk across the grass to the dance stage, which
was the altar for now. It was a cool, clear morning, the
sky blue with white, puffy clouds drifting across the
expansive view, mountains off in the distance.

The stage was decorated with white lights and wildflowers mixed with roses all in pinks, reds, yellows, and blues. Natalie wished she could have been here earlier to help out with the decorations, but everyone in the pack had assisted, from the guys building garden arches and a gazebo and hanging the lights to the ladies decorating with flowers, ribbons, and lace.

Brock approached Natalie before everyone dressed for the wedding. "The pack paid for the gazebo and arches as a wedding present. Since Aaron is so gracious about letting everyone come here for pack parties, it was the least we could do."

"That's really nice. Angie said one of your more senior wolves is walking her down the aisle. A former pack leader, she said."

"Yeah. When we were young, a fire spread through the area, killing most of Bella and Serena's family and some of the Greystoke pack members. Many of us were youngsters. At the time, Argos was our pack leader. He helped to gather our people and lead them to safety across the river, where we stayed until it was okay to return to our land and rebuild the homes that had been destroyed.

"Some of the homes had been spared, but no one could have remained there during the fire and lived; the smoke had sucked the oxygen out of the air. We buried our loved ones and started anew. Argos was a great and fair leader, until Volan fought him to remove him as the pack leader. But the wise old wolf continued to teach us how to live and prosper and always knew that Devlyn would one day have the strength to lead. Devlyn finally killed Volan, freeing the pack from his tyranny, and Bella proved she also had what it took to be a pack leader, showing a female gray she wouldn't rule at Devlyn's side as his mate. In honor of everything Argos has done for us over the years, Angie asked him to walk her down the aisle since she has no male relative to give her away. She said your dad would have, if he could have come to the wedding. Devlyn would have, had Argos not wanted to, but Argos was thrilled to be asked."

"That will be so special." Natalie noticed everyone was going to the guesthouse and the ranch house. "It must be time to get dressed."

"Yeah, see you in a little bit."

Everyone in the wedding party had dressed with a western theme for the big event: cowboy hats, boots, flouncy white skirts, and blue jean jackets for the bridesmaids; blue jeans, white shirts, and denim jackets for the guys. Angie was absolutely glowing in a lacy white gown with an overskirt of blue denim, the front of the denim cut in a V to show off the lace. She also was wearing a white cowgirl hat and boots. Natalie swore she was more nervous for her friend than Angie was for herself.

After everyone was dressed for the wedding, and before Angie walked down the grassy aisle between the chairs they'd set up for the event, she pulled Natalie aside in the house. "One of Aaron's other cousins was supposed to walk you to your place, but Brock insisted he escort you, and the good doctor, his cousin Heath, will escort another of the bridesmaids instead."

Natalie thought Brock was so sweet to insist. He was total SEAL wolf material.

Angie was looking at her curiously, waiting for a response.

"Sure. Good thing. He's serious about being my bodyguard."

Angie smiled. "That's what he said." Then she laughed. "Okay, just wanted to make sure you were fine with it, and he wasn't pushing to do this while you were unaware."

"Was the doctor upset with the change of plans?"

Still smiling, Angie shook her head. "He said he knew that while Brock was denying he would be hooking up with another woman in the next millennium, he really didn't feel that way."

"He's not hooking up with me."

"He kissed you, right? When you said you were trying to pretend you were 'together' together, I know he had to have kissed you. And I imagine Brock is like Aaron—a consummate kisser."

"*I* kissed *him*."

Angie laughed. "You go for it, girl."

"We're not hooking up." Though if Natalie had the chance to get to know Brock Greystoke, who knew how things might evolve?

"Uh, yeah." Angie winked at her.

"Time for everyone to line up," Bella said, getting the ladies ready.

Natalie gave Angie a big hug. "You are so beautiful. And I'm thrilled you met Aaron. He and the rest of the pack seem wonderful. I'm so glad for you."

"Could be you too. Just hang around and get to know some of the guys. They've been so warm and welcoming. You'd love it here too."

"They have been, but I've got to get back to work."

Natalie realized that was all she'd been doing the last couple of years. Even when Angie had wanted her to go skiing with her, Natalie hadn't felt she could leave her parents to run the garden center by themselves. For Angie's wedding, sure, but not just to have fun.

"You know what they say about all work…"

"They say you get to eat and pay the bills."

Angie smiled. "Right. But just think, you might have learned to ski under the tutelage of a hunky male wolf."

Natalie could just imagine how badly her parents would have felt if both she and Angie had left them.

Then Bella took charge and had all the bridesmaids line up. Bella was in the lead, and the best man and groomsmen came to escort the matron of honor and bridesmaids to their places. Natalie thought Brock looked right dapper in his western wear as he escorted her to the front, her bouquet of roses and wildflowers in her hands.

Argos led Angie up the aisle next, and she truly was beautiful. The elderly man looked as pleased as could be to give the bride away.

It was lovely here, so special, and perfect for her friend who loved horses. Natalie got to thinking that when she married, she wanted to have a garden wedding. And a honeymoon in the tropics.

Brock was glad the wedding had gone off without a hitch. Now everyone was ready for the afternoon feast and then dancing. He couldn't help seeking out Natalie once the ceremony ended. He saw her talking with some of the ladies, and he didn't want to intrude. But he was watching his bachelor cousins and some of the other males in the pack, ready to intrude if *they* made a move toward her.

Vaughn joined him before they all took a seat for the feast. "Taking your duty to heart?"

Brock should have known his brother would be watching him observe Natalie.

"Yep. Can't call myself a bodyguard if I'm not guarding my client's body."

Vaughn smiled. "She's safe here. Well, mostly. You just have to watch out for our bachelor cousins. If she falls for one of them, you'll have to see her all the time and know you didn't get the girl because you were still riled over the old flame."

"She wasn't a 'flame.'"

"Not like this one could be, I betcha."

"If I asked Natalie to be my mate, you would be shocked."

Vaughn smiled at Natalie.

"You *would*."

"Yep. I told you that you were thinking of her in that way."

Aaron joined them as one of the pack members took pictures of the bride with her bridesmaids. "Thinking of who in what way?"

"Nothing." Brock gave Vaughn a look that told him to quit talking about it.

Vaughn looked at Natalie but didn't say a word.

"Ahh, I should have known. The ladies always fall for the SEAL wolves," Aaron said. "I was damn lucky Angie hadn't met you."

"Not this time. She was much more interested in a rancher type," Vaughn said.

Aaron laughed. "Looks like the weather is going to be perfect. We won't have to move to the barn for the feast and dancing."

Aaron had converted a large, red barn into a place the pack could use for social gatherings. In anticipation of good weather, the tables were set outside for the feast. Blue flax, wild rose, western wallflower, and columbines in the surrounding field provided a spectacular mass of color for the festivities, with the mountains nearby snowcapped, the sky blue, and the sun bright. A gentle breeze was blowing as the barbecued pork ribs and chicken, steaks, corn on the cob, potato salad, coleslaw, rice, and baked beans were being served. The large wooden stage was ready now for dancing, and band equipment was already set up.

Natalie was smiling pretty for pictures with Angie, giving her a big hug for one of the shots and turning to see Brock watching her. She smiled at him, and that made his day. As much as he hated to admit it, his brother was right. If Natalie hooked up with one of his cousins or any of the other bachelor males in the pack, he wouldn't like it. She wasn't anything like Lettie. She had no hidden agenda. She was here just to celebrate her friend's wedding. Natalie wasn't trying to snag a male wolf's attention either. And that intrigued him all the more. How could he win over the she-wolf who could only think about getting back to her parents and helping them out at the garden center?

Family meant the world to him, and he appreciated that she felt the same way about hers.

He winked at her, and she blushed.

Natalie had been afraid she wouldn't fit in, that Angie and her mate would be too busy to spend a lot of time with her. They were, but Brock was always there for her instead. And she really appreciated that. He was cute when it came to serving as her bodyguard, yet she thought there was more to it than that. The scoundrel winking at her made her blush to high heaven, and she noticed that Bella's sister had snapped a picture of her and Brock. She sighed. Nothing could ever come to anything between them with them living so far apart. Still, she loved how he had made her visit here even more special.

As soon as she headed to get in line at the buffet, Brock joined her. They filled their plates with all kinds of great food. She glanced at all the starch on his plate: corn, biscuits, rice, and potato salad. Plus a steak, pork ribs, and chicken. She smiled. Typical male wolf.

They took their seats at a long table with glass jars filled with wildflowers and bright-green linen napkins on plates decorated with wallflowers, which Natalie would love for her own wedding if she ever got to that point in her life.

"Don't tell me I eat too many starches." Brock cut up his steak.

Natalie glanced at him and laughed. "My mom always tells my dad that when he cooks. 'You can't fix corn and rice when you have mashed potatoes,' she'd say."

"I know that look. My mom always said that to me when we ate at buffets."

"Well, if it's any consolation, I wasn't going to say a word." What Brock ate was his business. Besides, *he* looked good enough to eat, so whatever he was chowing down on appeared to be good for him.

"Good, because I'll burn it off anyway. You do realize that gram for gram, starches contain fewer than half the calories of fat of many other foods, and they provide energy, fiber, et cetera."

"I didn't realize that. My mom always said all that starchy food would make you fat."

Brock shook his head. "Not true. Speaking of exercising, you're ready for some dancing after we finish eating, aren't you?"

"I haven't danced since I was a little girl." Natalie had thought some of the other single males would finally approach her and ask her to dance, though she hadn't for eons, and she'd probably be kind of awkward.

"No problem. You'll get the swing of it."

"Don't bet on it, but I'll give it a try." She would always try things once, or twice. She didn't want to look as if she wasn't enjoying the celebration.

After everyone was seated and champagne was served, toasts were made.

Both pack leaders made a speech, saying how fortunate Aaron was to have found a wolf mate who was as crazy about horses as he was and welcoming Angie to the pack. All his cousins ribbed Aaron about being the one they figured would take the longest to find a mate, but he had beat several of them, to their chagrin.

Even Natalie got up to speak, hoping she wouldn't tear up, but she knew she would. "To my best friend and her mate, I wish you many, many years of good cheer, lots of little wolf pups, and all the love you deserve. I'll miss you so much, but I'll be back!"

Everyone clapped. Brock smiled at her, thinking she'd made the nicest speech of all while he, his brother, and his cousins were giving Aaron a rough time.

Natalie was thinking how neat it was to be with a pack like this. Her dad had been so mistrustful of them that she hadn't known what to expect. He'd warned her she could have trouble if a bunch of males were interested in her when she went to Angie's wedding, that there could be fights even, but that hadn't happened. Oh sure, the bachelor males all smiled and were polite, looking highly interested, watching her a lot, but she swore they were staying clear of her because Brock was around her so much. Which she appreciated. Not that Brock was even thinking of being her mate. She thought the other men were being ultra-considerate not to overwhelm her.

She loved how the wolves in the pack could go for wolf runs together, how they had a big party place for everyone in the pack. How wonderful to be able to have other friends who were here to enjoy their company. Even when Angie had her own kids, she could be part of a wolf community, not doing things on her own. With a mate, of course, but he wouldn't know anything about raising babies either. Not like another she-wolf would who had already given birth. It wasn't the same as having strictly human friends who didn't know anything about their wolf half. How could a she-wolf mother talk about the issues of when their babies were running in their wolf coats with their mom, unless she was with a pack? Natalie could see the benefits of knowing others were close by to help out.

Even here, the other wolves were watching the kids of varying ages. Not just mothers caring for their own kids, but older kids assisting the younger kids, and some of the moms with babies were sitting together chatting it up. Some of the men were doing babysitting duty too. Just as wolves would.

"Angie said she had invited your parents, but they said they couldn't come. She said you all have been like family to her, so I was surprised about that," Brock said, catching Natalie's attention.

She cut off another couple pieces of steak. "My parents don't care for pack politics. At least when they were living with the last three. After the last one, they really swore off them. As to Angie's wedding, mostly, my parents haven't had any luck hiring anyone competent enough to run their business so they can leave. They'd do it if I were there. Angie and Aaron are staying with them when they come back from their honeymoon to celebrate their wedding there instead."

"That will be great. From what Aaron's said, she is really close to your parents too. I understand all about pack politics though. We had Volan, a beast of a wolf, in charge of our pack after Argos. Everyone wanted to get rid of him. A few died trying. No one was strong enough to best him. Not until Devlyn was old enough. Bella and Devlyn loved each other from the time they were young and growing up in the pack together. Devlyn had saved her from the wildfire where most of her family perished. Anyway, Volan planned to make her his mate, but Devlyn fought him for the right to rule the pack and offered his love to Bella."

"How romantic." To find a mate at a young age would really be something special.

"I agree. More recently, we discovered her twin sister

had survived. When Serena came home, she mated one of our cousins. Everyone was thrilled to have her join the pack."

"Oh, how wonderful. I noticed they are both red wolves. It's amazing how similar, yet dissimilar the two sisters are. I bet Bella and her sister were thrilled to find each other again. I always wished we had a bigger family. It's just my parents and me. Mom's sister died young due to a cougar attack when she was little. Dad's brother was struck by lightning when he was a teen. Just weird tragedies that befell their families when they were growing up. I had a twin, but she didn't survive the birth. Because of that, it's just the three of us. I can't imagine having all the cousins you do."

"We've enjoyed a strong friendship over the years. My brother and I left the pack to join the navy and became SEALs, just to do something patriotic. Shawn and a couple of his brothers were in the army. We had been gone a long time. We only recently came back and started our PI business, and then Vaughn went to work for the USF. It's a great organization, but I was ready to settle down with the pack permanently and run the PI partnership with him here. Not that my job doesn't allow me to visit other places, but I like going home after I finish a mission. He's asked me to join up with them repeatedly, but I like where I'm at." Brock drank some of his champagne and leaned back to study her.

"I don't blame you."

"What happened with the three packs your parents had belonged with?"

Natalie scoffed. "The first pack didn't want Mom and Dad to mate each other. You know how it is when wolves find their mate. It's more than a human interest in another human. Dad was a newcomer, and he and Mom just fell in love. Everyone believed Mom should have mated one of the pack members once she joined them. Her own pack had been lost in a flood. With the shortage of females, they weren't happy about Dad capturing her heart.

"Mom and Dad left the pack and mated. They finally found another pack, believing it was safer to stay with one rather than be on their own. There was so much infighting that it was like a civil war between the wolves, with two alpha males posturing to fight each other for the role of leader. Both factions wanted Mom and Dad to side with them. My parents didn't know who should be in charge since they were so new to the pack. They finally left, figuring the pack would have to sort it out for themselves."

"That would do it for me. What about the last one?" Brock drank the rest of his water.

"My parents finally found a new pack, which was important because my mother was pregnant at the time. We stayed with them until I was seven. Then the pack leader announced I would mate his son when we were both the right age. Can you imagine anyone being so unreasonable?"

Brock smiled. "If I had been the son, I would have wanted the same thing."

"I doubt it. It's ludicrous since we mate for life."

"You must not have been impressed with his son."

"I wasn't. He thought, just because his father was the pack leader, he was some kind of prince of the pack. He didn't have the alpha personality or leadership qualities to lead the pack. Last I heard, someone else had taken over from his father, and the son got mad and left the pack. If I'd mated him to keep peace with the pack, I'd be stuck with him in God knows where. After that, my parents just decided that they didn't need to be with a pack."

"No princes here. We have a great pack. I think even your dad would approve."

Was the wolf who wasn't interested in a she-wolf changing his mind about her?

Chapter 5

BROCK WAS CERTAIN NATALIE AND HER FAMILY WOULDN'T like joining a pack, which was the reason he wasn't going to get emotionally entangled with her beyond being her friend. "I don't blame your parents for not wanting to be with a pack after all they've been through." It was just as Brock had suspected. Her parents probably wouldn't want to come here to stay with his pack, no matter how reasonable his leaders were. Brock had been gone for so long that he enjoyed being around his cousins and their mates again. Even Bella and Devlyn's triplets. "Since you're isolated from packs, how do you find anyone to date?" He wondered if she only dated humans.

She shrugged. "I've done some traveling, run into wolves of different wolf packs. I dated a couple of the guys at Silver Town where I did a lecture on gardening for the pack. The guys were nice, but I don't think they were ready to settle down with anyone any more than I was. They were twin brothers, ski instructors. Funny, nothing serious, and that was it. Every once in a while, I've run into a lone wolf where we're living, but nothing sparks between us. Maybe we'd have a meal out or something, but that is all. Other than dating a wolf who was pretending to be interested in me but only interested in our garden center, long story. What about you?"

"Actually, I've dated a lot of humans, no she-wolves in the navy that I ever met. It was hard finding she-wolves to date most places I lived. The last one I was seeing turned out to have a hidden agenda."

"Oh?" Natalie sounded intrigued.

"Yeah, I was tracking her brother down for a crime he'd committed, and she knew it beforehand. I didn't know she was his sister. Not until I had a showdown with him. It was either him or me, and I wasn't about to let him get the best of me. Man, was she furious with me. That's when she let me have it about how I'd killed her brother. That's also when I realized she'd been using me, trying to learn what I knew about him and warning him to hide somewhere else every time I got close. I was such a dope that I didn't put two and two together about how the guy kept figuring out I was onto him and always staying a step ahead of me."

"I understand how you would feel, but I can also see why she was protecting him."

"Hell, here I thought she had the hots for me."

Natalie chuckled. "It would be easy to see why a she-wolf would—and not because she had some hidden agenda."

Surprised she'd say so, Brock smiled at her.

"What are you going to do about the counterfeiter? I know you're not going to just drop it," Natalie said.

"Once the partying is over, I'm going to begin looking into it. Since I'm driving you home instead of you flying, what time did you want to get started?"

"My flight wasn't leaving until late afternoon. I didn't want you all to think I was ungrateful and running back home right away. I figured I'd have breakfast, then head to the airport, so no rush. But…if you're going to look into this guy while I'm here, I could stay a little longer. Maybe a day or two. I don't have anything scheduled."

"All right then. We'll look into this situation with the guy, you tell me when you're ready to leave, and we'll figure out some fun things to do while you're here, if you'd like. You could even ride a horse. I see you have the boots for the job."

She stuck out her cowboy boot and examined it. "I wear them sometimes for fun, but I've never ridden before."

"We'll remedy that. Get those boots broken in right proper."

Everyone's dishes were being picked up, and they were getting ready to photograph the bride and groom cutting their cake. It was a seven-layer white cake, and the topper had two gray wolves howling, him with a bow tie, her with pearls and a veil. Blue, red, yellow, and pink sugar flowers decorated the cake and looked too pretty to eat, Brock thought.

They were just starting to do the first cut, Aaron's hand over Angie's as they sliced into the sweet confection, when a gust of wind out of nowhere blew across the field, catching Angie's veil and whipping it toward the cake. She grabbed for her veil and teetered, knocking into the cake. Aaron was grabbing her, others rushing to stop the toppling cake.

For a moment, it was chaos, and then with the cake mostly back in place, and the photographer snapping pictures happily, everyone began to get pieces of the cake to stabilize it, and disaster had been averted.

They all were laughing, and Brock thought the best pictures would be of the near disaster.

"Well, it is sure good," Natalie said after eating a bite of her cake. "Good thing it didn't all end up in the dirt!"

He laughed. "You know there has to be one thing that

goes wrong at a wedding. It looks like Aaron and Angie got as big a kick out of it as everyone else did."

Aaron was licking off the cake on Angie's veil, and she was laughing.

"When I have my wedding, I think I'll keep the cake inside. It's the best part of the wedding."

He smiled. "Not the groom?"

She blushed again.

"Been giving it some thought?

"No, not really. Not until I came to Angie's wedding. I don't ever think of it. Not when I haven't been dating anyone lately." She eyed his nearly empty dessert plate. "I know you had all those starches so you probably don't want to get any more cake, but…did you want to get me another piece?"

He chuckled. "Yeah, but I'm getting some for me too, so if you're trying to hide the fact you're eating a second slice, it won't work. Besides, this is energy food for the dance coming up."

"I'll go along with that."

Brock soon returned with two more slices of cake. "Everyone's eating second pieces. The cake artist is delighted."

"Oh, good."

They both finished off their cake, and then the guys in the band started warming up.

Natalie glanced at the stage. "Are they some of the men in your pack?"

"Yep, they sure are."

The waltz "Faithfully" played first, and Aaron and Angie began the dance.

"They're beautiful together," Natalie said. "I really

didn't think she'd met 'the one' when she first told me about Aaron. Until she wouldn't quit talking about him. That wasn't like her. When he came home to visit and meet my parents, he wanted their approval, and he charmed both of them. That's when we figured this was going to be a mating, not just a passing fancy."

Brock agreed. "We teased the living daylights out of Aaron, saying any she-wolf he'd meet at the airport on her way to ski at the resort wouldn't come back here to mate him. One of the days, we all went up to the ski resort to harass him about it, good cousins that we are, but we knew when we saw them together it was a sure deal. We were afraid we might have messed things up with her wanting to be part of our pack, but she thought we were really funny and loved that we planned to give our cousin a hard time. Especially when it backfired on us."

Natalie laughed. "I can imagine that it would have won her over. She has a good sense of humor, and she's always wanted a big family."

"Well, she's got it." Brock took their cake plates and dumped them in the trash, then came back for Natalie and led her up to the wooden dance stage. "The barn's also used for dancing in inclement weather, but it's so nice out, everyone just wanted to be outside."

"This has been fun. I guess you do other shindigs out here?"

"We sure do. We have a dance for every season. The winter and spring ones tend to be indoors. We often have snow on the ground." He pulled her into his arms and began to waltz and was impressed by the way she was so light on her feet. "You seem to know how to dance just fine."

"It seems to be coming back to me, but I'm sure it also has something to do with my dance partner."

Man, this was nice, breathing in the intoxicating floral and feminine scent of the she-wolf, feeling the heat from her body, and though he was trying not to keep her really close to his body—as in claiming Natalie for his own—they ended up close. Their pheromones were swirling around each other's in a much-too-interested way. Not that Brock minded, but he was more concerned about how she was viewing this.

She rested her head against his chest.

Okay, so that was really stirring things up further south. At least she was telling him she felt comfortable with the closeness. He wondered if she was just tired from all the activities last night. He couldn't control his traitorous body, which was rising to the occasion, or his thoughts about how he wished she lived in the vicinity and he could see her further, for a lot more of this.

When the dance ended, one of Brock's cousins asked her to dance. Brock had the hardest time releasing her, but he did, to prove to himself his brother was wrong. He wasn't hooked on the she-wolf.

Natalie looked a little apprehensive, maybe worried that she couldn't dance well with a new partner. Or maybe she was just shy around men in general, and now she was out of her comfort zone.

Heath smiled down at her in a warm and welcoming way, waiting for her to agree. It was a good thing, because if he hadn't, Brock was going to tell his good-natured cousin her dance card was full. When Natalie took Heath's hand, Brock finally left the dance floor and sat it out, not wanting anyone to get the impression he wanted to mate her. He just hoped she'd have fun while she was here, no matter who she was with.

When the dance ended, she thanked his cousin but headed straight to the table where Brock was sitting. And that had his heart rate accelerating, knowing she wanted to be with him before anyone else approached her on the dance floor. He was glad Heath hadn't asked her to dance again. Maybe it had to do with the growly looks Brock had been giving him, though he'd tried damn hard to pretend he wasn't bothered by the fact that his doctor cousin was dancing with Natalie and he wasn't. He did worry she might see the doctor as being a perfectly eligible prospect.

"Are you done already? Just one dance?" she asked, offering her hand to Brock.

He was over the moon. He immediately rose from his chair, nearly knocking it down, and hurried to catch it.

"Now that I remember how to do this, I want to keep on dancing until the clock strikes midnight or the band goes home," she said.

His whole countenance uplifted, Brock laughed and took her hand and led her back to the dance floor. He hoped his pack mates weren't watching their behavior, but he was certain they would be. Every last one of them. They were wolves, and the way individuals interacted with each other was always important.

It might be Angie and Aaron's wedding, but Natalie was a single she-wolf, and the pack had so many eligible bachelors who were looking for mates. Everyone was just waiting to see if this business between Brock and the lady was heading toward something more permanent. Of course, it was just for the time she was here. Then again, if she came to visit her friend, would he just work his jobs? Or would he put them on hold so he could "be around" for her visit? He knew the answer to that. He hoped she'd give him enough notice of a visit—or that Angie would relay the information to him—so he could make arrangements to be around.

"You're a scuba diver, eh?" Brock asked, wishing she was going to be here longer so he could go diving with her.

"Yeah, Angie just had to tell that story."

Brock suspected it was because Angie wanted to make sure he knew he and Natalie had something in common. "We have Carter Lake, Chatfield Reservoir, Blue Mesa Reservoir, Turquoise Lake, and others to scuba dive in."

"Really."

"Yeah, you don't have to go to some exotic place to dive."

"Same in Texas."

"Really," he said, surprised. He was thinking he might just have to check out some of the diving locations in Texas if she wanted to have a dive partner to go with.

After the dancing, Angie and Aaron were photographed as they drove off for a hotel in Denver. They would catch their red-eye flight to Hawaii later that night.

Everyone else visited and cleaned up after the party, and then Natalie and Brock went to the ranch house while everyone else left for their homes.

Brock had never expected to be alone with Natalie when Angie had first mentioned her coming. He had assumed someone else, their pack leaders maybe, would have her stay with them for the night so she wouldn't be left on her own.

"I'm going to change into something more comfortable," Natalie said to him.

"All right. I will too." He changed out of his jacket and trousers in a spare guest room and put on a pair of jeans and a T-shirt, socks, and boots, then sat on the couch in the living room. He opened his laptop and began searching for clues about Marek.

Natalie joined him in the living room, wearing a pair of jeans and a T-shirt, her feet bare. He liked that she felt so comfortable around him. He especially liked the saying on the shirt: *Hot to Trot*, featuring a horse in a dress, one front hoof on her mane, looking sexy—for a horse.

"I really didn't think you would get started on searching for clues this afternoon."

"No time like the present."

"Sounds good to me." She brought them glasses of water and sat down next to him on the couch—close, their legs touching—so she could see his laptop.

Her touching him made his attention drift to her again. Hell, he had to get his mind on business. She wasn't here to seduce him, just to see what he was finding on the internet. Yet he couldn't help breathing in her sweet scent of vanilla and peaches.

"His name could be fake." Brock didn't want to get her hopes up that he might locate the guy right away. He began to search for the guy's name in the databases he had access to as a PI. "Okay, we have one Marek Jones in the database who lives in…Amarillo, Texas. He's been there just a couple of weeks."

"No."

"Yeah. Here's a picture of him on his Texas driver's license. It's him." Brock showed her the picture.

She frowned. "No fake ID. Which is good."

"He must not believe anyone is going to catch up to him, or he would have changed his name." Brock pondered the situation for a moment. "Criminals come in all different kinds. Ones that are too stupid to live, like the guy who put on a mask right in front of a convenience-store camera, then tried to steal money from the register. Or the type who cover most of their bases, who are more methodical, yet still leave some things to chance. Then you have the ones who are super cautious, who cover all their bases. Considering the fact that he was drinking too much and being so obnoxious at the airport and getting kicked off the plane, then using his own name, I'd say he was in-between: not the most careful, but rolling the money in wrapping paper to transport it… That was clever. So it wasn't just a spur-of-the-moment criminal act."

"I still wonder about the drinking. Was it related to some issue, like he was angry with the people he's working with or doesn't like to fly, and not just because he has a drinking problem?"

"Or got dumped by a girlfriend."

Natalie's lips parted. "Okay, that could be. Is there any way to see if he has a girlfriend?"

"Yeah, doing a search for anyone who was receiving mail at his residence in Denver." Brock smiled when he found a hit. "L. C. Storm, a wallpaper hanger by profession. She had the same address in Denver, but she's receiving mail in Boulder as of a couple of weeks ago."

"A breakup? Why would they both leave? Why not just one or the other? Seems odd to me, unless he couldn't handle her being gone and had to leave the memories behind. How long has she been receiving mail in Denver?"

"For two years."

"So they've been together for a while. Is she a wolf?" Natalie asked.

Brock chuckled. "We can learn a lot through these databases but not whether the individuals are wolves. Her house in Boulder is only about a half hour from Denver, maybe too close for his liking if they broke up."

"But why would he go to Amarillo? No new girlfriend there, right?"

Brock checked. "A woman is receiving mail there by the name of Eugenia Jones. Marek doesn't have a job. He still has a bank account in Denver and one in Amarillo."

"A relative or a mate Ms. Storm didn't know about?"

"Checking. Not sure on Eugenia yet."

"Any former jobs?"

"Yeah, he was working at a wallpaper company in Denver. L. C. was working at the same company for the same length of time. They had been working there for two years. She has her own business now—the Wallpaper Lady."

"Well, that leaves him out of the picture. You know what? I've never been to Boulder."

He smiled at her. "You don't have a sudden yearning to see a lady wallpaper hanger, do you?"

"Yeah, I do. Could she be participating in the counterfeiting? Or is she oblivious? Maybe she learned about it and didn't want to have any part of it."

Once a criminal... It was hard to give up a life of crime when there was easy money in it, Brock was thinking. "Or she's working with others up in Boulder, spreading the business out a bit."

"Here's another thing I hadn't considered before.

Why, if he could just drive here from Amarillo, would he fly? It would cost lots more, and though it's still a drive, it would be safer than risking transporting the fake money on the plane. Especially when he couldn't carry the bag on the plane with him. You'd think he would have just driven instead."

"Unless he had a deadline." Brock continued to look for any information he could on Marek. "He purchased a car in Denver and has a former residence there."

"Don't you imagine he's with a group of people who are doing this? I would guess so, because we smelled other wolf scents on the wrapping paper."

"Yeah. An operation like this would require several people if they wanted to really make money at it."

"Make money. Right. What if he still has friends here in Denver? Business partners? Maybe the other wolves' scents on the rolls of paper belonged to them. What if he moved to the new location—Amarillo—so they weren't all in the same area? And it has nothing to do with his female roommate moving away. Maybe they thought they could move the money without getting caught if they weren't all in the same place." Natalie leaned her head against Brock's shoulder.

He glanced down at her shiny hair all in curls against his shirt. "Possibly. I'd sure like to know who else is implicated in this. None of us have run into any wolves we don't know when we've visited Denver, or we could have recognized the scents. When I drive you to Amarillo, I'll pay Marek's residence a visit. Are you sure you really want to go to Boulder with me in the morning?"

"I do. We can do a bit of conning ourselves. Do you have a room you'd like to have wallpapered?"

Brock laughed. "No. Let me ask you this: why would we go all the way to Boulder to find someone to do a wallpaper job when we could just hire someone in Denver?"

"She started her business in Denver." Natalie was looking at her phone. "Tons of good reviews. We could say I preferred having a woman do the job. She does consultations on Sundays. Tomorrow. Perfect. See? Do you have any rooms that are wallpapered?"

Brock looked up from the database where he was searching for Eugenia Jones. "A bathroom."

"Old wallpaper? Something new?"

"It's been there for twenty years, but it's fine." He realized how grouchy he sounded, but he was a bachelor male, and he supposed he was kind of set in his ways. Not that any of this was for real.

"Let's go see it. It's still early."

Brock frowned at her.

"We need a cover story."

Brock didn't see that they needed to go to his place to verify he needed to change his wallpaper. He didn't want to admit he was afraid Natalie really wouldn't like it. What did it matter if she didn't? He realized he already wanted to present a good image to her. It didn't mean he was willing to change his decor.

"And we can come up with more of our story. Maybe even lead her on to believe we might want another room done if the bathroom turns out like we dreamed it might. For the baby, you know." Natalie rubbed her flat tummy.

Brock clamped his gaping jaw shut. Never in a million years had he expected her to come up with that. The thought of making babies with her had his cock stirring.

Brock lifted his brows. "Don't let it get out to the pack that we're having a baby anytime soon."

Natalie smiled and hopped up from the couch. "I'll get some shoes." She headed upstairs and then came back down wearing a pair of sneakers. "Come on, Brock. Let's see what we can do about that bathroom of yours."

"My bathroom is fine. I'm not changing it." Brock was thinking Natalie would make a good con artist herself. He escorted her out to his Humvee and glanced at her rental car. "We need to drop off your car at the airport since we'll be using mine from now on."

"Okay, we can do that after we come back from Boulder."

"Sounds good." He drove her to his place, which was about a half mile from Aaron's ranch house. Brock had a big place too, in case he ever found the right mate and they had kids. Though he and Vaughn had shared the home before his brother found a mate and moved out when their house was built.

"Wow, this place is about as big as the ranch house. Room for all those babies, I see."

Brock laughed, parked the Humvee, and escorted her to the front deck. The covered wraparound deck was perfect for viewing the mountains, forest, and wildflowers in the meadow nearby, and he noticed she was admiring it too.

"You could have horses here," she said.

"I could, but they're a lot of work, so I just ride at Aaron's place when I want to. I'm off running around on jobs, and it's easier not to have to worry about the horses' care." He unlocked the front door and she stepped inside, the lights coming on automatically.

"Beautiful. Nice and open from the living room to the dining room and kitchen." She examined the walls.

"No paper, no need." Painting walls was much easier than papering them.

She chuckled. "It's only for a cover story. Show me the bathroom."

He led her to the first guest bathroom, which had a black, embossed pattern.

"Dark and outdated," Natalie said. "Yes, we definitely need something lighter to brighten up the room."

He turned on the light switch.

"Still too dark."

"I like it." He had no intention of changing it.

"Where's the baby's room?"

"For twins?" He smirked. "Triplets?" He glanced down at her flat belly. "You're not showing yet. Did we just learn we are pregnant?"

She touched her belly and sighed. "Yes. Today. We won't know if it's more than one baby or not for a while. Same with the sex."

"So we need a unisex color in the baby's room." He had never actually visualized converting a guest room into a nursery.

"We'll wait until we know what the sex of the baby is. And whether we're having more than one. Which will give us a good reason why we're waiting on papering the room."

"I have four guest bedrooms and the master bedroom." He led her down the hall and motioned to the rooms.

"Should we have the baby's room closer to ours, or farther away? When they're young, I'd want them close, but as they get older, they could play in their room and it would be nicer for them to be farther away, don't you think?"

"We can get a phone app that will let us monitor their room. It can be at the other end of the house, so we can keep an eye on them."

Natalie looked into the first of the rooms. "Checked into this already, eh?"

"I've had babysitting duty for Bella when the triplets were younger. The app comes in really handy."

"Good to know. This is a nice room. The furniture will have to go to make room for the cribs." She snapped some pictures with her cell phone. Then she moved back down the hall to the papered guest bathroom and took some more photos. "Is this the only papered bathroom you have?"

"I have a second guest bathroom and the master bath that are papered. But you don't need to see those." If she didn't like the paper in this bathroom, she wouldn't like the others.

"I'd love to see them."

He sighed and headed back down the hall. She paused to peer into each of the guest rooms and his office.

"They're all painted. No papering required," he said.

When he turned on the light for the second bathroom, she smiled. "Okay, so you papered both bathrooms with the same paper. Don't tell me you got the paper on a good sale."

"You'd make a good detective."

"Thank you." She took some more pictures. "The other bathroom?"

"Same wallpaper."

She chuckled and headed down the hall to the master bedroom.

"It's the same wallpaper," he repeated, exasperated, following behind her.

"Yes, but it might look just fine in the master bathroom if it has enough windows and it is bigger."

He didn't think she'd like it in there any more than she liked it in the other bathrooms, more windows or not. He could imagine her wanting frilly, pastel, floral wallpaper instead, because she was a gardener. A master gardener.

He turned on the light, and she eyed his king-size bed and the black comforter on it. He could just imagine the comforter would have to go, if Natalie had anything to do about it—and there would go his neat, orderly life. From super masculine to flowery and feminine.

She walked into his master bathroom and turned on the light. She sighed. "It's not as bad as the rest, but this could be changed to make an improvement." She took a picture.

"I'm not changing them." He packed an overnight bag for staying at the ranch house for the night and for traveling to her place and back.

She smiled at him. "This is just our cover story. If I were you, I wouldn't change them either."

"But if it were you, you would."

"Absolutely. A change in color and texture or print can make a world of difference from so-so to spectacular. Just like rearranging or adding to a garden. Big bed."

He glanced at his king-size bed.

She laughed and headed out of the room. "If the pack knew I left with you and we never went back to the ranch, can you imagine the rumors that would go flying?"

"I would be reprimanded for sure," Brock said. *By everyone!*

She smiled. "All for a good cause, if we make any headway on this Marek guy."

They drove back to the ranch. When they arrived after a few minutes, they walked inside.

"It's six. Do you want to grab a bite to eat and take a wolf run?" he asked, heading for the kitchen.

"Yeah, I'd love that." She looked in the fridge. "Well, we have some leftovers from the wedding." She began bringing out assorted dishes, though other pack members had taken some of the food home with them.

After they heated up the food, they ate their fill and visited for a while longer. Then they cleaned up the dishes and decided it was time to run. They stripped and shifted and tore out of the house. Brock had thought he'd be sitting at home alone after the wedding, maybe having some of the leftovers, certainly not working a case and not running with a beautiful wolf. They explored the land for a couple of hours, with him taking her around the area so she'd feel comfortable there, and he wanted to share the sunset with her again.

By the time they returned to the house, they found Jillian had made up a bed for him on the couch while they were gone. She must have returned to make sure he had everything he needed, even though he'd slept there the night before. She must have forgotten that part. Jillian had already left, but he smelled her scent on the sheets. His laptop was sitting on the coffee table.

He pulled on his boxer briefs, and Natalie pulled on her long T-shirt.

"I hope you don't get in trouble because Jillian came and didn't find us here," Natalie said.

Brock shook his head. "I'm sure she and Vaughn will

be speculating away, but they won't tell anyone else in the pack." He sighed. "No good-night kiss? After all the discussion of being 'together' to make the cover story more plausible? And…the kisses we've already shared?"

She laughed and went up to her bedroom.

He smiled. So much for having a nursery set up anytime soon. "Night, Natalie," he called after her. He climbed under the blue-and-white covers. Normally, he would be thinking of the case at hand, planning his next move. But all he could think of was Natalie and how different she was from any other woman he'd ever known. None of them would have wanted to accompany him to investigate a case, let alone go to such lengths to create a charade. It was a shame she lived in Amarillo. Most of his friends didn't scuba dive, so he'd gone with his brother. And with Jillian now too because she was into scuba diving. But he would have enjoyed doing that with Natalie. If she'd lived closer.

He just hoped nobody learned of the ruse they planned to use on the wallpaper lady.

Chapter 6

NATALIE LOVED GARDENING MORE THAN ANYTHING ELSE IN the world. She hadn't thought helping with a PI investigation could be so much fun too. Poor Brock. She was just playing the game, setting up a cover story for them. He was happy with his decor, and that was all that mattered. If it were her place, she would definitely redo the wallpaper in the bathrooms to lighten them up and add elegance or western appeal or charm, just something that would give them more…character. But if the black paper was him, then by all means, he should leave it.

Her dad was the same way about doing anything different. Except for gardening. In the nursery, he was all for changing things up to make it more profitable. Even adding the water gardens and a few cats to provide entertainment for visitors to the gardens. Those had been her idea, but he had been eager to design the water gardens himself. The koi in one of the ponds really added a special touch. But in the house? He hated it when her mom moved things around or overhauled decorating schemes. So she understood Brock's need to keep things the way they were.

She stared up at the ceiling in the guest bedroom. She had wanted to kiss Brock before she went to bed. Even now, she was thinking about his masculine lips on hers, making her blood heat and her heart pound, but she knew this wasn't going anywhere between them. She didn't want to keep thinking about him when she was home and he'd left there for good.

Yet she kept thinking about him, his hands on her as they had danced, their bodies snug, his whispered breath on her ear while he talked to her over the loud music, making her think of sizzling nights and sexy encounters. He was just plain hot.

The problem for wolves was they didn't have a huge population of partners to choose from, not like humans did. Narrow that down to the few she had encountered, factor in eligibility, sexual interest, commonalities, and being with the wolf forever and ever, and with them aging one year for about every human thirty, and it was damn hard to find the right mate.

After tossing and turning for what seemed like forever, Natalie finally drifted off to sleep, and it felt as though she had barely fallen asleep when she heard people up and about in the kitchen. She glanced at the clock in the bedroom. Eight o'clock already? She never slept in that late. She hurried out of bed, showered—so nobody would smell Brock on her—and dressed.

She wondered who would be having breakfast with them since so many of the pack members lived in the area.

Natalie reached the large western kitchen, which featured marble counters and beautiful mosaic tile on the wall beneath the microwave of painted ponies running across a field of purple flowers. Brock was opening cabinet doors, looking for something. The aroma of pancakes and scrambled eggs filled the air, but there wasn't any sign of the food.

"Good morning. Did everyone eat and then leave?" she asked Brock.

"Morning. I told them we had a late night trying to run Marek down and that we've gotten a lead in Boulder. His ex-girlfriend, presumably. They had other things to do, but if we would like, my brother and his mate want to have dinner with us tonight. They were glad you slept in a bit and are hanging around for a while longer. I am too."

Natalie smiled. "Sure, sounds good. And then we can head to Amarillo tomorrow. And check on Marek's house."

"Sure thing." Brock looked a little surprised that she'd want to continue helping him with trying to solve this case and not just go back to working her job.

She wanted to know if this guy was operating alone there. Or if other wolves had moved into the Amarillo area and would cause trouble for them if they learned Natalie had seized Marek's bag at the airport and knew what had really been inside it.

"Did you want to make an appointment with the wallpaper lady?" Brock asked.

"Yeah, I'll do that." Natalie was excited he was including her on the mission and pulled out her phone.

"What would you like to eat?"

"Um, what are you having?" She glanced over to see what he was getting ready to prepare.

"Ham-and-cheese omelet. Does that appeal to you?"

"Yeah. Sure. You cook too. That's nice." Natalie opened up the website for Ms. Storm's wallpapering services and made an appointment on the online form. Then she received an email verification and submitted the confirmation. "We're in."

"Good. Do you want anything else on your omelet? Bell peppers? Onions? Mushrooms?"

"Everything but the onions."

He was soon serving their breakfast at the kitchen table while she poured them both cups of coffee. "So what color scheme do you want in the bathrooms?"

"I thought we were doing just one." Brock raised a brow at her.

"We might as well do all three."

He smiled and shook his head. She thought if she mentioned all the bathrooms, the woman might be more willing to talk.

They sat across the table from each other, and he took a bite of his eggs.

"I think blue would be nice. It would pick up the blue in the tile in the first bathroom." She scooped up some of her omelet. "Not sure on the other two."

Brock didn't say anything, just continued to eat his eggs and drink his coffee.

She was amused. "Don't you think we should agree on this beforehand?"

"No. Don't you think it would sound more realistic if we don't agree on it?"

She laughed. "Okay, I'll buy that."

After they ate and cleaned up the dishes, they drove to Boulder. Since they were early, they went to a building supply shop to look at wallpaper, to give them an idea of what they might say to the woman. "Do you like any of these?" Natalie pointed out a selection in blue.

"I don't see any that look like the paper I already have."

"You're no help." She pulled up her phone and looked at the picture she'd shot of the first guest bathroom. "I think this will work."

Brock glanced at the picture and then the wallpaper. "I like mine better."

She chuckled. "You're going to have to agree to something, or we won't be able to hook her."

He was looking on his phone at the woman's website. "She needs two months to get to a job."

"Well, if we did schedule something with her so you could learn what you needed to from her, you'd have time to cancel on her."

He shook his head.

"Hey, it's about that time. Ready to see the woman and learn if she's a wolf?"

"Yeah, I am," Brock said, and they exited the building supply store and parked around the corner from her shop, just in case.

Then they left the Humvee and headed to the woman's shop. A green-and-white-striped awning shaded the windows in front of the redbrick building, with a hand-painted sign in the window to match. As soon as Natalie drew close to the green door and smelled a she-wolf, Brock motioned for her to stop and quickly moved away from the shop's door and beyond the sight of the windows.

"What?" she whispered, figuring the PI/SEAL had an indication something wasn't right, but what?

"Let's go. This isn't going to work."

Natalie didn't question him further until they rounded the street corner and she hurried back to the Humvee with him. "Okay, what's going on?"

"Either my former girlfriend used this woman's services to wallpaper her place and that's why her scent is there, or L. C. is Lettie. Lettie didn't go by the last name of Storm when she befriended me."

"Oh, wow, the one who was trying to save her brother from you?"

"Yeah."

"Okay, well, I've got to meet her alone then. You and I haven't touched each other today, so she won't know I'm with you. Do you have a picture of her so I'll know if it's her? I didn't smell her at your house."

"We always met at her place. Afterward, I figured she didn't want to meet any of my pack members or me at the house, since she was seeing me for devious reasons. Here's the picture of her." Brock pulled up a picture of Lettie's driver's license.

"No boyfriend-girlfriend pictures," Natalie said, thinking he might have gotten rid of them already.

"No. I didn't realize until later that she never wanted pictures of the two of us together or of her alone either." Brock frowned at Natalie. "This isn't going to work. I'm supposed to be your bodyguard and protecting you at all times."

"I'll be fine. I just need to verify if she's the same woman. If so, she was most likely Marek's girlfriend. I'm going to be late. Just stay here and I'll meet her, then let you know what happens."

"Don't tip her off."

"I'll try not to." Though Natalie wanted to remind him she wasn't trained for espionage work, and she couldn't guarantee that she wouldn't make any mistakes.

She hurried back to the shop and entered it, the doorbell jingling on the green-painted door. A perky brunette wearing a blue knit sweater, blue slacks, and high-heeled boots greeted her. "Welcome to my shop." The woman was the same one pictured on the driver's license Brock had of Lettie. She was a wolf with a big smile.

"Hi, I'm Natalie, and you must be…" Natalie almost said *Lettie* and felt her face flush with warmth.

"I'm Lettie. And you're… Well, how refreshing."

Natalie knew she meant to say *a wolf*.

"Come in here, and you can look at all the wallpapers I have. You can tell me what your interests are and the color scheme you're thinking of." Lettie led her into another room.

The whole little shop was wallpapered smartly, and Lettie had tons of shelves housing large books of wallpaper. A couple of long tables were available to set the books down and look through them. Lettie opened a couple of them for her.

Natalie was glad Lettie hadn't been to Brock's house where she might have seen the guest bathroom. Natalie showed her the picture of the first guest bathroom.

"Hmm, black and white. And you want something different?" Lettie asked.

"Yes, I was thinking something blue to match the blue tiles." Natalie pointed at the tiles.

"Oh, absolutely. So many new bathrooms are all in beige. It's fun to see the older tile that has more color, and it's important to embrace it." Lettie brought out some more of her wallpaper sample books. "Floral? Geometric shapes? Textured?"

"I'm thinking a textured wallpaper would be the nicest. One of those grass-textured wallpapers in blue. So it's not too busy but picks up the color of the tile and looks like it was meant to be there, not just some sale paper stuck up there."

Lettie laughed.

"But I have to get my mate's approval before I decide. After we do the one bathroom, maybe I can convince him to also do the other two." Natalie ran her hand over her stomach. "He and I will be having a baby or more in the future, and if the bathroom turns out well, I'll be back to pick out wallpaper for the baby's room, depending on what sex the baby is and if we have two or more."

"Oh, well, congratulations. You're from Denver, right?"

"Yes. I looked up reviews and saw that you'd been in Denver too. I really liked the idea of having a woman wallpaper the bathroom. It's really not too far for you to drive, is it?"

"The distance is no problem. I still have a lot of repeat customers from Denver. I lived there for a couple of years."

"Oh, super. Do you have a mate?" Natalie wondered if Lettie had a new boyfriend yet.

"Nah, just had a boyfriend. But we broke up."

"Oh, I'm so sorry to hear it. I didn't see any reviews for your Boulder location, so you must have moved here recently." Natalie continued to look through the wallpaper samples.

"Yeah, we'd been fighting a lot. I just needed to end it."

"I've had that happen before," Natalie said, trying to connect. "It seemed we couldn't agree on anything. Is your ex-boyfriend still living in Denver? I don't blame you for moving."

"Nah, he moved to Amarillo. Best for both of us. I just wanted a change of scenery."

"Well, that's a shame, but I hope you love it here." Natalie pulled out her phone and took a picture of blue wallpaper that looked similar to the color of the tile. Not that she was going to go through with this, but she had to make the trip seem real. "I think that this would be the right one. Do you have a sample of it? I'll have to show it to my mate and compare it to the bathroom when I get home, and then I'll get back with you."

"Yeah, sure. Be right back." A few minutes later, Lettie came back with a sample.

"Thanks. Okay, you are backlogged for two months before you're ready to do a job, correct?" Natalie tucked the wallpaper sample in her purse.

"Yeah. I'm booked up. Sometimes I get cancellations and then I can move clients up earlier in the schedule. I'd have to measure the bathroom to give an accurate quote. Here's a quote sheet that gives you an idea of the cost of the paper per square foot and my cost of papering. You can do a rough estimate of the square footage to get an idea of the cost." Lettie smiled brightly at her. "It's so nice to meet another…wolf."

Natalie smiled back and thanked her. "I agree. I can't wait to do this."

Then she left the shop, not feeling guilty since the woman had used Brock and made him distrust women and relationships because of it. She hoped the woman didn't look out the window to see where she was going and notice Natalie wasn't parked nearby.

When she reached the corner, she didn't see the Humvee. She sighed and walked into a coffee shop nearby, ordered a white mocha, and sat down at the window. Then she called Brock. "Where are you?"

"I parked a couple of blocks from the coffee shop, in case she followed you."

"She didn't. I'm sitting at the coffee shop. I've been watching for her, but no one's followed me."

"Okay, walk down the street two blocks north and then turn right."

"Do you want something to drink?"

"Yeah, that would be great. White mocha."

"Are you kidding me? Once we agree on the wallpaper, we're going to mate."

He laughed out loud, and she loved that she could amuse him so.

"I'll bring it. Be there in a few minutes." Natalie got another cup of the white mocha and began to walk to where Brock had parked the Humvee. She soon reached him, and after she got in the vehicle, he drove off.

"Thanks for the drink. You like the same thing too, eh?"

"My favorite is the peppermint mocha during the holidays. But the white mocha is my go-to drink any other time."

"I haven't tried the peppermint mocha before. Sounds good. All right, tell me what you learned," Brock said.

"The woman on the driver's license you showed me is Lettie. When did the two of you part company?"

"Two years ago."

"That's about the time that she hooked up with Marek. At least she wasn't with him while she was seeing you."

"She would have had a hard time keeping me from smelling him on her. I hope you didn't tell her you wanted to do the bathroom in a new paper."

Natalie finished her mocha. "Nope. I told her my

mate had to agree, and I'd get back with her. But that we were having a baby—or more—and would get in touch with her later on that." Natalie explained everything they'd said. "Of course, my first question is, if her brother was caught up in criminal activities, and her subsequent boyfriend is too, does she just hang out with wolves mixed up in crime? Or is she participating in some of this stuff too? Wait, I have an idea. Let's go back. I'll text her and tell her I sent you a picture of the wallpaper, and you agreed it would work for you."

"But it doesn't."

She chuckled. "Right, but we're not going to actually have her wallpaper anything. I'll tell her I just couldn't wait a moment longer to arrange to have it redone."

"You really don't like it that much?"

She laughed. "I'll say I'm going to put a deposit on the job. I'll give her one of those fake hundred-dollar bills you kept. If she's on the team—"

"She could try to hurt you if she thought you were going to turn her over to the pack for her criminal activities."

"I'll keep my phone line open. You can come to my rescue if I need it."

Brock grunted, but he turned the Humvee around and parked where he had before so they weren't in sight of Lettie's shop.

"If she's not implicated, she'll just accept the money."

Brock frowned at Natalie. "Unless she suspects it's fake because she runs a business and she would be cautious about accepting that large a bill."

"If she figured out the bill was fake because she was more observant, she wouldn't call the police because we're both wolves. I'm not getting change back or free goods that could be returned for real cash, which would be a counterfeiter's goal. Or free meals, or whatever. It's going to be so long before she wallpapers the room that I wouldn't benefit from it. For me to intend to defraud her would be silly, because once she tried to deposit the bill at the bank, she'd know and have my name and everything. So if she's not participating in any of this, she would probably ask me where I got the bill, if she realizes it's counterfeit."

"What address would you give her?"

"What if I give the ranch house as the address? If anyone shows up there, they have ranch hands who can deal with the person or people. Wolves."

"If you use Aaron's last name, it's the same as mine. Same with the pack leader. Lettie will know it has something to do with me."

"If she knows my last name, she might be able to verify I don't have a home here, if she investigates this on her own. I just want to see her reaction, smell her scent, see if she gives herself away."

"One thing to know about Lettie… She has manipulation down to a science. I wouldn't be surprised if she took the money and pretended it was real, if she recognized it wasn't, and then got in touch with her cohorts, if she's involved. If she asks you where you got the money, feigning concern you were duped, what would you say? From your garden shop? But then you'd have to make up a garden shop that you don't own in Denver, and she could investigate that and learn you're a fraud."

"Okay, so I just make up a garden shop, make up a home address, show her the bill, and pretend I'm clueless, just to see her reaction." Natalie grabbed for the door handle.

"I'm your bodyguard for now, and a SEAL and a PI, and I don't like this plan."

"Stand near her shop, just out of view of the windows. And I'll scream if anything bad happens."

"I still don't like the plan, but let's do this."

"I'll go first. You stay some distance back." Then Natalie texted Lettie: Douglas agreed to the wallpaper, sight unseen. I can have whatever I want. He's the greatest. I'll come in and make the deposit. Be there soon.

"Douglas?" Brock said, looking over at her phone.

She smiled.

As soon as they reached the shop, Brock stayed out of sight of the windows while Natalie went to the door. She heard people talking inside and opened the door. A couple was speaking with Lettie, and Natalie waved at her in acknowledgment.

"I'll be with you in just a second," Lettie said.

Her palms growing sweaty, Natalie felt guilty that she intended to give the fake hundred-dollar bill to the woman. Then again, Lettie had used Brock in an effort to protect her rogue brother, so she wasn't all that innocent. And she could very well be implicated in all of this. Still, Natalie was taking deep breaths, trying to calm her nervousness. She realized how much *she* didn't like handling the money herself. She definitely wasn't cut out to pursue a life of crime.

"Just look at those designs, and I'll be right back with you." Lettie turned and joined Natalie. "Yeah, so you wanted to get that blue paper you were looking at?"

"Yeah. Douglas said it didn't really matter to him.

That I could do whatever I wanted. I knew there was a reason why I married him. Is a hundred-dollar bill okay for a deposit?"

Natalie fished the bill out of her pocket, her stomach muscles tense, ready to pounce if the woman tried anything physical with her. Then again, with customers in the shop, Lettie would probably play it cool.

"Uh, yeah, sure. I'll need to schedule an appointment to come out and measure the bathroom." Lettie pulled up a tablet.

Natalie wanted to get this over with, so she quickly handed Lettie the bill before she gave her an address.

Lettie stared at the bill for a moment, and then she ran it under a scanner, and her face turned dark with anger. "Where did you get this? Marek put you up to this." She was trying to keep her voice low, but she was angry.

Lettie knew Marek was into this business! If Lettie was engaged in it, Natalie didn't think she would have said what she did. But now what was Natalie to say?

"Take the money and get out of here," Lettie said, her voice low so her real customers wouldn't hear them.

"We…need to talk," Natalie said, relieving her of the bill.

Lettie glowered at her, and after what seemed like an interminable time, she finally nodded. "After my clients leave. Go to the coffee shop around the corner, and I'll let you know when to come back."

"Sure." Maybe they'd get some good intel on Marek. Natalie was really hoping that Lettie wasn't conning her. Natalie headed outside and joined up with Brock.

"You look pale. I heard what happened," Brock said.

"Yeah, it was nerve-racking, giving her the fake

money. And she was plenty angry about the money. But she implicated Marek right away. Do you want to go to the coffee shop with me, and we'll wait for her call after her clients leave?"

"I want you to go to the coffee shop and wait for her to contact you. I'll watch the door of her shop and make sure she doesn't run off."

"Okay. But if she sees you?"

"I'll be in the grocery shop across the street. They have a café there."

Natalie glanced at the store to see how far it was. It was close by. "Are you going to join us? She might not speak to me if you're there."

"I don't like the idea of you alone with her after she's learned this wasn't about a real wallpapering job."

"I'll keep the phone line open again. I'll scream bloody murder. You can come and rescue me. I'll see you in a little bit." Natalie hurried off to the coffee shop to wait for word from Lettie so that they wouldn't blow their cover, or Brock wouldn't change his mind about her going it alone.

Natalie hoped this didn't go sideways.

Chapter 7

BROCK SURE HOPED GETTING INVOLVED WASN'T GOING TO cause more problems for Natalie.

A half hour later while he was watching out the café window in the grocery store, he got a call from her. "Lettie's finished with her clients and wants me to go back to the shop. She doesn't have any more clients this afternoon. I'm leaving my phone open so you can hear us talking."

"Okay, good. I'll leave the grocery store and stand on the corner where she can't see me." He watched as the couple Lettie had been speaking with left her shop.

Then Natalie walked around the corner and entered the shop. Brock was glad she was keeping the phone line open again so he could hear if she had any trouble.

"Hi, Lettie. Yeah, we need to talk," Natalie said to her.

Once Natalie closed the door, Brock left the grocery store and walked to a location closer to the wallpaper shop instead, just in case Natalie needed his bodyguard services in a hurry.

He heard a crinkling noise that he suspected was the money she was removing from her pocket. "You knew this was a fake right away," Natalie said.

Pause. Brock's muscles tightened in anticipation of making a whirlwind dash for the store.

"How did you get this money?" Lettie was irate. She waited for a response, but Natalie didn't say anything.

"You're from Denver, and you're a wolf. You got it from Marek, didn't you? And he told you to come here and pay me for a job? The *bastard*. I knew he'd been seeing someone else behind my back. So why the hell are you here harassing me?"

Natalie didn't answer Lettie's question. Brock wasn't sure she'd be able to handle an investigative job without some training.

"Did you know he was making counterfeit money?" Natalie finally asked, sounding sympathetic, as if she was offering Lettie a shoulder to cry on, not as though she was accusing her of being in on the illicit business.

Once Natalie began questioning Lettie, Brock thought she was surprisingly good in the way she was handling it.

Lettie didn't answer Natalie at first. Brock was still ready to sprint for the door. He didn't like long periods of silence, afraid something bad was going to happen.

Lettie snorted. "Not that I knew of at first. Marek talked about creating the money, but I never believed he'd really have the brains to do it. Or the gumption." Again, another pause. "Are you his new girlfriend? Old girlfriend?" This time Lettie wasn't as hostile, as if the way Natalie was handling this had changed her tune.

Brock was glad for that.

"Hardly," Natalie said.

Another significant pause.

"Wait a minute," Lettie said. "Let me see that bill again."

Brock wondered what Lettie intended to do with it. He heard Natalie hand it over, but then he realized their whole cover was a bust.

"Ohmigod," Lettie said, smelling the bill and noticing Brock's scent on it.

Neither of them had considered that.

"It's Marek's money, but Brock's scent is on it too! Don't tell me you're a PI and you hooked up with Brock Greystoke." Now Lettie was angry again.

Hell. Lettie was smart. If Marek wasn't the brains of the operation, Brock could see where Lettie might have been.

"I should have known it! So what does he think? Brock can pin this on me now? Is he still mad at me for leading him on so I could save my brother? You know he killed him, don't you?"

"Your brother killed a woman and her child in a bank robbery. What did you think would happen to him? He was a dead wolf walking. Someone was bound to catch up to him eventually. Our kind couldn't let the human police capture him and have him tried for the murders. You know that."

"I loved my brother. You don't know anything about him. He would never have killed them on purpose. He wouldn't have!" A drawer slammed.

Brock started to move closer to the shop.

"Well, he *did* kill them during the commission of a federal crime. And *you* knew about it. Which makes you an accessory. You're as guilty as he was." Natalie was no longer Miss Congeniality.

Hell, Natalie. Brock bolted for the shop, worried she was going to push Lettie too far, and who knew how the woman might retaliate.

"I wasn't part of his business. I just loved him was all. And that's *not* a crime."

"Then you're shacking up with a wolf who's making counterfeit money? How much of the profits did he give you to set up your wallpaper business?" Natalie asked, really accusing Lettie now.

No, no, no! Brock was near the shop. Just a few steps, and he'd barge in.

"Marek bragged about making the money. I told you I didn't think he would be able to create it. I didn't have a thing to do with it. After losing my brother, I wasn't about to be with anyone who is implicated in criminal pursuits. Once I learned Marek really did make some of the money, I moved out. I have a legitimate business here, and I make an honest living at it. I didn't want to be caught up in all his shenanigans. Don't you dare accuse me of doing anything with that damn money!"

"When you left Denver, why did he leave too? Seems to me if he left the area, you wouldn't have any reason to."

Brock hesitated at the door. Natalie seemed to be okay, and she *was* getting information out of Lettie. Probably more than he would if he tried to question her because of the animosity between them.

"Marek said he loved me. Always had. He said he couldn't stay in Denver any longer. There were too many memories," Lettie said.

"Do you believe him?"

"I don't know. I mean, I'm sure the people he works with are in Denver, so it seems like living so far away would be an issue for him. Unless he's going into business with someone else located in Amarillo."

"What about how you treated Brock—lying to him, pretending to want something real with him? It could very well be that you are lying to me now."

Hell. Don't bring me into the picture, Natalie!

"No, I'm not lying. What do I have to gain from it?

Oh, and don't worry, sweetie. That bastard's all yours, if that's what you're really worried about." Another pause. "So what did Brock do? Send you to do his dirty work because he was afraid to see me himself?"

"He didn't have any idea you were Lettie."

Time to be part of this. Brock switched off his phone and barged into the shop.

When he threw the door open, Lettie shrieked. Natalie jumped, folded her arms, and rolled her eyes at him. Lettie grabbed a wallpaper sample book and threw it at him.

Which was just what he'd hoped for. He easily caught the heavy book, slipped a listening bug into the plastic holder on the front, and dropped the book on a table. "As long as you aren't mixed up with what Marek's doing, you're off the hook," he said, all growly. "But if you've lied, I'll be back for you. On the subject of your brother, when I dug deeper, I learned he had killed three more people during the commission of other armed robberies. He just didn't seem to give a damn. Kill the witnesses, seize the money, and run. You were informing him of any leads I had on him. When he got tired of trying to keep out of my reach, he and two other men ambushed me. He was bad news. The sooner you learn to live with that, the better."

Brock felt only animosity for the woman. Sure, the guy had been her brother. But pretending to be Brock's girlfriend to keep her brother safe was something Brock could never forgive because the guy was a killer. Brock suspected he felt so much hostility toward her because he couldn't believe she'd pulled the wool over his eyes so completely. He was also sick of hearing how her brother had only *accidentally* killed the woman and her child.

DJ had been a killer. He'd wanted the money, sure, and he hadn't cared who died while he was in pursuit of it.

Lettie snapped her gaping mouth shut. Maybe she hadn't known her brother had killed other people. Those were the only other murders that he had committed, as far as Brock knew. There could very well have been more.

"Do you know who else Marek might have been working with, who helped create the money?" Natalie asked, getting back to the real business at hand.

"No, but if I did, why would I tell you?" Lettie folded her arms, her face red, her brow furrowed with anger.

"You would because if they realize you knew about the operation through Marek, they may want to kill you, now that you and he aren't together any longer. They might think you'd want to tell someone what you know to get back at Marek. Who knows?" Natalie said. "These guys are making too much money to let anyone stand in their way. That means someone like you could be an easy target. No pack to back you up. You're all on your own. It would benefit you if we took care of them first."

"I told you already I didn't know he was really doing it. Until he showed me a fake bill." Lettie shrugged and began shelving her wallpaper books on a tall shelf. "I told him if he really was doing anything criminal, I wouldn't stay with him. He knew how I felt about my brother and the mess he got himself into. I wasn't about to go through that with a boyfriend. And I certainly didn't want to be accused of being part of it. I told him I was leaving and setting up shop away from all that. Away from Brock too. Even though I hadn't run into him in Denver, I knew he lived in Greystoke, and that was too close for comfort."

"Took you long enough." Brock couldn't help it. After what she had pulled, he couldn't believe she'd stayed in the area, or that *he* was the reason for her finally leaving two years later.

Lettie scowled at Brock. "I was seeing Marek then. Of course, I wouldn't have left. Not even when you were living nearby. Once I ended things with Marek, there wasn't any reason to stay."

Natalie let out her breath. "You met Marek in the wallpapering business?"

"Yeah, but he was friends with my brother before that. I had known him for a long time. We were all friends over the years. Maybe my brother talked him into doing something 'easier' to earn some money." Lettie threw up her hands. "This is all speculation. I didn't know, all right? If he'd been in on the armed robberies with my brother, Brock would have learned of it." She turned to Brock. "Right?"

"You're right. Marek wasn't on the last bank robbery. But in the other case where I learned DJ had killed the couple and their friend in the armed robbery? Maybe. There were three men. DJ was the only one who had been identified, but the police couldn't catch up to him."

"Okay, so who might have worked with Marek in the business of counterfeiting? Do you know any people he was hanging out with? Maybe even friends he wanted to spend time alone with?" Natalie asked, steering them in the right direction. She was good at this. "Maybe even friends of your brother and Marek that you know of."

"Yeah, of course he had male friends he socialized with," Lettie said.

"Any that you knew by name or that you can give us a description of?" Natalie asked.

Brock was about to ask the same question, but Natalie seemed to be doing fine and Lettie didn't seem as reluctant to share with her.

"Dexter Cartwright, Joe McKnight, and Benjamin Hayward. They'd all go together to the pub near our house. They weren't gone long, and Marek would come back in a cheerful mood, so it wasn't an issue with us. If he'd been gone for hours, drinking it up with his buddies, I would have left sooner."

"But it could have been time they used to make plans," Natalie said.

"Or just drink. You can find fault with everyone when you're really looking for it, you know," Lettie said.

"Any other names you might have overheard? Had Marek been acting suspicious, trying to keep what he was doing secret from you?" Natalie asked.

"He suddenly had a sick aunt in Amarillo that I knew nothing about. He kept driving down there to check on her. Stay a few days, then come home. I smelled the she-wolf on him, so he hadn't tried to hide that from me. You know we have faster-healing genetics, so I asked what was wrong, figuring if she was a sick aunt, she'd get better soon. He said she was an alcoholic and on dialysis. I wondered if he really had a girlfriend and was just lying. But he did it a few times, and then that was it. He said she was better. Which didn't make any sense. Being on dialysis wouldn't just stop, unless the person died.

"Then we broke up. I thought he figured he should move closer to her, and that's why he packed up and left for Amarillo. Or maybe she really is a girlfriend. He showed me a fake bill and was so damn proud of it. Made me sick. I work hard for my money. I'd be pissed off if someone gave me fake money to pay for my services." Lettie straightened. "That's all I know."

Brock was certain Lettie had been well aware of what had gone on. She wasn't that naive. Maybe the counterfeit money had been the last straw with Marek, and Lettie was afraid somehow Brock would learn of it and make her pay for it since they lived in the same area. He didn't get into Denver much, and where she'd been living with Marek had been in a part of town he never visited, or he might have run across her at some time or other.

"I don't know anyone else he might have been seeing. I didn't think he was acting suspicious about anything else. And I was damn busy trying to get my business off the ground," Lettie said.

Natalie nodded. "Is Marek prone to drinking too much?"

Lettie's brows shot up. Brock took that as a yes.

Natalie explained, "He got kicked off a plane for being drunk and disorderly."

Lettie's jaw dropped.

"Is he usually like that?" Natalie asked.

"Not around me. Well, when I said I was leaving him, he began drinking heavily. I figured it all had to do with me leaving. That he'd get over me soon enough, and it was just a temporary thing."

Natalie glanced at Brock to see if he had any questions for Lettie.

"I better not learn you're helping with this, once I check into these other guys," Brock said to Lettie.

"Or what? You'll kill me? In self-defense?" Lettie made a derisive sound.

"Don't do the crime, and you'll stay off my hit list. Ready to go?" he said to Natalie.

She looked as though she wanted to say something more, but then she nodded and left the shop ahead of him. He turned back to Lettie and said, "Do you want my card in case you recall anything more? Or do you still have it?" He smiled and walked out of the shop after Natalie.

Lettie slammed the door behind them.

"Why were you antagonizing her so much in there?" Now Natalie sounded hostile with *him*.

"And you *weren't*?" He shook his head. "She's a con artist. She's good at her job. I don't believe her when she says she didn't know what was going on all along. She may be in on the whole operation, and splitting up with Marek was just a ruse. She may be moving the operation up here."

"But he was angry at the airport. Breaking up with his girlfriend could certainly cause that. Did her brother really kill others beforehand? Lettie seemed surprised to hear that."

"Yes, he did. I discovered that right before I took him out. She might have known about it all along and was surprised to hear I'd learned about it. Or she might not have known and was as shocked as she appeared. It's not easy killing someone, despite whatever reason we have to. I looked further into DJ's background, in case he had committed other atrocities, but couldn't find anything else. Not that there wasn't, but just that there was no way to learn the truth.

"I also checked the backgrounds of the other two men who had ambushed me. They'd also been on the other job with DJ, but the police couldn't catch them. The only bad part about this is they'll be listed as cold case files now. But at least they're not robbing and killing any longer." He pulled out his cell phone and hooked earphones to it.

"What about family? Do you investigate their backgrounds to see why these men went bad? If they have some criminal element in the family? Were they with a pack?" Natalie was about to walk past the coffee shop, but Brock took her hand and steered her inside.

"They weren't with a pack, and the wolves were drifters. Their families hadn't seen them in years, and they weren't surprised the men had met a bad end. In the case of DJ and his cohorts, all three men had started out doing something criminal early on, and then the severity of their crimes escalated, from petty theft to stealing cars. In Lettie's brother's case, she'd kept in touch with him. The parents of all three men seemed likable enough, so the men had taken a wrong turn somewhere. What do you think about Marek having an aunt living in Amarillo?" Brock really liked that he could talk over the case with Natalie.

"Could be. Eugenia? The woman who's getting mail there? Or she could still be a girlfriend. Or maybe part of the criminal setup he had going there."

"I suspect Amarillo could be where they're making the counterfeit money. Why carry it from Amarillo to Denver otherwise? I'll be checking into Marek's background, looking at family and friends, seeing if any of them are also working on this." He led Natalie to a small café table away from everyone else and started listening on his phone.

"What are you doing?"

"I put a listening device in the pocket of the wallpaper book cover she threw at me. I couldn't have planned it better."

"Wow, I would never have guessed. You're really good at this. Do you want some coffee, brownie, water, tea? We need to buy something." Natalie looked back at the board that showed the menu.

Brock glanced at the menu. "Can you get me a coffee and a brownie?" He fished a bill out of his wallet, saw it was one of the fake hundred-dollar ones, shook his head, and shoved it back in his pocket. He reached into his other pocket.

She smiled. "That's all we need to do. Use the bad money to buy something, and get ourselves into trouble. I've got this." She took off for the counter to place their order.

Brock watched Natalie get in line behind three other customers as he listened to Lettie swearing up a storm in her shop, throwing things around, and pacing. Then she must have gotten on her phone. "Marek, how in the hell did one of your hundred-dollar bills end up in Brock's hands? Yeah, yeah, his PI partner used it to get me to talk about you."

PI partner Natalie? Brock smiled.

"I mentioned your three friends, all right? I didn't say anything about anything else, but if your friends are doing this too, tough. I'm not covering for them, and I'm not covering for you. You'd better tell that brother of yours to stay clear of Denver. So how did Brock get the money? His partner said you were drunk and got kicked off the plane. Have you lost your mind? Who would do such a stupid thing?" Pause. "Don't use me as an excuse for your damned drinking."

Lettie stomped around the store, slamming books down on the table.

"The money was in a suitcase? Ohmigod, a whole suitcase full? How much money was in it?" Significant pause. "Three million dollars? How did you make… Forget it. I don't want to know how you created the bills. How in the hell did you lose the suitcase? You think… you think a she-wolf has the suitcase? Well, hell, Marek. That must be how Brock got some of the money!" Another pause. "No, I couldn't tell the hundred-dollar bill was fake by looking at it. I could smell the fresh ink! I'm a wolf, for God's sake. And then I realized that not only was your scent on it, but so was Brock's!" Pause. "All that matters is Brock's like a dog with a bone, and he *always* takes down his prey permanently. You'd better quit what you're doing. Now. And leave Amarillo pronto."

Brock heard Lettie stomping around her store some more as Natalie brought over their coffees and brownies and sat down with him.

"So what are you going to do about it?" Lettie made a disgruntled sound. "You do know Brock has a whole pack to back him up in Greystoke, right? Yeah, yeah, I know he went after my brother alone. He also thought my brother was by himself out there. If you go after his mate, you'll be a dead man…"

Brock stiffened. He knew he shouldn't have gotten Natalie any more immersed in this than she already was.

"Well, whose fault is that? How come you and your luggage became separated? I would think you would have kept it chained to your wrist at all times…" Pause. "Well…if you couldn't… Marek, if you couldn't carry the suitcase on the plane, you should have driven.

"Yeah, so you had a deadline, but you missed it anyway! I can't believe you were drinking when you have a job to do. You are such a moron… Wait, if she was on the flight with you, she must have had you under surveillance. Unless she just grabbed the wrong bag at the airport. Which means it was an honest mistake. Same black bag? Same size?"

Lettie let out her breath in a huff. "No, you can't stay with me here. I'd clear out of Amarillo, if I were you. And I sure wouldn't stick around Denver. Your boss won't like it that you lost his money. If Brock doesn't find you, your boss will. Brock's checking me out now to see how I'm involved in this business with you— which I'm not, damn it! Don't call me again."

Lettie hung up and then paced some more. She moved some things around in the shop. The door to the shop opened with a sound of jingling, then closed with a clunk.

Brock turned off his phone, pocketed it, and took a sip of his coffee. "Lettie's still up to her usual tricks: warning the guy who's doing the crime that I'm after him. But it sounds like she wasn't actually on board in committing the crime. She knows he had a boss, though, and was supposed to turn that money over to him."

"Oh wow. So she did know about the operation, to some degree, which was probably why she so adamantly denied knowing anything about it. That means the boss will probably try to terminate Marek, and then he'll come looking for me and the money."

"That's a good bet, which means you're stuck with me until I deal with this bunch. And Marek has a brother. Apparently, he's with the counterfeiters. How much trouble would it be for you and your family if you didn't go home until we resolve this?" Brock was sticking by her side. He couldn't believe the woman he hadn't wanted to get to know initially had become his mission. And he was certainly rethinking the part about not getting to know her.

"It would be way too much trouble. I have talks scheduled for the next couple of weeks, either at the nursery or at other locations in the area. We have a big garden show coming up next weekend where I'll be selling plants and gardening tools. Mom and Dad will continue to run the nursery. Besides, what if the boss, or Marek, learns where I'm from and where I work? He could go after my parents."

"Okay, then we'll go to your place. But I'm not leaving there until we resolve this."

"How will you eliminate these guys in Denver when you are in Amarillo?"

"I'll ask Vaughn and Jillian to look into the situation here. We all have a stake in this. They can advise their boss with the USF that they have a situation right at home that they need to resolve. He'll most likely add it to their workload. In the meantime, we'll look for Marek's place in Amarillo, see if anyone comes after you, and deal with the fallout in Texas. I'll be at all your garden talks as your assistant, watching out for you, if we still haven't dealt with this by then."

"What about my parents?"

"I'll see if one of my cousins can stay with them and help out around the nursery. He can watch them at night at their place. Do you all live at the same home?"

"Not in the same house, but close by. The nursery is in front of the main house, and I live in the carriage house to the west."

"Okay, so we'll have two places to watch, but at least they're on the same property."

"Right. Are we leaving here?"

"Yeah, let's go."

"Okay. I'll let my parents know what's going on." Natalie got on her cell as they left the shop and headed down the street to Brock's Humvee. "Hey, Dad, I have some bad news."

Brock wondered if her dad would rethink the business of not being with a pack. A pack could be a good thing when dealing with rogue wolves.

Chapter 8

"YEAH, DAD. WHAT WOULD BE THE ODDS? THIS DOESN'T mean that anyone will come after us. Especially if they believe we destroyed the money, which they would have to figure we would do if we're not rogues. If we were rogues, we'd probably decide to go into business for ourselves." Natalie explained everything that had happened up to this point to her dad.

"But if this Marek believes you *are* going to use the money? That you *didn't* destroy it? You said Brock kept some of it as evidence to work on the case. Since you showed it to his former girlfriend, and she told Marek, he might figure you still have all of it. I think having Brock and his cousin come here to watch out for you and us is an excellent idea. I also think word needs to get back to Marek that the money has been destroyed."

"I agree, but, Dad, let these guys handle it, okay? Mom needs you to help her manage the nursery. She doesn't need you getting into this business as if it were your new mission."

"I'm retired," her father said, but he sounded as if he was itching to get back on a case. "The younger guys can handle this. Besides, it's not a murder investigation."

That wouldn't make any difference to her dad. When it came to solving crimes, he loved it. He'd driven Natalie and her mother nuts with all the nights he'd stayed up late, puzzling over some evidence or other while he still worked as a homicide detective. Or he'd be checking out another lead and miss meals and everything else going on in their lives. Though he wasn't supposed to discuss cases with them, he was a wolf, and wolves were close-knit. Both Natalie and her mom were the perfect sounding boards for him. And a few times, he'd even come up with a solution because of their input. Even today, he was fascinated with true crime stories and swore he was going to sign up to work on cold-case files at a local police department one of these days to help out.

"Okay, Dad. We're coming in tomorrow. Just be on the lookout for any trouble until we arrive."

"Will do. And, Natalie, send us a picture of this guy who's offered to be your bodyguard."

"He's just helping out." She wanted her parents to know nothing was coming of this business between her and Brock. She could just imagine them worrying about her leaving home too. She wouldn't. Not without them.

"Yeah, but your mom wants to see what he looks like."

"I will. Tell Mom I love her. You too, Dad. See you tomorrow." They ended the call, and she glanced at Brock. "Dad's glad you and your cousin will be helping out."

"What did your dad do before he retired?"

"He was a homicide detective."

"I can imagine what that means. He's ready to help solve the case." Then Brock frowned. "You're afraid he's going to try to do more than just work at the garden shop while we're there?"

"Yeah. I could hear the excitement in his voice. He's eager to help with the case. At least he knows how to handle a gun. He taught my mom and me too, in case we ever needed to protect ourselves, which was something he worried about. She's only needed to once. Since we're a small business, we never know when someone might try to rob us. We don't have a lot of cash on hand, like we did early on. Most people pay with credit cards. But we do have some money in the register." She smiled. "Don't take this personally, but my mom wants me to send her a picture of you."

Brock laughed. "Wait until we get home, and you can get a shot of my good side."

"Here I thought all your sides were good."

He smiled at her.

When they arrived back at Aaron's ranch house, Brock called Vaughn to see if his boss would allow him and Jillian the time to work a case there. After that, Brock ended the call and spoke with his cousin. "Hey, Shawn, got a mission for you. I'll run it by Devlyn, but if you can spare some time, I need you to come with me and help safeguard Natalie's parents at their garden center in Amarillo." He smiled and glanced at Natalie as she brought them glasses of water, and they sat down in the living room. "Yeah, her parents. I have Natalie's back. I'll firm up details with you later. Bye."

"Are you sure you don't want to swap places with your cousin? Is he as well trained as you?" Natalie asked.

"Yeah, he is. But no, I don't want to exchange places with him. You're already paying me to be your bodyguard."

"You wanted the job for free, you said," she reminded him.

"Right, just room and board."

Using her cell phone, she snapped a shot of Brock, then texted someone.

"Did I look sufficiently growly for that picture? That's why your mom wants a picture of me, right? To see if I can handle the bad guys?"

"Knowing Mom, she's wants your photo so she can see if you are mate material as far as passing on good genes to prospective kids."

Brock laughed. Then his phone rang. He was surprised to see the caller ID showed it was Marek—the counterfeit-bill carrier himself. Brock quickly answered the call. "Hey, Marek. I'm putting this on speakerphone so my mate can listen in." He figured since he and Natalie were going with that story, he'd stick to it. "What can I do for you?"

"Hand over the bag you took from the airport. And we'll call it even."

"Sentimental value? I don't have it."

"What did you do with the money?"

"Burned it. No way could we let you keep it. You know what happens to rogue wolves dealing in crime."

"I have to turn over the money. I don't have a choice. My life depends on it."

"Weren't you listening to me? It's gone. The money made a great bonfire for a cookout. Rogue wolves don't live long, one way or another. If you play the game and get caught, you have no one to blame but yourself. The money's gone. You'll have to square it with your boss. You shouldn't have been drinking and gotten thrown off the flight. Sure messed things up for you and put you squarely in our territory to deal with. Good thing for us, though, before the police caught you at it."

Carrying laptops and looking ready to work, Vaughn and Jillian walked into the ranch house, and Natalie signaled that Brock's call was on speaker. They nodded and silently took seats in the living room.

"Marek, are you still there?" Brock asked.

"Yeah. Okay, so what if I tell you the boss's name? And you get rid of *him*?"

Brock was surprised at this turn of events. "What about you?"

"You let me go, and I won't get into any more trouble. Hell, I'm not cut out to be a criminal. Every time I try to do anything illegal, I screw it up. The other thing is…you don't hassle my friends. Lettie told me she mentioned their names to you."

"Are they in this business with you?"

"No."

If they weren't, then what difference would it make if he and Natalie questioned them?

"You'll let me go? Just pretend I don't exist?"

"Only if you keep your nose clean and nobody's already been hurt by what you've done. Why did you move to Amarillo?"

"Lettie left me. Then the boss said he wanted me to move to Amarillo because we've got a couple of guys working on the money who live there. I was supposed to oversee the operation and get the real dollar bills. Then the others would bleach them and print them. I had to put up my own money for this operation. Ten thousand one-dollar bills. All gone now because of you."

"Hell, sounds like you're running the operation. What does the boss do?"

"Gets the ink, set up the printing operation, hired these guys. Ink Man, who does all the artwork. The printer. The boss is in thick with the middleman who finds stoolies, humans, to spend the money, then return the goods and get real money, and he gives them a percentage of the cash. But they don't know who any of us are. He changes up the drop-off point all the time."

"Have you put any of the money you've created in circulation yet?"

"Some. I was supposed to give this batch to the middleman, and he was going to pay me my capital back and a hearty return on my investment. I started out with ten thousand and would have gotten thirty thousand in hundred-dollar bills. Then I begin the process again."

"Have you been doing this for a while?" Brock asked again, not believing this was a one-time occurrence. It sounded like they'd been in operation for some time.

"Just got started."

"If you get into anything more than this, you go down. And I mean for anything else criminal. Not just for making funny money."

"Are you going to handle him? The boss? You'll have to remove the middleman too. The boss wouldn't say, but I think he's a relative of his. Cousin, brother, or something. If you don't eliminate him, *he'll* be looking for blood."

"We will if we can. The boss is living here in the Denver area?"

"Yeah. Carlson Johnson."

"Address?"

"Denver area. He would never say where. We'd meet at a specific location he came up with to talk about how far we'd gotten on the printing job. The guys we found who could actually do the artwork and printing live in Amarillo, and they wouldn't move their operation to

Denver. I had to bring the real money there to them. Does the boss use a fake name? Probably. Is he a wolf? Yeah. So are the other men on the crew."

"I'll need the names of the other men."

"Are you…you going to eliminate them?"

"Buddies of yours?" Brock wondered if Marek just wanted to keep his crew for more of the same work later but wanted Brock to remove the boss and the middleman so he could be in charge.

"No. First time I ever met them. I don't have a name for the one. He goes by Ink Man. And the other is Antonio. No last name," Marek said.

"Are they with a pack?"

"No. Not me either. Don't think Carlson is either."

Packs could make it easier—or harder, if the pack was participating in the crime. If the pack wasn't taking part in criminal activities, they would handle the wolf themselves, and that would make the situation even easier.

"Whether I terminate them depends on how they react. Are they getting out of their life of crime? Going to keep it up? Will they try to kill me? We do have the offer of a facility to incarcerate shifters. The jaguars run it. We might end up putting the lot of you there if you don't cooperate. Since you say you're quitting the business, where are you going now?" Brock asked.

"I'm leaving. Getting out of the country."

"How's your brother tangled up in all of this?"

There was a prolonged silence, and Brock assumed he'd shocked Marek to the core by knowing anything about his brother.

"He's not."

"Okay, listen, we know he is. And the same goes for

him. If he continues doing this crap, he's a dead wolf. Is he still in Denver?"

No response.

"We'll find him. Don't do anything illegal anywhere else."

"I won't, but leave my brother out of it." Marek hung up on him.

Brock didn't believe the man would give up his life of crime, not with the setup they had. He and Natalie needed to find not only the boss and his brother, the middleman, but also Marek's brother, who must be just as involved in all this mess. Not to mention that Ink Man and Antonio needed to be dealt with.

Then Brock's cousin Shawn showed up at the ranch house. His gaze quickly singled out Natalie.

"You have the parents to protect," Brock reminded him. "The lady is mine."

Shawn smiled.

Yeah, Brock knew how it sounded. He hadn't meant to say it quite that way, certainly not in front of Natalie or his brother and sister-in-law.

Vaughn and Jillian smiled from where they were sitting nearby on another couch, their own laptops open.

"Hey, one of our cousins is going to drive your rental car back to the airport for you, if that's okay with you," Vaughn said to Natalie.

"Oh yeah, that would be great. Thanks. We were going to do that after we left Boulder but got distracted. I'll grab the keys." Natalie went up to her room and pulled them out of her purse, then went back down to the living room and handed them to Vaughn. "Thanks again."

"No problem. It saves you guys having to drop by the

airport before you get on the road tomorrow morning," Vaughn said.

That was one great thing about the pack and Brock's family. They always had someone willing to help out.

"Do you believe Marek's going to give this business up?" Natalie asked.

"No. I don't think he'll be after you or your parents though. He wanted the money. With it gone, the counterfeiters only have to worry about me. Well, and Vaughn, Jillian, and Shawn, if we catch up with them."

"Do you think Marek gave you the real names for the boss and the other men working in this operation?" she asked.

"If they aren't using fake names already."

Natalie got on her phone and called someone. "Hey, Lettie? I'm so sorry to be bothering you again, but Marek said the boss is Carlson Johnson. Do you know where he lives?" She put the call on speaker.

Brock was surprised at how much Natalie seemed to be enjoying her part in all this.

"No. I don't know him, or where he lives. I told you, I know nothing about their operation."

"You don't know Antonio?"

"No! I was never into any of that."

"But when I handed you the hundred-dollar bill, you knew that it was a fake bill right away. You knew who was responsible for it. I mean, I could have been the one who was making them. Or I could have been paid for something and got stuck with the bill, thinking it was real."

Lettie didn't say anything.

"You knew all about the operation, didn't you?"

"No. I. Didn't. Not until Marek was running late

coming home one night, and I accused him of seeing another woman. Some cute little thing he was hitting on at a café. I didn't know he had given her a tip that was a fake bill. He explained to me why he'd done it, just to see if it would pass."

"He gave her a hundred-dollar tip?"

"No. He was making fives, tens, and twenties. I didn't know he had graduated to hundred-dollar bills. It might take longer to get his money back, but most places don't pay any attention to the smaller denominations. Just think, you hand over a five that feels like the real paper because it is, when you actually started out with a one-dollar bill, and you 'make' four dollars on the deal. Yeah, it's not the same as ninety-nine dollars on a dollar bill, but it's a lot less risky."

"So he wasn't passing out hundred-dollar bills?"

"No. He's too cautious for that. I'm sure he's giving the bills to someone else who can pass them off."

"I thought you didn't know anything about the operation."

"I didn't. He told me when he was trying to explain why he was being so friendly to the waitress. That was the living end for me. Is that all?"

"Are you sure you don't know Antonio or Ink Man?"

"Yes."

"What about...Marek's brother?"

"Jimmy? Don't tell me he's actually doing this too. I've known him for as long as I've known Marek. He thinks he's a real lady's man, and he didn't like it when I wouldn't give him the time of day. But I didn't know he could be doing this too."

"Where is he now?"

"Amarillo. Marek might not like it that his twin brother hit on me whenever he could, but he knew I wasn't interested. The guy is a real jerk. When Marek was supposedly checking on his sick aunt, would Jimmy go with him? Or go instead of him? Nope."

"What does he do for a living?"

"Tattoos."

Natalie glanced at the others. They were listening with rapt attention while Brock was making notes.

"You know, go figure. Wolves don't wear tats. It would be too dangerous if a wolf were caught wearing tattoos under their fur. But he's into that and…" Lettie paused. "Art. Ohmigod, maybe he's the one who's designing the money for them." She snorted. "Live fast and die young. Is that all?"

"Thanks. Yeah. Talk later."

"Not if I can help it." Lettie hung up on her.

"So he's passing bills of other denominations," Brock said, thinking Natalie needed to be in the PI business with him. "And Jimmy, brother to Marek, could be Ink Man."

"Sounds like it. Did Marek pass a phony bill just the one time, or is he doing it on a regular basis?" Vaughn asked.

"If he's got the setup, he could print out any denomination. Does the boss know he's doing this on his own? Using smaller print denominations? If you find and eliminate the boss, Marek has free rein to do what he's been doing. Especially if the boss already paid for the equipment and ink. Marek would get the lion's share of the profits. He's already using his own money," Jillian said. "Oh, but you'd also have to eliminate the middleman, who could be Carlson's relation. And Marek's counting on it. Then who's at fault? Not Marek. *You*."

Brock agreed and began looking at his laptop. "No wonder Marek didn't want us going after Ink Man, if that's his brother. He probably doesn't figure we'll be able to learn who he is."

"Unless his brother riled Marek one too many times by hitting on Lettie when she was dating Marek," Natalie said.

"True. Okay, so no Carlson Johnson listed anywhere in Colorado on the database I pulled up."

"Fake name then," Natalie said.

"Most likely. Or Marek made up the name, not intending for us to find him," Brock said.

"Or," Vaughn said, "the boss doesn't exist. Marek made him up, and he was really coming here to deliver the money to the middleman who will distribute it. Only we had a bonfire with it."

"Could be," Brock said. "That's the trouble with dealing with criminals. They lie."

"I can't believe anyone would do something so stupid as to make all this money and then try to pass it off as the real deal. It would be easy to get caught, I would think," Natalie said.

"It's big business. The funniest case I ever heard of involved the con men getting conned by con men. You know, if something sounds too good to be true, it probably is," Brock said. "In this one case, two brothers from Spain put a down payment on a famous Goya painting. It had a certificate proving its authenticity. Did the brothers think they were paying a low price for a painting worth millions because it had been stolen? Not sure, but probably. In any case, when they learned it was a fake, they tried to sell it to an Arab sheikh through an Italian middleman for four million euros. They paid the middleman three hundred thousand euros in broker's fees as a commission that they'd borrowed from a friend. The payment they received was 1.7 million Swiss francs as a down payment.

"When they took the money to a Swiss bank, they learned the bills were just photocopies. Customs at the border discovered the counterfeit money in their bag. Fake sheikh, fake money, fake painting. The middleman had conned the brothers and ended up with the only real money in the deal—the three hundred thousand euros. The brothers went to jail. The fake painting was confiscated. And the sheikh, if there really had been one, and the middleman disappeared with the real money. Which teaches the moral, if you're going to do a con, make sure you're not the ones being conned," Brock said.

Natalie and the others laughed. "Sounds to me like these guys had been conned twice already, which meant they should have stopped while they were behind."

"Exactly. And my point is if Marek has been having trouble being successful in criminal ventures—his own words—he should leave well enough alone. You also see how the criminal mind works. If one thing doesn't succeed, try and try again. The Spanish brothers had been conned once. Instead of giving up, they figured they might as well con someone else. It doesn't stop." Brock was sure of it where Marek was concerned.

"You still want us to locate the boss and the middleman, and you'll go to Amarillo and find the others?" Vaughn asked.

"Yeah. If we can discover where their printer and the rest of their crew are, we can stop the press. You remove the boss and the middleman. And learn what you can about anybody else being with them in this venture."

"Okay, will do. When are you leaving tomorrow?" Vaughn asked.

"After we have breakfast. We'll get in that afternoon then," Natalie said.

"Works for me," Shawn said. "You don't need me here tonight, do you? I'll go home, pack a bag, and meet you here tomorrow."

"Yeah, that sounds good," Brock said.

Shawn said goodbye, and then the others settled down to look up anything else they could find on their laptops about the counterfeiters.

"We'll have dinner with you, then head home," Jillian said to Brock and Natalie. "We'll keep you posted on what we learn while you're in Amarillo."

"Same with us when we get there," Brock said.

Vaughn was working on his laptop when he leaned back against the couch and nodded. "Hey, Marek's got a flight to Amarillo tomorrow. He arrives there at three thirty."

"Hell, that's good news. We'll be sure to be there then," Brock said. "Shawn can meet up with the Silvertons either at their house or at the nursery."

"Are we going to confront Marek at the airport?" Natalie asked.

"No. We're going to conduct surveillance. Low profile. We'll see if he goes home or if he drops by the place where they're printing the money. Even if he really does plan to lead a straight life from now on, we need to find the printer and anything else they're using to make the money."

"You don't really think he's going to move to another country, do you?" Natalie asked.

"I doubt it."

"Could you send a picture of your cousin Shawn to my mother? That way, she'll know who he is when he arrives," Natalie said.

"I'll send a picture of him and of Brock, in case the two of you get separated," Vaughn said.

Natalie gave him her mother's email address. "Thanks, Vaughn. My dad will probably still give Shawn the third degree when he arrives, what with all that's been going on."

"Shawn can handle it," Brock said.

Brock and Vaughn smiled conspiratorially. Brock noted Natalie didn't tell Vaughn she had already sent Brock's picture to her mom at her request.

Chapter 9

"Is everyone up for some hamburgers for an early dinner?" Brock asked.

Natalie was thinking about how growly he had been with Lettie. Would he be that way with her, too, if she annoyed him?

Normally, she wouldn't be thinking along those lines, but she couldn't help it where he was concerned. He was one hot and sexy wolf. "Sounds good to me. And a run as a wolf afterward, if it's safe while it's still light out?"

"Yeah, we can do that."

"Do you want to do this on the grill?" Vaughn asked, already getting the hamburger meat out to make patties.

"Yeah, sure," Brock said.

"We'll supervise," Jillian said, escorting Natalie out to the back deck.

"It's beautiful here." Natalie enjoyed the view of the mountains.

"Yeah, and watching the sun set and then seeing the millions of stars sprinkled across the inky sky is really spectacular."

"You're fairly new to the pack. What do you think about them?" Natalie asked Jillian.

"Devlyn and Bella are good pack leaders, fair and impartial. Devlyn has a lot of cousins in the pack, including my mate, but he doesn't treat Vaughn any different from anyone else in the pack. Both Devlyn and Bella are fighters and will protect the pack with their lives. They want only the best for all of us. They were thrilled when Vaughn and I decided to mate and my family moved closer. Everyone keeps teasing me about having babies soon, but we want to hold off a while, get to know each other better, and continue to fight against the rogues who threaten our security."

"I don't blame you. It's a big responsibility to have children and still do a job you love." Natalie overheard Brock telling his brother he needed to make the burgers thicker. She smiled.

"They're always like that when they get together," Jillian said. "I have a brother, too, and he and Vaughn and Brock are like brothers now."

"That's great. I have Angie, who's so much like a sister. I'm not used to seeing brothers hassling each other. They're cute. You and Vaughn aren't here a lot of the time though, are you?"

"In our jobs, we travel all over, but we also have a lot of downtime after a mission. We end up here when we need time with the pack. We come back for special celebrations, too, and holidays. There's nothing more fun than having a wolf pack to celebrate with. All the little ones dressed up for the holidays, the feasting, games, dances."

"I bet that's nice."

"It is. Before that, it was just my parents and my brother and me. But I was off doing my own job after I left the service, and I didn't have a pack."

Natalie was thinking it would really be fun to do all the things the wolves did in this pack. To be with *lupus garous* more her age. To be part of a wolf community.

"I guess we should help the guys out a little bit. Looks like we're about ready to eat."

She and Jillian went inside and gathered the condiments, lettuce, tomatoes, cheese, and buns for the burgers, along with paper plates. Then they each began to fix the burgers the way they liked them. Brock went back to the house for a bottle of Bordeaux and wineglasses.

They all sat down to eat at a big picnic table on the deck, and Brock poured glasses of red wine for each of them.

"Now this is great," Vaughn said, lifting his wineglass in a salute. "Family and friends. Just perfect." He wrapped his arm around Jillian's shoulders. "Absolutely perfect."

Natalie was thinking the same. It was really fun being with Brock and his brother and sister-in-law.

"Yeah, I couldn't agree with you more, Brother," Brock said, touching his wineglass to Natalie's.

She could certainly see the allure of being here with this pack, with *this* wolf and his family.

After they finished eating, they cleaned up.

"Wanna run?" Brock asked, helping to put away the condiments in the fridge.

"Yeah," Vaughn said.

"Sure do," Natalie and Jillian said in unison.

Natalie noticed everyone's hesitation, waiting for her to retire to the guest room she was staying in, but it was just the four of them, and she didn't want it to look like she was a she-wolf prude.

She began pulling off her boots, and Brock whooped, making them all laugh.

They all hurried to strip, though Natalie thought it

was cute when Vaughn helped Jillian with her boots and kissed her knees. They were definitely newlyweds.

Natalie glanced at Brock as he pulled off his shirt. He was sooo hot, every muscle toned to perfection. She smiled at the gloriously beautiful hunk, then pulled off her bra and panties. She shifted, the others all following suit.

It was so incredible out here, so peaceful as they left the ranch house and ran through the woods and down to a creek. They all swam, then left the water, shaking off on one another. Jillian nipped at Vaughn's ear, and Brock rubbed up against Natalie affectionately. She licked his nose, and he licked hers back.

Brock nuzzled her again, and after an hour of running, smelling scents, and enjoying nature as wolves, they stopped to see the sun setting over the mountains. They sat and enjoyed the yellows and pinks reflecting off drifting clouds. And then as the sun set, the sky turned a darker blue—the blue hour—before darkness settled around them and the stars began to appear.

It was magical, lying down on the ground with the other wolves, looking up at the twinkling stars. And then Natalie saw a shooting star and wished with all her heart they'd be able to get rid of the bad guys without anyone from the Greystoke wolf pack being hurt.

Brock licked her muzzle and she licked him back, and then they headed to the ranch house. No matter what else happened, Natalie would always remember this special time she'd had with Brock and his pack.

Back at the house, everyone shifted and dressed, and then Vaughn and Jillian said their goodbyes, wishing them a safe trip and the best of luck in dealing with Marek and whoever else they had to confront. They wished Jillian and Vaughn the same in running down any wolves in the counterfeiting business in Denver. And then the couple went home, and Brock and Natalie were left on their own.

"That was so nice," Natalie told Brock.

He pulled her into his arms. "Yeah." He sighed deeply. "I sure could get used to this." He drew her hand up and moved his mouth over her wrist, her skin soft and warm. He gave her a gentle kiss on the lips, and she moved her mouth over his—the feeling intense and real.

Their pheromones hummed as their tongues tangled. She tasted of fresh raspberries and blackberries, the bouquet of the Bordeaux adding to her own delicious scent and taste. Brock wanted this closeness for the rest of the night. If Natalie wanted the same.

She wrapped her arms around his neck and pulled him close. All her soft curves fit against his body, and he relished the contact. He didn't want to let go of her, sure she'd want to go to bed alone as soon as he suggested getting some sleep. He couldn't believe the way he was thinking, wishing she was thinking the same. Their lips were locked, and he wanted to carry her to bed and join her there.

Before he could say anything, she pulled away from him, but she was still holding on to his hips in a way that made him think she was having trouble letting him go. "Let's go to bed."

"Your bed?" He smiled, hoping he didn't look as wolfish as he was feeling.

"Of course, unless you want to sleep on the couch again."

"Hell no."

She laughed, pulled away, and ran up the stairs. He chased after her. She squealed when he touched her back as if he was getting ready to tackle her.

As soon as he reached the landing, he scooped her up and carried her to the bed.

"We don't tell anyone about this," Natalie warned, frowning and looking damned serious.

"Scout's honor."

She laughed, and he set her down on the floor. Then he began to remove her clothes, and she helped him with his.

Natalie grabbed her pj's from her bag, slipped them on—telling him she wasn't ready to go very far—and climbed into bed. "Coming?"

He'd love to. He smiled, and she blushed. Then he climbed into bed wearing his boxer briefs and gathered her in his arms. "I think I like this new job."

She kissed his naked chest. "I hope this doesn't cost me anything more." She snuggled against him, her silky hair falling over his chest.

"Just think of it as one of the perks you get from my bodyguard service: a bed warmer on chilly Colorado nights."

She licked his nipple, and he sucked in his breath. She slipped her hand over his stomach. "I'm glad you're not looking for a girlfriend or a mate."

"I might be rethinking that." He couldn't believe he might be, but Natalie had him thinking of real possibilities. He groaned when she nuzzled his chest with her mouth.

"This is strictly temporary. We live too far away from each other to do anything about it."

"Uh-huh." He didn't figure she was any more immune to him than he was to her.

She kissed his mouth, then settled against his chest. "Right, Brock. Thanks for helping me out."

That was it? All right. He didn't want to push things and force her to tell him to get lost. Not when things were going so well for them.

He kissed the top of her head. "My pleasure." And he meant every bit of it.

"I hope I don't…shock you if…I tell you I want a bit more than just your protection tonight." She traced her finger around his nipple.

"This isn't a test to see if I can make all the right moves, is it?"

She smiled. "You're not worried, are you?"

"Hell yeah. I have a reputation to uphold."

Smiling, she raised a brow.

"I don't mean sexual exploits. I mean proving to you that… Well, hell, enough talking before I ruin a good thing." He moved her onto her back and began kissing her.

And she began sliding her fingers all over his naked back, then lower until she was pressing her hands against his buttocks. They couldn't have consummated sex or they'd be mated wolves, but he was more than willing to pleasure her. Sitting astride her, he ran his hands over her pajama-top-covered breasts, feeling her nipples peak beneath the soft fabric.

She slid her fingers underneath the back of his waistband, and he felt his arousal jump. He wasn't sure if she wanted to get naked and do a whole lot more, but she could always say no and he'd back off. *He* wanted a whole lot more. He slid his hands up her shirt and caressed her breasts—beautiful, soft, malleable, the nipples pebbled beneath the palms of his hands as he massaged.

The scent of her pheromones swept over him, triggering his own to answer the call of duty. He eased her top up and over her head and tossed it to the floor. He couldn't believe they were doing this, yet from the moment she'd had contact with him, he'd been intrigued, just from the way she'd interacted with him on the phone while lost in Denver.

She'd needed his aid, and he liked feeling needed. Even now. To fulfill some sexual craving.

She slipped her hands down his boxer briefs further, and he loved the way her touch was spurring him on. Groaning, he leaned down to suckle a breast. She moaned and tightened her hold on his ass.

He licked and suckled the other breast, running the palm of his hand over the first. Arching against him, she sucked in her breath. He kissed her mouth, and she tackled his back, full of passion, her hands wrapped around his neck, holding him, wanting him. Sliding his body against hers, he was claiming her for now, his scent mixing with hers, telling anyone else she was his.

Their tongues tasted and teased each other's, again sharing their scents. She reached down to remove his boxer briefs, tugging at them. He was past ready to deal with the throbbing desire he had for her and was sure she was feeling the same craving.

He moved off her and slid his boxer briefs off and threw them aside. Then he kissed her soft, flat tummy and was reminded of her comment about being pregnant and wallpapering a room for the baby or babies. Not that he wanted to think about that now, but it did come to mind and it amused him. Then he ran his fingers over her blue silk panties, his thumb sliding down the center of her.

Her dark hair splayed across the pillow, her lips curving up slightly. She looked pleased, and that pleased him. He slipped her panties off and moved against her again, their bodies sliding against each other, rubbing, exploring. Being with her like this felt like nothing he'd ever experienced before with a woman, a mixture of wolf need and human desire, the feel, taste, and scent of her ratcheting up his hunger for her. His blood was on fire, their pulses racing.

Not wanting to delay this further, he moved aside so he could stroke her, his hand sliding down to the juncture of her thighs. Then he began rubbing her clit, drawing the wetness from her center and encircling her sensitive tissue. She melted against the mattress, her blue eyes smoky with desire, a small moan escaping her lips. Then he began to stroke, her dark curly hairs drenched with anticipation.

It was hard to hold back, to keep this from being a consummated sexual experience, as much as he wanted to push his pulsing cock into her. He leaned down to kiss her mouth again, his fingers stroking her clit hard and fast. She parted her lips and cried out, his mouth covering hers, kissing her, loving this with her. He didn't want to go there, but he couldn't quit thinking about how much he wanted to do this with her again. Pleasure her. See her come apart under his ministrations. Feel the exquisite friction between them. He pushed a finger between her feminine folds, felt her ripples of climax gripping him, and smiled.

But she quickly pushed him down against the mattress and began to stroke his cock standing at attention, waiting for her touch, and he was in heaven.

———~~~———

Brock was some hot wolf. Natalie loved how gentle and focused he had been in pleasuring her. Now it was her turn to bring him to completion. She couldn't help thinking she wanted more of this. All of this. That was the problem with being wolves. And the good thing too. They had to be so sure that it was forever between them.

For now, this was all they could have, and she put her heart and soul into it. She began stroking his cock, watching his lustful expression—the pleasure, the torture—at what she was doing to him. Wringing him out. Drawing out the expectation, the rising need for climax, his body straining, just as he'd done to her. Payback of the most pleasurable sort.

He started running his hand over her thigh, and she swore if he didn't quit, he was going to make her come again. Yet she wanted to. She spread her legs so he could touch her again, and while she was stroking his cock, he began inserting a finger between her feminine folds…and then he growled as if his own release was near. His body tensed with need, and then he threw his head back and howled, spilling his seed at the same time. But he wasn't giving up on her—for which she was profoundly grateful—and rolled her over on her back so he could finish her off. Their pheromones were on fire as he brought her to the top again, and she cried out, something she never did, feeling pure joy wash over her like a blazing-hot shower.

He rolled onto his back and pulled her into his arms and just held her close, as if touching her further satiated more of his need for intimacy. She felt so relaxed, filled with contentment, but she had been thinking that after this beautiful encounter, they'd better put the brakes on. She fully intended to stay on her side of the bed the rest of the night—to get a good night's sleep, not cling to him as if she'd never had such an unbelievably wonderful sexual experience and wanted to prolong the intimacy.

With humans, it could be nice, but she couldn't ever have a lasting relationship with one, so she'd been careful not to give the guy the wrong impression. It hadn't been hard because most had just wanted to sate their own needs. With wolves, she had never gone this far. But with Brock? She was feeling so much more. She didn't want to end it here.

"Want to shower?" Brock finally asked, his hand sliding in gentle caresses down her bare back.

"Yeah," she said softly, tired and gratified, still feeling the white-hot glow of climax filling her to the marrow of her bones. But then she raised her head and smiled at him. "But no more hanky-panky."

He chuckled darkly, like a hungry wolf would. "I'm making no promises I can't keep."

She smiled back just as wickedly. He knew all the right things to say. Then they were climbing off the bed and racing to the shower.

Chapter 10

NATALIE AND BROCK WERE JUST CRAWLING OUT OF BED early the next morning when she heard Vaughn, Jillian, and Shawn arrive at the ranch house. Her first thought was that they'd know Brock hadn't slept on the couch last night. Oh sure, maybe she was overthinking it, knowing the truth and believing they would too. He could have already been up, put away the linens he had on the couch, and be getting ready in the bathroom. Only he wasn't. He was in the bedroom with her, smiling and waggling his brows at her as he pulled on his clothes. *The wolf.*

She had thought of setting an alarm on her cell phone last night but had dismissed the idea. She never slept late. Ever. She never needed an alarm. And certainly not when she had important business to attend to. Then again, after she woke Brock last night to have more unconsummated sex—and heck, they'd done the same thing in the shower!—she should have realized she would need some extra sleep this morning. He was totally addictive, and she felt like a nympho, wanting to enjoy this…outlet…with him before they had to end it for good.

"I hope they won't tell the rest of the pack about us," she said quietly.

"They wouldn't dare." Brock's words were just as hushed, and he gathered her in for a hug and a kiss.

"Don't worry. I wouldn't kiss and tell either." He sighed. "But this sure changes things."

"It doesn't. We still live hours apart. I have a job to do. You have a job to do. It wouldn't work out." She slipped out of his arms and headed for the bathroom. "Meet you downstairs."

He smiled. "I had the best sleep ever. I never wake up this late."

She chuckled. "You should have told me to go away when I woke you in the middle of the night."

"Hell no. When a lady's in need, a SEAL wolf does the honorable thing and focuses on her."

Natalie laughed, shook her head, and retired to the bathroom. She didn't want to hear what Vaughn would say to Brock about all this. In private. Later.

Brock knew nothing would get past his brother and his cousin Shawn. Jillian might not know Brock well enough to recognize the cues. Then again, she was as wary a wolf as any of them and an intuitive woman.

No one said a word to him as they made pancakes and he fixed himself a cup of coffee. Hell, he wished someone would say something. Not about him and Natalie, but about anything else. He couldn't come up with anything to say, not when all he could think about was Natalie and what an incredible night it had been with her. And how he wanted a lot more of that with her.

Everyone was smiling, not looking at him, and in the worst way, he wanted to say something about not reacting like they were reacting, but not when Natalie might overhear them.

"Good day for the trip," Vaughn said finally. Weather was always a safe topic.

"Yeah," Shawn said. "I filled up my gas tank. What about you, Brock?"

Hell...yeah. Brock hesitated too damn long in responding—which should teach him not to have his mind where it shouldn't be—and everyone chuckled.

As Natalie came down the stairs, everyone looked at her, just a natural reaction, and she blushed. Brock quickly got her a cup of coffee. "Milk? Sugar?"

"Yes, mostly milk and two teaspoons of sugar."

He brought her the doctored coffee, and she thanked him. "Pancakes?" he asked.

"Yeah, that sounds good."

They soon sat down to eat their breakfast and began talking about the mission. Vaughn and Jillian said they'd wash the dishes after everyone finished eating. They said they'd check into who might be dealing in the counterfeit money in Denver and wished Brock, Natalie, and Shawn a safe journey.

The three of them wished Vaughn and Jillian luck in locating the bad guys too.

Then Brock and Natalie took off, Shawn following them in his black pickup.

"Okay, so we can do this one of two ways. I can go to the airport in Amarillo alone and look for Marek, while you go with Shawn to the garden center, and he can watch out for you and your parents. Or, you can come with me. He'll continue on to the garden center to help out your folks, and I'll still be keeping you safe. Though if we run into trouble, you could be in harm's way," Brock said to Natalie as he drove his Humvee on the interstate to Texas.

"I'll stay with you. I'm still on vacation, and sometimes I like to live dangerously."

He chuckled. "Really?" He couldn't imagine living dangerously while working at the garden center, unless she cut herself while clipping plants or something.

"Yeah, any time I use the GPS, no telling where I'll end up."

Brock smiled.

"I noticed you didn't ask Marek for the location of the printing press," she said.

"There was no need to. If he'd told me, I'm sure it would have been someplace else. Besides, I didn't want to spook him. I'd have no way of knowing who Antonio is. And no way of locating him and Marek's brother. The only way is to follow Marek and see if he'll lead us to them. It could be days, weeks even, though I imagine he'll want to be overseeing the printing process so the other guys don't use the money instead."

Natalie didn't say anything for quite a while, and Brock hoped she wasn't regretting what they had done last night. He wasn't. He was trying not to think ahead too much, just play things by ear, but he was much more of a tactician, which meant he couldn't help thinking about tonight and how things would go. He didn't want to do anything to upset her. Not just because she was Angie's best friend and now Angie was part of his family, but also because he cared too much about Natalie to want to make her feel bad about anything.

"Are you okay?" he finally asked.

She scoffed. "I didn't get enough sleep."

Neither had he, but he'd do it all over again, given the

choice. "Why don't you crawl in the back and lie down for a while."

"Then we could switch off?" she asked.

"Yeah, and get some lunch when I get low on gas."

"Yeah, sure." She glanced back at Shawn's truck. "Do you think they know? Your brother and Jillian and Shawn? About us and what went on last night?"

"Yeah. Not that anyone said anything, but you know how it is."

She sighed. "As long as my parents don't get wind of it. I should have set my alarm."

"I was thinking the same thing about my phone." He hoped her parents didn't get upset with him about having been with Natalie, if they suspected what was up between them. Maybe she would want to cool it with him while he stayed with her. He preferred being with her, but it would be completely up to her how she wanted to handle this.

She reached over and patted his arm. "Don't worry. My dad won't bring out his shotgun."

Brock chuckled, glad for that at least.

After they had each napped on the way to Amarillo, Brock was driving again. "Did you want to get hamburgers for lunch?"

"Sure. Maybe Shawn needs some rest, and one of us can drive for him for a while."

"We can ask, but I suspect he'll say no."

"My dad can spell Shawn tonight on guard duty. In fact, Dad will love helping with this. He'll probably put Shawn to work in the nursery, and Dad will be the lookout for any rogue wolves."

Brock laughed. "It could work. Your dad would know the customers better than Shawn would, and he could concentrate on watching for anyone who shouldn't be there." Brock paused. "If Marek believes you were only visiting Amarillo, he probably won't be looking for you or any connection you would have there. We have that working in our favor."

"True."

"I see a place ahead where we can stop." Brock called Shawn on the Bluetooth to tell him they were stopping at the next service station for gas and lunch. Shawn was ready for a break.

While they got a bite to eat, Natalie asked if Shawn needed her to drive his vehicle for the last two and a half hours.

"No way. I can drive fifteen hours straight."

"Okay." Then she told Shawn about her father and what might happen at the garden shop.

"We'll work it out just fine. I can do a lot of the grunt labor and still watch both of your parents. I was a multitasker before anyone came up with the term." Shawn took another bite of his double cheeseburger. Then he began to munch on some of his french fries. He finished off his lunch with a strawberry milkshake.

Brock was smiling at her. "He eats too much too, doesn't he?"

Natalie shook her head. "He must need to eat all that to make him look that good."

Shawn laughed out loud. "I bet she doesn't tell *all* the guys that."

"Nope." She finished her chicken sandwich.

Brock just kept smiling at her. Giving his cousin a

hard time in front of Natalie had backfired big time. He and his cousins and brother were so used to the banter back and forth that he couldn't have stopped himself if he'd tried. He sure hadn't expected her comeback. She smiled at Brock.

---∿---

When they were on the road again, Brock drove the rest of the way until they reached a service station right outside Amarillo. She had already given Shawn directions to her parents' garden shop on the outskirts of town. Since she and Brock had to go to the airport, they would be heading in a different direction.

As soon as he parked the Humvee at the gas pump, Natalie stretched. "Here's where we'll split off. Shawn can meet up with my parents while we do some surveillance work."

When they got out of the vehicle, Brock tossed the empty water bottles into the trash, and she saw her chance to pay for the gas as she'd intended. She slid her credit card in the machine.

Glancing back at her and looking surprised, Brock immediately said, "I was going to get that."

"No you aren't. You wouldn't be driving all the way to Amarillo if it hadn't been for me. Plus, you can't do a paying job if you're stuck doing this for me."

Shaking his head, Brock filled the tank. "I'm not *stuck* doing this job for you. I wouldn't have wanted any other job in the world right now."

"I'm still paying for your gas." Natalie went over to the other pump where Shawn was, but he'd already started pumping the gas. She offered him forty dollars, but he shook his head. "Unlike Brock, I'll pay my own way."

"But you're also here because of me." They hadn't let her pay for lunch, and she'd only paid for the gas for the Humvee this time because Brock had been busy cleaning out the car, which she thought was commendable.

"Free meals, Brock told me," Shawn said.

She laughed. "Yes, and a free room. From here, you'll need to go south, and the garden shop is just right off the highway." She showed him the directions on her GPS.

"You let me know if you have any trouble at the airport."

"I'm sure Brock will update you right away." She was both thrilled and apprehensive with anticipation of what might happen. They just couldn't let Marek see them, or he'd most likely assume they were after him.

"Ready to hit the road again?" Brock asked, joining them.

"Yeah," she said.

They said they'd see Shawn later and then headed for the airport. Natalie was glad they arrived an hour before Marek's flight landed.

"He won't be going to baggage claim, most likely, since we took his bag, unless he picked up another," Natalie said.

"Agreed. We should wait where the arrivals are coming off the plane, in any event."

They waited in an inconspicuous place. Tons of people were arriving and departing, which helped to conceal them. Natalie was afraid they'd missed Marek until she finally saw him coming out of the men's room.

"There," she whispered to Brock.

"I see him. We need to watch where he goes. We have his home address, so if he doesn't head straight to his place, we'll have to make sure we don't lose him."

They followed Marek out of the airport. The way he was walking so fast, he seemed to be in a rush.

"What if we lose him when he gets in his car? We might not be parked anywhere near where his vehicle is."

"We'll get his license plate number, car make, and model. He's got only one way out of the parking tower. There," Brock said. "Black Toyota." He took a picture of the license plate.

They sprinted for Brock's Humvee, which was on the same floor of the parking tower but a long way away.

Natalie was worried they'd lose Marek and miss the chance to learn where the other men in the counterfeit business were located.

"If we lose him, we can stake out his house," Brock assured her as they jumped in the Humvee and headed for the exit.

She liked how Brock always had a backup plan.

They didn't see Marek's car on the way out, but on the road, they spied it. And the chase was on. She couldn't believe she was helping Brock, but this part was fun. Brock followed him, keeping his distance so Marek wouldn't realize Brock was on his tail, but staying close enough to ensure he didn't lose him.

Natalie was looking up the GPS for Marek's house address. "He's not going straight home."

"Hopefully, he's not just going to a grocery store or something, and instead, he'll lead us to some of the other men in the operation."

Marek signaled and turned right on the next street. Brock followed him. "Grocery store up on the right."

"Yeah, but if he's really leaving the country, he wouldn't need groceries." She thought she was pretty good at this.

"Exactly. I knew he wasn't going anywhere."

Marek parked his car and walked into the store. Brock parked the Humvee in the side parking area, out of sight of the front windows of the store. "Okay, I'm going to put a tracker on his car. Let's hope he takes a little time to grocery shop. You stay here."

"All right."

Brock hurried out of the Humvee and walked straight to the Toyota, dropped his keys next to it on the pavement, and planted the tracker on the car. He picked up the keys and walked back to the Humvee.

"That was quick."

He climbed into the driver's seat, and they waited. "Yeah, you have to be quick if you're going to do this right. Did you notice I stayed on the side of the vehicle where no one could see what I was doing on a security camera?"

"Yeah, though I just thought you went to that side because it was closer. For the kind of work you do, I guess you have to think like a criminal to catch one."

"It certainly helps."

Natalie was anxious to learn more but hoped they wouldn't get caught at it.

―⁓―

Half an hour later, Marek came out of the grocery store carrying a couple bags of groceries, got into his car, and drove off.

"Toward home this time?" Brock asked as he drove out of the parking lot to follow Marek.

Natalie was watching the GPS. "Yes, which is understandable if he has perishable items and needs to refrigerate them. Or something like chocolate that might melt if it's left in a hot car. His house is in the development where he's turning now."

"No need to follow him then." Brock pulled into a service station nearby.

"What now? If the rogue wolves are going to meet up with him at his house, we won't know who they are."

"We'll watch who enters the development, and if anyone looks suspect, we'll follow them and turn off on another street. If he drives off, we can follow him to his next location."

"I'd rather be gardening."

Brock glanced at Natalie. He felt bad he hadn't considered she might get tired of all the waiting for something to happen, a hazard of this business. "I can drop you off at your garden shop."

She chuckled. "No, I'm fine. If we missed him, I would be upset with myself. I'm just saying that sitting in a car watching for someone to do something isn't as much fun as gardening. Though the espionage stuff is thrilling. My adrenaline was pumping hard when we were waiting at the airport and then again when we didn't want to lose him in the parking tower. Does it give you a heightened sense of excitement doing stuff like that?"

"Yeah. Like it gives the bad guys a rush to commit their crime, I get one when I'm trying to catch them at it."

"I'll admit that getting an adrenaline rush from gardening doesn't happen very often."

He smiled. "I bet when the first flowers of spring bloom, or if you create a new cultivar, you're thrilled."

"That's true. When the flowers begin to appear, I love it." She got a call from her mom, and she answered it. "Is everything all right?"

"Yes. Shawn arrived, and you didn't tell me what a charmer he is. We can see why Angie fell in love with the Greystoke pack, if Shawn is anything like the rest of his cousins. Anyway, your dad has him doing a hundred chores, and Shawn is eager to help. You know your dad. He's got some fresh labor, so he'll make good use of the extra help. How are the two of you coming along?"

"We're on a stakeout, but nothing is happening right now."

"You'll be home for dinner, won't you?"

"As long as we're not in the middle of anything, we will be. Any problems there?"

"Nothing out of the ordinary. Okay, dear, well, I've got customers so I'll let you go. Good luck with catching up to this guy and his partners. And be careful."

"Thanks, Mom. We will. Talk later."

"We've got movement," Brock said. "Here comes the car."

"Too bad you couldn't put a listening device in his home."

"I could, but for now, I'd rather follow him and see where he's headed." Again, Brock kept his distance.

Natalie agreed and was thinking there was an art to tailing someone. Brock often ensured a car or two traveled between them, while she was keeping an eye on the vehicle and Brock had to watch for traffic too.

Marek headed out toward Canyon, Texas.

"I hadn't expected him to leave Amarillo," she said.

"If he is meeting up with these guys, they could be waiting about anywhere."

There was still a lot of traffic on the highway, which Natalie was glad for. Otherwise, Marek might have realized they were following him.

They had to fall back a bit when he turned off onto another road and began to drive out into the countryside. "He can't be going for a wolf run out here," she said.

"Maybe one of the guys he's dealing with lives out in the country."

She began doing a search for land for sale in the area. "Lots of farmland and ranch property out here. Expensive too. I'm kind of surprised. If one of the guys works with him, maybe he's rich off the illegal money or drugs or something."

"Could be. Or Marek has lied about all of it. Maybe his boss owns a palatial ranch house, and Marek is the middleman."

"Which is why he was carrying the money to Denver. To sell it to a street team or mobsters."

"Agreed. You know, we need to get your car and use it to track him in the future in case he saw my Humvee at the Denver airport. If he sees me following him, he might realize we learned he was going to be here."

"I agree. We can switch out vehicles next time. He's pulling into that ranch." She got the address.

Cactus and live oaks dotted the ranchland, with the ranch house way off in the background and two smaller ranch houses to the right. Marek drove down the road past the property, kicking up a dust storm.

"Now what do we do?" Natalie asked.

"We go to your garden shop, and while you're doing whatever you need to do, I'll see what I can learn about the guy who owns the property."

She gave a fake hearty sigh. "Somehow, I knew the fun was going to end, and I'd be working with plants again."

"I thought you said you preferred that."

"Yeah, when we're just sitting around, doing nothing. But when we're tracking someone and trying not to be seen? That's fun."

He smiled and found a different road out of the area so he didn't have to drive back by the ranch house. Though if anyone was watching traffic from the main house, they'd need binoculars to see from that distance.

"Okay, now you can direct me to your place."

"You don't want to try setting up a bug at Marek's house?"

"Not in broad daylight."

When they finally arrived at the garden shop, Brock was impressed. He'd expected a small mom-and-pop garden center, not several acres of plants, greenhouses, fountains, koi ponds, and waterfalls. But it also meant her family looked to be well settled into the area and wouldn't have any intention of moving anytime soon.

"Dad kept adding more features to sell more plants. But I think a lot of it has to do with just wanting to create a little slice of paradise here."

"It's beautiful. I really hadn't expected anything this grand." He saw Natalie's mother at the register, checking out a man pulling a wagon of plants behind him. She was an older version of Natalie, dark-brown hair threaded with a few silver hairs, clear blue eyes, her hair swept up in a bun, her smile contagious.

Then he saw Shawn loading trees into a customer's pickup truck. Brock chuckled. His cousin probably hadn't thought he'd get this much of a workout on the assignment. "Looks like you could use some more help."

"We'd hire wolves, but there were none that we could locate around here. Angie was a great help at the garden center, so we'll be missing her."

"I'm sure she'll be feeling the same way about you."

"Ha! She's so wrapped up in Aaron, I doubt she'll miss being here for a moment. But I'm truly glad for her."

Brock saw an older man adding peroxide to a fountain, Natalie's father, most likely. Brock frowned. "Won't that hurt the birds?"

"Nope. Best-kept secret. Works better at cleaning out algae than any of those store-bought brands that could harm animals in higher doses. You just need to add the proper amount of the peroxide to the water. Distilled water is supposed to help too."

"I hope you don't sell the stuff that doesn't work."

"No way. We tell all new owners of our fountains how well it works. That's Dad, if you hadn't guessed it." Natalie motioned to her father, who was working on another fountain.

He was a spry, older man, dark-haired with strands of gray hair, and when he glanced up and saw the two of them, he smiled broadly. He looked just like Natalie when she smiled.

Then he joined them, shaking Brock's hand and slapping him on the back. "I'm Connolly Silverton, and you must be Brock Greystoke, Shawn's cousin. Thanks for coming to watch over Natalie and the rest of us."

"You're welcome. I guess she told you that these

people don't know where you are living. Most likely, they believe Natalie's with me in Denver and we're mated."

Connolly laughed. "Good thing we finally got the news."

Natalie smiled and hugged her dad. "Yeah, well, it isn't for real."

"Too bad. We could use a strapping young man like Brock to help in the garden."

"He's a PI, Dad."

"Even a PI can do some real work sometimes."

She laughed.

Brock smiled. He liked the guy. Her dad had his kind of sense of humor. Brock could see what he would be doing in his spare time when he wasn't working a job if he was mated to Natalie—assisting with the family business. Which he wouldn't mind. That was the thing about a pack; everyone helped out.

"Are you here to work for a while, or do you need to do something else?" Connolly asked.

"I'm here to work. What do you need me to do?" Brock hoped Natalie's dad didn't believe he could answer customers' gardening questions. He would do more research on Marek tonight.

"Natalie, can you show him the gardens so he knows where stuff is? Then he can load customers' plants into their vehicles."

"Yeah, Dad, sure." She escorted Brock to see her mom first. They waited while she rang up a purchase, and then her mom gave Natalie a hug. "Mom, this is Brock Greystoke, and Brock, this is Juliet, my mom."

"Pleasure to meet you, ma'am." Brock meant to offer

his hand in greeting, but she put her hands over her heart and just smiled at him.

"He looks every bit as handsome as his picture." Juliet reached out and gave Brock a warm hug too. "And good, hard muscles."

"Yeah, Dad already put him to work."

"Naturally. Shawn's good-natured about it, and he seems to have been around gardens, so he's a real help. What about you, Brock?" Juliet asked.

"Uh, mowing a yard and trimming trees. That's about it." Brock didn't want to give misinformation about his skills as a gardener, but for once in his life, he really wished he knew more about it like Shawn did. So many of the wolves in the early days had kept their own gardens to produce food for the table. Once he had grown to manhood, gardening had been a thing of the past for him.

"He's got a beautiful house in Greystoke. Lots of acreage. It could be a really lovely piece of property if landscaped a bit," Natalie said.

Smiling, Brock glanced down at her. "First, the wallpaper in the bathrooms has to go, and now I need to landscape."

Natalie smiled up at him. "That's a start."

Her mom was eyeing them speculatively, probably wondering why Natalie had seen his house and was already "redecorating" it. But then Juliet got a customer, and before Natalie could show Brock the gardens, he offered to haul the customer's shrubs, flowers, and bags of potting soil to her pickup, with Natalie going along with them.

"Oh my, the Silvertons never had this much assistance

here before. And the new help is quite...lovely," the older woman said, winking at Brock.

Natalie chuckled and loaded the flowers in the back of the truck bed to protect them from the wind. Brock set the bags of soil on the bed to keep them from falling over, then loaded the shrubs.

"Well, thank you both," the woman said, handing Brock a five-dollar tip. He was going to hand it back, but the look Natalie gave him made him reconsider.

"Good luck with your plants, ma'am."

"They'd do even better if you'd come over and plant them, I'm sure. I might just have to come back soon to ogle the new help."

He laughed.

Natalie was smiling. "Thanks," Natalie said, and they waved to the woman as she left.

Brock handed the money to Natalie, but she wouldn't accept it. "I think we'll have to hire you for real, just so we have more paying customers. And maybe some good tippers too. You might even exceed what you earn as a PI if you keep making good tips." She squeezed his bicep. "Maybe you and Shawn could wear muscle shirts."

Smiling, he took her hand and led her back toward the gardens. "Show me the whole place, and then I'll get to work. What will you be doing in the meantime?"

"Watching you? You didn't need any help loading the lady's flowers, but I was there if you needed rescuing."

He chuckled. "She did have me worried. You too. I was afraid you'd offer my services to plant her flowers and shrubs to give your garden shop an even better reputation."

"No way. Then customers would come expecting you to landscape their places for them. And you'd have no clue what to do. Sure, dig holes, but…" She shrugged. "Besides, then you'll be gone, and all we'd hear is 'Where are those nice hunky guys you had working for you?' Sales would drop off because they would search other garden shops trying to find you."

He chuckled. "Hunky, huh?"

"Did you see her wink at you? Positively shameless."

"Yeah, I've never had that happen while on a PI job. I must be in the wrong line of business."

"Wait until all her gardening friends hear about it." Natalie took him through the rose gardens and herb gardens, showing him the numerous fountains they had on display.

The whole place was beautiful and made Brock rethink his own plain yard. Not that he had a need for a showcase place, but she did make him think about aesthetics.

Four cats—an orange tabby, a black and white, and two tan and white—lounged in various places in the garden.

"They don't try to eat your koi?" Brock asked, surprised.

"They're well fed. Between mice and cat food, they're not really interested. They get treats, we have them all fixed, and they have all their shots. They're like family. They come in out of the heat in the summer and the cold in the winter. Usually, they end up with my mom and dad. Customers adore the cats, for the most part. Unless the customers have cat allergies, but being outside, the cats don't pose a real problem. And they don't bother anyone, just lie around and look majestic."

Natalie had no sooner said that when one of the tabbies leaped off his stone perch, landed on the stone walkway, and joined them. He rubbed his body against

Natalie, and then circled Brock, rubbing against him the whole way around.

She looked down at the cat. "Well, that's a first. George has just welcomed you into the family. I wonder if he welcomed Shawn too."

"Maybe he can smell I'm different, like you."

"Hmm, maybe. I hadn't thought of that." Natalie greeted a couple who were loading a wagon with potted flowers in the flower garden. "Do you need any help?"

"No, we're good, thanks."

"You're welcome. Just let us know if you need anything." Natalie was walking Brock one way when he saw an intriguing path off to his left, red roses trailing over the top of a wrought-iron arbor, the walkway leading to a wooden gate under another wrought-iron arbor.

"You know it would be easy to forget you're here to shop for plants." Brock steered her to the other path.

"We created 'room dividers' of tall, narrow holly in the shrub area to showcase what can be done with plants. That's the goal. To create several landscaped niches to show what can be done with the ponds, fountains, and plants. It gives some customers an idea of what to do that they might not think of. When we started this a couple years ago, we had just the usual garden shop with every inch filled with plants in an organized way: trees there, flowers here, shrubs over there, shaded plants under shade, et cetera." They paused to watch the colorful gold and orange koi swimming in the pond.

"But I always wanted something more. A little bit of Eden to enjoy. It's nice and relaxing after a day of work. And it's special because we created the gardens ourselves. Not only did we end up with tons more garden sales, fountains and ponds included, but we also ended up with a couple of additional sales features.

"Individual photographers had come here to pick up some potted plants for photo shoots. They were so impressed with the beauty of the gardens that they began to pay us a fee to photograph their clients here after we close. You might have noticed that we have garden lighting all over for nighttime. It makes the gardens quite magical, and we sell the outdoor lighting too. We close at six, so there's still light until late in the evening in the summer. In the winter, we have the lights on. We have a bulletin board in the shop where photographers share the pictures they shot of their clients around the gardens. Between that and the photographers sharing their pictures on social networking sites, the word has spread like wildfire. The fun thing is we decorate for every season, so we always have a slew of scheduled photography sessions, even if plant sales are down in the off-season.

"We even set up an eating area with a roof and a view of a waterfall spilling into one of the koi ponds for receptions. We don't do any of the catering. But we're paid for the use of the gardens."

"You've done a remarkable job. And what a great way to extend your marketing skills and sales." They continued on their way and came to a bench on one side and the quaint gate with an arbor over the top that had intrigued him. "What's beyond the door?"

"That's the path to my personal gardens and the car-riage house."

In the worst way, Brock wanted to see her house and gardens. He wanted to learn if she had floral wallpaper throughout. To discover if her "yard" was as much a garden as the nursery was. To see what her place looked like and learn if it suited her. He had to admit he felt at home here in the garden setting. But it also made him feel as though it was private, despite the number of customers roaming about the place. He could hear some of the customers discussing what they wanted to buy, but he couldn't see them.

She took his hand and led him away from her gate. "Later, you can see my house. After we close up today, you can drive around back and park. We'll drop off your bag and have dinner at my parents' house. Depending on the day, sometimes I just eat at my place, but most of the time, we have dinner together and have fun sharing our stories of what went on during the day. We might not be a pack, but we still are a family."

"Totally understandable. Vaughn and I lived together until he found his mate. We often ate with others in the pack, the bachelors, mostly." He glanced back at the gate. "Does it lock?"

"No. We have locks on the gate in front so when we're closed, no one can drive into the place. That way, we don't have any plant thieves come and steal our plants."

He looked skeptically at her. He couldn't imagine anyone stealing plants from a garden store.

"Ohmigosh, yeah, it's unbelievable. We've been lucky, but then we have a really good security system with motion-detector lights. If anyone's creeping around the place, they come on. And we live on the property, so we can hear what goes on. That acts as a deterrent. If someone drives up and gets through our locked gate, we'll hear them. They wouldn't be able to carry a lot of stuff out of here unless they have a vehicle close by. And they don't know we're wolves, so we can hear better than they can.

"We've only had one attempt at theft. Four men in ski masks figured they could steal a couple of our fountains. Dad had his gun out, Mom was on the phone to the police, and I was a wolf. They were armed and so considered dangerous. The lights were on all over the place, the security cameras catching them in the act. Dad told them to get on the ground, but one of the men pulled out a gun. Dad shot his hand, and the thief dropped the gun. Another went after his gun, and I came around the corner and leapt at him, knocking him down.

"Mom came out with a shotgun and was ready to shoot anyone who didn't do what they said. The two other men eyed my parents with a look that said they thought they were bluffing. One of them went for a gun, and I leapt at him, knocking him down. 'Down now, or I shoot,' my dad said."

"I guess you were afraid to bite the men," Brock said.

"Yeah, we had the security videos running, and we didn't want it to look like we were in the wrong. What if I'd bitten someone and turned him? That would have been a disaster. The police might have tried to quarantine the wolf, dog, whatever they thought I was. We were trying to get the thieves' cooperation without getting ourselves in trouble."

"And?"

"They heard the police sirens. The man with the injured hand was groaning, cupping it, whining that he was going to bleed to death. The man I had knocked down was getting to his feet. I growled and barked at him. He smelled of fear and sweat. He ran, and I took him down, one pounce, slammed into him, and he was pinned to the gravel road. The other three got down on the ground, but two of them were still armed. Dad always had a pocket full of ties for plants, or in this case for thieves. Mom held the shotgun on the men while Dad tied them up, and then he confiscated their guns. I just stood there wagging my tail and growling. When we heard the sirens wailing, I was ready to head back to the house. I waited until I saw the police cars' headlights though, afraid to leave my parents alone with the men."

"Hell, what happened to the would-be thieves?"

"They were all charged with attempted armed robbery. Two of the men were on parole, and they went to prison. I think it helped us because we never had another problem. Too much security here. Too many guns. And one badass wolf."

Brock chuckled. "You are my kind of wolf. Somehow I didn't think a master gardener would be such a wolf."

"You don't know the half of it."

"But I'm sure eager to learn."

Chapter 11

THAT EVENING, AFTER THEY'D CLOSED THE GARDEN CENTER, Brock moved his car to park in front of Natalie's house. Then they walked over to her parents' two-story home, which featured a nice wraparound porch. Inside, Natalie's mom had cooked a pot roast, potatoes, and carrots in a slow cooker, so the meal was ready when they closed up the garden center. The aroma of the roast made Brock's stomach growl in anticipation as he and his cousin, Natalie, and her parents were about to sit down to eat at the long oak table.

With a twinkle in his eye, Shawn made a move to sit beside Natalie, but Brock stopped him quickly enough. Smiling. Knowing his cousin was trying to prove Brock was being mighty territorial for a wolf who wasn't interested in courting another.

Of course, everyone noticed the maneuver. Wolves watched one another for actions and reactions. It was part of their wolf heritage and made them more aware of cues they were giving off. Not to mention they also smelled the change in the wolves' scents—from congenial to slightly aggressive.

Natalie let out a big sigh and sat down beside Brock. He didn't know if she was resigned to considering courting him or annoyed he'd been posturing so his cousin couldn't get near her for the meal. Brock couldn't help it. He was a wolf.

Her dad dished up roast beef that was falling apart, it was so well cooked. Brock thought he should invest in a slow cooker: great, easy way to cook a meal while he was off doing surveillance and such for a job in Denver and going home to Greystoke for the evening.

"What do you think about our garden center?" her dad asked, looking straight at Brock for an answer.

Before Brock could speak, Shawn did. "You get a lot of exercise, that's for sure. I like working out in the fresh air and sunshine. Right now, I work at the leather goods factory the pack owns. This is a really nice change of pace."

Brock thought her dad was more interested in *his* viewpoint on working at the nursery, maybe because Natalie's parents thought he could be a prospective mate for Natalie. There was no hiding the chemistry between them, even if he'd wanted to.

"And you, Brock?" her dad asked.

"Good, honest labor. I'd like it better than working at the factory." Brock did enjoy working at the garden center. He enjoyed being outdoors as much as the next wolf.

"But not better than your PI job?" her dad pointedly asked.

Brock smiled. Natalie's cheeks were suffused with color. "I do like being a PI. Sometimes, I can even use the military skills I learned as a SEAL. As a gardener, I wouldn't be able to. Unless you had someone looking to rob you. And then? I'd be first on the line to deal with it. But I love solving the mystery of the cases I'm on."

Connolly sighed. "I understand. I loved solving murder investigations. Too bad you're not into the garden business. We'll just have to hire Shawn."

"He's got a pack back in Colorado," Natalie reminded

her dad. But it was more than that. She was scowling at her father as if she didn't like him trying to set her up with Shawn.

At least that was what Brock figured her dad had in mind. Or maybe he was trying to force the issue of Brock seeing Natalie.

"But Shawn would have an opportunity for a mate here, maybe. Someday." Her dad looked meaningfully at her, as if to remind her she wasn't getting any younger and there were no marriageable prospects in the area.

"It could work," Shawn said, giving Brock a cocky smile. He poured some gravy on his meat and potatoes. "Except for one thing. The SEAL has already surrendered to the lady."

Everyone looked in Brock's direction to see what he had to say about the matter.

He just smiled and shook his head. He would get his cousin back, but for now, it was time to change the subject. "The dinner is great."

"Thanks," her mom said. "It's a great way to have a dinner all ready to go after a long day at the nursery."

Everyone else agreed that the food was delicious.

"What would it require for someone to join a pack like yours?" her dad asked Brock, surprising him, especially because of what Natalie had said about the problems they'd faced with other packs. He also didn't think they'd want to uproot and move to Colorado. Not when they had such a beautiful garden center here.

Natalie's jaw dropped, but her mother didn't look surprised to hear Connolly ask the question. Brock suspected her parents had discussed the topic with each other, and Natalie hadn't been in on the conversation.

"Bella and Devlyn would have to agree to allow a wolf or wolves to join the pack, but if you're talking about you and your family, you already are a shoo-in with Angie mating one of our cousins and becoming a member of the pack. Aaron will vouch for you too. I would. I'm sure Shawn would, so I imagine our pack leaders wouldn't hesitate to accept you," Brock said.

"We've had difficulties with being in other packs," her dad warned, cutting into his roast beef.

"Natalie discussed them with me. You haven't been with *our* pack. Would you want to relocate to Colorado, leaving all this behind? Your place is beautiful, and it looks like you're doing well with your business." Brock couldn't imagine wanting to start from scratch all over again. What a job that would be! Though, in all fairness, the Silvertons would have lots of wolf help if they did want to move to Greystoke.

"Angie is like a daughter to us. She'll have kids one of these days, and we don't want to miss out on the joy of being 'grandparents.' We already missed her wedding because we were tied down here. A pack could help us with running the business if we needed to enjoy a break for a bit."

"Are you seriously considering moving close to their pack because of Angie?" Natalie asked, her eyes wide.

Brock could usually read people. This time, he was having a hard time knowing if Natalie was happy or apprehensive about the prospect of a move.

"Yeah. You girls will miss each other too much. Your mom and I can't have you leaving to see her all the time. And you know when she has children, you're going to want to be part of that too. If we had a place there, we could hire more reliable wolf help. We've already hired Shawn, and he'd still be close to his pack."

Brock glanced at Shawn. He thought that was all a joke.

Shawn smiled at him. "Hey, sounds good to me. I'd love to work full time at the nursery."

"Mom, you agreed to this?" Natalie asked, sounding surprised.

"We've been discussing it ever since Angie brought Aaron home to meet us and we knew she was moving to his ranch in Colorado. So yes. We figure if the pack doesn't suit us, we can always establish another garden center somewhere else. Closer to Greystoke, but not in their territory. But we're thinking of you too. We've been selfish, not considering your situation and Angie's. There are no decent male wolf prospects around." Her mother forked up some of her potatoes. "Last year when we had the attempted robbery, if we'd had a pack to help out, we would have been much better off. We could have been seriously injured or worse. And we worried about it for months afterward. All of us did." She paused. "How do you feel about moving, Natalie?"

"Like I've been left out of the loop. Why didn't you tell me what you were thinking?"

Her mom sighed. "We wanted you to meet the pack first. If you were completely against the move, we'd stay here. We were going to discuss it with you once you came home, to see if you liked the pack. You arrived here with two of the pack members instead, so"—her mom shrugged—"we discuss it now."

"You'll have to go meet the pack," Natalie said. "You can't join them until you're sure you will be fine with them." She sounded like she didn't trust that her parents would find them acceptable.

"That was just our thought. If Brock, Shawn, and you can hold down the fort, we thought we could enjoy a mini vacation and visit with Bella and Devlyn. Then we can decide. But we want your approval on this venture first."

Natalie lifted a shoulder. "You know me. I'm always ready to try something new and different. But it's going to be a lot of work to set up anything this grand in a new location. We'll have to learn about plants that thrive in Colorado. It's a big move."

"You'll have a whole pack to help you," Brock said before Shawn could. Brock couldn't help feeling elated, as though he were floating in the clouds. He'd been trying not to think about the situation with Natalie living so far away, as much as he'd been feeling more and more territorial with her. He thought she really had gotten along well with the rest of the ladies in the pack, so joining wouldn't be a problem for her. She'd been more reserved around the men, but he was sure that had to do with her not wanting any of the bachelors to think she was interested in them. Her parents might be more of an issue, given the bad experiences they'd had with other packs.

But what if she thought one of the *other* bachelors suited her better?

He'd have to make sure they didn't.

"Hell, I guess I'd better let Devlyn know I'll be quitting work at the leather goods factory," Shawn said in a salute with his glass of wine.

"Maybe you should wait until *after* my parents see the pack leaders," Natalie said.

"We'd kind of like to meet with them quickly, before you need to leave, Brock," Natalie's mom said.

Brock was thinking he could hang around here until the family was ready to move, maybe even advertise to do some PI jobs, once he resolved the issue with the counterfeit money ring.

"But we don't want to leave you in the lurch over this counterfeit-money situation," her dad said.

"It could be some time before we could eliminate the menace." Shawn stabbed a carrot with his fork. "I say we go for it. You could leave tomorrow and see the pack, spend a few days, and we'll handle everything here. We can keep checking into the counterfeiting guys, and when you come back, maybe we'll have that resolved."

"Will you be able to manage both if you have trouble with the wolves?" her dad asked. "I'd be more than willing to stay and help."

"Maybe when you arrive home," Brock said. "I agree with Shawn. We can do it. Did you want to leave tomorrow?" He hoped they could manage the place like her parents wanted. Everyone had their own way of doing things, and the Silvertons might not be happy when they came back. Then again, if they planned to sell the place and move, they probably wouldn't care as long as everything was maintained properly—meaning the fish and plants didn't die.

Her mom and dad exchanged glances, smiled, and nodded. "If it won't be too much of an inconvenience," her dad said. "Natalie knows how to operate the place by herself, but she'll need your help."

"She's got it," Brock said. "And I was thinking I could pick up some other PI work here while you're trying to sell the place, or whatever you need to do until you're ready to leave."

Now Natalie was looking at him, her lips parted in surprise. He wanted to lean over and kiss them.

Her mom and dad were smiling.

"Yeah, you have a good time with the pack. Don't worry about us. You can check on us as much as you like while you're gone to make sure we're doing everything right," Shawn said.

"Boy, will I have you working hard for your money," Natalie said to Brock and Shawn and laughed evilly.

Brock and Shawn chuckled. Brock was ready.

"If you cook as well as your mom, I'm ready," Shawn said.

"I can't believe my parents were discussing all this behind my back," Natalie groused to Brock on the way back to her carriage house after dinner. "That's why they were so insistent I hang around with your pack a while longer after Angie and Aaron went off on their honeymoon. They were hoping I'd enjoy being around your pack members and maybe even find someone I might like to date."

"Well, it worked, didn't it?"

She took hold of his hand. "I thought they were joking about hiring Shawn. Were you serious about doing some PI jobs here until we can move?"

"I am. I've been giving it a lot of thought. I had assumed your parents were joking about hiring Shawn too. I was afraid they were disappointed in me for wanting to continue working as a PI. They floored me when they asked about joining the pack. But I can see their reasoning. Their two lovely daughters—"

Natalie lowered her chin and raised her brows at him.

"Well, one 'daughter' departed the area, and with the prospect of her having babies, they didn't want to miss out. But they're just as concerned you might hook up with a wolf like me and leave them behind too. Just think if you ended up with a wolf of another pack somewhere far away. Then they'd be split between the two of you. And with running their own business, that makes it hard to get away to visit either of you. I can tell they're pack-inclined, but they just haven't found the right pack to settle down with."

"What do *you* think about us joining the pack?" she asked, opening the door to her house.

"Truthfully? I couldn't be gladder. You'll find lots of help for your garden center, all of us would be customers, and we'll provide security so you won't have any more theft or attempted theft problems. Not with a whole pack to back you. Angie and Aaron will be thrilled too. We have a pack doctor for when Angie and Aaron have babies. We don't have anyone in the pack who runs a garden center. It's always nice to expand our businesses to include wolf customers and humans. You won't believe how much marketing the pack would do on social media to help boost your sales."

"Wow, I hadn't even thought of that." Now she was really smiling as she shut the door.

"Shawn will talk their ears off about all of it. The rest of us will be eager to help out."

"Will Bella and Devlyn consider the trouble my parents have had fitting in with other packs as a bad sign?"

Natalie thought it sounded bad to an outsider, though she knew her parents had good reason to pull up stakes and move each time.

"Given the issues they had with other packs, no." Brock pulled Natalie into his arms. "You have to know I'll be the happiest of all that you're joining the pack."

She slid her hands around his back and hugged him tight to her body. "We haven't made it to that point exactly. But if we did, and my family moved there, what if I found one of your other bachelor males...intriguing?"

"You won't."

She chuckled. "You're certainly sure of yourself. But you're right. I wouldn't. Not after hearing your sexy voice over the phone when you were giving me directions to the restaurant. And you weren't laughing at me for being so excited to find my way there. That said a lot in my book."

"I was only glad Angie asked me to help out."

"You must have been close by when she asked you for your assistance."

He laughed. "I wasn't. She was waving frantically for me, and I rushed across the room to join her, thinking there was a real emergency, the way she was frowning. Of course, Aaron was smiling, and I should have known better."

Natalie chuckled. Then she pulled him down for a kiss, only this time, it was more. Much more. Erotically deep and emotionally charged. She'd never felt this way with a wolf or human before. After last night, she was certain they had the kind of wolf connection that meant this was worth exploring a whole lot more. She suspected her mother already knew it. Her dad too. Both were instinctual enough to know something was going on between the two of them.

Brock's hands caressed her shoulders and her arms, his mouth expertly on hers, kissing her, exciting her. His tongue licked her lips, his mouth nuzzling hers. The heat ratcheted up between them, and their pheromones were ablaze. She cupped his buttocks and pressed his heavy arousal against her.

She ached for him, wanting him inside her, but they couldn't go that far yet. She had to know for certain that her parents really did want to move and join the pack. She just couldn't leave them behind like Angie had done. Angie had been adopted by the family, but Natalie was their own flesh and blood. They would be devastated if she abandoned them for the Greystoke pack if they didn't want to join them.

"God, you're hot," she whispered against Brock's mouth. "Combustible."

"So are you. And beautiful." He kissed her back, their hearts beating frantically.

She wanted to haul him to her bedroom and explore every inch of his tantalizingly naked body again, but she gave him a soft kiss, signaling an end to this madness. She drew away…reluctantly. "I…guess we should get our laptops and do a little research before we go to bed." She wanted to continue this, but she thought it was prudent for her parents to like Brock's pack first.

"Uh, yeah, we've got some bad guys to terminate." He smiled at her and grabbed his laptop sitting next to his bag. He seemed to understand how she was feeling and didn't view it as a rejection.

She was glad for that.

She brought her laptop in from the dining room and sat down to do some research in the living room. She had planned to leave some room between them on the brown velour couch, but she really didn't want to and sat so her leg was touching his. He smiled at her closeness and opened up his laptop.

Yeah, she was going to keep her distance from him until her parents decided the pack was good for them. *Right*. She would enjoy the time they got to spend together, no matter what her parents decided.

She began looking for information on the ranch property out near Canyon. She found a ranch near Marek's friend's ranch house that was for sale. "Okay," Natalie said. "I told you those properties were high-dollar value. That ranch where Marek went? The one near it costs $1.8 million. That doesn't mean theirs is that fancy, but then again, maybe it's even more expensive."

Brock whistled. "Hell, he's got some money. I just located information on a Eugenia Jones residing at the same house as the one where Marek lives in Amarillo. In fact, it shows they're co-owners."

"A mate? Or the aunt he supposedly has?"

"Looks like she's the aunt or some other relative. According to her driver's license, she would be the right age to be his aunt or mother. The house isn't a new purchase. Eugenia bought the home fifty years ago, and she's the original owner."

"Who owns the fancy ranch Marek visited?" she asked.

"Let me look." Using the address Natalie gave him, he found the record. "Dexter Cartwright. And you're right. According to property values, it's worth $3.5

million, which includes the main house and two other ranch houses on the property."

"Wow. Okay, that's one of the men Lettie said hung out with Marek in Denver. What's he doing here?"

"Living in a big ranch house, it appears. And it makes me think Lettie might have given us some good information. Maybe she's not as bad as I thought after all." Brock was looking for the name of anyone else who lived at the residence. "Dexter has a wife. And he has a black Ford pickup and a red Porsche. Got the tag numbers too." He did another search and swore. "Damn it." He rubbed his chin, frowning, deep in thought.

Natalie glanced at the driver's license picture of Dexter Cartwright—black hair, black eyes, unsmiling, clean-shaven, tan, tall. She didn't recognize him. "What's wrong?"

"He shot me three times, and I thought I'd killed him."

"What?"

"Yeah, last year. He was dealing drugs, and Vaughn and I took down his ring. We had a hell of a firefight, and I shot him five times. The bastard. I can't believe he made it out of the warehouse alive."

"How bad were you hit?"

"It wasn't good. The only good thing was I wasn't as bad off as someone who doesn't have our healing genetics. I was hospitalized for a week in my cousin's clinic. Luckily, Dexter hadn't hit me anywhere that would have made me bleed out at the scene. Even our healing genetics won't work fast enough to stop that from happening."

Still, it meant Brock had suffered significant wounds, or he wouldn't have been hospitalized for that long.

"You didn't seem to recognize his name." She wondered what other injuries Brock had suffered over the years in the line of duty.

"He had a different name back then."

"Was his brother into all this?"

"Not that we knew of. From what we learned, we'd gotten rid of all of them. But I guess his death was faked so I wouldn't go after him again."

"Once you were healed up."

"Yeah, right."

"What if Dexter's the boss? If his property is an indication of his wealth, he should have the money to set this all up."

"True. Unless he's in debt up to his eyeballs. Why would Marek be transporting the money to Denver?" Brock was looking through his databases for Dexter's old residences.

"Maybe Dexter had a couple of houses. One in Denver, and one in Canyon. Dexter knew Marek in Denver—and his brother is the middleman still living there. And that's who Marek was transferring the money to," Natalie said. "Then Marek has this aunt in Amarillo, so with the breakup between him and Lettie, he moves to Amarillo for good."

"Could be. Yeah, here's what we're looking for. Dexter had a home in Denver, and now he has the ranch in Canyon, newly purchased. He sold the one in Denver, so it appears he's not living there any longer. I wonder why Marek would have to invest his own money in the venture when Dexter lives so well."

"Maybe because he had to do something big to participate in this venture," Natalie said.

"I'll ask Vaughn to check out the other two friends Marek hung out with in Denver. It makes me wonder if they're all in on it."

"You should call Marek too."

Smiling, Brock rubbed his hand over her leg.

"Yeah, call him and ask if he's got the printing press at his house and that's where he makes the money. Or if it's at Dexter's place. We could set up surveillance and see if anyone tries to move it."

He laughed. "Not happening."

She let out her breath. "I don't think I have the patience for this job. I'd want to push it forward. Get a reaction. Take them down right away. Like gardening, doing something physical, getting the job done."

He chuckled and rubbed her back.

She ran her hand over his leg. "I'm sorry for what my dad said during dinner. I've only dated a few human men, for the most part, nothing I planned to make permanent. I think Dad was always afraid I might turn one of the guys into one of us. I had no intention of doing that. But finding wolves in the places we've lived has been difficult, to say the least. Then I dated the wolf who was really into gardening. He treated the whole family like they were his best friends and he adored them. He brought my mother flowers when he came to dinner, brought my dad's favorite brandy. He was—"

"Almost too good to be true?"

"Yeah. Exactly. I'd never been with a wolf who acted like he wanted to court me. I thought, well, I thought maybe this was what it was supposed to be like. That we had this connection because we were both wolves. And because of our shared love of gardening. He was so caring and considerate. But…I…didn't feel the emotional attachment for him like my parents feel for each other. I kept thinking it would happen, like, someday soon. Then I…I don't know. I began to get suspicious. He'd have mysterious calls that he had to answer when he ate with us. And once he took me to a movie and left in the middle of it for another phone call. I started thinking he was concealing some secret life—a girlfriend, criminal activity, something. I asked who was calling, but he would just say it was business."

"What did he say his occupation was?"

"He was an investment broker, but he knew everything about plants. He said his mother was big into gardening and taught him everything he knew. Kind of like Shawn. I was thrilled to meet another wolf who knew so much about gardening. Since I had my suspicions, I began to follow him to see where he hung out during the day. I saw him pull into a new construction site for a business. He was there, looking over the foundation they were pouring. I didn't know what it was for though. It could have been for anything, and he might not have been the owner.

"When he left, I parked and asked one of the men working on the building what they were putting in there. He said they were building a garden center. One of the superstore franchises. And he told me the name of the owner—the guy I was dating. We were a small, privately owned garden center, and we couldn't stand up to the competition. I don't think I've ever been angrier in my life." She knew she should let go of the resentment, but she couldn't.

"Hell, I would have been too."

"Even though we didn't think we'd be able to match their prices or the stock they were carrying, we tried to compete with him. Some of our loyal customers continued to shop with us because they liked the family-run business and the personal touch, but it wasn't enough. The betrayal was what hurt the most. After that, I wished I could read minds and know just what a guy was thinking so I wouldn't be used like that again. It wasn't just about me though. He ruined our business, and we had to move. He hurt my parents too."

"You didn't tell me you were into PI work on your own earlier." Brock smiled.

She chuckled. "Yeah. That was my first case."

"And you learned just what you needed to know and didn't get caught at it. That's something to be proud of." Brock stretched out his legs. "I felt the same kind of betrayal from Lettie, so I know how you feel about someone lying to you."

She frowned at him. "Have you investigated my family to make sure we're all on the up and up?"

Brock smiled. "No. Vaughn did ask Aaron if he wanted us to look into Angie and her family, just to hassle him. He said hell no, and if we did, he'd disown us. We all just laughed."

"Good. If you had run a check on us, you'd be finding a hotel and heading back home tonight."

Brock smiled again. "You have to admit after what we both went through, it makes you feel like you need to check out other wolves you're dealing with."

"Other wolves. Not mine."

He chuckled. "You're cute, you know. You're some of the good guys, just like we are."

She cuddled against his shoulder. "Tomorrow will be here soon enough. I guess it's time to go to bed."

"Which bedroom did you want me to sleep in?" He sounded hopeful she'd have him stay with her, but he was letting it be her call.

"I only have two. The first one is yours." Natalie had to keep her mind on business and ensure her parents were all right with the pack before she got too tangled up with Brock. She got off the couch, and he grabbed his bag. She led him to the first of the bedrooms. "Night, Brock." No matter what she wanted, she needed to give them a breather.

He pulled her in for a hug and a kiss. So much for some distance.

"Hey, we're not just connected by being wolves. There's a hell of a lot more to us than that," he said.

"I agree, but I want to make sure my parents feel comfortable with your pack before you and I go any further."

He gave her a frustrated sigh. "All right. It's going to kill me, but…all right." Then he gave her one of his charmingly wolfish smiles.

She chuckled, kissing him, then left him at the guest room.

But later that night, while she was sleeping, the motion-detector lights came on, and she was fully awake in an instant.

Chapter 12

AT TWO IN THE MORNING, NATALIE HEARD THE WOLF DOOR squeak open and shut. Immediately, her heart began pounding. She yanked off her pj shorts set, shifted, and ran to the guest room. The door was wide open, black boxer briefs were on the floor, and Brock was gone.

Maybe he was a night prowler, couldn't sleep in a new place, and went for a wolf run outside. But she was certain the motion-detector lights had woken him too, and he was in full wolf-protector mode.

As soon as she was outside, she saw the motion-detector lights shining all over the garden. She headed in their direction. It could be just the cats, an armadillo, or any number of things. Nothing sinister.

If someone was trying to steal something, she didn't want Brock dealing with it on his own and possibly getting hurt. She still couldn't believe he'd been injured so badly that he had been laid up at the clinic for so long. It was a reminder that their kind were not invincible.

As a wolf, she preferred moving through the darkness and sneaking up on would-be thieves, but now she was setting off the motion-detector lights herself. Brock suddenly came around a hedge, likely checking to see who had set off the lights in this direction, as Shawn abruptly appeared as a wolf to join them.

Brock shifted into his glorious naked human self, and Natalie couldn't help but eye his whole gorgeous body—from his broad shoulders and chiseled muscles and six-pack to the dark curls surrounding his semi-aroused cock and his well-muscled legs.

Brock smiled at her. "Did either of you see anyone?"

They shook their heads.

"I heard a car door open and shut, and tires crunching on gravel."

Shawn shifted. "All I saw was the lights going on all over the place. I told your parents to stay inside their home, Natalie, and I'd check it out. But I didn't hear anything."

"All right. Well, I looked for a vehicle, but it was gone. I suspect I didn't hear it until they were leaving. Probably the lights scared them off," Brock said.

"Did you smell anyone?" Shawn asked.

"No. Which bothered me. I didn't smell anyone. Humans or wolves."

Natalie wondered how that could be when Shawn said, "Hell, they're wearing hunter's spray?"

"Yeah, they had to have been, or I would have smelled them. Which means they're wolves and they know we are too, or they wouldn't have bothered. They're up to no good," Brock said.

The only wolves in the area that they knew of were Marek and his cohorts. How had they discovered where Natalie lived? Where her parents lived?

"Should we pull guard duty the rest of tonight?" Shawn asked.

"No. Just stay in the house, and be alert and watch over things there. I suspect they were checking out the security here and realized it was a little more than they'd bargained for. The lock on the front gate was cut. Do your parents have another?" Brock asked Natalie.

She nodded.

"I'll get the lock from her parents, since I'm staying there, and replace it on the gate," Shawn said.

"I'll go with you," Brock said.

Natalie wasn't walking back to the carriage house on her own.

Both men shifted, and they all headed for the main house.

Shawn went in through the wolf door while Brock and Natalie stayed outside and watched for any movement. When Shawn appeared, he was dressed in jeans and boots, carrying a gun and a padlock.

"Come on. Let's go," Shawn said.

They ran a ways from him so they were all spread out. When they reached the gate, Natalie saw it was open, the padlock cut and thrown onto the ground. She growled in anger.

Shawn quickly locked the gate. He grabbed the cut lock, and they all went back to the house.

"Night," Shawn told them.

Both woofed at him, and Brock and Natalie ran off to her house. Now the rogue wolves knew they lived here. Just great.

After she and Brock were inside, Natalie raced to her bedroom, threw on her pajama shorts set, and went into the guest room, where Brock was already dressed in his boxer briefs.

"If it's Marek and his men, how did they learn about us?" she asked.

Brock pulled her over to the bed, and they sat on the end of it. "The problem is criminals can access information as easily as we can, if they have the means. That's the unfortunate truth of the matter. They must have learned who you were at the airport and that you didn't live with me in Colorado. Marek probably assumes you're just dating me. They could smell my scent here and probably realize we're coming after them."

"What about my folks leaving tomorrow to check out your pack? Should they stay instead?"

"No. I think them leaving for Colorado is the best for everyone concerned. They'll be safely away from here, and the rest of my pack can watch out for them. They'll be fine. It would be safer there for them than being here."

Natalie sighed. "I'm not sure my dad will go along with it after what happened here tonight. And if Dad doesn't go, Mom won't either."

"It's up to them, but I believe they'd be safer in Greystoke. And we'll deal with these men here."

"No ulterior motives, right?" She smiled at Brock.

"Oh, hell yeah there are. The sooner your parents meet with the pack and agree it's the one for them, the quicker you and I won't have any obstacles in our path to courting."

She sighed. "What do these men hope to do? I mean, like you said, some members of the pack are out to get them, but if they hurt you, the whole pack will come down on them."

"They probably don't have any idea how big the pack is. Lettie didn't know. She never wanted to meet anyone. I should have realized there was something wrong there. I think she figured she had me so wrapped around her little finger that I wasn't thinking clearly. But if any of the pack members saw her, they'd straighten me out about her."

"And me?"

"All the bachelors would love to get to know you better. And they can. Once we're mated."

She laughed. "If we don't get some sleep, we're going to be worn out when it's time to work in the gardens before customers arrive. I didn't hear anyone or anything, not until you went out the wolf door."

"The wolf door squeaks."

"On purpose. I don't ever lock it, but if anyone came in, I'd hear them. That's why I don't apply oil to the hinges. Not that I'd ever expect anyone to show up and barge through my wolf door. Speaking of which, I guess with wolves on the prowl, I should lock it."

"I'll get it." Brock left the room.

Fully intending to share the bed with Brock this time, appreciating his dedication to caring for them and not wanting to be apart from him, Natalie climbed under the covers of the guest bed.

Brock returned and stared at her lying under the covers, then smiled and joined her.

"Since I can't seem to hear anyone driving up the drive, but you can, I'm sleeping in here." As if *that* was the only reason.

"With me, right? You don't want me to switch rooms with you, do you?" Brock sounded as if he was afraid she hadn't intended to join him in bed.

She cuddled next to him. "You stay right there. If you hear anything I don't, you can wake me."

Natalie's phone ringing in her bedroom woke Brock, and he realized he was still snuggling with the she-wolf of his dreams. She stirred. They'd cooled it last night, but he was damn glad she had wanted to stay with him, to share the space, to maintain the intimacy. He glanced at the clock. Holy hell, it was seven already. They were supposed to be having breakfast at six. He pulled free of Natalie and headed for the bathroom.

She was right behind him. "I can't believe we overslept."

"I'm sure your parents figured we needed a little extra sleep due to all the running around we did last night because of your unwelcome guests."

"Right." She went into her bedroom, and he heard her speaking on the phone to her parents. "Yeah, Mom, we'll be right over. Brock's showering, and I'll get a quick one too. Sorry for oversleeping. See you there in a few minutes."

With a towel wrapped around his waist, Brock walked back into the guest room and pulled on his underclothes, jeans, a T-shirt, and a pair of boots. By the time he was fully dressed, Natalie came out of her bedroom dressed in similar clothes, but her green T-shirt had flowers on it and the name of the nursery. She glanced at his black T-shirt.

"You look like you're ready for a SEAL mission. When we get to Mom and Dad's place, we'll get you and Shawn each a garden center T-shirt so everyone will know you're working here."

"No being anonymous, eh?" Brock was used to being knowledgeable about any job he worked, so this was a change.

She laughed. "Nope."

Then they headed over to the main house, and Brock felt guilty for oversleeping. He never did that. He thought it had to do with cuddling with Natalie all night and not wanting to let go of her this morning.

The food was already on the table when they arrived: eggs, ham, toast, hash browns, and coffee. Brock was famished and hurried to eat before they had to run over to the garden center. At least it was within walking distance. Shawn was already wearing the green garden-center T-shirt, and one was resting on the back of Brock's chair for him.

Brock probably should have changed shirts out of view of the family, though he often removed clothes in front of others when they were shifting. But since the older wolves weren't part of his pack, and they were Natalie's parents and he was trying to put his best foot forward, Brock wasn't sure why he whipped off his black T-shirt and pulled on the green one at the dining table. Maybe to show he wanted to please them by being part of the garden team.

Natalie's mom was smiling and blushing. "Oh my, I remember when you were like that, dear," she said to her husband, patting his stomach.

He ran his hand over his chest. "I still am, dear."

Juliet chuckled. Natalie was laughing. Smiling, Shawn was shaking his head.

"Shawn said he thought we should still visit with your pack and leave today," Connolly said. "What do you think?"

"I agree. It would be safer for you if we could handle these men while you're gone," Brock said.

"But what about running the garden center? Can you do both?" Juliet asked.

"Yeah. They won't be here messing with us during

the day, and we'll be ready for them at night." Brock finished off his ham.

"But you were so tired this morning," Juliet said, glancing at Natalie, as if wondering if she'd had anything to do with it.

"We'll set an alarm on our phones." Natalie spread honey on her toast. "We won't wake up too late."

"Yeah, I'll make sure of it too," Shawn said.

"Shawn said the ones who trespassed have to be the wolves you're after because they used hunter's concealment," Connolly said.

Brock ate another slice of toast. "Right. Wolves who aren't trying to cause trouble wouldn't show up wearing it. It's the only explanation for why I wouldn't have smelled them at all—human or wolf. There can't be that many of them, or I'm sure you would have run across them some time or other."

"Are you sure you don't need our help?" Connolly asked.

"He wants you to see the pack sooner and fall in love with them so we can start courting," Natalie said, surprising Brock by mentioning it.

"We'll go," Natalie's mother said, patting her husband's hand and casting him a stern look.

"All right, but I hope you let your pack know if you need help right away so they can send reinforcements," her dad said. "I'll come back too."

"Absolutely. I've been keeping them informed of what's going on here. I checked with my brother, Vaughn, but he hasn't located any of these guys back in Denver yet," Brock said.

Connolly finished his coffee and set his mug down

on the table. "Maybe most of their operation is here in Amarillo."

"It could be. And Marek might even be a new partner in this business. He might not have been with them all along." Brock finished breakfast and rose from the table and started clearing dishes.

"Run along. Connolly can get you started, and Natalie will join you soon. She'll cashier while you all do what you need to do, but we don't need anyone cashiering for another hour." Juliet started putting the dishes in the dishwasher.

Natalie kissed Brock, and he kissed her back. "See you soon," she said.

He caught sight of her parents and his cousin watching them, smiling. Good. He was glad everyone seemed to approve, because as long as Natalie was agreeable, they were going to be mated wolves.

Brock headed out with Shawn and Natalie's dad to the garden center.

"A delivery truck will be showing up soon. Once you off-load the plants, Natalie will verify we received everything we were supposed to get," Connolly said. "She can show you where to move them to. If you have any questions, just ask her. Open the gate at eight, and then you probably won't be very busy until around ten or eleven. You can take turns grabbing something to eat at lunchtime, since that's our busiest time. I'm going back to the house to get us on the road and send Natalie out to oversee things. And thanks, fellas, for helping out with everything. I'm sure the pack will work out for us just fine. I know they need to look us over and learn more about us, just like we do them.

Would it be too much to ask if we can be away as long as three days?"

"You will have just arrived and practically turned around and come home. Make it at least five days, which includes your two travel days. That will give you three full days to meet with the pack and see the area. But spend more time away if you need to. We'll be sure to run everything right." Brock really wanted them to enjoy the pack, but if they had any issues or concerns, he wanted them to have time to hash them out too.

Natalie joined them. "I'll make sure we handle everything, Dad." She gave him a hug and a kiss. "Go. Mom's waiting at the car already, eager to get me mated off."

Her dad chuckled and hugged her back. "Just don't get into any trouble while I'm gone."

Brock suspected that was just what they were going to do as soon as they ran into Marek and his men.

After her mom and dad drove off, Brock said, "I was surprised they didn't worry about leaving the place in our hands when we might have some trouble. Especially since your dad is a retired homicide detective."

"I think *I* was more of a concern for them." Natalie glanced in the direction of the road where an eighteen-wheeler was driving toward their garden center.

"I'm all for ridding them of that worry."

She just smiled at him and ran her hand over the garden-center logo on his shirt. "Nice abs. You gave my mom a real thrill."

"I should have moved out of view of the dining room table. I was just thinking we were in a hurry to eat and get over here, and I wanted to show your parents I was happy to wear the center's T-shirt."

"Mom appreciated it."

"And your dad?"

"He was amused." Natalie waved at the truck driver. "It's time for the delivery of new garden plants. We'll have to move them to their various locations once they're off the truck." Natalie led the way and opened the gate so the truck could pull up closer to the center.

Then they all got busy off-loading the plants. After Natalie confirmed delivery, the truck left and Shawn locked the driveway gate. They each had a cart to move plants to their temporary homes, starting with the shrubs.

Brock and Shawn followed her lead.

"Listen," Brock said as they hauled their carts full of hollies, "these guys, or at least one of them, could very well visit the garden center with the ruse of shopping for plants to check the place out during the day. And to learn who all works here."

"Or they might even send a woman to check out the place—and us—so we don't suspect anything." Natalie motioned to where they needed to off-load the hollies.

"Marek won't be coming. We also know what Dexter looks like, but he wouldn't know that. I still can't believe it's the same bastard I thought I'd killed. I suspect he won't come if he's running the show. He'd more than likely send one of his henchmen." Brock finished unloading his cart and headed back to the delivery area.

"Unless others are working with them, that would leave Ink Man and Antonio, the printer. I wonder if Dexter thought you were dead too." Natalie followed Brock and began loading roses on her cart.

Brock and Shawn did the same with their carts.

"Dexter might have thought I died after he shot me so

many times," Brock said. "I'm sure he'd love to finish the job."

"They'll be wearing hunter's concealment, don't you think?" When they reached the rows of roses, Shawn moved some of them around.

"I'm sure of it, or one of us would smell the wolf." Brock set the last of his rosebushes down.

Brock and Natalie watched Shawn rearrange the potted plants.

"They weren't color coordinated. The red roses and orange ones clashed," Shawn said.

Brock smiled. He never would have thought to organize the colors, but if Shawn was trying to earn brownie points, he was doing a good job of it.

"Isn't that right?" Shawn asked Natalie, ignoring Brock.

"You're absolutely right. You can reorganize them to your heart's content."

"I'll move the rest of them after we put the other new plants where they need to go." Shawn tugged his cart behind him.

"My folks are going to love having you work with us. If you have any other ideas to make things look more appealing, let any one of us know."

"I will. Thanks."

Brock was surprised his cousin was really getting into the gardening bit. Not just as a job, but as a viable member of the team. He hoped that didn't change Natalie's and her parents' opinions of him with regard to Natalie. He didn't mind doing all the grunt work, but designing gardens wasn't really his thing.

"My mother had prize roses when she was alive. I

used to give her a hand in the garden all the time. And I helped grow the vegetables." Shawn shrugged. "It was just something I did and enjoyed. I hadn't remembered how much until I was assisting your mom and dad in the garden center yesterday."

"How wonderful. Working out here always makes me feel good," Natalie said. "What about you, Brock?"

"Yeah, it's always good to get out of the house and enjoy nature. It's beautiful here, and it's nice seeing customers who love plants just as much." Brock listened to the birds tweeting in the nearby trees, bees buzzing around the flowers, butterflies fluttering about, all something he didn't really pay a whole lot of attention to normally. "I guess I don't get out and enjoy gardening like I might if I took the time to do it." He finished loading the cart of ferns and other shade-loving plants. They began hauling their carts into the shaded part of the garden. "There hasn't been any pressing need. Just mow, trim trees, that's about it. Now, if I had a mate who happened to be a master gardener, I'd be a lot more interested, because she could teach me what I needed to do to turn my yard into a showcase garden."

"Good. Another new customer."

Brock laughed. "You're going to make me pay for the plants?"

"You'll get a family discount."

Shawn laughed.

"You too," Natalie said to Shawn.

When they finished moving all the plants, Shawn began reorganizing the roses.

"What do you want me to do?" Brock asked Natalie,

pulling her into his arms for a hug before the place opened for business and he wouldn't get another chance.

She smiled up at him. "Water the plants. I've got to get the cash register ready in about half an hour. You can open the gates then."

He kissed her, his arms wrapped around her in a hot-blooded embrace, wanting to clear up a matter with her. "You really don't mind that I'm not going to be working at the garden center like my cousin plans to, do you?"

"No. You have an exciting job. I don't blame you for wanting to continue to work at it. Besides, you'd probably get tired of me telling you what to do."

"It depends solely on what you're asking me to do." He kissed her again, more deeply this time, emphasizing that when it came to this, showing her just how aroused she made him, she really didn't even need to ask. He took a deep breath, not wanting to release her, but the place would be open before they were ready if he didn't. "Okay, so I'll go in back and water, but when we open up, I'll water out front, just to keep an eye on you and the customers."

"What do we do if we suspect a customer could be one of Marek's cohorts?" she asked.

"Call or text me. Just tell me I need to water the plants out front if I've moved away to help someone. I'll already have done so, and that way, I'll know you've spotted a potential rogue wolf."

"This is going to be so strange. All the time I've worked here, I've never felt like I'm an undercover cop, viewing anyone who visits the center as a potential rogue wolf."

Brock rubbed her arms. "Are you okay with it?"

"Oh yeah. This is a real change of pace for me. Makes it even more exciting."

He chuckled. "You'll have to go on some of my cases, just to make your life a little more thrilling."

"After the center closes for the night, sure. I'd love to. And I would love to help you research on the computer too."

"Sounds like I've got me a part-time PI partner." If he had a full-time mate.

"Okay, go off to water, and I'll open the register in a bit," Natalie said.

It wasn't long before Brock was opening the gate before it was time because three vehicles were already waiting to drive in and park in the lot. He knew how it was when he was waiting for a shop to open. He always appreciated the shops that opened a little early to accommodate their customers.

"You need to open earlier," an older man wearing a navy cap said as he climbed out of the cab of his black pickup. "The major chains do."

"I'll certainly suggest it to the owners," Brock said, taking the man's comment seriously. He was usually up before dawn himself, so he understood the man's needs. Go to the garden center early before it was too hot out, carry the plants home, put them in the ground, and enjoy the rest of the day pursuing other interests.

"Thanks, young man." The gray-haired man motioned to Brock's shirt. "You need a name tag."

"I'm Brock, sir. I see you were in the navy. Thank you for your service."

"Thanks. Some great times, some rough times."

Brock wasn't going to mention his own time in the

SEAL WOLF SURRENDER 197

service because he figured he needed to work, not chat it up with the customers too much. He could see the gardens being in ruins by the time Natalie's parents returned if he didn't do what needed to be done.

"Mr. McCormick, Brock is a Navy SEAL," Natalie said, having overheard their conversation.

The older man turned and smiled at Brock. "You don't say. Well, I know this young woman's got you working hard, but why don't you come along with me? We'll talk along the way, and"—he glanced back at Natalie and winked—"you can sell me on a bunch of plants."

Great.

Natalie and her parents knew all about gardening. Shawn knew some stuff, but when it came to plants, Brock didn't know much at all. He was clueless on how to care for them, if they were low maintenance, high maintenance, or did well in this area. Hell, he wasn't even from this area. He hoped it wouldn't be too obvious when he stopped to read the cards on the plants if the gentleman asked him anything specific. He also hoped Natalie didn't have any trouble up front while he was wandering all over the gardens, pulling a cart behind him for Mr. McCormick while shooting the breeze about the navy.

But then he caught Shawn's eye, and his cousin realized what was going on, waved, and headed up front.

Chapter 13

Natalie thought Brock looked a bit panicked that he'd have to actually help a customer pick out plants. But she knew Mr. McCormick, who was as well read on gardening as she was. He just wanted to talk to a fellow serviceman about his war stories. She figured Brock would enjoy it too.

She saw Brock catch Shawn's attention and send his cousin to watch over her, which showed no matter what other tasks Brock had to perform, his mission to keep her safe was his utmost priority. She appreciated his sense of duty, though she didn't think anyone would try to harm her while the garden center was open.

Shawn began watering the plants near her, and since customers were off wandering around in the distance, he said, "Did you think Brock looked worried when he had to help the customer find the right plants for his garden?"

She laughed. "A little. But he doesn't have anything to worry about. Mr. McCormick has a mind of his own. He'll pick out everything he wants. And who knows, just so he can revisit the old days, he might even buy more plants this time."

"You won't miss this place if you move?" Shawn asked.

"No. We've created three of these since we started the centers, and each time, they've been perfectly unique and suited to the area. We always do well, and our former businesses sold well because they were so profitable, except for the time my ex-boyfriend ran us out of business with his franchise garden center. Of course, buyers wanted to know why we were quitting at the other locations, and Mom and Dad usually used me as an excuse."

"Oh?" Shawn moved to another area to water potted plants.

"Yeah. I was getting married and leaving, so they wanted to be close to where I was. Or sometimes they'd say that about Angie."

"Seems like that might really be the case this time," Shawn said.

"I think it could work out well for us, if my mom and dad are happy with your pack."

"I hope they are." Shawn finished watering. "What do you need me to do now?"

"Just wander around and see if anything needs to be rearranged to improve merchandising. I'm fine for now. The center is kind of slow first thing in the morning. And by the way, you and Brock are garden advisers, not the hired help."

Shawn smiled. "Works for me. I think Brock needs a little more training."

"He'll get it if we join forces. Even if it's just hearing me talk about plants during meals."

"He's a good guy. I'm surprised he took an interest in anyone of the female persuasion when he was so adamant about not doing so. I guess it's true that when a wolf finds his or her mate, it's the real deal."

"I think we both lucked out."

"Yeah, but I didn't." Shawn winked and then headed off to reorganize some of the flower displays.

Natalie thought Shawn was cute, and if Brock hadn't swept her off her feet, she might have fallen for his cousin. Then again, Brock unsettled her whole world. No one had ever done that to her. Being with him just felt right.

She began checking out customers and then had a lull again. Her mom loved handling the register and cheerfully talking to the customers at checkout, but Natalie preferred working in the gardens and giving lectures. Her dad never liked working at the register, so when her mom needed a break, Natalie always took over her job.

But this time, she had an additional duty that held her interest—watching anyone new who arrived. She suspected if one of the bad guys showed up, he wouldn't come real early. He'd wait until he figured there'd be more people around as more of a distraction for Natalie and the Greystoke cousins. She'd even considered not having one of the cousins wear the center's green T-shirt so he could fade into the background more. Then again, two men moving plants, watering, and helping customers with their purchases wouldn't look like they were anything but part of the staff.

Brock and Mr. McCormick came to the register to check out, Brock pulling the cart and the older man removing his credit card from his wallet. "You owe this man a commission for all the aid he was in helping me to decide which plants to get. I wouldn't have gotten half the plants if he hadn't given me so much advice."

Brock was smiling. Natalie wondered if he had stepped up to the plate and really helped Mr. McCormick decide, but from Brock's look of amusement, she thought not. The retired navy man never purchased this many plants at one time. It was important to be helpful, knowledgeable, and friendly with their customers, not so busy with caring for the plants that they didn't show an interest in the customers who shopped here. The only way their garden center could compete with the big ones was by giving a more personal customer experience.

"He started yesterday and already got one big tip," Natalie said, proud of Brock. She knew he felt out of place here, as far as plant knowledge went, but he was such a likable and helpful guy that she figured most of her customers wouldn't care.

"Is that allowed?" Mr. McCormick asked, not sounding serious in the least.

Natalie chuckled. "Not necessary, but it's nice and he tried to give me the money."

The older man nodded with approval. "Keep him on. I like him." He paid for his purchases, and then Brock loaded the plants into his truck for him. "Great meeting a fellow serviceman."

"Likewise, sir."

Then Mr. McCormick spoke with him for a moment, shook his hand, and got into his pickup and left.

Natalie did feel bad about giving up their customers—at least, the vast majority of them. There were always one or two who were a royal pain, arguing about all the trouble they had with the plants and returning plants that had died for lack of water. Their center gave a reduction on the price on a new plant to replace those. They couldn't afford to give a free plant for ones that had died, unlike many of the bigger plant franchises that did so for up to a year after purchase.

Brock joined her as she finished checking out a lady

who was buying two pots of hanging flowers. "See anyone yet?"

"Not yet. I suspect we're just not busy enough right now. A little later though. Maybe when we have our lunch breaks."

"Okay, so everyone else is someone you've seen before?" Brock asked.

"As much as I could watch them, yes. Sometimes I get distracted with checking customers out."

Brock glanced over at Shawn, who was chatting with a customer.

"You did good. Mr. McCormick purchased three times what he usually does when he shops here," Natalie said, impressed with Brock.

"All that war talk helped. I had to say my dad had been in some of the fights Mr. McCormick had been, because I would have been too young at the time otherwise."

That was the problem with their longevity. Wolves lived so much longer than humans that they had to disguise the fact they weren't aging as fast. They either had to move or just pretend they were younger versions of an older relation.

A woman was pulling a cart of roses, and Brock smiled at her and stepped aside. "Can I load those for you?"

"Oh sure, thanks." The woman paid Natalie, and Brock rolled the cart to the woman's car and loaded the plants.

If they did become mated wolves, would Brock help at the garden center when he didn't have a case? Natalie wondered. She sure liked working with him here.

He finished loading the car, and then the woman tipped him.

Natalie chuckled. She wondered if Mr. McCormick

had given him a tip. When her dad loaded plants in someone's vehicle, no one tipped him. It must have been because Brock was such a hunky wolf. She wondered if Shawn would get tips too.

Shawn helped her next customer, and then it was time for one of them to have a lunch break. She realized one of the guys would have to man the register. She figured Shawn could because he'd actually be working for them.

"Would one of you like to have a lunch break before it gets too busy?" she asked Shawn and Brock as they returned to see what else she needed them to do.

"I'll go make us some sandwiches with the leftover roast your mom made for us, if you'd like," Brock said. "Then we can take turns eating."

"Sounds good to me," Shawn said.

Natalie agreed.

"Just…watch out for things," Brock said to his cousin.

"Will do."

Brock strode off toward the back gate that led to her parents' home.

"Former SEAL," Shawn explained to Natalie. "He always thinks us non-SEAL types need more guidance."

She laughed. "I'm sure he can use your expertise in the garden."

It wasn't long before Brock came back with an ice chest he must have found in the garage and filled with sandwiches and bottled water, chips, and chocolate chip cookies.

"Wow, I've never had a picnic out here before. This looks great," Natalie said.

"Did you want to eat first?" Brock asked.

"I was thinking I could eat when it was busier, so the two of you would still see if anyone showed up... You know," she said cryptically when she had another customer approach, ready to check out.

"I'll eat first, unless you're starving, Shawn," Brock said.

"Yeah, go ahead. I'll grab a bite after you do."

Natalie had rung up three more customers when Brock offered to relieve her or Shawn for lunch.

"That was quick," she said.

"I'm used to eating fast on some jobs. Have you seen anyone who appears suspicious?"

"Not yet. I really thought they might try to check things out during the day, but then again, maybe they'll only do it at night, afraid we might catch onto them otherwise. Wait, that man just getting out of his pickup... He's not a regular customer, and he doesn't really look like the gardener type."

"How can you tell?"

"He's not looking at the plants. He's looking at the motion-detector lights up above."

He was dark-haired, of average height, with a scruffy beard and wearing old jeans, sneakers, and a brown T-shirt. She might be wrong, but he didn't look like a gardener.

"Okay, I'll just follow him around a bit and then ask if I can help him...maybe. I'll try to pick up a scent trail first."

"Good. I'm so glad you're here."

"Me too. For lots of reasons." Brock moved off to fill in the hole where some plants had been purchased while Natalie tried to look anywhere but at the man she thought appeared suspicious.

The guy walked past her and into the gardens in the back, and then she didn't see him any longer. Brock hurried that way.

Shawn joined her, and she waited to finish with a customer before she told him Brock was checking out a guy who looked out of place.

"Did you want me to help Brock?"

"No. That might appear too conspicuous."

"Did you want to eat?"

She didn't. She wanted to know what Brock had learned, but she figured it was better to eat before it got any busier.

"Yeah, thanks. Can you handle the register?"

"Yeah, I work in the gift shop from time to time where we sell leather goods." Shawn took over the register.

"Okay, super." Natalie hurried off to eat as fast as Brock had done.

They had a little picnic area that overlooked a man-made waterfall, but they also used it to enjoy their lunch breaks. She wished she could sit next to the cash register while Shawn was checking customers out instead of hidden away; then, she could watch anyone who arrived. But it was a standard policy that they didn't sit out in the open and eat lunch while customers were shopping. It didn't look professional.

But she sure wanted to watch the suspicious guy and see how Brock handled him.

<hr>

Brock agreed about the man who wasn't looking at plants but was more interested in the layout of the place. Natalie had good instincts, and he thought talking over his cases with her might give him new insights into solving them.

The man headed for the gate that opened to Natalie's carriage house. Brock was keeping out of sight, using the tall shrubs' foliage to screen his view. Hopefully, the man wouldn't know he was being observed and would do whatever he'd come here to do. He opened the gate and peered at the carriage house. Then he took a picture of it.

Brock hurried to join him. "Can I help you with something?"

The man smelled human, not like a wolf, no hunter's spray used to conceal his scent. Did Marek's crew hire this guy so that he would give them information about the property?

The guy swung around and smiled. "You work here?"

Obviously. Brock was wearing the T-shirt with the company's name on it. "Yeah, can I help you?"

"I'm a photographer, Tom Jonas. I've been looking for old, authentic carriage houses, and when I was doing research, I found this one listed from before the Silvertons bought it. I've been fascinated with old carriage houses for years and just began writing a book about them and their history. Are you the owner?"

"No. Do you have a business card? I can have the owner get in touch with you."

Tom patted his jeans pockets. "Uh, no. I thought I had one on me. I changed jeans this morning. Must have been in my other pair."

"Give me your phone number, and I'll text myself the number." Brock closed the gate to the carriage house and swore he was going to affix a lock to it. If this guy wasn't on the up and up, he knew now the gate wasn't locked.

The guy gave him the number.

"Do you have a website? You're a published author, right?" Brock asked.

"Um, no, this will be my first book."

He seemed sketchier and sketchier. "Okay, so you said you are a photographer. Do you have a photography website?"

"Well, yeah, sure. I just thought you meant did I have a website for my published books."

Brock dragged out his phone and brought up Google. "Okay, give it to me."

"Vintage Photography. I update old photos to make them look more modern and create more vintage ones of modern photos. It's the kind of photography work I like to do. This garden center has advertised, a lot of word-of-mouth, too, for photographers wanting to photograph weddings and have other shoots here. That's how I heard about it, and when I realized it was originally the acre-age belonging to the main house and a carriage house, well, I got real interested. I don't do weddings and that sort of thing."

Brock looked up the site. It was just what the man had said it was, and the photographer was named Tom Jonas. But there was no picture of the photographer. This guy could just be reading off a script, for all Brock knew. There was no mention on the site of work on a book featuring carriage houses.

They headed back to the checkout counter to meet with Natalie to see if she could get a feel for him too.

"This is Tom Jonas, who's interested in your carriage house to include in a book on the subject. I've got his contact information on my phone."

"An author." Natalie breathed deeply of the man's scent.

"A photographer who wants to write a book about them, yes," Tom said.

"Okay, I'll give it to my dad."

"You're one of the owners? Oh, your parents own it," Tom said.

"They do, and they'll give you a call."

"Thanks. I appreciate it." Tom shook Brock's hand and then Natalie's. He hurried off to his car, while Brock took a picture of him and the vehicle.

"What do you think?" Natalie asked as Shawn joined them.

"Slick," Brock said. "I don't trust him. He didn't have a business card. The website doesn't show his photo. It's one thing to forget the business cards or to run out, but if I was on a mission to do something like he said he planned to, I'd make certain I had a business card on me. Not only that, but he seemed nervous."

"He smelled nervous, but he's…only human." Natalie quit talking when she saw a woman approach with a cart of plants and then checked her out.

"Here, let me help you, ma'am," Shawn said.

The woman beamed at him. "If only my husband offered to help me as sweetly as you do."

Shawn looked pleased to hear it.

Natalie smiled as the two of them walked to the customer's car. "Did you get a tip from Mr. McCormick?" she asked Brock.

Brock nodded. "He said I ought to marry you."

"He wouldn't have said that." Natalie glanced around to make sure she didn't have another paying customer.

"Yeah, he did. I'm always surprised when I meet a super-intuitive human. He said it was like when he met his wife forty years ago. The same banter, smiles shared, same intimacy. He said he figured I wanted to be out front, staying near you, rather than out back in the gardens, talking to him about our navy days. Though I let him do most of the talking."

She chuckled. "I'll miss him if we move." She motioned to Shawn, who was coming from the parking lot. "You haven't eaten yet, have you? I don't want anyone to say we starve our plant advisers."

Shawn laughed and went to have lunch.

Business was brisk after that, without much of a break in between customers. When it was getting near closing, Natalie saw a woman who looked perplexed as she considered some annuals sitting on a stand out front. "Do you want to man the register while I see if she needs anything?" she asked Brock.

"Sure thing. Much better than if I try to advise her."

Natalie went off to talk to the lady, and Brock watched her as she talked about a variety of plants, then moved to another stand of plants and showed the woman the card on those but added to the information. "They love it here, and they're perennial, so they come back each year. And they'll spread out even more. Annuals are beautiful and provide an abundance of color for the season, but once they're done, they...usually don't come back. If you don't deadhead the flowers, sometimes the seeds will sprout during the next growing season. Sometimes even a couple of seasons later, and somewhere you hadn't planted them initially. With the perennials, for the most part, they'll keep growing, coming

back each year, and you'll have dependable color—"
She abruptly stopped speaking when she saw someone
enter the garden center, a blond-haired woman dressed
in jeans, a T-shirt, and sneakers.

Nothing that would indicate she was trouble, Brock
didn't think. Since he was on cashier duty, he couldn't
just leave to check her out. He caught Natalie's eye, and
she motioned slightly with her head at the new woman.
On his cell, Brock called Shawn, who was finishing up
his lunch.

"Hey, what's up?" Shawn asked while Natalie continued to talk about plants to her customer.

Brock kept an eye on the blond woman as she moved
around the place, touching plants, and then walked
toward the back gardens. "I need you to work the register. I've got to pursue a potential suspect."

"Be right there." Shawn headed over. "Got it. Which
one?"

Brock moved out from behind the register. "The
woman over there who's headed into the back gardens.
Nothing made me suspect her, but Natalie seemed
suspicious."

"All right. Go get 'er."

Brock grabbed a cart sitting near some shrubs and
moved through the shop where planters and gardening
tools were on display and headed into the back gardens.
At first, he didn't see the woman, and he felt a bit of
a panic that he'd already lost her. But then he saw her
looking at the motion-detector lights and cameras on the
building up above, then moving around the plants and
farther along until she was next to the fence. Now he
was suspicious. All the plants in the rows were the same

from the front all the way to the back. Unless a customer was super picky and wanted to see every shrub in the row and pick out the ones he liked best, there would be no reason to walk all the way to the fence.

She wasn't armed with a cart either. And like the man claiming to be a photographer, she'd been checking out the security around the place. Something Brock wouldn't think of doing if he were just here as a garden enthusiast.

Chapter 14

NATALIE WISHED SHE WERE A PI. SHE WANTED DESPERATELY to call Brock to tell him the woman he was checking out had driven Marek's car here, but she was still trying to help her customer decide which plants she wanted to buy. Normally, Natalie never minded. But in this instance, she wanted to chase after Brock and the woman and question her.

"Okay, you sold me. I'll get ten of the daylilies, five of the salvia, and ten of the phlox."

"Super." Natalie didn't want to appear to be rushing her, but she tried to load the plants the customer picked out as quickly as she could.

"Oh, and a red rosebush. Which do you recommend?"

"They're in the back garden." Yes! "We can walk back there, and you can see which variety you might prefer." Natalie would give her more specifics, but she was hoping she could see Brock and the woman while she sold her customer on a rosebush.

Natalie hoped there wasn't an altercation between Brock and the woman he needed to check on. How would that look? Brock being nasty to a customer in front of other customers when he worked for her parents' company? Not good. Sure, he was a professional, but no one knew how the woman might react if she thought Brock suspected her of being in league with Marek and the rest of the counterfeiters. She could create a scene and look completely innocent of any wrongdoing, and Brock and the Silvertons' garden center would look bad.

Brock was chatting it up with the woman in one of the rows of shrubs that were only a couple of feet tall. He was nodding, smiling. The woman laughed at something he said and touched his arm, sliding her hand down it in an intimate caress. Natalie frowned. Didn't he get that the woman was a spy?

"I like the true red ones," the customer said to Natalie, drawing her attention back to where it should have been all along.

Natalie hoped Brock knew what he was doing.

"Those are a great variety for our area. Blackspot resistant, mildew resistant for hot Texas heat, and they even last well in snow. Mine were covered in snow, and they didn't die at all. They didn't bloom again until it began to warm up some more, but they're super-reliable."

"Oh, that's good to hear. I had a different variety, and all of them had blackspot and powdery mildew. Destroyed my whole hedge. That was when I lived in Oklahoma, so I didn't want to go through that again. They're like family, you know."

"Oh, absolutely. Do you want this one?" Natalie said, trying to hurry her customer along.

"Yes. Do you think I should have more than one?"

Natalie schooled her expression so she didn't show her exasperation. She wanted to overhear what Brock and the other woman were talking about. And she really wanted to make her presence known, a hazard of getting hooked on a male wolf when another she-wolf was batting her eyelashes at him.

"It depends on your landscape." It would have been easy to tell her customer that she should get a couple, because massing the color would be more spectacular. But Natalie didn't want to give her the wrong advice just to get another plant sale or to free herself so she could check on the suspicious woman. "Did you need just an accent rosebush in one place, or maybe a couple of places? This one grows a little bigger, so it's about four feet tall. But if you're looking for something smaller, the Drift is around two feet tall," Natalie said.

Her customer proceeded to pull out her cell phone. Natalie was tempted to pull hers out and text Brock, but she was afraid the woman he had under surveillance would think he had to do some work, and the woman would let him go so she could get back to whatever she was doing. Then what? He couldn't follow her around the place, because she obviously wasn't really there to shop.

Her customer showed Natalie a picture of her front yard. "Wow, it's beautiful. Where did you think you would like to put a rosebush?" Even in her own garden, Natalie was guilty of picking out something that was so pretty and planting it, then wondering why she picked it out for the garden in the first place.

"Right there," the customer said, pointing at a spot in her flower bed.

"I'd plant the lower variety so it doesn't encroach on too much of the flower bed and hide the flowers you have in the background."

"Okay, then I want this red variety."

"Good choice." Natalie hated to ask, but she had to. "Is there anything else you'd like to look at?"

The customer studied her cart of plants. "No, I think

this will keep me busy for a while. Thanks. I'm ready to check out now."

"All right. Super." Natalie loaded the rosebush on the cart and took it up front for her. She was going to let Shawn ring the woman up, but then she sighed. She didn't need to load the lady's plants, but that was what made a smaller garden center do well against the big ones. Customer service was so important.

Natalie towed the cart behind her and then loaded the customer's plants into her small SUV.

"Thanks, dear. I'll be back for more, I'm sure. I need to get these planted first and see what else I can use."

"We'll be here," Natalie said cheerily. Once the lady went around to the driver's side of her vehicle, Natalie hightailed it to the back garden, pulling the cart behind her just for show.

Brock and the woman had disappeared! Natalie glanced around and saw them walking to the section with fruit trees, but before she could head in that direction, a man stopped her. "I can't find a Steeds holly. Do you have them? The big chain stores don't have any."

"Oh, of course. They're wonderful in a landscape, easy to care for with practically no maintenance, keeping their beautiful pyramidal shape without needing to be trimmed." Natalie hated hearing people mention how they shopped at the big stores and only came to theirs in the hopes of finding something they couldn't at the others. On the other hand, it helped their business when they had plants that didn't compete with the major chains. "Come right this way."

Natalie figured she wasn't going to be able to meet up with Brock and the woman, as much as she was dying to. Not when she had to put on her master gardener hat and let Brock do his job. Then she had a break. The man looked over the Steeds holly and nodded. "Just what I was looking for. Thanks."

"Do you need anything else?"

"No, this will be it, thanks." He began loading the cart. Natalie found a spare one down one of the aisles, grabbed hold of the handle, and walked in Brock and the woman's direction.

Natalie kept glancing at rows of plants as if inspecting them, making her way toward Brock and the woman in as subtle a manner as she could.

He finally saw her coming and waved at her. She wasn't sure what he meant by it. To say he saw her? That he wanted her to join them?

She took it to mean he wanted her to join him. Even if he didn't, she could just drop by and say…something and then mosey off close by to overhear them. She really could get into some of this PI snooping business.

As soon as she drew close enough, Brock said, "This is Natalie, our master gardener."

Natalie was surprised to smell that the woman was a wolf. She hadn't even bothered to hide her scent. How bold could she be? Then again, the woman wouldn't realize they knew what Marek's car looked like either.

"Natalie, this is Kittie Canton."

"Hi, shopping for some trees?" Natalie asked as if they needed some of her gardening expertise.

"Aww, well, not really. I was looking for a plant for my mom, but then Brock came over to see if I needed any help, and I realized he was one of us. We just got to talking. He said the garden center is"—Kittie glanced around and, not seeing any humans nearby, finished—"wolf-run. I hope I'm not keeping you both from your work. But I was just so excited to find others like us here."

"Do you know any others in the area?" Natalie asked, baiting her.

"No. Just my mom and me. Like I was telling Brock, we live out near Canyon, but I wanted to replace a flowering plant my mom had that died. Anyway, we just got to visiting about wolf stuff, so we moved over here where no one was shopping to talk more…privately."

"What was the flowering plant that died?" Natalie didn't like the coy way Kittie was acting, the close proximity to Brock that indicated a desire for intimacy, and that Brock was allowing it!

Kittie finally said, "Oh, a…a rosebush."

Most people called a rosebush a rosebush and not a flowering plant, unless they didn't know what it was.

"Would you like me to help recommend one for you?" Natalie asked, continuing to be way too business-like when she should have pretended to be glad to see a fellow wolf.

Kittie gave her a fake smile. "Brock's helping me. But thanks so much for the offer."

Brock opened his mouth to speak, probably to get himself out of this one and tell Kittie that Natalie was the expert gardener again, but Natalie quickly said, "Great. I've got to get back to work anyway. We're getting ready to close soon." Brock didn't ask if he was needed up front. Natalie reminded herself again that he was doing his job. "Nice meeting you," she said. Then she hurried off.

"Guess I'd better hurry and pick out what I want,

then," Kittie said to Brock, loud enough that Natalie could hear her, though she didn't appear to be in any hurry to check out.

She'd better not be making a play for Brock.

So much for secretly listening in on the conversation.

They normally didn't remind people they were closing. They let them shop for however long they needed, within reason. But the woman totally irked Natalie. What kind of a name was Kittie for a wolf anyway? It was probably an alias.

Natalie left the cart with a row of others and joined Shawn at the register. "Here, I can man the register, and you can help customers with their purchases, if you like." She was trying to say it in a nice, congenial way, but Shawn raised his brows slightly, indicating he heard the annoyance in her voice.

He probably knew what she'd been up to. "Are you okay?"

"Yeah, yeah." Thankfully, she didn't have any customers at the moment. But she noticed an older couple loading some flowers onto a cart. "Did you want to see if they need any help?"

"Yeah, sure. Are you certain you're okay?"

"I am." *Not.* She appreciated Shawn's concern though, and then she got a text from Brock. Shawn hung around, waiting to hear what was up.

I want to invite her to dinner, Brock texted.

Absolutely not! Natalie texted back: She's Marek's girlfriend, or stoolie, or something. She's driving Marek's car.

Natalie waited for a reply, but none was forthcoming. Then she had a customer, and Shawn went off to help the older couple with their plants. Her cell dinged that she had a new text message, but she was in the middle of ringing up the lady's purchases. She had three more people get in line, her regular customers knowing it was almost time for closing.

Her cell phone dinged again. Brock again? She didn't look to see this time.

Shawn returned with the older couple's cart and hauled it to the end of the line. While they were waiting to get checked out, he went up to the cashier's desk and asked if Natalie wanted him to check the text messages on her phone.

"Sure." She handed it to him, and he checked the messages, then smiled.

Natalie didn't. No way did she want that woman in her house or her parents' home. Kittie was with Marek, and by virtue of her association with him, no matter in what capacity, she was one of them. Besides, she'd lied about not knowing any other wolves in the area. Was her name even Kittie Canton? Probably not. Did she have a mother who lost a flowering plant? Natalie doubted it.

She was dying to hear what else Brock had to say in his texts. Having Kittie stay for dinner when the center was closed for the evening could be a good way to really grill her privately about her connection with Marek, but the woman still irked her.

Why? She shouldn't have. Then again, Natalie realized it wasn't so much that the woman was most likely bad news, but that she was acting like she was making a play for Brock!

Natalie had never thought she'd be one of those controlling women who was afraid her mate would see another wolf as more intriguing than her. But the woman was a wolf, and she knew she'd been pulling Natalie's strings. Didn't Brock see that? Men could be so clueless when it came to a woman's wiles. Had he figured Kittie was part of the gang, or at least involved in it somehow? Natalie had smelled a slight amount of Marek's scent on the woman. Probably because she'd been sitting in his car, if she'd been careful not to hug on him before she showed up here.

Natalie wondered why Kittie wouldn't have driven her own car here. It was a mistake on her part to drive Marek's vehicle. Though once they discovered she was a wolf, they would have been suspicious of her anyway.

When they got to the end of the line of customers, Shawn helped all who needed assistance to carry their plants to their vehicles. Three cars were still parked in the lot.

"We're closed now," Natalie said to Shawn. "If you don't mind, could you man the gate until everyone leaves? Just close it, or people might think we're still open."

"Sure thing." Shawn handed her phone back to her. "He invited her for dinner. He's a PI. He knows what he's doing."

Natalie growled under her breath.

"Does this mean there might be hope for me yet?" Shawn smiled and headed for the gate.

Natalie was hungry, and she'd been looking forward to dinner. If Brock thought she was going to fix a nice dinner for them, he had another think coming.

Two more customers left, and Shawn smiled as he opened the gate for them. She really liked working with him. He seemed to love the job, and he enjoyed talking to the customers. She glanced in Brock's direction to see him walking with Kittie to the checkout. Kittie *didn't* have a plant she'd picked out *either*.

If the woman was going to pretend to be friends with them, she could at least buy a plant. Especially since Brock had invited her to dinner.

Shawn headed their way. "I ordered a couple pizzas—meat lover's and cheese deluxe."

"Oh, what a terrific idea." Natalie loved that he had been thinking ahead. She hoped someone would eat the cheese pizza. Wolves loved their meat. She was so glad Shawn had thought of a way to avoid anyone fixing a meal for Kittie.

"Why don't we eat out in the gardens?" Natalie said, not waiting for anyone's agreement. Not that she had asked the question as if she was looking for anyone's consensus.

"Sure," Shawn said. "The gardens are beautiful this time of year. Perfect for outdoor dining. That's back in that direction, right? Where we had our lunch breaks?"

"Yes."

"Okay, great. I'll wait at the gate for the pizza delivery. It should be here in about forty minutes, maybe longer, but if the delivery person is quicker, I want to be there to pay them."

"It might be too hot and buggy outside, don't you think?" Kittie asked Brock, as if *he* had anything to say about it.

"Nah. We've been working outside all day. We're used to it," Natalie said, not about to allow the woman into either her home or her parents'. Did she want to case the places? Natalie suspected she did, and she'd give a description to Marek and his buddies.

"I haven't been outside all day, and I'm used to air-conditioning," Kittie said, fluttering her eyelashes at Brock as if he'd invite her inside one of the places when Natalie was being hard-nosed about it. Then Kittie fanned herself as if it was just too hot out here.

Natalie gave Brock a look that said if he offered to move the venue inside, he'd be leaving for Greystoke tonight. And Kittie could go with him.

He cast her a small smile, appearing amused that she was having a meltdown over him.

"We have ceiling fans out there and citronella candles for the mosquitoes, so no problem." Natalie was annoyed at herself for having made the comment. If the woman didn't like it, she could leave. Natalie was biting her tongue about Kittie driving Marek's car and the reason she was really here, but Brock knew what he was doing, so Natalie was trying to play along. As much as she could. Besides, he might have talked to her about a lot of this already.

On the deck that overlooked the waterfall, Natalie fetched Styrofoam plates and paper napkins for the meal from a cabinet, waiting for Brock to question the woman. Maybe he was putting it off until Shawn joined them.

"Oh, Brock, would you get us some bottled water from my house?" Natalie asked.

He hesitated, as if he was afraid Natalie would screw up their dinner by questioning Kittie!

"I can help you, Brock," Kittie said, flashing a provocative smile at him.

Natalie fumed, but she plastered on a smile. "That's

okay. You probably wouldn't know where to look, Brock. I'll leave the two of you to get better acquainted."

"Why don't you make that wine," Kittie said. "And real wineglasses."

Natalie was about to say she was fresh out of both, but then again, if they could get her drunk, maybe Kittie would tell them what they wanted to know. "I'll see if I have any."

"Gotta have wine with pizza. Or beer," Kittie said as if everyone should know that.

Natalie turned on her heel and left without another word before she blew her top.

When she reached her house, she went inside but decided everyone would have water. What if she gave everyone wine and the guys got too talkative instead?

She returned with the bottles of water and saw Shawn walking toward her on the connecting path with pizza boxes in hand. She was glad the pizzas had come so quickly so they all could eat, learn what they could from Kittie, and send the woman packing. "Hmm, smells great. All meat for me," Natalie said.

"I'm an oddball. I love the cheese deluxe. Just in case, I ended up ordering a large meat one and half cheese and half meat on the second one."

"Thanks." She smiled up at him. "I would have paid. I wasn't thinking about it at the time."

"No problem. You had other things on your mind."

Yeah, like one she-wolf who was annoying the hell out of her.

When they brought the food and drinks to the table, Kittie frowned. "Oh, such a shame you don't have any wine." Then she said, "Oh, I'm so sorry. I didn't realize you could have a…well…drinking problem. I just never think of that. Forgive me."

The woman was a consummate actress.

Brock managed a smile. Shawn chuckled.

"Not me," Natalie managed to say. Brock was awfully quiet, and Natalie wondered why he wasn't giving Kittie the third degree.

Instead, everyone ate the pizza and drank their water, not offering much in conversation at all.

It wasn't long before Kittie said, "Do you mind if I use your restroom?"

Natalie thought there was a pattern here. Kittie kept wanting to explore one of the houses. Luckily, they had a restroom out here for both customers and staff. "Sure, I'll show you the way."

"Brock sure is sexy," Kittie said as Natalie led the way to the garden shop. "Oh, it's not a porta-potty, is it? I can't handle those."

"It's a regular restroom, and you're right about Brock. Shawn is too. So what is Marek to you?"

"What?"

Hadn't Brock asked her about him? "The guy whose car you were driving? Marek Jones, who's creating counterfeit money. Who knows what else he's into that's illegal."

Kittie didn't say anything. Trying to come up with a quick story to explain it all?

"I thought you said you didn't know any other wolves. Just your mom here," Natalie said.

Kittie shrugged. "He just moved out near where I live, so I didn't… Well, I didn't want to mention him in case Brock and I…" She gave a wicked smile. "You know. I'm not interested in Marek. He might be interested in me. I don't know. My car broke down and is in the shop. He loaned me his. He's a nice wolf. How do you know he's making counterfeit money? I haven't heard a thing about it."

"Really? What about Dexter Cartwright? Did he just move into the area too? And he's a nice wolf?"

Kittie's jaw dropped a little, but then she recovered with a smile. "I don't know any Dexter Cartwright. Is he a friend of Marek's?"

"Not sure if they're friends, but they're in on the counterfeiting business." As if Kittie wasn't taking part in all this. Natalie led her into the store and motioned to the restroom. "You know it's not safe to be around wolves who commit criminal acts."

Kittie looked at the restroom for a moment, then said, "Yeah, I know that. I can find my way back."

Sure she could. But Natalie wasn't leaving her to do whatever she planned to do. "Sure."

Natalie left the shop and walked off, but then sneakily checked to see what Kittie intended to do. Kittie had entered the restroom, used the facilities, and then stayed in there awhile. Texting her cohorts in crime?

Kittie finally left the restroom and wandered around the shop. She'd better not even think of stealing from them, though Natalie suspected the woman wasn't the least bit interested in gardening.

Then Kittie headed back to the path to the picnic area, and Natalie slipped down another path to beat her there. Natalie frowned at Brock, who was talking to Shawn about gardening when he needed to focus on questioning Kittie!

He gave her a brilliant smile as if he was truly happy to see her arrive. That sexy smile of his nearly made Natalie forget her annoyance about him and Kittie, but then Kittie rejoined them and that was all Natalie could focus on.

<hr>

Once they sat down, Brock continued to question Kittie, aware that Natalie thought he was falling for the she-wolf's ploy with her fluttering eyelashes and constant moves into his space. Which worked damn well for him. He suspected Kittie would keep her distance, so he was surprised when she moved in so close to him. He was astute enough to realize how fake she was, but it afforded him the opportunity to slip a bug into the open side pocket on her purse. He just didn't know how to let Natalie in on what he was up to, or what he'd already questioned the woman about, without clueing in Kittie.

He'd figured having a nice dinner would make every-one relax bit. Now he was ready to ask Kittie more direct questions and not beat around the bush as much. He was certain Natalie would have questioned her, too, when she took her to the restroom, which could have helped them to unravel the mystery. Natalie had already proved she did well with dealing with a woman under suspicion after questioning Lettie.

He couldn't believe the woman had stayed for dinner. He suspected she hoped to see the layout of one of the homes, and that was why she kept wanting to go inside.

"So why did you really come here?" Brock asked Kittie.

Natalie took a deep breath and let it out, as if she realized he had this under control.

"I told you. I was looking for a special rosebush for my mom to replace the one she lost, but then I realized you were all wolf, and that sidetracked me." Kittie smiled sweetly at him.

"Yet you didn't buy a replacement rosebush for her," Natalie said, her tone of voice annoyed.

"You didn't have any that were special enough." Kittie gave her a simpering smile, then turned to Brock. "But your manager was so nice with all the special care he gave me while *trying* to find the right one." She shrugged. "Too bad you didn't have anything that worked out."

Shawn was quietly eating more pizza, listening, smiling a little.

Brock was thinking the woman was pure poison. "You said your mother's name is Elizabeth, but I looked and I didn't see her listed anywhere on the internet. You know how it is. You can look up anyone and find their name, address, and phone number sometimes. It's amazing what's out there."

"Why would you look her up?" Kittie asked, feigning surprise.

"I've been burned before on wolf relationships. I like to know if everything's on the level. So you said you live with her."

"I do. Well, I guess if that's the way you treat a new wolf friend…"

"What do you know of Marek's counterfeiting operation?" Brock asked, not about to let her go.

"I don't know anything about that. Are you sure he's caught up in something like that? I just *can't* believe he is."

"Yeah, I'm certain. Since you're driving his car, I can only assume you know something about it."

"Listen, the pizza was great, and I want to thank you for having me to dinner," she said to Brock, "but it's getting late and I need to leave." She rose from the table.

Brock and Natalie followed suit.

"Yeah, to return his car. Hope you find the rosebush you're looking for and aren't part of this counterfeiting business. You know criminal rogue wolves need to be dealt with," Natalie said.

Kittie smiled at Natalie. "Of course. I'm sure one of the bigger garden centers will have what I'm looking for." She ignored the rest of Natalie's comment. She didn't look worried about Natalie's threat either.

Brock had expected her to defend herself or ask who was planning on taking the counterfeiters out, but she acted as though they had no worries from Brock and the others here.

Brock escorted Kittie to her car while Natalie and Shawn cleaned up.

"You never did explain the reason I couldn't find your mom's name anywhere in the Canyon area," Brock said to the woman.

"She goes by Smith, not Canton. That's probably why you couldn't find it," Kittie said.

"Smith," he said. There were probably tons of Elizabeth Smiths in the area. He was surprised Kittie hadn't used that as *her* last name too. "I didn't see your name listed either."

She shrugged. "Can't help that. What's your interest in Marek anyway? You're not a wolf cop, are you? I mean, you're working at a garden center."

"Nope, not a cop, but if I know of a wolf who's

pursuing criminal activities in my territory, I have an obligation to handle it."

Kittie's lips parted a little, and she appeared to be surprised. "The Lone Ranger, eh? Think you can handle the criminal element? With what? A garden shovel?"

He just smiled.

"What about the others?" Kittie asked.

"Natalie and Shawn? They aren't into all that."

"So you're the alpha."

He raised his brows. "All the way."

She ran her finger down his chest. "What if you learned I was in on any of it? You wouldn't hurt a she-wolf, now, would you?"

"Just don't let me learn you are in any of this, or you'll have to face the consequences. We can't afford to have our kind go to jail."

She chuckled. "What I wouldn't give to have a wolf like you on my side." Then she got into the car, and he opened the gate for her. She drove off in a hurry.

Once he'd locked the gate, Brock headed for the picnic area to help clean up, but Shawn and Natalie had already left.

He suspected Natalie was riled over the whole Kittie business. He hoped she wouldn't be this way if he was working on an undercover case. He wouldn't sleep with a human woman that he was investigating. With a she-wolf, it was a given—no sleeping with her in any shape or form. He just didn't want to worry Natalie would be all out of sorts if he smelled of a woman when he came back from a mission.

Chapter 15

"NIGHT, SHAWN. I'LL SEE YOU IN THE MORNING FOR BREAK-
fast," Natalie said, the drawer of cash in hand as she
walked toward the gate that led to her house while Brock
was sending off their "guest."

"Do you want to wait for Brock to walk you to the
house?" Shawn asked.

"No need." Natalie still couldn't help feeling annoyed
about the woman. Would she have felt the same way
if Shawn had been the one Kittie was making all the
moves on? No.

"Then I will."

"I'm sure it's not necessary, but thanks."

"Brock knows what he's doing with the woman,"
Shawn said, walking Natalie through her gate. He shut
it behind them. He wasn't letting her walk to her house
alone, and she appreciated his concern.

"I'm sure he does." It still didn't lessen her annoyance.

"Did you see him being...rather intimate with
Kittie?" Shawn was so sweet, seemingly worried about
her feelings.

"Is that how he solves his cases? Gets intimate with
female strangers? Softens them up?" Natalie didn't like
it, but she guessed if it worked for him and he wasn't into
the woman for real, it shouldn't be a big deal. She suspected the reason she was feeling out of sorts about it was
because Brock and she weren't formally mated wolves.

"He was planting a bug somewhere on her clothes, or maybe her purse. I'd bet my salary on it."

Natalie frowned at Shawn as he led her to her front porch, not having suspected that was what it was all about. She should have though.

"Yep. I suspect he'll want to follow her and see where she ends up once she leaves here."

Natalie glanced back at her gate. She wanted to go with him. He might not even want to bring her with after she'd acted so annoyed with him. "Okay, thanks, Shawn. You did a great job today. Everyone loves you."

"I enjoyed it. This is just the kind of place where I need to work."

She got a call and thought it would be Brock, but it was her dad. "Hi, Dad, did you and Mom get in all right?"

Shawn stuck around to hear what her dad had to say.

"Yes, this afternoon. We didn't want to bother you earlier while you were managing things at the center, but we figured you would be closed now and have had dinner already. Did any of the rogue wolves show up?"

"A human male, possibly, who might have been casing the place. Brock questioned him. And a she-wolf, but she denies any involvement. She was driving Marek's car though."

"Sounds like she's taking part in it if she's at the center and knows Marek."

"I agree. Too much of a coincidence. The man said he was interested in writing a book about carriage houses and wanted to include mine, but he seemed like a phony. Since he was human, I'm not sure about him though. How are things going there for you and Mom?" Natalie hoped they loved the pack.

"It's been unbelievable. Bella and Devlyn put on a full-pack welcoming, nothing like we've ever had before. They gave us a tour of the leather goods factory and the doctor's clinic. We went for a wolf run around the acres of woodlands and across a number of streams to see what all the wolves owned. It's really impressive and beautiful. Aaron's horse ranch was great too. We're going horseback riding, just like in the old days.

"We've met most of the wolves in the pack already. They told us where we could establish a garden center and are eager to help us in any way that they can. Several of the wolves expressed an interest in you giving classes to the younger wolves about plants. I told them you give classes like that now for all ages. Some of the wolves are even interested in growing a community garden, if we could mentor them."

"That sounds wonderful. So you're liking the pack?"

"Yes, very much. Your mom found several women around her age who have crochet and knitting circles. She's in heaven. I've been talking to Vaughn and Jillian about some of the USF work they've been doing and some of their former PI cases. They've been just as interested in the murder cases I've investigated. It's really great talking with other wolves about getting rid of the bad guys."

Natalie was thrilled. She loved the idea of moving closer to Angie and her mate. "Are you going to do it?"

"We want to, but we have agreed we'll wait until we're done with our visit here and then make the decision."

"Okay, sounds good, Dad. We're doing well here, and Shawn has introduced some nice changes. He's a real asset to the business."

"We knew he would be. What about Brock?"

"Doing great. He's been getting lots of tips too."

Her dad laughed. "Well, we have a dinner to go to. We'll talk again tomorrow after you're closed for the night. Let us know if you have any trouble with these counterfeiters in the meantime."

"I will. Have fun!" She was thrilled the pack was treating her parents so well and that they were enjoying their time there. "Night, Dad." When she ended the call, she told Shawn, "My parents are loving your pack. I've never heard them praise a pack like that."

"Hot damn. What about you and Brock?"

She saw Brock heading toward them.

"We're good," Brock said, and she wondered how much he'd overheard. He smiled at her in a way that said he had good news for her.

She felt some of the tension leave her.

He drew close, retrieved his phone, and punched in something, then handed his cell to her. "Kittie's talking to Dexter."

Ohmigod! Natalie could hug Brock. She slipped her arm around his waist as she put his cell on speakerphone.

"Why the hell didn't you tell me they knew what car Marek was driving?" Kittie said to Dexter. It sounded as if she was still driving and on the Bluetooth.

"Why the hell didn't you drive your own car, Kittie?"

"It was in the shop!"

So that much was true.

Brock wrapped his arm around Natalie's waist and smiled down at her. He *was* good at his job. And he was still hers. She leaned in to him to show she appreciated the intimacy.

Shawn was smiling at them. Yeah, he knew Brock and Natalie were the ones for each other.

"Marek wanted me to get this done tonight. Hell, *you* wanted me to get this done tonight. So two male wolves are there, the owners were gone, and their daughter is there running things," Kittie said.

"Did you get into either of the houses?"

"No. I tried several times, but the one wolf followed me around. I tried to make a play for him, to see if he'd fall for it, but I think he's hooked on the she-wolf."

Brock nodded. Natalie smiled at him. She should have known he was just working the job.

"The one named Brock said he'd take you down," Kittie said to Dexter.

So Brock had talked to Kittie about the whole business already.

"No damn way. How the hell did he know my name? I was using a different one when he tried to kill me, unsuccessfully, the last time. Though I sure as hell thought I'd killed him."

"Brock didn't say how he knew you were doing the counterfeiting."

"And you didn't ask? He's signed his own death warrant. What about the others?"

"He said the others won't be doing anything about it. He said he's the only alpha of the bunch."

Shawn and Natalie chuckled.

"You'll have to break into their places on your own to learn what you need to. I don't know who lives at which place or if they have security alarms on the houses. The two males didn't appear to be leaving the center, like they lived somewhere else. So they're probably staying there. I didn't see any other vehicles there. They've got security cameras at the garden center and the motion-detector lights that you discovered yourself. They may not have any on the houses. Or they might, if they're that security-conscious," Kittie said to Dexter.

Shawn glanced up at the security cameras on the carriage house. Yeah, after the men tried to steal from the Silvertons, they had put up all kinds of security measures.

"Okay, listen, I've got to go. It's your problem now," she said.

"You're getting a pretty penny from it, darlin', so you'll do what I say, or else." The call ended.

"Shit," Kittie said. Then she told her Bluetooth to call Antonio. "Antonio."

"Yeah, what's going on?" he asked over the Bluetooth.

"We have a real problem."

"Shit. Don't tell me this is more bad news about Marek losing the money. He's such an ass."

"Yeah, this is about the wolves who know what Marek's up to."

"Do they know about me?"

"No, they don't know who you are yet, but we need to get out of this, pronto, or we're dead wolves. Dexter's pretty hot about it. I wouldn't put it past him to get rid of all of us and start over so he doesn't have any loose ends. Though they know about him. So they'll be after him. Which means we need to pack up and leave."

"Hell, Kittie, this is too lucrative a deal to give it up. We'll have to move our operation somewhere else, but it will be a lot of work. We're in the middle of cleaning this money and printing the new stuff."

It sounded like "the crew" was ready to dump Dexter, who must be the boss.

"Where would we move to? Can we do it without Dexter's backing and Marek's money to convert into the fake money?" Kittie asked.

"We've made enough. We can start over somewhere else. We've been working on something new anyway. Marek's an ass. He's gotten us into all kinds of hot water with the wolves over this. We just have to convince Jimmy to go with us, or it's a no-go. Without the artist, we can't do this on our own."

Jimmy was Ink Man then, as Brock and Natalie had assumed.

"He's like a brother to you. Convince him already," Kittie said.

Silence.

"Listen, if they catch up to you and the others, you're all dead," Kittie said. "Me too, if they know I'm really taking part in this."

"Unless we take them out first. We can make the bodies disappear. They're not part of a pack here. No one will be the wiser. We could even work the garden center and pretend we're the owners."

"The garden center? You're crazy. Everything would die within weeks of you or me having anything to do with it."

"We'll hire real gardeners or put the place up for sale."

"You're forgetting one thing. The owners and their daughter aren't part of a pack, sure, but that guy Brock is. Marek said he's part of the pack out of the town of Greystoke, Colorado. I don't know about the other guy they had working there."

Antonio didn't comment.

"We need to leave. Let Brock handle Marek and Dexter. Or Dexter can deal with Brock and the others. Let it be on Dexter's head. We can start over again somewhere else. If we get the lion's share of the proceeds from the money, then we won't have any trouble starting up in a new location."

"That's saying Marek or Dexter won't kill us for leaving. They need us. But if we're going to run out on them, I'm sure they'll just terminate us," Antonio said.

"We could give Brock some clues on where they are."

Shawn raised his thumb in a sign to Natalie and Brock that said it worked for him. They nodded in agreement.

"And while they're removing those guys, we leave with the printing press and everything else we need so we can keep making the money," Kittie said.

"I don't know, honey. If Dexter got word of us double-crossing him, he'd kill us himself."

"We have to do something, act now, or we're going down with the whole lot of them. Make up your mind. I'll talk to you later."

Silence ensued.

And then there was nothing more but Kittie muttering under her breath.

"They're coming for us, or we're going after them," Natalie said when Kittie didn't say anything after that.

"Right. Which puts us in the better position?" Shawn asked.

"The home front. Dexter's house is way out and probably has security to the gills. Marek lives with his aunt. It would be better if we let them come to us, since it seems that's their intention anyway," Brock said.

"Should we all stay together then?" Natalie wasn't used to pack warfare. She didn't know the best way to handle this.

"Shawn and I will stay outside your house, hidden. We'll keep an eye out for any sign of movement," Brock said.

"But the motion-detector lights will go off, and they'll see you."

"We can disable the ones where we'll be. They won't see us. Believe me," Brock said.

Which reminded her he was a SEAL and Shawn was an Army Ranger.

"And me?" Natalie didn't want to be relegated to the house and doing nothing.

"You stay inside and monitor my phone for any more conversations Kittie might have. If she's too far away from her purse, we might not pick up on them. If she's close by and reveals something crucial that we need to know, you can come out and tell us," Brock said. "You can monitor the security cameras on the garden center and the houses too. You'll be our tech person."

Now she felt better. She agreed and liked that plan. Nothing she hated more than when she felt she couldn't help out in a situation where they could all be in danger.

"The same goes for seeing anything on the security monitors. If you see movement around your parents' house, let us know. If you see it around your house, we'll be on it."

"All right."

"Do you have a couple of locks for the walk gates? They might not come that way, but if they do, we'll hear them trying to remove the locks," Brock said.

"Yeah, in my garage. I've got a lot of leaves I just put into the composter. We could spread those around so you can hear if anyone's walking around on the dry leaves." Natalie led them to the garage and opened a storage cabinet.

Brock and Shawn each grabbed one of the locks.

"I'll meet you out at the shed where we keep the wheelbarrows." She motioned in that direction.

"Okay, we'll lock the gates and join you." Brock and his cousin took off for the gates, and Natalie went to the storage shed to pull out a couple of wheelbarrows.

She moved one toward the composter nearby, and Brock soon caught up to her.

"So you heard from your parents?"

She opened the composter. "Yeah. They seem to love the pack, but they're going to give it a few more days before they actually join."

"Hallelujah." Brock smiled. "If you're no longer angry with me over Kittie—"

Natalie handed him a rake. "Why would I be mad about the she-wolf?" She tried to make light of it.

He chuckled. "I don't blame you. If some guy was hanging all over you, and you were laughing and smiling and not moving out of his space, I'd have felt the same way."

"It did look bad, though I was trying to tell myself you were working a mission."

"I was. So about us…" He began loading the wheelbarrow with dry leaves.

"Well," she said, waving at Shawn and motioning to him to grab the other wheelbarrow next to the shed, "do you really like the black wallpaper in the bathrooms?"

Brock laughed out loud. "Hell, you can change them to anything you want. Seriously. Man, I thought it would be a lot harder to win you over."

She laughed, pulled the rake out of his hands, and leaned it against the wheelbarrow. Then she wrapped her arms around his waist. "A woman knows what a woman wants."

"That makes me one damn lucky wolf."

Shawn wheeled his wheelbarrow up next to the composter and began to load it. "Don't mind me."

They didn't, and Brock began to kiss her. She loved the way he kissed her, his hands cupping her head, their tongues lingering in a sensual dance, but knowing the trouble they could be in, they separated with regret and got back to work. She was thinking how she wasn't going to wait to learn what her parents officially decided about the pack. She was certain they had already made the decision, and if she told them she and Brock were mated, they wouldn't wait to confirm they were joining the pack.

They finished filling the wheelbarrows and spread the dry leaves around the two houses. It was enough for a light cover. Hopefully, if a man or wolf stepped on some, they'd hear him.

"I doubt they'll show up until it's really dark out and they think we've gone to sleep," Brock said.

"So we can relax until then?" Natalie asked. Relaxing wasn't really what she had in mind.

She remembered seeing him standing in front of the fountain outside the wedding rehearsal luncheon, looking good enough to eat, and him wanting to protect her all the way to Texas and until this was resolved...

Yeah, he was the wolf for her.

Chapter 16

"SHAWN, WILL YOU BE ALL RIGHT BY YOURSELF FOR A LITTLE while?" Natalie asked, grasping Brock's hand and tugging him toward her house.

Brock hadn't realized Natalie wanted to get on with what he hoped was a mating, but he'd been serious when he'd said he was certain these people wouldn't make a move until later.

"Hell yeah. I'll keep watch but stick close by to warn you if anything goes down. And I assume congrats are in order."

"They are," Natalie said, confirming what Brock was certainly hoping for.

"Hot damn!" Brock said. "And thanks, Cousin." Brock swept Natalie up in his arms and hurried her inside. He didn't want to rush the mating, but he wanted to be ready for any contingency. And, like Natalie, he didn't want to put this off.

"You're sure about this? You don't want to wait to see if your parents like the pack well enough to actually join?" he asked her as he carried her into her bedroom.

"I know my parents. Even though Dad said they'd wait to make the decision in a few days, they've already decided. I'm sure they figure I've already fallen hopelessly in love with you, and that means both Angie and I would be gone. I mean, sure, we could stay here, if you were all right with it, but I want to be with a pack when we have children. So eventually, we'd end up having to move."

"Good deal. I wondered how long I could hold out."

She laughed. "You don't have to wait any longer."

"I'll help you and your parents in the garden center every chance I can get and would love it if you'd want to help me with my cases." He set her down beside the bed.

"I'd love that. But I have to tell you that my dad will want to also. Since my mom and I helped my dad with his cases for so many years, don't be surprised if this becomes a family affair."

"Why didn't you tell me that before? I would have insisted on you mating me when we first met."

She laughed and began unbuckling his belt.

"You are so good for me, Ms. Natalie Silverton." He sat her down on the bed to remove her boots.

"You are so hot and sexy, Mr. Brock Greystoke. If you'd left without me once all this business was cleared up, I would never have gotten you out of my mind. I'd only think of being with you. You don't know how much it was killing me not to wake you last night and have crazy sex with you again."

He laughed. "I woke a couple of times, but I was afraid you really needed your sleep and it might backfire, and you'd kick me out of bed."

"No way."

He laughed, then pulled off her socks. She tackled his belt again and unzipped his zipper. He hurried to sit on the bed to remove his boots, but she crouched in front of him to make fast work of them.

Then she slipped his shirt off while he ran his hands

over her shirt, feeling her nipples stretching against the palms of his hands. He groaned. "I love you."

She hauled her shirt off, but before she could unfasten her bra, he was doing it for her. "You're easy to love."

"So are you." He removed Natalie's bra, and she straddled him on the bed. He didn't want to think of anything but the she-wolf he loved who wanted a mating with him.

He kissed Natalie's breasts and moved his hands down to unfasten her jeans. Then he rolled her over on her back so he could pull them off. He quickly dispensed with his own jeans, then removed her panties. Once he slid his boxer briefs down and kicked them aside, he moved his aroused body over hers. He kissed her mouth, tasting the essence of her, feeling drugged by her arousal. Their pheromones were zinging all over the place, telling them this was meant to be—a mating between two wolves forever. He felt the power of their connection, the way they worked together, played together, made love together.

He kissed her navel and moved his hand down her waist, until he reached her sensitive clit and began to stroke.

"Ohmigod." She breathed out. "We...shouldn't... have waited...last...night."

He chuckled and kissed her tummy but continued to stroke her, licking her navel, watching her come apart under his touch. The way she was arching her back and pulling at him to join her, he figured she was about to come. "Ready?"

"Yes," she growled, "now!"

He didn't hesitate, pushing his cock deep between her feminine folds. And then he thrust, taking pleasure in making Natalie his mate, enjoying the intimacy they shared and the unbreakable bond between them. He adored her, loved how territorial she'd become with him when he worried she might be irritated by the way he'd become possessive. Which all went to show they were meant to be together.

"God, you're beautiful," he said, kissing her cheek, her nose, her forehead, before his mouth captured hers again.

She groaned with release, and he continued to thrust, his hand sliding down her leg and up again, cupping her ass to pull her tighter against him. And then he climaxed, realizing too late that if they'd wanted to wait to have children, he hadn't thought of it in time.

He continued to pump into her until he was spent, and then he cuddled with her, loving the way she fit against him, her arms wrapping tight around him, not letting go.

"Love you, Brock," Natalie said, still holding him securely to her.

"I hope you're not mad at me." He was serious. It was a stupid mistake to have made, if she had wanted to wait. Sure, she might not become pregnant the first time, but what if she did?

She smiled up at him. "Why? Because you forgot to use a condom? I'm ready for children."

Relief washed over him. He loved her. "Let's get a quick shower. We've got to get going."

"Yeah, let's do that. And don't worry about it if little wolves are on the way. We'll just have to get that spare bedroom papered sooner rather than later."

He chuckled. "You had this all planned from the beginning, didn't you? You were just waiting for me to agree to the wallpapering jobs."

She laughed.

They hurried into the shower to clean up quickly. He started it, and they soaped each other up and rinsed off.

"You're the only one for me." Natalie sighed, shutting off the shower, kissing Brock, then grabbing a towel. "We'd better check on Shawn and make sure he's okay."

Then they hurried to dress. Only this time, Brock went back to the guest bedroom to grab a black T-shirt while Natalie dressed in her room.

He poked his head outside and saw Shawn sitting on the deck in the dark, armed with a rifle. "Hey, I'm going to do some research on this Tom Jonas, the supposed photographer."

"Yeah, sure, go ahead. I'll just wait out here and watch for anything. It's been quiet."

"Holler if anything happens." Brock entered the house, and Natalie joined him.

"What are you checking for?" she asked as he brought out his laptop, sat down on the couch, and opened it.

"An email address or a phone number on Tom Jonas's website. Just a way to contact him."

She sat down beside Brock.

"Here's an email address. I'll send an email, or you can. We can see how he responds. If he wasn't here, we'll know the guy used his identity."

"Okay. I'll do it." She pulled out her phone and emailed the photographer.

Hi, I'm Natalie Silverton. I would like to know more about this book you're writing. You can email me at this address and talk to me about it. Thanks, Natalie.

"Hell, the car doesn't belong to the photographer. I took a picture of the car he was driving. I just ran the plates, and it belongs to a Paul Schwartz," Brock said to her.

"Well, we kind of expected he wasn't the real photographer." Her cell phone beeped, indicating she'd received an email. She checked it and smiled. Brock peered over her shoulder to see the message. It was the *real* photographer responding to Natalie's email.

I'm sorry, you must have mistaken me for someone else. Why did you think I was interested in writing a book?

She emailed back.

Someone came to visit me today about a carriage house I own and used your name and website as his contact information. Thanks. At least I know he's an impostor, and if he comes back, I'll have him arrested.

Sorry someone did this to you. Glad you contacted me to verify. Best of luck. Tom

"Okay, so now what is the *real* guy up to?" she asked Brock.

"The guy must be working for Dexter. He has to be."

Later that night, they were ready for the bad guys in case anything further happened. Brock and Shawn had set up in places outside the carriage house where they wouldn't be seen, both wearing wolf coats, while Natalie watched the security monitors and listened to Brock's phone to learn if Kittie revealed anything of importance. Natalie kept hearing sounds, music playing in the background, pots and pans banging in a kitchen, she figured, but no conversation. She wished she knew where Kittie was. At Marek's house? Or somewhere else? Dexter's maybe? Her own with her mother? As if her mother really was in the area with a dead flower bush.

Then Natalie heard sounds on the listening bug: a door squeaked open, and footsteps hurried across a tile floor.

"Marek," Kittie said. "I thought I was supposed to pick you up from The Inking Spot."

"Antonio dropped me off. Did you learn anything about the security at the garden center and the houses there?" Marek asked.

"No. Not a damn thing. Where are you going? You just got home."

"I've got to drive my car back to the garden center. We're going to be in a hell of a lot of hot water if we don't deal with this. Don't wait up for me. I don't have any idea how long this is going to be."

So Kittie was Marek's girlfriend. Natalie wondered if Lettie had been right about him. He'd been seeing Kittie for a while. But now she was seeing Antonio behind his back?

Natalie headed outside and called out, "Marek's coming!"

Brock met up with Natalie and shifted.

"By himself?"

Natalie shrugged. "He said he was coming back here. I don't know if it means he's bringing a force with him. I imagine so."

"Okay, let us know if anything else is said."

"All right." Natalie walked into the house to watch the security monitors.

"Hey, one of Eugenia's social security checks was direct deposited to the account," Kittie said.

"Don't spend it. I need it for the business." The door slammed shut.

Eugenia's checks? The aunt who was supposedly on dialysis and who owned the house? It sounded like she was dead and they were still spending her checks.

Not much time had passed when the listening bug caught the sound of the doorbell ringing and footfalls headed for the door. The door squeaked open, and Natalie kept thinking if it had been her own front door, she'd have greased the hinges already.

"Dexter. What are you doing here?" Kittie sounded surprised to see him, and a whole lot worried.

After what Kittie had said to Antonio about getting away, Natalie thought she *should* be worried. She didn't imagine Dexter was someone who would be easy to cross.

"Don't ask me to do anything like that again. If you don't like what I did or how I did it, do it yourself," Kittie said.

"You'll do what I tell you to."

"You're such a damn control freak. You think you can do better, go do it yourself. They wouldn't have been any less wary of you. What about that other guy you sent? How well did he make out? Huh? Obviously not well at all, because then you sent me. If Marek and the others hadn't spooked them last night, they wouldn't have been suspicious of me," Kittie said.

Natalie was surprised Kittie would be so belligerent to Dexter if he was the one in charge.

"What are you going to do about Lettie?" Kittie asked. "You know Marek confided in her. And that means she could be spilling her guts to these wolves. Maybe that's how they knew so much about Marek. What else do they know? Your name? Your brother's? The rest of the team's?"

"Shit. One more damn loose end to deal with." Dexter didn't say anything for a few minutes, then said, "Hey, Trenton, I need you to handle a loose end for me… tonight in Boulder. *Lettie*. Yeah, she could be a real liability now that she's split with Marek, and she's been talking to a wolf with the pack in Greystoke… Well, hell, after you meet with him then. Tell him the money is coming. The guys are working through the night on the bills. But I want this other situation resolved tonight. We don't know how much Marek told her, and we can't have her sharing what she knows with anybody else. And do it yourself. Don't ask the other guys… Yeah…yeah, I'm sure they'd do as good a job of it, but I want you to *personally* handle it. Call me when it's done. Out here."

Oh no. As much as Natalie knew Brock didn't like Lettie, she had helped them learn more about who might be in on this operation, and Natalie suspected he didn't want her killed over it.

"What about your mate?" Kittie asked Dexter. "The rest of us are risking our necks in this venture, and she's not doing anything."

"You leave my mate out of this," he said. "She knows nothing about any of this, and it stays that way."

Man, Kittie had to have a death wish.

Natalie jumped up from her couch and ran outside to warn Brock and his cousin what was about to go down. Brock was at her side in a heartbeat. "Dexter is having his brother, Trenton, do away with Lettie. He's doing the job tonight."

Brock ran inside the house, and she called softly to Shawn. He joined her, and they entered the house.

Brock shifted and yanked on his boxer briefs. Since they were listening to his phone to hear what else transpired between Dexter and Kittie, she handed Brock her own, assuming he'd want to call someone to protect Lettie.

He did, and she was proud of him. He called his brother and said, "Vaughn, get someone to pick up Lettie. Dexter's ordered a hit on her. His brother's name is Trenton, and he's the one who has to oversee it. He might have more men with him. Just put her in protective custody until we eliminate this ring. Putting this on speakerphone so Natalie and Shawn can hear."

"You're not thinking of recommending Lettie join the pack after what she pulled, are you?" Vaughn asked.

"Hell no, but I may need her services to wallpaper some rooms."

Natalie frowned at Brock. She needed to tell her parents they were mated. First. At a decent hour.

Brock quickly cleared his throat. "At some time in the future," he reiterated.

Vaughn laughed. "Okay, I was getting ready to announce the news to the pack."

"Just see that Lettie's safe. Don't let her talk you out of removing her from her place."

"I have an even better idea. We'll lie in wait for Trenton to show up. We can move her before that happens, if we're not too late. But if she won't leave, we'll protect her and deal with him."

"Take enough men to do the job, just in case more than one shows up to eliminate her."

"You know it."

"Okay, gotta go and listen to what else Dexter is planning."

"I'll give you a heads-up when we've removed Trenton and his men from the equation," Vaughn said.

They ended the call, and Shawn went back out to watch for any sign of intruders while Brock stayed inside to listen to Dexter and Kittie. Brock ran his hand down Natalie's arm as she cuddled with him. "Sorry, I sort of let that slip out about the papering business. I didn't want Vaughn to believe I had any interest in Lettie."

Natalie smiled at Brock. "That's okay. I just didn't want him announcing it to the pack before I tell my parents."

Kittie began speaking again, and Brock and Natalie grew quiet to hear what she had to say.

"Okay, Dexter. So what about that guy pretending to be Tom Jonas, the photographer? I don't know why you would have called on him to check out the garden center," Kittie said to Dexter as he reclined on Marek's sofa. She was standing there, her arms folded across her chest, head tilted to the side, a little bit of arrogance and defensiveness mixed into one.

"Not that it's any of your business, but I thought a human wouldn't raise any suspicions, and he owed me." Dexter normally wouldn't have explained himself or his actions to anyone, but he liked playing a game a bit, and he wanted to clear the air before he eliminated her. He thought it only fair to give his crew members a chance to explain themselves before he ended their miserable lives.

"Wait, he's the guy who hadn't paid you for some of the counterfeit money he was supposed to exchange for real cash?" Kittie shook her head, as though she couldn't believe he was so stupid. "Hitting the bars at night was a great idea. Pay with a hundred-dollar bill in a dark bar when the bartender is busy with customers, can't see the money, and he gives a whole bunch of change back. So why didn't the guy give you the good money?"

"He spent it gambling," Dexter said, and man, was he pissed about it. "He screwed up, but it was a great scheme, if he'd paid me. I was giving him one last chance. He won't be doing that again. Ever. Past tense. Then there's you. You screwed up when you took Marek's car to the garden center. That's what clued Brock in that you're with us."

She shrugged. "All right already. I used Marek's car. What was I supposed to do? Show up in your wife's car? A bright-red Porsche? Like I wouldn't have stood out driving that. No one else drives your pickup but you. So what would you have suggested?"

"You could have told me you didn't have a car, and I would have sent one that wouldn't be traceable to any of us." He could not believe how shortsighted she and Marek were. "Hell, you even smell of Marek."

"I used a towel on the seat, and I didn't touch him."

"If you got close to Brock or the woman, both would have smelled Marek's scent on you, even if they hadn't recognized his car. They'd already met him at the airport," Dexter said to Kittie.

"Brock's the one who offered me assistance, as if he knew I shouldn't have been there. I couldn't do anything but pretend I was there to shop."

"Who was the other man working at the nursery?"

"A wolf named Shawn. They didn't give a last name, and I thought it would seem odd if I asked."

Dexter needed to learn what he could about the other man. Was he just the hired help, another wolf, or was he as highly trained as Brock? Hell, nothing was going the way Dexter had planned.

Shawn woofed outside, and Brock said to Natalie, "Warn us if Dexter says anything else we need to know in a hurry. I'll keep watch with Shawn outside."

"Okay."

Brock kissed her mouth, rose from the couch, and ditched his boxer briefs. Then he shifted and ran out the wolf door.

"So then they asked about Marek and how you know him. How you're tied in to his counterfeiting. Marek screwed up first by losing the money. Now you. I can't have any of this get back to us. Not only that, but I've heard you and Marek are thinking of leaving me and leading the rest of the crew to a new place to set up your own operation," Dexter said to Kittie.

Natalie was still watching the security cameras at the garden center for any sign of intruders, but she glanced at the phone and barely breathed when she heard Dexter's dark tone of voice and what he had accused Kittie of. This didn't sound good for Kittie or Marek. In fact, it reminded Natalie of a homicide case her dad had worked where the boss in a criminal conspiracy had killed two of his coconspirators when he learned they were planning on running off with the drugs and the money and setting up shop elsewhere. Only it sounded like Kittie intended to do it with Antonio and Ink Man, the men who really knew the nuts and bolts of the operation. It appeared Kittie planned to leave Marek to fend for himself. So what was her real role in the whole operation?

"Do you think the two of you can manage on your own? Hell, that would be the day," Dexter said to Kittie, knowing she and Marek couldn't have a setup like this without him running things, even if they took the rest of the crew with them. But they were too stupid to realize that. He had thought they made a good team—until Marek lost the bag of money at the airport.

"I don't know what you mean." Kittie had been so belligerent, but now she sounded scared, her voice softer, more anxious. It didn't become her.

"Don't play coy with me. Do you think I haven't been monitoring you, Marek, and the others all this time? I haven't been in this business this long without safeguarding myself." Dexter had learned that the hard way when one of his men spilled the beans to Brock, and he'd hired men to help him take Dexter down. That had nearly been the end of Dexter. He would never trust the men—or women—he had working for him. He kept everyone under surveillance.

He pulled Marek's gun out of a holster under his jacket. He'd found it in the bed earlier when he'd arrived, just where Marek told him he always kept it, and perfect for what Dexter had to do next.

"I'll…I'll disappear. You don't have to kill me. You won't ever see me again," Kittie said, her expression horrified.

"Too late for that. No one betrays me. And you and Marek are loose ends I can ill afford." Dexter was glad to have sent Marek on his way so he could deal with one of them at a time. No mess, no fuss that way. He shot Kittie twice, and she collapsed on the floor.

He set the gun down on the coffee table, made sure she was dead, her heartbeat stopped, and then wrapped her in a shower curtain he had tucked under the couch earlier. He dragged her body back to the bedroom and laid her in bed, then covered her with the comforter, arranging her head on the pillow as if he were a devoted boyfriend and had just killed her and then would kill himself. Dexter would make sure of it.

He carried the shower curtain out to his truck and shoved it under the front seat, then went into the house to wait for Marek. He cleaned up the tile floor, glad she hadn't gotten any blood on the throw rug. Once he was done, he sat down on the squeaky recliner and waited. It wasn't long before he got a call.

"Yeah, Marek?" Dexter said.

"Hey, I'm here and the guys are here. I'm going to shift into the wolf in just a few minutes to watch how things are going, and then I'll report back to you."

Dexter resettled himself on the recliner, and it squeaked again. "I told you you're in charge of this operation. They're human. They can deal with the heat and the blame. Brock's pack won't tie them to you. You have my word. Just see that it gets done and go home. I'll meet you at your place. Don't screw this up... All right. Do it." Dexter smiled to himself as if he wasn't already at Marek's place with a dead Kittie. He was waiting for his next victim to show up. He just hoped Marek would get it right this time so that would end Brock's meddling in his affairs. Otherwise, damn it, he'd have to handle this himself.

Surprised, yet she shouldn't have been that Dexter would kill Kittie, Natalie had to warn Brock and Shawn that Dexter was sending armed humans, not wolves. That meant they needed to handle this in a whole different manner.

She dashed through the house to the front door, threw it open, and called out in a hushed voice, "Brock! Shawn!"

Brock raced to meet up with her, Shawn following a few paces behind.

"Dexter is sending armed humans."

Both men shifted and began to dress and arm themselves. They didn't want to try to fight armed men as wolves.

Natalie explained the rest of what happened while she watched the security monitors.

Brock leaned over the monitor, rubbing her back. "With humans taking part, we can let the police handle this."

"What if they name any of the wolves responsible for this?" Shawn asked.

"Sounds to me like Dexter plans to eliminate Marek, and I suspect the hired killers don't know who else is in on this," Brock said. "If they even know who Marek is."

"Then if Dexter is waiting at Marek's house for him, we need to go over there and deal with him," Shawn said.

"It would be a good idea before Marek warned him their plan was a bust, but I don't want to risk having us split up at this point," Brock said. "Not with armed gunmen planning to hit here soon."

Natalie got a call from Vaughn on her phone. "Your brother." She put it on speaker, hoping Vaughn and whoever he'd taken with him weren't injured and that they had arrived in time to protect Lettie.

"We're in Boulder. Six of us. Devlyn didn't want us to risk losing this battle. Lettie refused to leave her home and shop. She was shocked to learn you were the one to orchestrate this, Brock, and said you couldn't be all that bad. She figured your mate had something to do with mellowing you out, believing you're mated wolves. Anyway, we're all staying here, safeguarding her and watching for Trenton or anyone else who might be planning her murder. We are all wearing hunter's spray so they won't know we're here to protect her."

"Thanks, Vaughn."

"I'll get back with you once this is resolved. You let me know as soon as things are resolved between you and Natalie too."

Brock smiled at her. "I will. Be safe."

"You too."

They finished the call, and Natalie said, "I'm proud

of you for doing that for Lettie. You have every right to be angry with her, especially since her warning her brother of your movements could have meant more people would have died at his hands. And she could very well have led you to your death when he and his cohorts ambushed you. But you rose above it."

"When she said she loved her brother, I don't know, something just hit home. If my brother was guilty of committing crimes, I probably would have felt like she did. Protective, loyal."

"Even if he had murdered innocents?"

"Probably not then."

Natalie glanced at the security camera monitor and saw movement. "Ohmigod. They're here," she warned, pointing to the monitor showing the back of her parents' property and three men moving around wearing camo fatigues, boots, and black hoodies, all armed with semiautomatics.

"Call 911. We'll incapacitate them without killing them before they can harm any of us," Brock said.

Natalie glanced at Shawn. "You too?"

"Yeah, me too. I didn't retire from the military like Brock, and I wasn't one of those guys with flippers."

Brock smiled and checked his ammo.

"But I was an Army Ranger for twelve years. So yeah, I can fight."

Natalie patted her 9mm. "Okay, good. I'll be ready here."

"All right, you stay here. If anyone comes before we can secure them, you shoot. Try not to make it fatal, but if they're shooting, do what you have to do. The law's behind you on this," Brock said to Natalie and gave her a hug and kiss.

She gave him the same back. "Be safe, both of you."

Then she called 911, and Brock and Shawn headed out into the dark. She prayed the guys would remain safe as she talked to the 911 operator.

Brock moved left, and Shawn went to the right of her parents' house. He hoped to hell none of these guys breached the carriage house while Natalie was there by herself. And that the police would be there quickly to pick up the vermin once they restrained them.

He saw the first of the men coming around the side of the house, peering in the main house's kitchen window. The guy looked like he was special ops, not that it meant he really was. Some of these guys tried to look the part. Either that or Dexter could afford to hire some real guns.

At a crouch, Brock ran toward the man. He ran like a wolf, quiet, even when moving as a man, and reached the armed gunman before he heard him. Brock slammed his fist into the guy's head before he could cry out and took him down. He tied the gunman up with plastic ties and gagged him, then headed around the other side of the house to try to neutralize the other guy.

But then shooting started at the north side of the main house, sending a chill up Brock's spine.

He ran full out to reach the area where he feared Shawn was in a firefight. A man was shooting at Shawn. *Hell and damnation.* Where were the police when they needed them? Still, they were all being caught on candid camera, so the wolves had to do this right. They had to protect themselves and turn these men over to face the human justice system.

He saw the man hiding behind a storage barn, shooting in the direction where Shawn had to be. He was pinned down. Brock took aim and fired, catching the man in the hand, and he dropped his rifle.

The man yelled out and dashed around the building. It didn't mean he wasn't armed to the teeth with other weapons. From warfare training, Brock and Shawn knew they had to make the shot that would keep their opponent from being ambulatory and able to continue to fight. But they didn't want to kill the humans.

They heard sirens and raced after the man, but then a shot was fired near the carriage house. *Hell.*

Shawn called out to Brock. "Go. I've got these two."

"Gotcha." Brock took off running to reach the carriage house, worried to death Natalie could be injured or worse. That was when he found a man groaning in pain on her front porch, mouth gagged, arms tied behind his back. The front door was wide open, and there was no sign of Natalie.

"Natalie?" Brock called out, letting her know it was just him, his voice harsh and anxious.

"I'm fine. Watching the security monitors. Go. I've got this one under control."

Not trusting she was okay, Brock poked his head in the door and saw she was armed and still on the phone, watching the security monitors for any more movement.

She mouthed *911* and motioned with her phone, which meant she was keeping the line open until the police arrived. Good.

More shots were fired, and Brock said, "Okay, running to help Shawn." He wanted to eliminate all these men, to ensure Dexter knew Brock, Natalie, and Shawn wouldn't be that easy to neutralize. Brock would be coming for him next. Not to mention he wanted to remove these men from the streets so they wouldn't come back to finish the job.

Another shot was fired as Brock reached Shawn, who was hunkered down behind a stack of planters, and then cars screeched to a halt farther out on the property, and police were shouting to the gunman they could see, "Drop your gun, now!"

Shawn and Brock slipped back to the carriage house to help protect Natalie in case there were any more of the gunmen out there. At the carriage house, they laid down their weapons and waited for the police to come for them and to haul off the tied-up guys.

"Everybody, down on the ground now," the officers told Brock, Shawn, and Natalie as they approached, guns drawn.

"I'm the one who made the 911 call," Natalie explained as Brock and Shawn showed their IDs. "These two men are currently working for my parents and me at the garden center. My parents took a trip, so Brock and Shawn are here to protect the place because we've had problems before, and I'm dating Brock." She showed her ID to the officer.

"We notice you have security cameras," the officer named Coffman said, writing everything down.

"Yeah, I can send the video to you." She explained about the cousins' military training, which was why they were able to handle the intruders.

They all had to give their statements to the police, and then the armed trespassers were rounded up, treated for wounds, if they had any, and hauled off to jail.

"Did you get all three of the shooters?" Brock asked Coffman, the officer in charge, wondering what had happened to Marek. He'd probably fled the scene when he heard all the shooting. If Dexter was true to his word, he'd kill Marek for them.

"All three. Some mighty fine shooting," Coffman said.

"Thanks. We were trying to keep them from killing us without killing them," Brock said.

Coffman nodded. "You don't have any idea why these men would come in shooting? They were armed to kill." He gave her his email address.

"Not at all, Officer," Natalie said. "I can't imagine that a competing nursery would do this. No one I know of or that my dad or mom—or me, for that matter—has had a run-in with." She emailed the officer the security video.

"Hell, I know your dad. A decorated homicide detective. He was on the news about that homeless strangler serial killer in New Mexico. Now *he* could have enemies. What about the two of you? It appears the trouble didn't happen until you arrived," Coffman said to Brock and Shawn while writing notes. "Except for the other incident two years ago. But those were strictly armed robbers. These guys looked like they were hired for a hit, not a robbery."

"Not unless Natalie has a jealous ex-boyfriend," Brock said, wrapping his arm around her shoulders.

"No, no boyfriend here. Or…anywhere." Natalie placed her arm around Brock's waist.

Shawn shook his head. "No one has a beef with me around these parts. Brock and I just got here."

"Okay, well, we'll have to have your testimony against these guys if they end up going to trial."

"I sure hope they do," Natalie said, frowning. "If Brock and Shawn hadn't been here, and my parents and I were alone, we could have been murdered."

"Understand. The men will be questioned, and hopefully we'll learn something useful."

Hopefully not about the wolves' involvement.

"Thanks, Officer," Natalie said.

Coffman and the other officers said their goodbyes and left.

Once Brock, Shawn, and Natalie went inside, they checked the security monitors to watch the police officers as they collected more shell casings and then left.

"What about Marek?" Natalie asked.

"I didn't see any sign of him, nor did I smell him," Brock said.

"Me neither, though he probably was wearing hunter's spray." Shawn took a seat in the living room with them while they continued to watch the security monitors in the event Marek tried coming for them once the police were gone.

"Want something to drink?" Natalie asked.

"A beer, if you have any," Shawn said. "Unless, of course, you don't have any alcohol in the house because you have a drinking problem."

Natalie smiled at him and got up from the couch. "I was so going to mention Marek to Kittie when she said that."

"You did good, Natalie, with the guy who reached the house. I'm sorry you had to deal with that," Brock said, joining her to help out.

"I saw him coming to the house via the security cameras. I didn't want him breaking down my door or smashing a window. Luckily, I caught him when he lifted a plant pot in one hand, ready to strike a window. I threw open the door and shot him before he could drop the pot and aim at me. I just hoped I wouldn't kill him outright, and that I was able to stop him so he couldn't terminate me. The round struck him in the shoulder, and he dropped his rifle."

Brock pulled her into his arms and kissed her. "I didn't think Dexter would hire human hit men."

"He's making too much money. And he doesn't want to leave his mansion of a ranch house behind," Shawn said.

"He's an idiot if he thinks the pack wouldn't retaliate," Brock said.

Natalie shook her head. "He must not have been with one. Maybe he doesn't realize how close-knit they can be. He might even believe that if the crime was out of the pack's jurisdiction, they wouldn't come after him. Besides, he has a grudge concerning you."

"True." Brock helped her carry the beers into the living room, while she brought a bag of chips.

They were still monitoring the listening bug Brock had left in Kittie's purse.

"I was glad when Brock learned you were all right and helped me out. Those guys were definitely military-trained," Shawn said, drinking his beer.

Brock grabbed some chips. "Yeah. I think the only reason we got the better of them was that they didn't realize we could see them in the dark or smell their scents. And we could hear them moving around too. It really helped to give us the advantage."

"You know, the good thing is the police will be able to learn who these guys are from their military records if they served in the armed forces." Shawn took a handful of chips.

"Yeah, and if they haven't registered their weapons in Texas, they can be charged with that. Just using the guns to commit a crime should get them some time. The only problem is that they didn't steal anything or injure any of us, so they might not get much time for it." Natalie bit into a potato chip with a snap.

"Glad they didn't injure any of us," Brock said. "At least they'll have arrest records. If they do get out, they probably won't try to come here again."

Motion-detector lights went on near her parents' home, and they watched the security cameras to see what had made them come on. Brock pointed to the culprit. "One of the tabbies prowling around."

Natalie frowned and got up from the couch. "The cats should have scattered, but I want to make sure they're okay."

"I'll handle it," Shawn said.

"Will they come to you?" she asked. "They can be shy around new people."

"Yeah, I've made friends with all of them. Do you have something I can use to entice them to come to me?"

"Yeah, sure." She headed into the kitchen and brought him out treats and a little bell. "Just jingle this, and they should come running."

"Okay, thanks." Shawn headed outside with the bell and the treats.

She and Brock continued to watch the monitors and saw Shawn jingling the bell and heard him calling for the kitties. She smiled. He was good with cats. They started to appear, and not only were there the four they were caring for, but a new one appeared out of the blue.

"Yours too?" Brock asked. He didn't remember seeing more than the four cats.

She chuckled. "Nope. Looks like we have another new cat. We'll have to get it fixed and get its vaccinations."

Shawn was close to the carriage house, petting the cats as they wrapped their bodies around his legs. Once he had finished feeding them, he rejoined Brock and Natalie in the house. "That's all of them, right?"

"Plus one," Natalie said, smiling.

Then they heard a door slam—the sound coming from the listening bug on Kittie's purse.

They all sat up and listened.

—⁓—

"What happened?" Dexter asked Marek, so angry about all the damn foul-ups. Hell, couldn't anyone get anything right? Though he knew with Brock fighting him every step of the way, it wouldn't be easy to get rid of Brock, the she-wolf, and the other man, which was why he'd hired the best. He wondered who the other man was. Another damn SEAL? Without a last name, Dexter couldn't learn who he was.

"Hell, I thought you said these men were supposed to be damn good at their jobs. Brock and the others took them all down. I stayed around in my wolf form so I could listen in, and one of the cops said the woman even shot one of the men!" Marek sounded furious. "I thought she was just a damn master gardener."

Dexter swore. He'd paid top money for those men.

At least enough to get the mercenaries to agree to do the job. Thankfully, the rest of their fee wasn't to be paid until they'd finished the job. And it was good damn money. "The police arrested *all* of them?"

"Yeah."

"At least they can't tie this to any of us." Dexter started to pace.

"Where's Kittie?" Marek asked, sounding surprised not to see her there.

Dexter stopped in place. "She went to bed. Said she had a headache." He began walking again. "You and I need to have a talk. Let's go in the kitchen and grab a beer."

"Yeah, sure." Marek sounded a little wary.

He ought to be. Damn fool.

"Did you try to kill any of them after the police left?" Dexter asked, pulling a beer out of the fridge for each of them. He opened his and took a swig.

"Are you kidding? The three of them were armed and staying together as a team. If the hired guns couldn't remove them as a threat, you think I could have? I'm sure they must have seen the hired gunmen on the security cameras, because Brock and the other guy didn't come out as wolves, like you thought they would." Marek guzzled down his beer.

"The gunmen I hired were supposed to disable the damn security cameras!"

"They did. I saw them cut the wires to several of them."

"Decoys then?" Dexter's property had security all over the place, but he hadn't expected the garden center to have that much.

"Hell. Maybe."

Dexter and Marek were quiet for a few minutes, drinking their beers.

"And you stayed out of sight? None of them saw you?" Dexter asked Marek.

"Yeah. If the gunmen had any inkling I was out there, they would have only seen a wolf, figuring I was a dog. But they didn't see me. I'm sure they would have shot me if they'd thought I was the owners' dog and would warn the owner and the rest of them."

"Hmm."

"What do we do now? Should we go as wolves?" Marek asked.

"I want to know what this business was with you and Kittie planning to go solo, leaving with the rest of the team. Not my brother, of course. He'd see you dead first."

Silence.

"I...I don't know what you're talking about," Marek finally said.

"See, here's the thing. First, you screw up big time. I mean, none of this would be happening if you hadn't missed your flight and lost your bag and our money. My brother had to deal with the fallout in Denver, and he's still waiting for the new money to hand over to the guys who are waiting impatiently. These guys you don't want to cross. Not that you want to cross me either."

Dexter couldn't believe that she-wolves could stir up so much trouble. It appeared Kittie had been the force that had changed his crew's loyalties. Not to mention the trouble Dexter was having with Lettie in Boulder—and his damn brother better make this right, or Dexter would have his head too—and that she-wolf Natalie grabbing the bag of money and getting Brock involved in the first place.

"No. Hell no," Marek said, his eyes wide.

"All right. Then your girlfriend has one little job: learn about the security systems in the houses. What does she do? She drives *your* car. Whose lame-ass idea was that?"

Marek didn't say a thing, and Dexter knew the guy had to figure he was in deep shit.

"You didn't know?" Dexter asked, sounding as if he didn't believe it for a moment.

"No."

"Her car was in the shop, she said. She didn't have another car to use, so you told her to use yours," Dexter said.

"I didn't."

Dexter knew Marek was lying to save his own skin.

"Where were you? You left your keys and car behind? While she had a mission?"

"All right. Antonio picked me up so I could help him clean bills because of the time constraints on this batch of money. She took my car and put a towel on the seat so she didn't have my scent on her. They didn't know what my car looked like."

"But these wolves did know what your car looked like. They ran the plates, found out the car belonged to you, and the connection was made. She's a wolf, your girlfriend, and now they know you're both implicated in the counterfeiting scheme and where you live, and after someone trying to take them out, they'll want blood. Your blood." Moron.

"Uh, uh, okay, we'll leave. Go to Mexico. Disappear." Marek set his empty beer can on the counter.

"Here's the thing, Marek. Your girlfriend was seeing your brother. They planned to leave you to hang for this."

Marek sputtered, "Jimmy? I'll...I'll kill him."

"I don't blame you. I'd feel the same way. Especially since she's got something going with Antonio too." Dexter was well rid of the bitch. "I still need your brother and his friend. You, not so much. But if you really want to leave, I think it's a good idea. Being the good-natured sport that I am, I'll help you." Dexter pulled out the gun.

Marek stared at it in disbelief. "What...what are you going to do? Is...is that *my* gun? It was my money I lost, damn it. And I said we'd leave. Like now."

"Oh, you will. You can join Kittie." A shot sounded as Dexter pulled the trigger. Then another. Marek crumpled to the kitchen tile floor. "No one crosses me and lives to tell about it," Dexter said. "Ever."

Chapter 17

NATALIE SAT BACK AGAINST THE COUCH. "THAT DOES AWAY with two of them. Now, if Dexter would eliminate Antonio and Jimmy for colluding with Kittie, we'd only have to terminate Dexter and his brother. If Dexter is getting rid of loose ends, Jimmy will most likely be on his hit list so he doesn't come back for revenge. Unless Marek and his brother are on the outs with each other. Since Jimmy was seeing Kittie, it sounds like they were."

"Agreed," Brock said.

"I wonder what this guy's going to do about the dead bodies," Natalie said.

"He used Marek's gun. How much do you want to bet he's going to try to make it look like Marek shot his girlfriend and then killed himself?" Shawn asked. "Her body wasn't where Marek could see it. If I were up to no good and wanted to frame someone, that's what I'd do. Carry her to bed, make her nice and comfortable, cover her as if I adored her, clean up the mess in the other room, then shoot myself."

Natalie smiled. "Good to know."

Shawn smiled at her. "At least that's how I figure Dexter must have done it. I doubt he would have buried her. He has to make it look like a murder-suicide."

"No suicide note though?" she asked.

"Dexter might have even done that. It would be easy to write because Marek's girlfriend had been unfaithful to him," Shawn said. "About the security cameras... You had decoys up around the houses?"

"Yes. The fake security cameras give any intruder a false sense of security. Once they thought they'd sabotaged the real ones, they didn't look any further for any others." Natalie took a deep breath and let it out. "Once you've had armed trespassers, it makes you wary of it happening again. Though I never expected something like this to happen."

"I would never have thought it. They looked like the real thing to me," Brock said.

"Oh, and another thing," Natalie said. "They were spending Eugenia's social security checks. I wonder where the older lady has gone."

Shawn snorted. "Died? And they're spending her checks? But did she die naturally or otherwise?"

Brock thought Shawn's explanation sounded reasonable when he finally got ahold of Vaughn. "Hey, have you learned anything about the other men Marek was associating with in Denver, particularly the ones he was meeting at the pub?"

"Yeah, I did what you suggested and offered each of them a hundred-dollar counterfeit bill to tell me all they knew about Marek. Of course, they wanted to know why I was asking, and I told them I was a PI trying to track him down for committing a crime. They're wolves. I didn't have to say anything more than that."

"Did they notice the money wasn't real?"

Vaughn chuckled. "No. Which was a good thing for them. I was certain they didn't have anything to do with what he was participating in. I told them Marek was working with another of their friends. Dexter Cartwright.

Now *that* got a reaction. The two men looked at each other. They said if anyone was doing something criminal, Dexter would be the one to put it together. They said Dexter was always talking about coming up with the perfect crime."

"What about Dexter's brother?" Brock asked.

"I'm still trying to locate Trenton. He must be using an alias. No luck so far."

"You didn't leave the fake bills with the other men, did you?" Brock asked.

Vaughn chuckled. "No. I told them what they were, and the men were shocked and impressed. But not enough to be mixed up in any of it. I took the money from them though."

"Good." Brock told him what was going on with them. "We've learned Ink Man is actually Jimmy, Marek's brother. Nothing going on there?"

"Not yet. What about you folks?"

"Three human assassins, all in police custody."

"Hell, Jillian and I should have been there helping out."

"We're still listening in to the drama at Marek's place, so I'll let you go. And you still have a mission there. Stay safe."

"Okay, talk later." Then they ended the call.

Dexter was talking on a phone at Marek's place, the listening bug in Kittie's purse picking up half the conversation. They wished they could hear the other man's part of the conversation.

"Hey, Jimmy, just calling you to let you know Marek and his girlfriend have been cut out of the business," Dexter said, pacing around the room.

Brock was surprised Dexter would tell him that.

"Don't worry about them. If you screw up like they both did, then you're out of here." More pacing. "Let me ask you something though. Did either of them ask you if you wanted to go into business with them? And cut me out of the process?" Pause.

"Well, why the hell didn't you tell me?" Dexter was irate.

"I'm confused," Natalie said. "Kittie called Antonio, and he was calling her 'honey.' So was she really having an affair with both Antonio and Jimmy? I didn't think she could get away with it without one of the men catching on."

"A threesome, maybe," Shawn said.

Dexter cleared his throat, catching their attention. "Kittie wasn't serious? Sure, she was. Better be glad you said no to her. I'd hate to lose my Ink Man."

"I can't believe Jimmy wouldn't want to kill Dexter for murdering not only his own brother, but also the woman he had been with," Brock said to Natalie and Shawn as they listened to the conversation via the listening bug. Brock was damn glad he'd slipped it into Kittie's bag and nobody had been aware of it. It was better than being a fly on the wall.

"What about Antonio?" Dexter asked Jimmy. He paced some more. "Okay, good. Loyalty is rewarded. You've got the new money, so I expect it to get done right, no foul-ups, and on time... The problem wolves? Don't worry about them. Marek wouldn't have been stupid enough to tell them anything about the rest of us. He told them he was just the middleman and had clandestine meetings with the man in charge but didn't know who he was. And that he didn't know anything else about the operation—in other words, about you and Antonio."

Then the front door squeaked open and slammed shut. Brock, Natalie, and Shawn listened, but they didn't hear Dexter saying anything anymore, nor did they hear him moving around the house.

"Sounds like Dexter finally left Marek's house," Shawn said. "Sure wish we had a bug on him."

"What about the aunt? If she's dead, did Marek bury her in the backyard? If she was buried in a cemetery, they'd have to have a death certificate, and Social Security would have been notified and the checks would have stopped," Natalie said. "The house is in both her and Marek's names, so he could stay there indefinitely."

"Unless she's off on a vacation somewhere, but I doubt it. Not when they're spending her money," Shawn said.

"Let me see." Brock looked her up on one of his databases. "No record of her being deceased."

"Here's an idea. What if Marek didn't use his own money to create the counterfeit money? Maybe he's using her checks," Shawn said.

"That would make sense. That's why Dexter didn't seem worried about her being around or that she might suddenly show up when he murdered Kittie and Marek. Though she could have been out of town on a trip, and he knew that. But we still have the comment Kittie made about cashing Eugenia's check." Brock looked up Marek's bank accounts. "Marek still has a bank account in Denver and one in Amarillo, joint account with his aunt."

"As long as no one knows she's dead, he could spend

her social security checks and any other checks she might get online in the joint account, no questions asked," Natalie said.

"It happens. Hell, on one case I checked into, the guy was a drug addict and his mom was an alcoholic and they were both hoarders. They lived together, and they'd been so abusive to other family members when they checked on their welfare that no one visited them any longer."

"I'm surprised the family would hire a PI to check into it," Natalie said. "Why not just call the police?"

"They'd had their own run-ins with the police. Money is always a good motive too. There was a sizable inheritance that the mom should have had, and truth be told, that's what the other siblings were more interested in—payment for all the abuse and neglect they'd suffered while in the care of their mom. I found the man lying on the couch in her home, dead. He had died weeks earlier there, a drug overdose. I could smell another body too. I made my way through the narrow aisles they'd left to reach the bathroom and two bedrooms and was heading for the bedroom where I smelled the odor of another decomposing body.

"I opened the door, and she was in bed, dead, just a skeleton and gray hair, covered with the comforter, the whole room filled with boxes of stuff, only a small path from her bed to a dresser, the closet, and the door. She was still wearing a nightgown. There didn't appear to be any violence, just that she had died in her sleep. Maybe. Unless she'd overdosed on drugs too. But the son had been cashing her disability and social security checks for years when she had been dead all that time."

"How do you know for certain how long it had been?" Natalie asked.

"Sitting on the bedside table, a diary was open, and the last entry was dated five and a half years earlier."

"Ewww. Can you imagine living in a place like that? With a dead body? Your own mother?" Natalie shook her head. "Did the other kids get the inheritance?"

Brock smiled.

"What? If she'd been a horrible mother, they could have at least received some money for it," Natalie said.

"Between paying the utilities and taxes, and the son's drug habit, no. I asked his siblings if they knew how he managed to keep up with his taxes, utility bills, et cetera. I figured someone would have removed him from the property and disposed of the house. They said the house was paid off, and other bills were on auto-pay out of his mother's and his bank account and had been for years. But the taxes hadn't been paid for the last year. He was looking at losing the house if he didn't pay them. The police would have found his dead mama and him then."

"Gross," Natalie said.

"Yeah, but it goes to show you that it's done—a relative stealing the funds of a dead person, whether they caused their death or it was of natural causes. Too easy to just keep cashing those checks. I can't imagine living with a dead body in the house for long, but for years?" Brock shook his head.

Natalie was still looking for things on her laptop while Brock was doing his own searches. She suddenly turned her laptop so Brock and Shawn could see it. "Hey, here's a listing for an Ink Man Tattoo Artist on Facebook. His shop, The Inking Spot, is located in

Amarillo, Texas. Maybe he does tattoos as his regular business, and the counterfeiting is on the side."

"Hell, Natalie, if you weren't a top-rate gardener, you should join me in the PI business full-time." Brock gave her a hug.

She beamed.

"His first name wouldn't happen to be Jimmy, would it?" Shawn asked, moving closer to see the screen.

"No, it doesn't list it. That would be too easy. Since wolves don't wear tattoos, he must love to do artwork on humans." Natalie shrugged. "It could be a way to stay employed while having other...pursuits of a shadier nature."

"It's worth checking into. He's got a phone number and address. Inking done by appointment only." Brock leaned back on the couch. "We ought to call and ask for Jimmy and see what kind of a reaction we get."

"He might run if he doesn't recognize your voice and he thinks you might be one of the wolves who are causing trouble for this group of counterfeiters," Natalie said.

"Yeah, it would work even better if we looked him up at his place of business. We could smell that he was a wolf and—" Brock said.

"See if his scent was on the money in the bag I took!" Natalie said.

Brock smiled at her. He loved how excited she could get when she was helping them solve the puzzle. He hadn't thought of it as quickly as she had, but she was right. Ink Man most likely had handled the money.

"Yeah, but the problem with that is he'll recognize we're wolves, know we're not coming for an ink job, and suspect why we're there," Shawn said.

"Right. And then he'd alert his 'master,' and Dexter would be on our case again. Though I really don't believe Dexter would hire the hit men and then give up on dealing with us after we turned them over to the police. I'd say he'll be even more determined to eliminate us," Brock said. "Though I feel the same way about him, after he tried to kill me while dealing in drugs."

"I don't blame you at all. Do you think he paid them in real money?" Natalie asked.

The guys laughed.

"It's probably more like you get half the money to sign up for the job and the rest when the job is done. Since they're assassins, I'd say he wouldn't risk giving them fake money. Good way to have them come back to eliminate him." Brock thought some more about how they were going to deal with this. "Rather than try to speak to Jimmy personally, we can break into his ink shop when he leaves. Then we can smell his scent and learn if the ink, money, and printer they're using are in there."

"But you heard Dexter," Natalie said. "They're going to be working on the money. And he wants it done soon. They may be at it all hours of the night until they're done."

"That's true. We need to go," Brock said, "and try to catch them at it then."

"All of us?" Shawn asked.

"Yeah, I don't want to leave the two of you here if Dexter plans another attack at the garden center. Natalie's right. Jimmy and Antonio could be working on this now at the ink shop, if that's where they have their operation set up. It might even be at Dexter's ranch."

"Then we can confiscate the money, printer, ink, everything if it's at the ink shop. Good deal," Shawn said.

"And the men?" Natalie asked. "You don't want to just…kill them, do you?"

"If it's us or them, we'll handle it. *If* they'll cooperate, we'll turn them over to the JAG policing force. They'll incarcerate them in their special facilities, but if they're out to kill us, that deal's off the table. Hell, maybe we can even confiscate the money before they bleach off the ink from the real money, and they can use it to help pay for their incarceration," Brock said.

"Sounds good to me," Natalie said.

Thankfully, they had more guns, since the ones they had used on the gunmen had been given to the police for now.

Brock rubbed Natalie's back as they headed out to his vehicle. "We'll get this done and get back to more pleasurable business."

She nodded. "I sure hope so."

They headed in Brock's Humvee in the direction of the ink shop, all the way across town in a seedier part of the city filled with bars, pawnshops, tattoo parlors, and triple-X-rated movie theaters. Brock didn't like having Natalie with them, but he sure as hell wasn't leaving her behind in case Dexter retaliated while he and Shawn were away.

"Are you okay?" Brock asked her as he drove through the area, looking for the right shop.

"Yeah. I mean, sure, I'm nervous. I'm not into all this kind of work like you are. I don't have the combat training, and I feel out of my element to an extent. But I'm okay. I can use the gun to defend myself."

"Should one of us go as a wolf?" Shawn asked.

"They won't be wolves if they're working on the

money. It's better for us to be armed with guns, rather than with wolf teeth," Brock said.

"There's the shop." Natalie pointed at it. "Looks like they've got some muscle."

Two big, muscular guys were smoking and leaning against the brick wall of the shop. They were talking to each other, casting a glance around at anyone walking on the sidewalks.

"Yep, they're definitely the muscle. They probably are there to ensure no one bothers the geniuses at work." Brock was disappointed but not completely surprised the counterfeiters would have some other men working for them.

Shawn snapped a couple shots of the men. "Wolf or human?"

"After Dexter sent the humans, it's a fifty-fifty toss-up. But those men definitely are protecting the shop, and they're being obvious about it, not hiding in the shop to wait on the unsuspecting criminal," Brock said. "I suspect they'd be in the shop if they thought we might come here. They'd be lying in wait for us."

"Dexter must have truly believed Marek's lies and doesn't think he spilled his guts to us," Natalie said. "He's not as bright as I thought he was."

"Looks that way," Brock said, "which is a good thing for us."

"Now what?" Shawn asked as Brock drove on by the shop.

"We'll see if there's a back alley and another way in."

Chapter 18

BROCK PARKED THE HUMVEE IN THE ALLEYWAY BEHIND THE door to The Inking Spot. There were no windows or security cameras, just a metal door. Brock had lockpicks—most *lupus garous* did, in case they needed shelter to shift—so he figured he'd get in without any trouble as long as opening the door didn't trigger an alarm.

"Why don't you stay in the Humvee with your cell phone ready to call 911 if we don't come out in a reasonable amount of time. I'll leave you the keys in case you need to hightail it out of here," Brock told Natalie.

She didn't look happy about the prospect of being left behind, but it was bound to get ugly inside, and she wasn't trained for this.

"Just keep the doors locked. Call the police if you have any trouble with thugs in the area harassing you. The Humvee was bulletproofed after I'd been on some tough assignments."

"Did he tell you how many times he's been shot?" Shawn added. "After that, he opted for a bulletproof Humvee."

"There were other situations than when Dexter shot you?" Natalie asked, looking worried.

"That was the only time I took so many rounds." Before Natalie asked about the other times, Brock said, "We'll be back as soon as we can."

He got out of the vehicle, and Shawn joined him.

Brock prayed no one learned Natalie was in the Humvee in the back alley, and he and his cousin didn't get themselves shot.

"If I hear shooting?" she asked.

"Don't call it in. Hopefully, no one else will either," Brock said. "If we're wounded, we'll make our way out to the Humvee and leave with you."

Then he used his special lockpicks and unlocked the back door. Inside, heavy metal was playing. Good. It would help cover the noise they made when they entered.

Brock opened the door and the damn thing creaked, but no one seemed to hear them.

He slipped inside and heard a printing press running upstairs. Shawn followed him inside. The hall led to a restroom, the door open, and no one was inside. A staircase was off to the right. Up front, a couple of chairs and a table were situated for tattooing. No one was there either.

Brock motioned he was going up. He just hoped the damn steps wouldn't creak as much as the back door did. He was again glad for the deafening music. He couldn't believe they'd play it so loud. The wolves had enhanced hearing, but if they listened to loud noises like this, their hearing could be affected permanently, just like a human's.

Then a man said, "Shit, we got company."

Security cameras. Damn.

Brock bolted up the stairs, not wanting to be shot where he had no cover, while Shawn took cover downstairs.

A dark, shaggy-haired man came out of an upstairs room shooting. He looked a lot like Marek. His brother, Jimmy, most likely.

Brock dove into a room filled with rubber tubs containing bleach. Money was sitting in several of the tubs, and the chemical burned Brock's eyes and throat. He hid behind the plastic tubs.

The guy came around the corner, shooting into the room, the rounds striking the rubber tubs, the bleach pouring out of the holes.

"How many?" another guy asked, his voice harsh, frantic.

"Hell, it's a male wolf. I can't see him. But I can smell him." The man fired more shots at the rubber tubs. "He's in the cleaning room."

Brock lay low. He needed to get Jimmy's gun and use it on the other guy. He needed to make it look as if the two men had had a falling-out. But he was pinned down. He hoped his cousin remained safe until he could put at least one of the men out of action.

"I might have killed him," the man said and began slowly moving into the room.

Good. That was the best scenario Brock could hope for. He had only one chance to do this right if he wasn't going to get himself killed. He'd have to put his SEAL training to good use. He low-crawled around the tubs, angling himself so the shooter would approach the same way Brock had initially moved, his scent still in that area. But Brock was moving around to the other side, trying to get into position so he could tackle the man, disarm him, knock him out, and use Jimmy's gun on the other man.

"Jimmy?" the other man called out from the room where the printing press was running.

In the room where Brock was, Jimmy continued to move cautiously toward the tubs. Brock had to risk rushing forward before Jimmy reached the tubs and could see there was no one behind them any longer. He didn't want to shoot Jimmy with his own gun and was still too far away to just jump on him in one leap. He had to move several steps, and Jimmy would undoubtedly turn to shoot at him as soon as he saw movement.

Shawn began moving up the stairs, the wooden steps creaking.

Before the other man could shoot at Brock's cousin, Brock jumped to his feet and rushed to pounce on Jimmy with steely determination. Jimmy swung around to face Brock, but he was too late. Brock quickly grabbed Jimmy's arm and twisted his thumb, forcing him to drop the gun. Then Brock knocked him out with a well-placed strike to the side of the man's temple. Jimmy collapsed, and Brock grabbed his gun.

Whoever the other guy was, he was hesitant to come into the room shooting.

"Got company!" Shawn shouted when the shop's front door burst open. He raced up the remaining stairs, coming to help, no matter what the situation was up there.

The other guy came out of the printing room shooting, but Brock was ready for him. He fired three shots from Jimmy's gun, killing the man. Both were wolves. Were the musclemen too?

Shawn retrieved the other man's gun, and he and Brock waited for the musclemen to come up the stairs. The two men hesitated just inside the building near the front door. Then one of them slammed it shut.

"Antonio," one muscleman called out from down below but well back of the stairs.

"Come on down and tell us what you want," the other

guy said, probably assuming Brock and Shawn had taken the other men out.

There was no way that these men were going to give Brock and Shawn what they wanted without a fight.

"They came in the back way, and there's a Humvee out there," one of the guards said to the other.

Brock couldn't wait any longer for the men to approach him and Shawn, worried the musclemen would try to grab Natalie as a hostage, if they could.

He carried Jimmy to the stairs, holding the unconscious man in front of him, and moved down a couple of steps. One of the musclemen came out of his hiding place and began shooting, killing Jimmy. Using Jimmy's gun, Brock blasted away at the shaved-headed muscleman. He went down, and Brock released Jimmy. The dead man tumbled down the stairs and landed at the bottom.

Brock charged down the stairs and fired off Jimmy's gun. The second guard shot back, grazing Brock's arm. Shawn was above Brock on the stairs and fired two rounds into the muscleman's forehead. The man crumpled to the floor dead.

"What do we do with the money and printing press?" Shawn asked.

"Pull the money out of the containers of bleach, and throw it in a container we can carry with us. I'll round up the money they haven't tried to remove the ink from yet and the stuff they're printing so Dexter doesn't get ahold of it. We'll need to set up the guns to make it look like they had a shoot-out between them." Brock called Natalie while he dropped the gun off with Jimmy where he had fallen to the bottom of the steps. "Shawn and I are both fine. How are you?"

"I'm good."

"We're bringing money out."

"They saw your Humvee," Natalie said. "I'm glad you're both fine. I didn't call the police, as much as I wanted to when I heard all the shooting."

"Good. I've got to deal with the offset printing press, security cameras, and ink and such. Be there in a few." Brock knew Dexter could afford to buy another offset press, but finding another good counterfeiter would be a different story. Especially one who was a wolf. "Hopefully, they didn't have time to tell Dexter what was going on."

Brock rushed back up the stairs to help Shawn. His cousin was reading through a journal.

"What now?" Brock found a box to put the printed fake money into.

"Hey, this guy was an apprentice. The master counterfeiter could still be doing this crap, and if he's a wolf—"

"We've got to deal with him." Brock began dismantling the offset press, breaking the pieces to ensure no one could use it again. "Destroy the ink so they can't use that mixture again."

"How? I don't want to pour it into the toilet. Environmental concerns."

"Add it to the tubs with bleach."

Shawn smiled. "Why didn't I think of that? Hey, there's glue here too. And more paper, a whole roll of it, and cut paper that looks like regular paper but about half the weight of a bill. And…automotive paint?"

"Just pour all the ink, paint, and glue into the bleach. We'll bring the paper with us. That's the special paper used for making counterfeit bills."

After they demolished the small offset press and the other components the counterfeiters had used to create the fake money, Brock destroyed what he could of the equipment they had used for photolithography.

"What the hell is that?" Shawn asked, carrying a couple of butt rolls of paper to the stairs.

"He was using photolithography. It uses light to transfer a pattern to a surface for etching."

"You'd think he'd use an ordinary digital printer, the way some do," Shawn said. "Less expensive than an offset press, and less intensive work."

"But the quality isn't as good," Brock said. "These guys wanted to sell what looked like the real thing so no one would get caught. Not the criminal element they sold to. No one. And then they could sell more at a higher dollar amount. I've got the etched metal plates. We'll have to find a way to destroy them."

"That's how they were applying the ink onto the sheet of paper." Shawn glanced at the security monitors. "I'll grab the security cameras."

"Good. There are two: one in the front room and one up here."

"Handling it," Shawn said.

Brock rushed outside with the plates and a box of money. Natalie unlocked the car door for him.

"Hurry. With all the shooting—" she said.

"Yeah, I know. But in this neighborhood, it probably happens a lot." Brock ran back inside and helped Shawn carry the rest of the money out to the Humvee. There was more than a million in fake bills, plus the rolls of paper that would have been used to create more of the stuff. "Hey, if Dexter was monitoring these guys…"

Brock fished in a bag he kept in his Humvee and pulled out a device that would look for listening devices. "I'll be right back. I'm going to check for Dexter's listening bugs." He quickly searched the place and found four. He destroyed them, then locked the front and back doors of the shop and climbed into the vehicle with his cousin.

"What exactly happened in there? From all the shooting going on, I wasn't sure any of you would make it out without wearing a bunch of bullet holes," Natalie said as Brock drove out of the alleyway and headed down one street and then another, just in case they were seen…or followed.

"Jimmy tried to shoot me. Then Antonio tried his hand at it. I guess the musclemen guarding the place out front heard shots fired and barged into the place." Brock settled back against the driver's seat as he drove onto another street.

"Did you get all the money?" she asked.

"Yeah. The real money that hadn't been whitewashed, still one-dollar bills, the fake money, and the blank bills. But they had started a new process using a roll of paper. Looks like we'll have to have a bonfire cookout at your place," Brock said. "The musclemen were human."

Shawn was flipping through the journal. "Okay, bad news. Some guy called Picasso was Ink Man's mentor. Apparently, a 'master' teaches an apprentice all the ins and outs. Jimmy was an artist, stealing cars and dealing in drugs, until he was removed from the streets to be apprenticed by Picasso."

"Great. Is Picasso a wolf then? Or human?" Natalie asked.

"Um, hold on." Shawn flipped through several pages. "Okay, good. He's human. Jimmy wrote down some important notes on how to create the bills, but then began to create his own. Genius, really. He wouldn't have needed the money from Marek after a while. He was beginning to create his own version."

"He wouldn't have needed Dexter's backing either," Brock said.

"Doesn't look like it. But he would probably have kept Antonio on to do the printing or bleaching, whatever he needed him for. The two of them would have done this together. Too much work for one person. Maybe Kittie would have been working with them on all this."

"I wonder how much it cost him to create the money," Natalie said.

"That's a good question. If he was getting thirty cents on the dollar for one hundred thousand, that's not all that much money. Especially not when they had to share it. But it looks like they made a hell of a lot more money than that," Brock said.

"Man, this journal says it all. Jimmy posed as a Sunday school teacher at one of the paper plants and got free butt rolls, the end of a roll of the 'good' stuff they could use for making the bills. Dexter's brother has been selling the counterfeit money to the Chinese, Russian, and Italian mafia, drug organizations, you name it. He lost a sale to one criminal faction because they bought superbills, ones so superior they're incredibly hard to detect as counterfeit. But it's really hard to find them that good, so other criminal elements bought from Dexter's brother."

"Wow, I've never heard of superbills before," Natalie said.

Brock said, "The new stuff looks perfect."

"According to the journal, it is," Shawn said. "The

guy must have been OCD to write all this stuff down. Treating it as an art and a science, based on all the experiments he did to create the right ink for the job, he outlined every detail in here. The new money is close to being superbills. He says here that he stole one of the hundred-dollar bills Picasso made so he could spend it, going against the master's rules. Jimmy loved the power of being able to spend the money, after creating something that would pass for the real thing."

"Hell, I would think Picasso would have been pissed if he'd learned about it," Brock said.

"He would have, according to Jimmy. Apparently, that was one of the first rules—not to spend the money they made. That was a good way to get caught up in it. They had to resell it to another party and distance themselves from the money. The other thing he was supposed to do was live on the low, printing only around a hundred thousand in bills a year, so he'd end up with thirty thousand, not so much that it might be noticeable."

Brock shook his head. "He's making a hell of a lot more than that."

"Then he took on these partners, and he had to make a whole lot more. They must have a lot more distribution, too, so they can all earn enough."

"What's with the glue and automotive paint?" Brock asked.

Shawn flipped to another page in the journal. "Okay, get this. The paint mixed with the ink made the ink stand out more, giving it more texture. The ink is raised on real bills, and counterfeit bills are flatter. The automotive paint helped. You won't believe this, but two thin pieces of paper are sandwiched together. Then Jimmy added a security strip on the left side and created his own watermark on the paper, using a special glue that won't add too much weight to the twin sheets of paper. They discovered that using a counterfeit pen on the paper in a phone book would show yellow, rather than the iodine turning black. Black ink means the paper is counterfeit, not starch-free. They tracked down one of the printers of the phone books to locate the paper they used. The only problem with these is that in the heat and humidity of the south, the paper money can separate."

Natalie chuckled. "I can just see that happening in Texas. Go to buy some clothes, and your money begins to peel apart right in front of the clerk. It would be a sure giveaway that it's not the real stuff."

"That means they are making two kinds. One is being sold to northern locations, and the other can be sold in the south. The money that's bleached," Brock said.

"The one-dollar bills will be a nice gift to the Greystoke pack. How will the police explain the shootings?" Natalie asked, sounding worried.

"I took one of their guns and used it on the others. It will look like they had a quarrel among thieves. There was enough evidence to indicate the men were up to no good. The destroyed offset press, the chemicals. The police might believe someone got away with the money. I doubt anyone in the ink shop had time to inform Dexter of the trouble they were in, unless he was monitoring them. I doubt the musclemen even knew him."

"You're bleeding." Natalie touched Brock's shoulder above the blood on his shirt.

"Superficial. Nothing but a graze."

"What about you, Shawn?"

"I'm good. Brock didn't let me terminate but one guy. I did the same as Brock and used one of the perp's guns to shoot the last guard. If Dexter heard what was going on through the listening bugs, how much do you want to bet he'll be after us?" Shawn asked.

"No doubt in my mind. If it's like Brock's listening bugs, Dexter could listen on his phone, right?" Natalie said.

"Yeah, but only if he's listening to it at the right time. He might be making phone calls or not monitoring the bugs all the time. He'd be smart to run, but I suspect he doesn't want to leave his ranch behind, and he'll want us dead after all the trouble we've been to him and his operation," Brock said.

"Don't you think he'll want all his stuff back before we get rid of it? What if he and his men are already at the garden center?" Natalie asked. "If he's got any other men on the payroll?"

"He's got about fifty miles to drive to reach the garden center," Brock said, "if he's out at his ranch and not in Amarillo right now."

"I say we park out away from the garden center, Natalie runs as a wolf, and you and I go in packing to check out the situation," Shawn said.

Brock turned down another street. He had to rethink this whole business. "Okay, if he was in town when we were eliminating his crew, he'll undoubtedly have to get some thugs together to come after us. That's only if he was listening to the bugs to hear what Antonio and Jimmy were discussing and what went down."

"He might try to head us off so he can steal back all this contraband before we destroy it," Shawn said. "If it were me, that's what I'd do. Maybe going to the garden center isn't such a good idea."

"You're right." Brock turned onto another road and headed out of town on the route they'd travel to Denver.

"Wait, where are we going?" Natalie seemed ready to bail out and go home.

"Home to Denver. We've got to get rid of this stuff, but we need the pack as backup." Brock called Devlyn on the Bluetooth. He wasn't risking Natalie's life on speculation. "This is Brock. Natalie and Shawn and I are headed home with more than a million dollars' worth of fake money, real money, and the paper to make the money. And the metal plates they used to print it. Dexter will want our heads and his stuff back."

"What about the garden center?" Devlyn asked.

"It will have to be closed for the day tomorrow, or we can send a team of our men to intercept Dexter and anyone else he sends to the center. We just can't let him get ahold of all this. And Natalie is in danger if we try to go there tonight."

"I'll send six men to open the garden center," Devlyn said.

"They won't know what to do," Natalie said. "What if you send extra men, and we meet halfway, transfer all this stuff to another vehicle, and someone can drive back to your pack with it? In the meantime, we'll have the extra men to help us fight Dexter and whoever else he manages to call on, and we can go back to the garden center. Your men won't be able to run it without me there."

Devlyn said, "What do you think, Brock?"

Brock knew Devlyn was more worried about Natalie

than anything else. "All right. As much as I don't want to take Natalie there, with more men, we should be able to manage it. We need to get rid of this contraband too."

"Okay. Sending vehicles and men. One of the vehicles will continue with you, and the others will haul off the loot and come back home so we can dispose of it all properly."

"Thanks, Devlyn. We'll meet up with them in about three hours at a travel center at the halfway point."

Chapter 19

SHAWN SIGHED. "I DON'T THINK THERE'S ANY WAY YOU'RE stopping Natalie from helping you with this mission, Brock. You ought to just have her join you in your PI business."

Brock let out his breath. "I *really* don't want Natalie to be in the middle of this."

"I *am* in the middle of this already. As soon as I took Marek's bag, I got us enmeshed in this. I want to help you to see it through."

"Well, it's a good thing you *did* grab his bag, because if Marek had been caught with the fake money, it could have spelled real trouble for the rest of us," Shawn said. "Not to mention that the more wolf players there are, the more likely one of them would have been caught by the police sooner or later."

Brock glanced at her, worried she was feeling responsible for all this. "Shawn's right. You did all our kind a big service. If you hadn't picked up that suitcase when you did, no telling where this could have gone down the line."

"Part of me understands that, but I also feel that here my parents are, getting interested in joining your pack, and look at all the trouble I've caused you. You're wounded, for heaven's sake, and it's all because of me."

"This is just a graze," Brock reminded her. "It'll heal in no time."

"It's not the end of all this. Your brother and the others could be in real trouble too," she said.

"You have to understand that Vaughn and Jillian do this for a living. Both are hard-charging when it's time to deal with rogue shifters. This is their business. Frankly, it's all our business when we have rogues in our territory. My only regret is I couldn't just be with you as a newly mated wolf for days on end, enjoying our new status."

She smiled, and he was glad he could cheer her up a bit. But he was reminded she wasn't all that used to how a pack worked together. They had each other's backs, and they took down rogues when they needed to.

"I hope you're going to tell the rest of the pack about the two of you being mated soon. I hate knowing something like this and having to keep it a secret," Shawn said.

Brock chuckled. Shawn could never keep a secret about any kind of important news.

"Okay, I'll call my folks first to let them know. We've been kind of busy, and no time seemed right before. I don't want anyone else telling them before I do." Natalie got on her phone and called them, even though it was really early in the morning and she knew she'd be waking them.

Brock was glad she was finally telling them. He felt the same way as Shawn. He was having a hard time not howling about it to the world. He wanted to celebrate his mating with her, but also with the pack. Everyone would be thrilled. Which reminded him, he needed to discuss a wedding with her. He assumed she'd want to wait until after they moved to Greystoke and had their garden center operational so her parents could attend their daughter's wedding. He also needed to know where she wanted to go for a honeymoon. Anywhere with her would make it paradise.

"Hey, Dad, before the word gets out to anyone… Um." She glanced at Brock and smiled. "Yeah, we're mated. How did you guess?" She laughed. "Okay, we are." She took a relieved breath. "Thank goodness." She leaned against the seat, perfectly relaxed.

Brock wondered if her parents had decided to go ahead and tell Devlyn and Bella they were joining the pack.

"No, you need to stay there and just enjoy yourselves. Make arrangements if you need to for getting the ball rolling on setting up a new garden center. You don't need to be in Amarillo right now, with all that's going on. Yeah, we're being careful. Thanks. Yes, you can tell everyone you want to about us. A wedding? Once we get moved there. Sure. Love you and Mom. Thanks. Bye, Dad."

"They're joining the pack?" Brock asked, knowing it couldn't be anything else.

"Yes." She smiled at him and ran her hand over his leg. "They're thrilled and knew it would happen. They're going to get things in motion to buy the land for the garden center—they'd already picked out the perfect site—and check into who can begin construction on their home."

"We have members of the pack who can do all of that—licensed carpenters, electricians, plumbers, you name it."

"Wow, this is going to be wonderful."

Brock agreed. "You want to get married after we move you and your parents to Greystoke?"

"Yeah. After Angie did, I sure do."

"But after your parents are established there with their garden center first?"

"Yes. Right. After having so many wedding parties at the garden center, I can't think of a better place to have our own. I can tell you right now, my parents are going to be chomping at the bit to put the garden center and our homes in Amarillo up for sale, get moved, and start all over again. My parents always jump on a good thing and get to work on it right away. So yes, once they're moved, we can schedule it. But I'll need to stay with them in Amarillo to help out with the garden center and still do my lectures until we're moved."

"I'll help too."

"What about your PI cases?" Natalie sounded surprised he would give up his work just to help her and her family.

"I had thought I would work some cases in Amarillo if I needed to, but I'm not going to bother. I'll put my work on hiatus while I concentrate on doing anything I can to help all of you get things ready to move to Greystoke. You and your parents are my priority."

She smiled at him. "Thanks, Brock. We'll need to put the places up for sale, and then we can start to have sales to reduce our stock. No sense in bringing it with us. We'll just order all new merchandise in Colorado. We'll be carrying some different plants that suit the conditions there anyway."

"What about our honeymoon?"

"Hawaii. If that's okay with you. I've never been

there, and I'd love to run as wolves in the tropics. And go diving with you. As long as we have my parents' new garden center up and running first."

"We'll have enough staff to work there that your parents won't even miss you," Shawn said.

Brock smiled. "Shawn's right. Hawaii sounds like a great honeymoon spot. Diving and all the rest. You got it. Do you mind if I tell my brother we're mated? And then I need to tell our pack leaders."

"Go ahead. I know you're dying to."

"I am. But I know Vaughn's going to give me a hard time over it." Brock called his brother first. "Hey, are you still at Lettie's, set up and waiting?"

"Putting this on speaker so Jillian and the rest of our team can listen in. Yeah, Jillian and I and the other guys are still here, watching over both Lettie's house and the shop. No peep from anyone yet."

"Okay, well, Natalie and I have some good news."

"You're not mentioning Shawn, so don't tell me. The wolf who wasn't about to get hooked up with the she-wolf is mating her."

"Mated."

Jillian whooped. Brock smiled.

Vaughn laughed. "I knew it. Congratulations, Bro."

"I'm one lucky wolf," Brock said.

"Me too," Natalie said.

"I never believed you for an instant when you said you weren't interested in getting to know the lady. One look at her picture, and from everything Angie said about her, you were already sold," Vaughn said. "I'm glad you didn't wait long to come to your senses."

Smiling, Brock reached over and squeezed Natalie's hand.

"Yeah, well, any wolf who's willing to drive all the way to Texas to be my bodyguard makes for the perfect live-in mate. He's not bad at gardening either."

The guys laughed.

Natalie blushed. Brock loved her.

After they talked for a bit, telling them all that had happened to them in the interim, they let Vaughn and Jillian go so they could be prepared for whoever might show up at Lettie's place.

"So your parents are going to join the pack right away? No delay?" Brock couldn't believe how mating Natalie would make him feel so uplifted, and he was glad everything was turning out so well for them, if they could just resolve the business with this counterfeit ring.

Natalie nodded. "Yeah. Dad said there wasn't any reason to delay. They're ecstatic about us. I didn't know they'd been so anxious about me finding the right wolf. But apparently they were. Especially once Angie found a mate and moved in with him. Dad was afraid I'd be… I don't know. Depressed maybe? I wasn't. I was just glad Angie was so happy. But I did miss seeing her all the time. Dad said they knew this was the right move for all of us. They're just delighted. And they picked out a beautifully treed bit of acreage that will work well for the setting of their new garden center."

Brock was thrilled. "Are you going to tell Angie?"

"Dad said they would. They didn't want to disturb Angie and Aaron's honeymoon, but they know they will be just elated to learn the news, both about you and me, and about all of us joining the pack. It will put them over the moon."

Shawn piped up. "Hey, Brock, you'd better tell Bella

and Devlyn you and Natalie are mated. You know if the Silvertons tell them they're joining the pack, our leaders will assume the two of you are hooking up, but they'll want to hear it from you first."

"I'm calling them now." Brock knew Bella would want to set up a celebratory feast for the union between Brock and Natalie, but also for her parents for joining the pack.

As soon as he reached Bella, she called Devlyn to join her.

"What's up?" Devlyn asked, and Brock swore Devlyn knew this wasn't about the case they were working on.

"Natalie and I are mated wolves, and she'll be moving in with me after we handle whatever we need to back at her place."

"That's great news," Devlyn said.

"Congrats, you two. What about her parents?" Bella asked.

"If you're agreeable, which I assume you are, they're going to join the pack."

"Hallelujah," Devlyn said.

"That is wonderful news," Bella said. "When will you be joining us?"

"We're not sure. We need to handle this other business, put the garden center and houses up for sale, and whatever else we need to do. Natalie could move right in with me, and her parents can stay with us as long as they need to while they build a home and the garden center."

"Okay, just let us know how we can help make the transition go more smoothly," Bella said. "If they want to give the two of you more privacy, they'd be welcome to stay with us, or any number of other pack members."

"Thanks," Natalie said. "You don't know what a

change this is for us when we compare your pack with the other packs we've belonged to."

"Do they still exist?" Bella asked.

"The one that was fighting internally, no. They broke up. I don't know what happened to them. We don't know about the other two either. Thanks so much for all your help and how welcoming you've been," Natalie said.

"We're just thrilled my cousin found such a perfect mate and you are bringing your family into the pack too," Devlyn said.

"But who also brought all kinds of trouble to the pack," Natalie said regrettably.

"That couldn't be helped. These guys needed to be eliminated," Devlyn said. "They came into our territory with the counterfeit money with the intent of distributing it. You helped us to learn about it."

"Let us know when you'll be coming here so that we can schedule a celebration," Bella said.

"We will. Thanks again for allowing us to join the pack."

"Our pleasure," Bella said.

When they finally reached the travel center, Brock said, "We'll pull over up there and let the other folks know we're at the halfway point."

But he didn't need to. He saw his pack members coming out of the restaurant, waving. He was glad they were already there.

They quickly transferred all the money and paper to the car's hatchback, out of sight of the restaurant, and then wished Jacob well before he went back home. Brock noticed another pack member's car getting gas, four men in the car. They ignored Brock and the others, but as soon as Jacob got on the road, their car followed him. Brock was glad Devlyn had made sure Jacob had backup in case he ran into trouble. Brock and the others got into the two remaining vehicles and headed to Amarillo.

This time, two of Shawn's brothers, Heath and Tanner, rode with them.

"What's the game plan?" Heath asked. He was the doctor for the pack, but he was as rough and tumble, as ready to fight any rogue wolves, as the rest of them. And he could care for injuries if anyone got hurt.

"If Dexter and his men are at the garden center, we'll take them out," Brock said.

"Do you think Dexter tried to hit the garden center, discovered we didn't go there, and wondered if we headed to your pack in Colorado?" Natalie asked.

"It's possible. He might have assumed we'd do just what we did—get reinforcements and send the illegal goods back with some of our men." Brock loved how good Natalie was at figuring this stuff out.

"What if he continued on his way with some men to try to intercept the vehicle with the money and the rest of the contraband?" she asked.

"He wouldn't have had time to follow us. In any event, I made sure no one was. Unless he reached the travel station after we did and saw us transferring the money over, he wouldn't know we aren't carrying it. Dexter said he could get any kind of a vehicle, and no one could trace it. Does that mean he's into stolen cars too? Maybe. But it also means we would have a time knowing what he's driving. He most likely knows what I'm driving by now, the same with what you and your parents drive. If he's headed out this way now and sees us leaving, he could believe we did a transfer with our pack members and are going back to the garden center."

"Then he could just continue on toward Colorado to get rid of the other guy." Natalie sounded worried.

"Which is why another of our pack cars is following Jacob. One that didn't meet with us at the service station, in case Dexter did see anything. They'll be the backup for Jacob, in the event anyone goes after him. If someone had somehow seen the transfer, they won't know the second vehicle is with our pack."

"Is it just one driver too?" she asked.

"No. They have four men."

Natalie let out her breath in relief.

"Hopefully, we have all the bases covered. The game plan is we go to the garden center. Some of us will arrive as wolves, some armed as humans. The other vehicle will park out a way. I'll drive the Humvee to the carriage house because they already know I drive it and because it's bulletproof. We'll park in the garage, make sure the house is clear, then Natalie can watch the security monitors, and I'll stay with her while Heath, Tanner, and Shawn watch the house from the outside. The other men will check out her parents' place, and make sure it's all clear. One man will stay in the house to secure it, and the rest will do what you and Shawn are doing, watching and waiting for anyone to appear," Brock said.

Natalie turned to speak to Heath in the back seat. "Brock's injured, by the way. He won't let us look at his injury, so maybe you can."

Heath chuckled. "It must be nothing much, or Shawn

would have warned me about it, since Brock said nothing about it."

"It's just a graze. You know me. Unless I have three or more bullet wounds, it's not anything worth worrying about."

"Are you able to fight these guys, or are you here as the medic?" she asked Heath.

"Both."

"Then don't get yourself hurt."

Heath said, "Believe me, I intend to do the hurting if this guy and his men come here."

Chapter 20

WHEN THEY ARRIVED BACK AT THE GARDEN CENTER, NATALIE hoped this would end this morning, with all the bad guys gone and all the good guys safe and uninjured. Everyone had been taking turns catnapping on the trip to the halfway point and now the return home. "We need to get the cats in the house this time," she said.

Still not dawn, the motion-detector lights were going off. Some of the men were running as wolves as Brock drove into the garage and shut the garage door. He wouldn't let Natalie leave the Humvee until he and his cousins made sure her house was safe. "I'll get Shawn to gather them up, using the treats like he did before. He'll put them up at your parents' house?"

"Yes, thanks. And…I've got a gun," she reminded Brock.

"I know. Just humor me, will you?"

She sighed. "Go ahead, be my hero."

He leaned down and kissed her cheek. "I'm your bodyguard and your mate."

"And I'm thrilled for that." Even if she felt she could help out, he was a warrior and she was a gardener, so she understood his need to feel he had to protect her.

"Good." He gave her a reassuring smile and kissed her.

Then he shut her door, and he and the others entered the house, guns readied.

She sat in the garage, protected by the Humvee, trying to hear anything she could as the men walked through the house. The light in the garage was still on, but now it was fading. And then it was dark.

No one was shooting anyone, so that was good news. But she wanted to be with them, not sitting in the car where she couldn't see what was going on. She wasn't a sitter. She was a doer. But she wasn't foolhardy either. She waited for Brock to give her the all clear.

The door to the garage opened. Natalie readied her gun, but then she saw it was Brock, backlit by the light that was on in the house. She sighed and smiled.

He stalked to the Humvee and opened the door for her just as she was grabbing her purse and getting ready to leave the vehicle.

"Come on, honey. Everything's clear."

She left the car and hugged him. She hadn't realized how anxious she'd been about him and the others, particularly after the shoot-out Brock and Shawn had dealt with earlier. "Nobody's been here?"

"We can't determine if they have been for sure. They probably would have worn hunter's concealment so we wouldn't catch their scent." Brock held her tight, running his hand over her back in a comforting way. She loved how he made her feel protected and loved. But their intimate contact was getting other things worked up. Pheromones were coming to the forefront. She felt his cock stirring against her, and her nipples were beginning to peak.

He kissed her forehead. "It doesn't appear anyone has accessed either home. No broken windows or locks. Shawn called me from your parents' place. Dexter's men probably would have come here first, figuring this was where we'd brought the money." Brock's phone jingled as he led Natalie into the house and locked the garage door. "Yeah, Devlyn? Hell, that's good news. No one's here so far. We'll talk later. Have a great pack bonfire."

"They arrived safely in Greystoke with the money?" Natalie asked when Brock pocketed his phone.

"Yeah. No problem at all. And Vaughn called me before I went out to the Humvee to get you and said no one showed up to eliminate Lettie. The team is going to sit on her place for a couple more days, in case there's still trouble coming. Hopefully, we'll neutralize all the key players before long, but if not, she'll have to either move in with someone in the pack temporarily or hire protection. Our people can't provide her security long term in Boulder."

"She's lucky the pack members have offered her this much protection. I thought the world of you for sending your brother to protect Lettie, despite how she lied to you."

"You helped me see she wasn't so bad after all. You're a good influence on me."

She smiled wickedly at him, wanting to ravish him in the bedroom, but she was sure that wasn't on the agenda for now. "What do we do now?"

Brock led Natalie to her bedroom. "We'll work shifts through the day so we can get some sleep but still manage to run the garden center. You can help watch the security monitors, but for now, Heath will." Brock's hands massaged her shoulders, pulling the tension from them.

She felt like melting into the carpet. "And you?" She ran her hands underneath Brock's shirt, bare skin to bare skin. She loved feeling his toned muscles and smooth, warm skin, and she suspected he wanted to make love to her before things got bad. Which made him her perfect mate.

He smiled at her and combed his fingers through her hair. "I'm going to help alleviate some of the tension that keeps erupting between the two of us whenever we're hugging each other so you can get some sleep."

"You are *so* my hero!"

He chuckled, then began to kiss her, his hands slipping up her shirt and unfastening the clasp of her bra in front. Then he slid his hands over her breasts, making her already sensitive nipples scream for his touch. She moaned out loud.

"Wait."

No! She didn't want to stop this for even a second.

"Should have thought of this first." His voice was husky as he took a few strides toward the door and closed it. Then he rejoined her and took up where he left off, kissing her mouth, fondling her breasts beneath the T-shirt, making her feel sexy and wanted. "God, you smell so good," he said.

"And you." But that was all she could breathe out as he bent down to kiss her mouth again, their lips pressed gently at first, then more urgently. Her hands slipped under his shirt again, sliding over his hard muscles to his pebbled nipples. She had made them do that, arousing them, just like his cock was growing harder, pressed against her belly.

His hands moved to the bottom edge of her shirt. He lifted it to pull it off and quickly divested her of her lacy bra too.

For a moment, he looked down at her breasts, and then his hands tenderly stroked them.

He knew just how to get her motor running. Even now, she was wet and ready for him. And hot and needy.

Their heartbeats ramped up, and he nuzzled her face and nibbled on her earlobe, his breath hot against her ear, tickling her, and she smiled. He cupped her breasts and began to massage them. Her nipples were so receptive as she leaned into his hands, wanting more of the heat and friction of his touch. Her breasts were achy and heavy, and she loved the way he enjoyed touching her.

He rubbed his body against hers, and she felt his cock fully aroused, her blood already hot with desire. He was so sexy that she just wanted to eat him all up.

"Hmm," she said, wrapping her arms around his neck and rubbing her body against his swollen cock. Oh, she was so ready for this.

He groaned with need, and she licked his chin, telling him she felt the same as he did.

He pulled off his shirt and dropped it on the bed. Wanting him inside her now and attuned to every bit of him—from his tantalizing, musky male scent to the husky way he was breathing and the ravenous look in his dark eyes—she quickly jerked at his belt to unfasten it and unzipped his jeans.

"Boots," he said, his face taut with need as he scooped her up and set her on the bed and hurried to pull her boots off, then removed his.

They'd needed to do that first!

Socks were tossed, jeans were dumped, then they were back to kissing. Except that she still had her panties on, and he was wearing his boxer briefs. She slipped her fingers underneath his waistband to cup his buttocks. He did the same to her, sliding his hands down her panties to mold his hands to her bottom. Their chests were pressed together, their mouths kissing. But then she tugged his boxer briefs down over his narrow hips and smiled to see his cock free, and he hurried to slip the briefs off the rest of the way, and her panties too.

She climbed onto the mattress. He moved in beside her and began stroking her clit, making her hot and desperate to find release. He was so good at it, and with all the kissing and touching beforehand, she was already reaching for the heavens. He inserted a finger between her feminine folds, pulling out and then rubbing his wet finger over her clit, lightly at first, slowly, circling the clit, then harder and faster.

She groaned with the pleasure he was giving her.

He lowered his mouth to hers and kissed her deeply. His touch was exquisite, and she was enraptured by him. Her breathing halted as she climbed to the peak, her nails gently scratching his sides, her fingers digging into his hips as she came. She swore his whole body was even harder than before.

"Oh, yes," she said, her voice as hushed as she could make it under the circumstances, and he smiled warmly at her before he slid his cock deep inside her for the ultimate feast.

———

Brock thrust deeply into his mate, intoxicated with the sexy scent of her, the feel of her wrapped around him, and the taste of her as he licked her mouth and tongue. The heat and wetness of her hugged his cock, ripples of her climax stroking him. He skimmed his mouth over her jaw, then kissed her mouth. She opened her mouth to his and sucked on his tongue. He groaned.

Her fingers gripped his biceps as if she were falling off the edge of the world again. The muscles of her sex tightened around him, forcing a low groan to escape his lips. Their pheromones mixed it up in a wild tango, telling him just how right this was between them.

She was just what he needed in a mate. Just as needy as he was when it came to taking pleasure in each other. She arched against him, moving her hands over his naked ass, her bare heels hooking over the backs of his legs. He pumped into her, so glad they hadn't waited to mate. And then he felt the tumultuous explosion rock his world, and this time, she cried out, not holding back, and then blushed to high heaven.

He chuckled and cupped her face, his elbows propped on the bed on either side of her, and kissed her again. "As much as I'd prefer staying here with you, I'm going to make some rounds while you get some rest. I'll wake you later."

"Be careful, Brock."

"I will be." He kissed her again, and she kissed him back. She finally released her hold on him, and then he left. After the mention of him being wounded a few times, he was afraid that she would think he wasn't very good at dodging bullets. It just depended on how many of them were headed his way!

None of Dexter's hired guns showed up at the garden center that day. Several of the Greystoke men served as guards while Natalie, Brock, and Shawn ran the garden center, as everyone took turns getting some sleep during the day in case they had to fight that night. They were beginning to think Dexter had called it quits, packed up and left. Unless it was taking him some time to recruit more men to carry out his bidding. That night, they were preparing for the onslaught again.

Natalie closed her eyes and imagined Brock prowling around in the dark as a wolf with the others, and she couldn't sleep. She heard him tell Heath she was going to sleep for a while and he was headed outside. Heath agreed.

Then Brock must have shifted, because she heard the squeak of the wolf door.

Sleep wasn't about to come. Not when she was too keyed up about what Dexter might pull next. She left the bed, threw on a pair of jeans and a T-shirt, and padded out to the living room to join Heath. She was still feeling embarrassed over being so exuberant during her lovemaking with Brock and was thinking seriously of asking her mom and dad if they could stay with another family so she could have some newlywed time alone with her mate.

Heath glanced at her from where he was sitting, watching the security monitors. "Can't sleep?"

She shook her head.

"Brock believes Dexter didn't have enough men to recruit to deal with us. Or maybe he's not planning to hit us until around three or so in the morning when he figures we'll all be wiped out. If Dexter couldn't grab his money already, he'll probably figure you took it somewhere else. Maybe all the way back to the pack in Colorado. Then what? You wouldn't be returning the same day, most likely. Or if you were, it would take several hours more to make it there and back."

That's why Brock hadn't felt the urgency to help the other men keep up the surveillance. She loved how astute he was when dealing with an issue like this.

"True. So it sounds like Dexter didn't follow us to Colorado," Natalie said.

"No. Or he would have realized there were too many people to confront. He didn't follow us back or we would have known. We thought he might have sent someone to check to see what was going on at the garden center today, but no one suspected anyone was a spy that came to the business." Heath smiled. "We're so glad to have you in the pack, and I'm delighted you and my cousin are mated. Man, did he work fast."

She laughed. "It was mutual." She began watching the monitors, despite how sleepy she felt. She could barely keep her eyes open, but her brain wouldn't shut down.

They watched them in silence, but she was glad Heath was observing them too. She was afraid she might miss something, she was so tired.

Half an hour later, Brock walked into the house and saw her sitting up and watching the monitors with Heath. He shifted. "Hey, Natalie. Can't you sleep?"

"No."

"No one seems to be coming. Not that we're going to let down our guard. Let me grab my gun and some clothes." Brock came back a few minutes later, dressed and armed.

Heath rose from the couch. "I'll go out and watch for a while."

"Thanks, Heath. You don't want to go to bed?" Brock asked Natalie, sitting down beside her on the couch.

"No. I'd rather just watch the monitors with you." She snuggled up against him on the couch while he observed the security monitors. But she laid her head in his lap and closed her eyes.

He chuckled. "Well, this works too."

"It sure does." She felt comfortable, safe, loved, and she so loved Brock for it. He gently stroked her hair while she drifted off to sleep.

—⁓—

Brock was watching the security monitors but only seeing his pack members moving around in the dark, some as wolves, some still as armed humans, in case Dexter sent armed humans again. He was glad Natalie and her parents could see what being part of a pack meant. How they helped each other out, no matter what the circumstances.

After Brock had monitored the security screens for an hour and a half, Shawn came into the house. He smiled to see Natalie with her head on Brock's lap, sound asleep.

"Hey," Shawn said, his voice hushed. He motioned with his head to her and then waved to her bedroom down the hall. "I'll cover for you here. Why don't you get some sleep?"

That worked for Brock. And he really did plan on sleeping. Until he moved his sexy mate to the bedroom and she stirred awake and wanted more loving. And he was ready to oblige.

Chapter 21

BROCK WOKE TO A WOLF'S HOWL OUTSIDE THE CARRIAGE house and Shawn yelling from the living room that they had movement in the gardens. Natalie was out of bed in a flash and throwing on clothes. Then she grabbed her gun.

Brock hollered to Shawn, "Human? Wolves?"

"Wolves!"

"I'll watch the security monitors," Natalie said and headed for the living room.

Brock followed behind her. Shawn started to strip. Natalie sat down on the couch to monitor the security cameras.

"How many are there?" Brock asked, looking at the monitor.

"Five. Dexter and his men, if he's even with them, are outnumbered. He probably figures there are still only the two of us men and Natalie, instead of a combined nine of us," Shawn said.

"As long as there aren't more of them coming in late as backup," Natalie warned.

"Agreed. I'm going out to help our men." Shawn shifted.

He was definitely eager to get out and fight with the encroaching wolves. Brock considered joining the others too, but he needed to stay here and protect Natalie. They had enough men on the grounds to deal with Dexter and his men. Brock just didn't want anyone breaking into the house and putting Natalie at risk like the last time.

"I'm staying with Natalie." He shifted, and he swore she sighed with relief. He couldn't have helped her the last time they'd been separated when they had the fight here. His cousin couldn't have successfully dealt with the armed gunmen on his own. This time, his pack members should have the advantage.

Shawn woofed in acknowledgment and dashed out through the wolf door.

As a wolf, Brock sat beside Natalie, watching the monitor, but suddenly one of the security cameras went out, and all they had was static on the monitor.

"They found the security camera on my parents' home," she said, alarmed.

Then they saw a man's face get close to the security camera on Natalie's carriage house.

Brock shifted. "Hell, it's Dexter."

"He's not running as a wolf."

But then the monitor's screen turned to static.

"We couldn't see anything but his face. He must have shifted to obstruct the camera." Brock was dying to go out and deal with the guy, but he wouldn't. He was determined to stay here and protect Natalie.

"I'm not doing anything now while the cameras aren't working," Natalie said.

"You're armed with a gun. If anyone breaks into the house, shoot him."

Something suddenly crashed through the kitchen window. Smoke started to fill the house. *Damn it*. The rogue wolves were trying to smoke them out.

Two more windows shattered, and more smoke bombs were thrown inside. They had to leave the house, and Brock was certain they'd be attacked if they went out the front way.

"Guest bedroom window," Natalie whispered.

Brock nodded, and coughing, they ran toward the bedroom. Once inside, he shut the door. A female wolf was at a disadvantage fighting the heftier males, but ultimately, it was her decision to leave the house or maybe find a room where the smoke wouldn't be too bad, the garage even. "I'm going as a wolf. You?"

"I have my gun. I'll remove any gunmen."

"All right." He slid the window up. "I'll throw open the front door first, to make them think we're coming out that way."

"Okay. Just be careful."

"I will be. Then I'll go out this window first," he said, his voice hushed. He wanted to ensure she didn't become a target if someone was waiting outside.

"All right."

She barely suppressed a cough, but he was certain that, despite the growling and yips and barks on the other side of her parents' house, anyone near her house could have heard it. Humans, no, but wolves, yes.

Brock raced back through the smoke-filled house, barely able to see, coughing violently, his eyes tearing up. He reached the front door and opened it, immediately leaping aside so that he couldn't be hit if anyone was waiting to shoot at him.

No one did anything. He assumed they were anticipating Natalie and him exiting the house, and then they'd attack.

Stifling his coughing, Brock raced to the bedroom and closed the door behind him. "Okay, let's do this."

He shifted and leaped out the window, then began to search for anyone lying in wait. Natalie climbed out through the window and ran to a large tree, and to his surprise, she scrambled up into the branches. Great plan! The wolves couldn't climb. If she saw one of the rogue wolves, she could shoot him from her safe vantage point. Then he realized she probably didn't know all the wolves in his pack by sight yet.

Brock hoped she didn't shoot one of the good guys. He stayed near the tree, still in protective mode, figuring whoever had thrown the smoke bombs in the house would be coming for them when they realized Brock and Natalie weren't going out through the front door.

The smoke was drifting out of the broken windows, reducing visibility. Not to mention that the cool night air and the heat of the day clashed, producing a ground fog that was growing thicker. *Hell*. That was all they needed.

Brock could barely see anything far away, but he heard wolf footfalls against the light leaves they had scattered the day before. He smiled just a little, glad for Natalie's quick thinking to do that. He heard wolf fights farther away, some moving into the garden, some near Natalie's parents' home.

Brock worried about his cousins and other pack members still fighting the remaining wolves. Were there more than they had accounted for? Brock thought that would be the only reason his friends and family were still battling other wolves. That was probably why Dexter had knocked out the security cameras, giving

Brock's people a sense of power, thinking they had so few to deal with that they'd grow cocky. Then Dexter sent in more men.

Here, except for the sound of the one wolf cautiously approaching, pausing, moving again, it was quiet with a toad croaking some distance away, leaves rustling in the light breeze, his own heart pounding, and his breathing rapid.

His muscles tense, Brock waited for the wolf to approach, having to ensure it was a rogue before he attacked. The wolf was smelling Brock's and Natalie's scents and heading their way. Brock was feeling antsy, wanting to terminate the wolf now before he could initiate the fight, but forcing himself to wait and see if the wolf was friend or foe.

And then the wolf suddenly appeared, materializing out of the fog like a specter, as if his light-gray fur were partly fog itself. It was Dexter—the wolf who had tried to kill Brock by slamming three rounds into his chest in the confrontation some years earlier. He'd always wondered if Dexter had worn a bulletproof vest that day under his leather jacket. It was time to end the criminal wolf—once and for all.

Brock was glad he knew the wolf by sight, having done surveillance on him, and one of his men in human form had called out to him, identifying the wolf for Brock. So Brock knew just what the bastard looked like, both as a wolf and in his human form.

He growled softly. The wolf appeared apprehensive, glancing around, most likely searching for Natalie's whereabouts. But then Dexter swung his head around and lunged at Brock.

Brock wasn't surprised. The wolf was known for acting on impulse, being decisive, even if he put himself at risk like the last time they'd tangled. Maybe Dexter thought Natalie was hiding, trying to stay out of danger, and wouldn't be a threat.

Brock and Dexter clashed, the angry wolf snarling and biting. But then someone came toward Brock from the rear and shouted, "I'll get him, Dexter. Move out of the way."

The man's voice sounded so similar to Dexter's that Brock wondered for an instant if the wolf he was fighting wasn't Dexter. Since the gunman called out Dexter's name, the armed human had to be Dexter's brother. Or maybe a close cousin.

Brock continued to try to grab hold of Dexter's throat or something else vital so he could make the killing blow, but Dexter was wily enough to keep Brock from doing so. And Dexter was trying to grab Brock's throat whenever he could.

The armed gunman was probably the person who had broken the windows, knocked out the security cameras, and tossed the smoke bombs into Natalie's house.

The gunman fired off a shot in Brock's direction. He felt something nick his tail. Damn it. Brock glanced around to see the armed man. He not only sounded like Dexter; he looked like him too.

Brock heard movement in the tree and hoped Natalie didn't expose herself. He figured she was trying to position herself better so she could shoot the lone gunman. Suddenly, she was firing at the man. Five shots, and he went down.

Dexter was still trying to battle Brock, but from the

way Dexter's ears and tail drooped, Brock was certain the wolf was distressed about his fallen family member. Too bad. He shouldn't have gotten him into a life of crime, if that was the way things had gone. He figured Dexter had been the one to set this all up, and his brother had gone along with it. Then Brock wondered if the fallen man could even be Trenton.

Brock bit Dexter in the muzzle, and the wolf dodged away. Brock was relentless. This guy wouldn't be organizing any more criminal activities. The blood was pounding in his ears, his adrenaline rushing through his bloodstream as he tackled the wolf again. And again.

The wolf made a final lunge at Brock, a fatal mistake, just as another shot was fired from the trees, and Brock bit into Dexter's throat, dealing the death blow. Dexter collapsed, his body still a wolf, gasping for air. Brock hung on tight, his jaws clamped around the wolf's throat. Dexter took a final breath, his wolf form turning into a human's, and Brock let go. He was serious about ensuring this guy wasn't going to hurt anyone anymore.

He loped to where the other man was, and he looked so much like Dexter that Brock assumed he must be Dexter's twin brother, Trenton. Whoever he was, he had died.

A wolf howled from the garden. Shawn. Another wolf howled from the direction of Natalie's parents' house. Heath.

And then, each wolf howled, letting the others know where they were and that they were alive. Only one didn't respond. Brock's cousin Tanner. Brock knew everyone would be searching for Tanner, praying he was still alive. He'd mated Bella's sister, and Brock didn't want to believe anything other than Tanner was going to be okay.

Suddenly, Shawn barked and then howled. Shawn had found his brother, and several of the wolves took off to help him. Brock wanted to also, but he remained behind to watch Natalie climb down from the tree.

"Who's injured?" she immediately asked.

Brock shifted and reached up to pull her into his arms and set her on the ground. "Tanner, Serena's mate."

"Your cousin," Natalie said, tears in her eyes and her voice.

"Yeah, hopefully he's okay."

"What are we going to do about the bodies?" Natalie hugged Brock tight. She was shaking from the adrenaline and maybe from knowing she'd killed a man.

"The jaguar policing branch can pick them up. They're an amazing group. They have planes and a helicopter. They can carry the bodies from here and dispose of them. Are you okay?" He wrapped his arms around her and held on tight.

She was staring at the man she'd killed. "Yeah. He was going to shoot you as soon as Dexter was in the clear. I had to move from where I was so I could get a clear shot at him. All I had at my vantage point were tree branches and twigs. I was afraid when I started moving, he would hear me and aim in my direction, but he was concentrating on you too much."

"Thank God for that. Let me see if he has any ID. He sure looks like he could be Trenton, which makes me worry about Vaughn and the others at Lettie's place." Brock searched the man's pockets and found a wallet, opened it, and found his driver's license. "Yeah, it's

Trenton." He gave Natalie the driver's license, then as a precaution in case there were any stray mercenaries running around, he shifted into his wolf.

Natalie pulled out her phone and called Jillian. "Hey, it's me. Natalie. Is everything all right there?" She put the call on speakerphone.

"Yeah, we're still waiting on any action. Nothing's happening." Jillian sounded tired of waiting.

"Dexter told Trenton he was supposed to handle Lettie personally. No one else. Trenton was down here with his brother. So why would he be here if he didn't do what his brother ordered him to do?" And then as if a light bulb went on, Natalie's jaw dropped. "Ohmigod, what if Lettie and Trenton had a romantic relationship? And he wasn't about to do what his brother told him to. Can you ask her?"

"Okay," Jillian said, sounding resigned, "but she hasn't been totally cooperative."

"In what way?"

"She doesn't think Trenton would come to kill her."

Natalie's mouth curved into a smile. "Yeah, because she had a thing going on with him. Betcha, and Dexter didn't know about it."

"Or he did, and that's why he told his brother to handle this personally."

"That could be. We've got to go. Tanner's been hurt. We're going to see what happened. The men are carrying him to my parents' house, and Heath is there to doctor him."

"Oh no. Okay. Let us know about his condition as soon as you can."

"Will do."

Brock hurried Natalie into her parents' house after the rest of the men, not about to leave her alone outside while she was talking on the phone with Jillian. He thought they had eliminated all the rogue wolves, but he wasn't about to chance it. He adored her for being able to work with him so well. They complemented each other in everything they did.

Heath was bandaging Tanner, most of the men looking on as wolves. A couple of them left the house. Shawn threw on his clothes and took over, bandaging Tanner while Heath dressed. Brock shifted, then threw on a pair of boxer briefs and called Vaughn. "Hey, can you call whoever can do it to send a helicopter for several bodies and to get Tanner to Heath's clinic? Obviously, Heath needs to go with him."

"On it. You'll be at Natalie's parents' house?"

"Yeah. But a helicopter can meet us out in the parking lot of the garden center."

"Gotcha. How's Tanner doing?" Vaughn asked.

"He's half out of it. Bad bite marks. Doc's got him on an IV. Damn glad we have Heath in the pack," Brock said.

"Hell yeah. He's doctored us all more times than I care to remember. Is it over? Dexter and his men have been eliminated?"

"Yeah, as far as we know. It's done."

The last wolves left the house. Brock assumed they were going to wherever they'd left their clothes.

"Keep us informed."

"I will. I've got to let Devlyn know what's going on."

"Okay, one other thing. Jillian asked Lettie if Trenton was a friend of hers and wouldn't intend to kill her. She said yes. But that his brother might send backup in case Trenton didn't do what he was told to do."

"Well, Trenton is dead. It's up to you whether you want to tell her or not."

"I'll discuss it with Jillian. We'll stay here for another day, but then we're out of here. She'll have to find someone else to provide her protection. She should have told us Trenton wouldn't harm her. Then again, maybe she wasn't sure. Or maybe she was afraid Dexter would send someone else to do the job. See you soon."

"All right. Out here." Brock asked Heath, "Does Tanner need blood?"

"No, he should be okay. He's got a concussion, and I need to do a CT scan to make sure he hasn't suffered any real damage. The wolf knocked him into a stone bench, and Tanner hit his head pretty hard. Thanks for calling a chopper."

"Yeah, we have to get you and him back home to your clinic and get rid of all these bodies so the Silvertons can sell the place." Brock turned to Natalie and pulled her into his arms. "So we can get you and your parents to the town of Greystoke for good."

"Thanks to everyone for helping with this menace," she said.

"Wel…come," Tanner breathed out.

Natalie hurried over to him, held his hand, and kissed his cheek. "Get better soon."

Tanner gave her a small smile.

Brock rubbed her back. "Hang in there, buddy."

"Will. Serena…kill…me…if…I…don't."

The guys laughed and Natalie smiled.

Two men armed with guns walked through the area,

continuing to provide security in case there were still any rogue wolves out there. Everyone else continued to talk to Tanner to keep him awake. Before it was time for the helicopter to arrive, the men moved the bodies to one location in the parking lot to make it less time-consuming to load them. They used wheelbarrows and garden carts to make the job easier, then hosed down all the conveyances.

They heard the flapping noise of the helicopter's blades, and then it landed in the parking lot.

The jaguars had body bags, and the men began to put the dead bodies in them, then loaded the helicopter, everyone wishing Tanner well as he was carried inside and he and Heath left.

Shawn looked as though he'd wanted to go, too, and stay with his brother, but when Brock had told him to go, Shawn said, "No. The rest of my brothers will be there. My place is here, making sure that the garden center runs smoothly until the Silvertons can sell it and move the family to Greystoke."

Brock sure appreciated him for it.

"By the way, our men found three vehicles with Colorado plates. One was registered to Trenton. It looks like he brought the men with him," Shawn said.

"Then the operation in Colorado is over too," Brock said with relief.

"I agree," Shawn said. "I'm going to join the guys outside and give you some privacy, but we'll replace the windows on the house tomorrow and make sure it's aired out properly. Some of the men are going to drop off the rogue wolves' vehicles at Marek's place."

"Sounds good and thanks, Shawn."

Shawn left, and Brock closed and locked the door.

With the counterfeiting operation stopped, the men responsible for it gone, and plenty of security here for the rest of the night, Brock took Natalie to a guest room that wasn't occupied. He wasn't sure if she'd want to make love after killing Trenton. Brock was fine just cuddling with her or doing whatever made her feel right with the world after the ordeal.

"Thanks for saving my ass out there," Brock said, stripping Natalie out of her clothes. "I was certain I could eliminate Dexter, but not with someone shooting at my backside." He pulled off his boxer briefs, then led her to the bed.

"You had to deal with a vicious enough wolf as it was. I would have shot Dexter, too, if I could have."

"I'm sorry you had to kill him." Brock wanted her to know he understood if she was feeling bad about it.

"There wasn't any other option. Protect my mate or…" She shrugged. "Protect my mate. That was the only choice. I'd do it again if I was faced with the same challenge. He came into my territory and threatened to kill you, and I have no qualms about what I had to do."

Brock still wasn't sure that she wouldn't feel differently in the morning, or even sometime during the night. The adrenaline was still rushing through their veins after the big fight, and he worried she might crash and feel bad after it left their systems. No matter what, he would be there for her.

He climbed into bed, and she joined him. He only planned to pull her into his arms and cuddle with her, but she slid her body over his, held her body tight against his, and began to kiss his mouth. Fire engulfed him and his erection jumped, already throbbing with need. He hadn't realized just how much his body was craving hers.

And then he was kissing her back, thinking the world of her for being his mate and just as protective of him as he was of her. Anticipation of thrusting his cock deep inside her was mounting, yet he was holding off to pleasure her. Seeing the joy in her expression meant the world to him.

He treasured feeling her soft skin sliding against his, her breasts pressed against his chest, her legs parted as they spread over his hips. She was beautiful and precious to him.

Their mouths connected again, and he cupped her ass, reveling in the way she was pressed against him, arousing him. Their pheromones triggered his craving to bury himself deep inside her. But he was letting her set the pace.

Aching for her, he didn't expect her next move when she rolled off him. He groaned a little. When she moved next to him, he was thinking she wanted to just go to sleep after their ordeal after all, and he couldn't help but be a little disappointed.

She slid her hand over his chest and down to grasp his cock. Glad she wanted to go further, he couldn't have been any more eager to go the full course. He leaned over, kissing her between her breasts, then licked a rosy nipple and suckled. He moved higher to kiss her mouth, their breaths mingling, their tongues touching.

Their pulses raced, and he began stroking her clit as she slipped her fingers into his hair. He loved the way her fingers caressed his scalp while he stroked her clit. She was barely breathing, soaking up his touches, her body sinking into the mattress, then arching to the heated contact. He wanted them to come together, but he might have aroused her to the breaking point already.

He slid his cock into her warm, wet tightness. As soon as he began to thrust, she was bearing down on him, letting him know she was about to let go. Tightening her inner muscles, her eyes closed, her hands clamped on his arms, she appeared to be fighting release. He continued to dive in, wanting them to do this together, but she groaned and then cried out. "Ohmigod, yes!"

For a moment, she seemed enraptured, and then she began to match his thrusts, until he couldn't hold out any longer. Release came then, and he felt exultant in her tight, wet embrace. He pumped a couple more times and then relaxed. "Hot damn, woman."

She smiled up at him, her willful look telling him he wasn't done.

Damn, this was one hell of a way to burn off the excess adrenaline from the fight.

Being with Brock was magical, but when he slid his cock inside her and began to thrust, Natalie felt the wild passion of the wolf claiming her. Joyous, enchanting, beautiful. Now they were wrapped around each other, their legs entangled, her hair spread across his chest, breathing raggedly, enjoying the scent of their lovemaking and of each other—the wolf and human combination.

She didn't want to think too deeply about killing Trenton. She had been honest with her mate when she'd told him if she had it all to do over again, she would have done the same. But killing a man wasn't who she was. She loved life and creating life or nurturing it. Still, she'd only had one choice, and she was glad she'd done what she had.

"Are you all right?" Brock asked.

Suspecting he was still concerned about her killing Trenton, she loved Brock for his sensitivity. Some men would have felt she should be a wolf, suck it up, and go on with her life. But Brock was so caring, so considerate of her feelings. "Yeah. You were made for me, you know? If anyone else had tried to claim you, they couldn't have. Because you were made just for me."

He chuckled. "I'm damn glad Angie asked me to help guide you to the restaurant that day. After that?" He kissed her forehead. "I had rescued the damsel in distress. You were all mine."

She laughed. "For getting me lost that one time only, I'll give my GPS a reprieve. Who would have ever thought it would lead me to the mate of my dreams?"

He smiled and kissed her hair, holding her closer. "Angie must have known I needed you in my life as much as you needed me."

Natalie agreed. She would be forever grateful to her friend. "Don't fall asleep too deeply on me," she warned.

"Hmm." He traced his fingers over her arm. "I will never be sleeping so deeply you can't wake me for more loving."

He was one hot SEAL wolf for sure. And that was all she needed to hear.

Epilogue

BROCK WAS GRATEFUL THAT HIS COUSIN TANNER PULLED through without any lasting effects from the concussion he received during the big fight with Dexter and his mercenaries. Dexter's whole counterfeit scheme was history. And after three months, the Silvertons had not only sold their places but also built a new home and garden center on acreage the pack owned in Colorado, all with the help of the Greystoke pack. Stands of native aspen were already turning yellow, and native Colorado spruce and other evergreens made for a spectacular early fall backdrop for the garden center and wedding. Even the cats loved the new pack and the garden center.

Everyone was delighted the family was part of the pack, and the wedding was scheduled for Brock and Natalie for next week at the new garden center. Natalie had enjoyed giving lessons about plants to both wolf children and adults and helping to start a community garden. But she couldn't have been more excited about going to Hawaii for the honeymoon and scuba diving with Brock.

He was busy searching on his computer for clues concerning the location of a deadbeat husband who hadn't been paying child support while Natalie was at work at the garden center. Or so he thought.

Until she came home much earlier than expected, her smile infectious.

He left the couch to give her a welcoming hug, thinking maybe she was as horny as he was, and he'd sweep her right off her feet and carry her to bed. Yeah, he'd gotten rid of the black comforter, but they'd agreed on an aqua one. And the paper in the bathrooms had been changed—though they hadn't called on Lettie to do it. A couple of carpenters in the pack had said they knew just what to do and put up the blue grass wallpaper in all three bathrooms—for free.

No one was after Lettie any further, and she wasn't getting any of the Greystokes' business. Not to mention she'd been pretty hostile over learning of Trenton's death. Especially when she heard Natalie had shot him.

Natalie dropped her purse on the oak coffee table and pulled a couple of wallpaper swatches out of her bag. "What do you think?"

He frowned as he looked at the wallpaper samples. One featured baby foxes, wolves, deer, and owls peering around trees. The other had teddy bears, hot air balloons, and swans in the clouds. He looked up at her, and she was beaming.

"A baby?"

"Two. Maybe a boy and a girl, so your cousin says."

Brock felt dizzy with joy and quickly gathered his mate into his arms. "You are my life!"

"I thought we'd have a little more time to get to know each other, but…"

"We have a whole wolf pack to help out for date nights." He couldn't have been more thrilled once he got over the initial shock.

Natalie loved Brock and wasn't sure why she'd been so apprehensive about telling him about the babies, even though they hadn't used any protection the whole time they'd been mated. He'd looked so pale all of a sudden that she swore he was going to faint! She loved him. He was tough as nails, rock-solid, but when it came to being a daddy? So cute.

Hugging her, he looked at the samples again. "The wolf one, of course."

And then together they called her parents, her sister and brother-in-law, his brother and sister-in-law, and their pack leaders. Everyone was ready for a whole new celebration.

"The only bad thing is I won't be able to scuba dive on our honeymoon," she admitted regretfully.

He smiled. "Hell, we'll go back to Hawaii after the kids are bigger, and we'll bring wolf nannies with us. You better believe half the pack will want the job. We will enjoy snorkeling just as much this time around."

"True." She was so glad Brock wasn't disappointed they couldn't dive together.

"But you can go on your own with a group."

"No way. On our honeymoon? No way."

She laughed and dragged him back to the bedroom. "That wasn't the only reason I came home early from work." Then she glanced back at the living room. "Were you doing something important?"

"Catching bad guys can wait. This can't." He scooped her up in his arms and hauled her to the bedroom. "Twins," he said in awe. "A boy and a girl."

"Love you, Brock."

He set her gently on the bed as if she'd break. "You are the love of my life."

"You are mine, you hot SEAL wolf."

So much for not seeking mates. One GPS malfunction, and they were set for life.

Acknowledgments

Thanks to my lovely beta readers, Dottie Jones and Donna Fournier, who are always there for me and do such a great job! Thanks to Deb Werksman for all her great suggestions and loving my books! And thanks to the cover artists who do wonders when it comes to turning fantasy into reality.

About the Author

Bestselling and award-winning author Terry Spear has written over sixty paranormal romance novels and eight medieval Highland historical romances. Her first werewolf romance, *Heart of the Wolf*, was named a 2008 *Publishers Weekly* Best Book of the Year, and her subsequent titles have garnered high praise and hit the *USA Today* bestseller list. A retired officer of the U.S. Army Reserves, Terry lives in Spring, Texas, where she is working on her next werewolf romance, continuing with her Highland medieval romances, and having fun with her young adult novels. When she's not writing, she's photographing everything that catches her eye, making teddy bears, and playing with her Havanese puppies and her grandbaby. For more information, please visit terryspear.com or follow her on Twitter @TerrySpear. She is also on Facebook at facebook.com/terry.spear. And at Terry Spear's Shifters on Wordpress, http://terry spear.wordpress.com.

Also by Terry Spear

Heart of the Wolf
Heart of the Wolf
To Tempt the Wolf
Legend of the White Wolf
Seduced by the Wolf

Silver Town Wolf
Destiny of the Wolf
Wolf Fever
Dreaming of the Wolf
Silence of the Wolf
A Silver Wolf Christmas
*Alpha Wolf Need Not
Apply*
*Between a Wolf and a
Hard Place*
*All's Fair in Love and
Wolf*

Highland Wolf
*Heart of the Highland
Wolf*
A Howl for a Highlander
*A Highland Werewolf
Wedding*
Hero of a Highland Wolf
*A Highland Wolf
Christmas*

SEAL Wolf
*A SEAL in Wolf's
Clothing*
A SEAL Wolf Christmas
SEAL Wolf Hunting
SEAL Wolf In Too Deep
SEAL Wolf Undercover

Heart of the Jaguar
Savage Hunger
Jaguar Fever
Jaguar Hunt
Jaguar Pride
A Very Jaguar Christmas

Billionaire Wolf
*Billionaire in Wolf's
Clothing*
*A Billionaire Wolf for
Christmas*

White Wolf
*Dreaming of a White
Wolf Christmas*
Flight of the White Wolf

Heart of the Shifter
You Had Me at Jaguar

YOU HAD ME AT JAGUAR

First in the new Heart of the Shifter series from
USA Today bestselling author Terry Spear

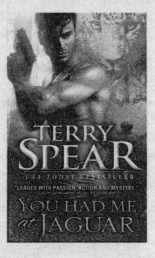

The United Shifter Force gives jaguar agent Howard
Armstrong an impossible task—to protect fierce she-
jaguar Valerie Chambers, when the last thing she wants
is protecting. They're going international to take down a
killer, and he can guard Valerie all day long. But guard his
heart? He doesn't stand a chance.

*"Packed with adventure...magnificently
entertaining."*

**—RT Book Reviews Top Pick for *Billionaire
in Wolf's Clothing***

For more info about Sourcebooks's
books and authors, visit:

sourcebooks.com

ALL'S FAIR IN LOVE AND WOLF

The Silver Town wolves return

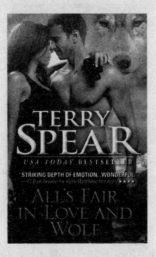

Wolf shifter Sarandon Silver's in trouble with the law, and bounty hunter she-wolf Jenna St. James is determined to bring him in for trial.

Lucky for Sarandon, the entire Silver Town pack is ready to fight for his innocence. But until the case is solved, Jenna's sticking to Sarandon like glue...

"Real depth and chemistry...a great read."

—RT Book Reviews for All's Fair in Love and Wolf, 4 stars

For more info about Sourcebooks's books and authors, visit:

sourcebooks.com

X-OPS EXPOSED

More thrilling action and sizzling romance
from *New York Times* bestselling author Paige Tyler

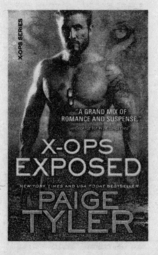

Lion hybrid and former Army Ranger Tanner Howland has retreated into the forests of Washington State to be alone. He's too dangerous to be around people—including his love, Dr. Zarina Sokolov. Little does he know, she's following him, determined to save Tanner with the antiserum she hopes will turn him human again. But a vicious ring pitting hybrids against each other for sport lies in wait.

*"Does it get any better than this?
Tyler...is an absolute master!"*

—Fresh Fiction

For more info about Sourcebooks's
books and authors, visit:
sourcebooks.com

A WOLF APART

Second in Maria Vale's strikingly original new series,
The Legend of All Wolves

Thea Villalobos has long since given up trying to be what
others expect of her. So in Elijah Sorensson, she can see
through the jaded, successful lawyer to a man who is
passionate to the point of heartbreak. But something inside
him is dying...

Elijah despises the human life he's forced to endure.
He's Alpha of his generation of the Great North Pack, and
the wolf inside him will no longer be restrained...

*"Brilliant... Vale's nuanced exploration of
werewolf concepts elevates this work."*

—Publishers Weekly

For more info about Sourcebooks's
books and authors, visit:
sourcebooks.com

COWBOY WOLF TROUBLE

A new evil will stop at nothing to tear their world apart

For centuries, the shifters that roam Big Sky Country have honored a pact to keep the peace. Even bad-boy rancher Wes Calhoun, former leader of a renegade pack, has given up his violent ways and sworn loyalty to the Grey Wolves. But his dark past keeps catching up with him...

Human rancher Naomi Evans cares only about saving the ranch that was her father's legacy. Until a clash with Wes opens up a whole new world—a supernatural world on the verge of war—and Naomi, her ranch, and the sexy cowboy wolf stealing her heart are smack-dab in the middle of it.

"Kait Ballenger is a treasure you don't want to miss."

—Gena Showalter, *New York Times* and *USA Today* bestseller

For more info about Sourcebooks's books and authors, visit:

sourcebooks.com

UNDISCOVERED

After centuries in darkness, the
Amoveo dragons are rising

A long time ago, Zander Lorens was cursed to walk the earth stripped of his Dragon Clan powers. Now, Zander relives his darkest moment every night, trapped in a recurring nightmare. By day, he searches for a woman who may be the key to ending his torment.

Rena McHale uses her unique sensitivity as a private investigator and finder of the lost. By day, she struggles with sensory overload, and by night, her sleep is haunted by a fiery dragon shifter. Nothing in her life makes sense, until the man from her dreams shows up at her door with a proposition…

"Bewitching, haunting, and deliciously carnal."

—*Night Owl Reviews* Top Pick for *Unclaimed*

SEAL WOLF
UNDERCOVER

USA Today bestseller Terry Spear turns up
the heat in her SEAL Wolf series

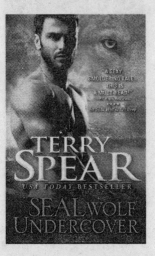

Special wolf agent Jillian Matthews has joined the jaguar-run United Shifter Force to track down a deadly criminal. She's even willing to work with PI Vaughn Greystoke— until the hot, growly SEAL wolf makes the mistake of getting in her way…

"Spear has captivated us with her striking characters and explosive chemistry."

**—RT Book Reviews for
SEAL Wolf Undercover, 4 stars**

For more info about Sourcebooks's
books and authors, visit:
sourcebooks.com